Nora Roberts is the #1 *New York Times* bestselling author of nearly two hundred novels. Under the pen name J.D. Robb, she is the author of the crime series starring Lieutenant Eve Dallas. With more than 300 million copies of her books in print and over 150 *New York Times* bestsellers to date, Nora Roberts is indisputably the most celebrated women's fiction writer today.

Praise for J.D. Robb's 'In Death' series

'Eve Dallas – the NYPD's tough, smart, and sexy lieutenant – leads the reader down mean streets and onto sacred ground to solve one of one of her most puzzling homicides in *Salvation in Death* . . . Another great thriller' Linda Fairstein

'Sheer entertainment' *Guardian*

'Gut-searing emotional drama' David Baldacci

'A thrills-to-chills ratio that will raise neck hairs . . . the epitome of great popular fiction' Dennis Lehane

'*Creation in Death* is a witty, dark, page-turning tale of futuristic crime fighting. Raymond Chandler meets *Blade Runner* meets *Silence of the Lambs*. The techno-toys may change, but evil never does' Jonathan Kellerman

'Curious corpses, ta   hs
Salvation in Death is a

D1340856

The World of J.D. Robb

'In Death' characters

Eve Dallas. Dallas is often injured in the line of duty and always has to be dragged, kicking and cursing, to hospital. Will only ever get her hair cut when she's ganged up on by Mavis and Trina. Never buys her own clothes – Roarke buys them for her and they simply appear in her wardrobe. Dallas can never hide her stash of sweets anywhere in her office without them being stolen by the mysterious 'candy thief'. She has the smallest office and most ancient computer in the squad. She is a Yankees fan and her drink of choice is coffee. The nicer the outfit Roarke buys her, the more likely it is to get destroyed in an explosion or a fight. Whenever her police car gets fixed, she ends up crashing it again in pursuit of a suspect, and she often borrows something to drive from Roarke's vast collection. Dallas still has nightmares about her past and does not sleep very well when Roarke is not at home.

Roarke. Has no first name. Multi-billionaire who owns many buildings in the city, has numerous companies and business meetings, but always has time to help Dallas with her investigations. He is an electronics genius and has an illegal unregistered state-of-the-art computer system which Dallas frequently uses to help sift the evidence. He likes fast cars and the poetry of Yeats.

Summerset. Roarke's butler, with whom Dallas has a love–hate relationship. Summerset reigns at the mansion where Dallas and Roarke live. Dallas and Summerset regularly sneer at each other, and enjoy their frequent arguments. When Roarke was a teenager, living on the streets of Dublin, Summerset rescued him – he is the father Roarke never had. Summerset has a medical background that he got in the Urban Wars, and Dallas would rather be treated by him than have to go to hospital.

Galahad. A fat cat. Previously owned by a murder victim, he tripped up a rampaging, homicidal maniac, which saved Dallas from being shot. He somehow ended up becoming a resident of the mansion where Roarke and Dallas live, and can be found keeping watch over Eve while she sleeps, especially if Roarke is away. He still occasionally trips people up and will sneak food off plates when no-one is looking.

Mavis. Dallas's first and best female friend. Has a wild and exotic sense of dress and wears high heels. When we first meet Mavis, she's a singer in a seedy bar. We learn that Dallas met Mavis when she arrested her. Mavis has a heart of gold. During the course of the series, her singing career, with a little help from Roarke, goes from strength to strength, resulting in her becoming a rock star.

Trina. Beauty consultant and friend of Mavis. Helps Dallas on cases when she needs to track down 'enhancements'.

Ryan Feeney. Short with 'rust-coloured' hair. Police captain, former partner to Dallas, and now head of the Electronic Detection Division. He trained Dallas how to be a police officer and is as close as she has to a father figure. Feeney has a rumpled 'lived-in' face. He's horrified by any kind of sentimentality. We know he has a wife, Sheila, but she never appears.

Commander Jack Whitney. Dallas's boss, he's been a cop for more than thirty years and is head of the police precinct ('Central') where Dallas is based. He's constantly balancing overseeing the detectives, the need to investigate crimes that may upset important people, and the politics of city hall.

Mrs Anna Whitney The formidable wife of Commander Whitney. Stern, sometimes unforgiving, she intimidates Dallas.

Delia Peabody. A few books into the series, Dallas appoints Peabody her Aide. They work together on cases, and eventually become friends. Peabody wears sturdy lace-up shoes, and is the child of 'Freeagers' (hippies). Now co-habiting with a fellow police officer, she dated Charles Munroe when he was still a 'licensed companion'.

Nadine Furst. A stylish reporter on a TV news channel, and the only reporter Dallas respects. She's often involved in the same cases as Dallas and is always trying to get an interview for the Five O'Clock News. Dallas and Nadine will sometimes help each other out with their investigations.

Leonardo. A talented and successful fashion designer, unusually tall. The love of Mavis's life. They have a daughter, Bella Eve.

Ian McNab. Detective with long blond hair and an earring. Dresses even more eccentrically than Mavis. Falls for Peabody, and they eventually become a couple. A genius with computers. He used to get jealous of Charles, who dated Peabody briefly.

Dr Charlotte Mira. Psychiatrist working for the NY police, and the best profiler in the city. Although it took a long time for Dallas to overcome her mistrust of psychiatrists, they have become friends, with Dallas often thinking of her as a mother figure. She enjoys drinking floral scented teas.

Charles Munroe. A handsome, high-class male escort ('licensed companion') turned sex therapist, who was once a suspect in a murder case. Now he's a source for Dallas, and could even be described as a friend. Dated Peabody a few times. Met and fell in love with Louise while helping Dallas on a case.

Dr Louise Dimatto. A strong-willed doctor, brought up in a wealthy household, now running a free clinic for street people and contracted to donate her services to 'Dochas', an abuse centre for women and children set up by Roarke in Eve's name. Met Charles through Dallas. Louise and Charles are now a couple.

Dr Morris. Chief Medical Examiner. Hard-working and efficient. Dallas treats him with respect. Plays tenor saxophone.

Donald Webster. Lieutenant in the IAB (Internal Affairs Bureau). Had a one-night stand with Dallas in her rookie year, which meant more to him than to her. Had a fight with Roarke over Eve. Gambles on the odd occasion.

Promises in Death

J.D. ROBB

piatkus

PIATKUS

First published in the United States in 2009 by G.P. Putnam's Sons,
a division of Penguin Group (USA) Inc.
First published in Great Britain in 2009 by Piatkus Books
This edition published in 2009 by Piatkus
Reprinted 2009 (twice)

A CIP catalogue record for this book
is available from the British Library

ISBN 978-0-7499-2897-1

Typeset in Bembo by M Rules
Printed in the UK by CPI Mackays, Chatham ME5 8TD

Papers used by Piatkus are natural, renewable and
recyclable products sourced from well-managed forests and certified
in accordance with the rules of the Forest Stewardship Council.

Mixed Sources
Product group from well-managed
forests and other controlled sources
www.fsc.org Cert no. SGS-COC-004081
© 1996 Forest Stewardship Council

Piatkus
An imprint of
Little, Brown Book Group
100 Victoria Embankment
London EC4Y 0DY

An Hachette UK Company
www.hachette.co.uk

www.piatkus.co.uk

Love itself draws on a woman
nearly all the bad luck in the world.
—WILLA CATHER

A little more than kin,
and less than kind.
—WILLIAM SHAKESPEARE

Prologue

She was dead the minute she answered the 'link. She didn't question the caller or the urgency of the request. In fact, pleasure and excitement rushed through her as she put aside her plans for an early night. Her movements both graceful and efficient, she dressed quickly, gathering what she needed.

She strode through her pretty apartment, ordering the lights to dim, and remembered to switch to sleep the little droid kitten her lover had given her as a companion.

She'd named it Sachmo.

It mewed, blinked its bright green eyes and curled into a ball. She gave its sleek white fur an affectionate stroke.

"Be back soon," she murmured, making a promise she couldn't know would be broken.

She glanced around the apartment as she opened the door, smiled at the bouquet of red roses in full and dramatic bloom on the table near the street window. And thought of Li.

She locked her door for the last time.

Following ingrained habit, she took the stairs. She was a slim, athletically built woman with eyes of deep blue. Her blond hair swung past her shoulders, a parted curtain for a lovely face. She was thirty-three, happy in her life, flirting around the soft edges of love with a man who gave her kittens and roses.

She thought of New York, this life, this man as a new chapter, one she was content to walk through, page by page, and discover.

She tucked that away to turn her mind to where she needed to go, what she needed to do. Less than ten minutes after the call, she jogged down the second flight of steps, turned for the next.

She had an instant to register the movement when her killer stepped out. Another for surprise when she recognized the face. But not enough, not quite enough to speak before the stunner struck her mid-body and took her down.

She came to with a shocking jolt, a burn of skin and blood. A rush from dark to light. The stunner blast had left her body numb, useless, even as her mind flashed clear. Inside the paralyzed shell, she struggled, she strained. She looked up into the eyes of her killer. Into the eyes of a friend.

"Why?" The question was weak, but had to be asked. There had to be an answer. There was always an answer.

She had the answer when she died, in the basement five floors below her pretty apartment where roses bloomed red and a kitten purred in sleep.

1

Eve stepped out of the shower and into the drying tube. While the warm air swirled around her, she shut her eyes and wallowed. She'd snagged a solid eight hours' sleep and had woken early enough to indulge in what she thought of as water therapy.

Thirty laps in the pool, a spin in the whirlpool, followed by a twenty-minute hot shower. It made a hell of a nice way to start the day.

She'd had a productive one the day before, closing a case within two hours. If a guy was going to kill his *best friend* and try to pass it off as a mugging, he really shouldn't get caught wearing the dead friend's inscribed wrist unit.

She'd testified in court on a previous case, and the defense counsel's posturing, posing, and pontificating hadn't so much as cracked a hairline in her testimony.

Topping off the day, she'd had dinner at home with her husband, watched a vid. And had some very excellent sex before shutting down for that eight straight.

Life, at the moment, absolutely did not suck.

All but humming, she grabbed the robe on the back of the door—then paused, frowned, and studied it. It was short and silky and the color of black cherries.

She was dead certain she'd never seen it before.

With a shrug, she put it on, and walked into the bedroom.

There were ways for a good morning to get better, she thought, and here was top of the list. Roarke sipping coffee in the sitting area while he scanned the morning stock reports on-screen.

There were those hands that had worked their magic the night before, one holding a coffee mug, the other absently stroking their fat slug of a cat. Galahad's dual-colored eyes were slits of ecstasy—she could relate.

That beautifully sculpted mouth had turned her system inside out, twisted it into knots of screaming pleasure, then left it limp and satisfied.

Just shy of two years of marriage now, she mused, and the heat between them showed no signs of banking down. As if to prove it, her heart gave a leap and tumble in her chest when he turned his head, and his bold blue eyes met hers.

Did he feel that? she wondered. Could he possibly feel that every time? All the time?

He smiled, so both knowledge and pleasure spread over a face that, she thought foolishly, must make the gods weep with joy over their work.

He rose, moved to her—all long and lean—to take her face in his hands. Just a flutter of those clever fingers over her skin before his mouth found hers and made a better morning brilliant.

"Coffee?" he asked.

"Yeah. Thanks." She was a veteran cop, a homicide boss, a tough bitch by her own definition. And her knees were jelly. "I think we should take a few days." He programmed the AutoChef for coffee and—if she knew her man—for the breakfast he intended her to eat. "I mean maybe in July. Like for our anniversary. If you can work it in between world domination and planetary acquisitions."

"Funny you should bring it up." He set her coffee on the table, then two plates. It seemed bacon and eggs was on the menu this morning. On the sofa Galahad twitched and opened his eyes.

Roarke merely pointed a finger, said, firmly, "No." And the cat flopped the pudge of himself over. "I was thinking a few weeks."

"What? Us? Away? Weeks? I can't—"

"Yes, yes, crime would overtake the city in July 2060, raze it to smoldering ash if Lieutenant Dallas wasn't here to serve and protect." Ireland wove misty magic through his voice as he picked up the inert cat and set him on the floor to make room on the couch for Eve.

"Maybe," she muttered. "Besides, I don't see how you can take off for weeks when you've got ninety percent of the businesses in the known universe to run."

"It's no more than fifty." He picked up his coffee again, waiting for her to join him. "In any case, what would be the point of having all that, and you, darling Eve, if I can't have time with you, away from your work and mine?"

"I could probably take a week."

"I was thinking four."

"*Four?* Four weeks? That's a month."

5

His eyes laughed over the rim of his cup. "Is it now? I believe you're right."

"I can't take a month off. A month is like . . . a month."

"As opposed to what? A chicken?"

"Ha. Look, maybe I could stretch it to ten days, but—"

"Three weeks."

Her forehead furrowed.

"We had to cancel plans for a quick weekend away twice this year. Once for your work, once for mine. Three weeks."

"I couldn't take more than two, even—"

"Two and a half. We split the difference." He handed her a fork.

She frowned at it. "You were always going for the two and a half."

He took her hand, kissed it. "Don't let your eggs get cold."

She'd squeezed confessions out of stone killers, brow-beaten information out of slimy weasels, but she would never come out a hundred percent on top with Roarke in a negotiation. "Where would we go during this famous two and a half weeks?"

"Where would you like to go?"

Now she smiled. Who needed a hundred percent? "I'll think about it."

She ate, dressed, happy that she'd left herself enough time to *take* her time. As she strapped on her weapon harness, she considered indulging in one more cup of coffee before she headed downtown to Cop Central.

Her communicator signaled. She drew it out of her pocket, and seeing "Dispatch" on the readout, went straight to full cop mode.

He watched it happen. It always fascinated him how those whiskey-colored eyes could go from easy, even laughing, to flat and empty. She stood straight now, her tall, lanky body braced, long legs spread, boots planted. Her face, all those delightful angles of it, showed no expression. The generous mouth that had been curved moments before, set.

"Dallas."

Dispatch, Dallas, Lieutenant Eve. See the officers, 525 West Twenty-third Street. Basement of residential apartment building. Possible homicide, female.

"Acknowledged. On my way. Contact Peabody, Detective Delia. I'll meet her on scene."

"Well, you had breakfast first," Roarke commented when she pocketed the communicator. He traced a finger, lightly, down the shallow dent in her chin.

"Yeah. I won't be getting that last cup of coffee. Then again, the female on West Twenty-third won't be getting any either."

Traffic clogged the streets. Spring, Eve thought, as she bullied her way through it, time for daffodils and fresh tourists. She carved her way over to Seventh, where she caught a break for a solid ten blocks. With her windows down she let the city-scented air blow over her and send her short, chopped-up brown hair flying.

Egg pockets and sludge coffee emanated from the glide-carts, stone dust kicked up from the crew that attacked a wide chunk of sidewalk with airjacks. The sound of them, the symphony of horns as she hit another snarl, the clatter of feet on pavement as pedestrians surged over a crosswalk, created the urban music she understood.

She watched street vendors, who may or may not hold licenses, pop their tables up in hopes of catching the early commuters or tourists up and about for breakfast. Ball caps and T-shirts replaced the winter's heavy scarves and gloves. Markets, open for business, displayed crates of fruit or flowers, colorful arrays to feed body and soul.

A transvestite, who easily topped six and a half feet, toddled along on skinny blue heels. She shook back her golden waterfall of hair as she delicately tested a melon for ripeness. As she waited out the light, Eve watched a tiny woman, well past her century mark, bump up in her seated scooter. The tranny and centurian seemed to chat amiably while they selected fruit.

You had to love New York, Eve thought when the light changed. Or stay the hell out of it.

She shoved her way into Chelsea, absolutely in tune with her city.

At 525, she double-parked and, flipping on her On Duty light, ignored the bitter curses and rude gestures tossed at her by her fellow New Yorkers. Life and death in the city, she thought, was rarely a smooth ride.

She hooked her badge on her jacket, grabbed her field kit out of the trunk, then approached the uniform at the main door.

"What've we got?"

"DB in the basement, female, round about thirty. No ID, no jewelry, no purse or nothing. Still dressed, so it doesn't look like a sex crime." He led her in as he spoke. "Tenant and his kid found her when they came down to get the kid's bike outta the storage locker. Kid's been grounded or something. Anyway, they called it in. Guy thinks maybe she lives here, or around. Maybe he's seen her before, but he ain't sure. He got the kid out pretty quick and didn't take a good look."

They headed down a stairway, boots and cop shoes clanging on metal. "Didn't see a weapon, but she's got burns here." He tapped fingers on his carotid. "Looks like she got zapped."

"I want two officers knocking on doors. Who saw what when. See the tenant and his boy are secured. Names?"

"Burnbaum, Terrance. Kid's Jay. We're sitting on them in six-oh-two."

She nodded at the two officers securing the scene, engaged her recorder. "Dallas, Lieutenant Eve, on scene at five twenty-five West Twenty-third. My partner's on her way. Find out if the building's got a super or manager on-site. If so, I want to see him."

She scanned the area first. Concrete floor, caged lockers, pipes, spiderwebs. No windows, no doors. No security cameras.

"I'm going to want any security discs from the entrances, and from the stairwells. Find the super."

Lured her down here, Eve thought as she opened her

kit for her can of Seal-It. Or forced her down. Maybe she came down for something and got jumped. No way out.

She studied the body from where she stood, coating her hands and boots with sealant. Slim build, but didn't look soft. The head was turned away, with long blond hair curtaining the face. The hair had a shine to it, and the clothes were good quality.

Not from the streets, she thought. Not with that hair, those clothes, the nicely manicured fingers on the hand she could see.

"The victim is lying on her left side, back to the stairs. No visible prints on the concrete floor. It looks clean. Did Burnbaum move the body?"

"He says no. Says he went over, took her wrist. Said it was cold, got no pulse, and he knew. He just got his kid out."

Eve circled the body, crouched. Something set off a low alarm in her brain, a kind of sick dread in her gut. She lifted the curtain of hair.

For an instant, one sharp instant, everything in her went cold. "Goddamn it. Goddamn it. She's one of us."

The cop who'd stayed with her stepped forward. "She's a cop?"

"Yeah. Coltraine, Amaryllis. Run it, run it now. Get me an address. Detective Coltraine. Son of a bitch."

Morris, she thought. Oh, fucking hell.

"This is her place, Lieutenant. She's got four-oh-five, this building."

She ran the prints because it had to be done, had to be official. The sick dread rose to a cold rage. "Victim is identified as Coltraine, Detective Amaryllis. NYPSD. This address, apartment four-oh-five."

She flipped back the light jacket. "Where's your piece, Coltraine? Where's your goddamn piece? Did they use it on you? Do you with your own weapon? No visible defensive wounds, clothes appear undisturbed. No signs of violence on the body but for the stunner burns on the throat. He held your own piece to your throat, didn't he? On full."

She heard the clang on the stairs, looked up as her partner came down.

Peabody looked spring fresh. Her hair flipped at her neck, dark sass around her square face. She wore a pink blazer and pink skids—a color choice Eve would have made numerous pithy comments on under any other circumstances.

"Nice of them to wait until we were almost officially on shift," Peabody said cheerfully. "What've we got?"

"It's Coltraine, Peabody."

"Who?" Peabody walked over, looked down, and all the rosy color drained out of her cheeks. "Oh my God. Oh God. It's Morris's . . . Oh. No."

"She isn't wearing her weapon. It may be the murder weapon. If it's here, we have to find it."

"Dallas."

Tears swam in Peabody's eyes. Eve understood them, felt them in her own throat. But shook her head. "Later for that. Later. Officer, I want you to take a man and check her apartment, make sure it's clear. I want to know either way. Now."

"Yes, sir." She heard it in his voice—not the tears,

11

but the simmering rage. The same that rolled in her gut.

"Dallas. Dallas, how are we going to tell him?"

"Work the scene. This is now. That's later." And she didn't have the answer. "Look for her weapon, her holster, anything else that might be hers. Work the scene, Peabody. I'll take the body."

Her hands were steady as she got out her gauges, went to work. And she froze the question out of her mind. The question of how she would tell the chief medical examiner, tell her friend, that the woman who'd put stars in his eyes was dead.

"Time of death twenty-three forty."

When she'd done all she could do, Eve straightened. "Any luck?" she said to Peabody.

"No. All these lockers. If the killer wanted to leave the weapon and hide it, there are a lot of places."

"We'll put Crime Scene on it." Eve rubbed the space between her eyes. "We have to talk to the guy who called it in, and his son, and take her apartment. We can't have her taken in until Morris knows. He can't find out that way."

"No. God, no."

"Let me think." Eve stared hard at the wall. "Find out what shift he's on. We don't let the morgue unit have her until . . ."

"The uniforms know a cop went down, Dallas. It's going to start spreading. Cop. Female. This address, or just this area. If Morris gets wind—"

"Shit. You're right. You're right. You take over here. The uniforms are sitting on Terrance Burnbaum and his boy in six-oh-two. Talk to them first. Don't let them take her off scene, Peabody."

"I won't." Peabody scanned the text on her PPC. "One thing good, Morris is working a noon to eight. He wouldn't be at the morgue this early."

"I'll go to his place. I'll do it."

"Jesus, Dallas." The words trembled. "Jesus."

"If you finish in six-oh-two before I get back, start on her apartment. Fine-tooth, Peabody." Steps, Eve reminded herself. Take all the steps. Think about the misery later. "Contact EDD, but give me a head start. All her communications, all her data. Uniforms are finding the super, so confiscate the security discs. Don't—"

"Dallas." Peabody spoke gently. "I know what to do. You taught me what to do. I'll take care of her. You can trust me."

"I know. I know." Eve struggled to let out a breath that wanted to stick in her throat. "I don't know what I'm going to say to him. How to say it."

"There's no easy way."

Couldn't be, Eve thought. Shouldn't be.

"I'll tag you when I . . . when it's done."

"Dallas." Peabody reached out, clasped Eve's hand. "Tell him—if it seems right—tell him I'm sorry. I'm so sorry."

With a nod, Eve started up. The killer had gone this way, she thought. Only way out. Up these same stairs, through this same door. She reopened her kit, unsure if she was stalling or just doing her job. But she took out the minigoggles, studied the lock, the jamb, and found no sign of force.

Could've used Coltraine's key card, Eve thought. Unless he was in first, jumped her when she came down.

Damn it, damn it, she couldn't *see* it. Couldn't clear her mind to see. She went up to the next level, repeated the process on the back door of the building with the same results.

A tenant, someone let in by a tenant—including the victim—someone with a master or superior skills at picking locks.

She studied the security cam over the rear door. Then shut the door, secured it as one of the uniforms jogged down to her.

"Apartment's clear, Lieutenant. Bed's made, no dishes around. It's neat and tidy. Lights were on dim. She, ah, had this droid pet—little cat. It was set to sleep mode."

"Did you see her weapon, her badge?"

His jaw tightened. "No, sir. We found a lockbox in her bedroom closet. Space for her sidearm and a clutch piece, holsters for both. None of them were there. Box wasn't locked. I didn't see her badge, Lieutenant. We didn't search, but—"

"What do you do with your badge when you're off duty for the night, Officer . . . Jonas?"

"Put it on my dresser."

"Yeah. Lock up the weapon, leave the badge on the dresser. Maybe on top of the lockbox, but easy access. Detective Peabody's in charge here now. I don't want her name out, do you hear me? I don't want a leak on this. You keep it contained here until I clear it. Understood?"

"Yes, sir."

"That's one of us down there. She'll have that respect."

"Yes, sir."

She strode out, then stood on the sidewalk and breathed. Just let herself breathe. She looked up, watched clouds crawl over the sky. Gray over blue. It was only right, she thought. It was only right.

She walked to her vehicle, keyed it open. Trapped behind it, a driver leaned his head out of his car window, shook his fist at her.

"Fucking cops!" he shouted. "Think you own the streets, or what?"

She imagined herself going up to the window, plowing her fist into his face. Because one of the cops he cursed was lying dead on a concrete floor in a windowless basement.

Some of it may have showed on her face, in the cold hard stare. He pulled his head back in, brought up his window, hit the locks.

Eve stared another moment, watched him shrink behind the wheel. Then she got in her car, flipped off her light, and pulled away.

She had to look up Morris's address, and used the in-dash computer. Strange, she thought. She'd never been to his place. She considered him a friend, a good one—not just a work acquaintance or connection. But they rarely socialized outside the job. Why was that?

Maybe because she resisted socializing like she would a tooth extraction? Could be it.

She knew he liked music, and was especially fond of jazz and blues. He played the saxophone, dressed like an uptown rock star, had a mind full of interesting, often incomprehensible trivia.

He had humor and depth. And great respect for the dead. Great compassion for those left behind by death.

Now it was a woman he'd . . . had he loved her? Eve wondered. Maybe, maybe. He'd certainly cared deeply for the woman, the cop, who was dead. And now it was he who was left behind.

The clouds brought a thin spring rain, the kind that spat rather than plopped on the windshield. If it lasted or increased, vendors would poof up with stands of umbrellas. The magic of New York commerce. Vehicle traffic would slow; pedestrian traffic would speed up. And for a while, the streets would gleam, shining like black mirrors. Illegals dealers would pull up their hoods and get on with business or huddle in doorways until the storm passed. More than an hour of rain? You could find a diamond on the sidewalk easier than finding an unoccupied cab.

God bless New York, she thought, until it ate you alive.

Morris lived in Soho. She should've guessed it. There was something bohemian, exotic, artistic about the man who'd chosen to doctor the dead.

He had a Grim Reaper tattoo, she remembered, which she'd seen inadvertently when she'd called him in the middle of the night, and he hadn't bothered to block video. Though he'd been in bed and barely covered by the sheet.

The man was hot. No wonder Coltraine had . . .

Oh God. Oh God.

She stalled, couldn't help herself, by searching out a parking spot along the street. Artists tented their wares or grabbed them from the little stalls to dash with them out of the rain. Those too iced to settle for trendy shops lived here, among the lofts and varied restaurants, the in-groove clubs and nightspots.

She found a spot, three blocks from Morris's place. And she walked through the rain while others dashed and darted around her, seeking shelter from the wet.

She climbed to the main door, started to push his buzzer. Couldn't. He'd see her through his screen, and it would give him too much time to think, or he'd ask, and she couldn't answer. Instead, she violated his privacy and used her master to gain entrance to the tiny lobby shared by the other lofts.

She took the stairs, gained herself a little more time, and circled around to his door. What would she say?

It couldn't be the standard here. It couldn't be the standby: *I regret to inform you . . . I'm sorry for your loss.* Not here, not with Morris. Praying it would come to her, it would somehow be the right way, she pressed the bell.

In the time that passed, her skin chilled. Her heart thudded. She heard the locks give, watched his lock light go from red to green.

He opened the door and smiled at her.

His hair was loose. She'd never seen it loose, raining down his back rather than braided. He wore black pants, a black tee. His exotic almond eyes looked a little sleepy. She heard the sleep in his voice when he greeted her.

"Dallas. The unexpected on my doorstep on a rainy morning."

She saw curiosity. No alarm, no worry. She knew her face showed him nothing. Not yet. Another second or two, she thought. Just another few seconds before she broke his heart.

"Can I come in?"

2

Art radiated from the walls in an eclectic mix from bold, bright colors and odd shapes to elegant pencil drawings of naked women in various stages of undress.

It was an open space with the kitchen in black and silver flowing into a dining area in strong red, which curved into the living area. Open silver stairs ribboned their way up to the second floor, again open and ringed by a shining rail.

There was a sense of movement in the space, maybe from the energy of all the color, she thought, or all the pieces of him and his interests displayed there.

Bowls, bottles, stones, photographs jockeyed for position with books—no wonder Morris and Roarke hit it off—and musical instruments, sculptures of dragons, a small brass gong, and what she thought was an actual human skull.

Watching her face, Morris gestured to the long, armless couch. "Why don't you sit down? I can offer you passable coffee. Nothing as prime as you're used to."

"No, that's okay." But she thought, yes, let's sit, have coffee. Let's just not do this thing.

He took her hand. "Who's dead? It's one of us." His fingers tightened on hers. "Peabody—"

"No. Peabody's . . . no." Only making it worse, she thought. "Morris, it's Detective Coltraine."

She could see by his face he didn't understand, he didn't connect his question with her answer. She did the only thing she could do. She plunged the knife in his heart.

"She was killed last night. She's dead, Morris. She's gone. I'm sorry."

He released her hand, stepped back from her. As if, she knew, breaking contact would stop it. Just stop it all. "Ammy? You're talking about Amaryllis?"

"Yes."

"But—" He stopped himself from making the denial. She knew the first questions in his head—was she sure? Could there be a mistake? There must be a mistake. But he knew her, and didn't waste the words. "How?"

"We're going to sit down."

"Tell me how."

"She was murdered. It's looking like her own weapon was used on her. Both her weapons are missing. We're looking. Morris—"

"No. Not yet." His face had gone blank and smooth, a mask carved from one of his own polished stones. "Just tell me what you know."

"I don't have much yet. She was found this morning, in the basement of her building, by a neighbor and his son. Her time of death was about twenty-three forty last night. There aren't any signs of a struggle at the scene, or in her apartment. No visible wounds on her, but for the stunner burns on her throat. She had no ID on her, no

20

jewelry, no bag, no badge, no weapon. She was fully dressed."

She saw something flicker over his face at that, a ripple over the stone, and understood. Rape always made murder worse. "I haven't looked at the security discs yet, because I needed to tell you. Peabody's on scene."

"I have to change. I have to change and go in. Go in and see to her."

"No, you won't. You tell me who you trust the most, who you want, and we'll arrange for them to do the autopsy. You're not doing it."

"It's not for you to say. I'm chief medical examiner."

"I'm primary. And you and I both know that your relationship with the"—she swallowed the word victim—"with Detective Coltraine means you have to step back from this part. Take a minute, take as many minutes as you need to come down to that. You can't work on her, Morris, for your own sake and for hers."

"You think I'll do nothing? That I'll stand by and let someone else touch her?"

"I'm not asking you to do nothing. But I'm telling you you won't do this." When he turned, started for the stairs, she simply took his arm.

"I'll stop you." She spoke quietly, felt the muscles in his arm vibrate. "Take a swing at me, yell, throw something, whatever you need. But I'll stop you. She's mine now, too."

The rage showed in his eyes, burned them black. She braced for a blow, she'd give him that. But the rage melted into grief. This time when he turned, she let him go.

21

He walked to the long, wide window that looked out on the buzz and vibrancy of Soho. He laid his hands on the shelf of the sill, leaned so his arms could hold some of the weight his legs couldn't.

"Clipper." Now his voice was as raw as his eyes had been. "Ty Clipper. I want him to take care of her."

"I'll see to it."

"She wore, always wore a ring on the middle finger of her right hand. A square-cut pink tourmaline, flanked by small green tourmaline baguettes. A silver band. Her parents gave it to her on her twenty-first birthday."

"Okay."

"You said the basement of her building. She'd have no reason to go down there."

"There are storage lockers."

"She didn't keep one. She told me once they charged a ridiculous price for little cages down there. I offered to store anything she needed stored, but she said she hadn't accumulated so much, yet, that she needed spillover space. Why was she there?"

"I'll find out. I promise you. Morris, I promise you I'll find out who did this, and why."

He nodded, but didn't turn, only stared out at the movement, the color, the life. "There's a place inside, when you're connected to cops—as friends, as lovers, even as associates—that knows the risk of that connection, of involvement. I've worked on enough dead cops to know those risks. But you have to put it aside, lock it away, because you have to keep that connection. It's what you do, who you are. But you know, you always know, and still when it happens, it seems impossible.

22

"Who knows death better than I? Than we," he said, turning now. "And yet, it seems impossible. She was so alive. And now she isn't."

"Someone took the life from her. I'll find them."

He nodded again, managed to get to the couch, sink down. "I was falling in love with her. I felt it happening—that long, slow drop. We wanted to take it slow, enjoy it. We were still discovering each other. Still at the stage where when she walked into the room, or I heard her voice, smelled her skin, everything inside me sang."

He dropped his head into his hands.

Comfort wasn't her finest skill. Peabody, Eve thought, would have the right words, the right tone. All she could do was follow instinct. She moved to the couch, sat beside him.

"Tell me what to do for you, and I'll do it. Tell me what you need, and I'll get it. Li—"

Maybe it was the use of his first name, something she never used, but he turned to her. When he turned, she held him. He didn't break, not yet, but kept his cheek pressed to hers.

"I need to see her."

"I know. Give me some time first. We'll take care of her for you."

He eased back. "You need to ask. Turn on your recorder and ask."

"Okay." Routine, she thought. Wasn't that a kind of comfort? "Tell me where you were last night between twenty-one and twenty-four hundred."

"I worked until nearly midnight, clocking some extra hours, clearing up some paperwork. Ammy and I planned to go away for a few days next week. Take a long weekend. Memphis. We booked this old inn. We were going to take a garden tour, see Graceland, listen to music. I spoke to several people on the night shift. I can give you names."

"I don't need them. I'll check it out, and we'll move on. Did she tell you anything about her caseload? About anyone she had concerns about?"

"No. We didn't talk shop a great deal. She was a good cop. She liked to find answers, and she was organized and precise. But she didn't live the job. She wasn't like you. The job was what she did, not what she was. But she was smart and capable. Whenever we had our jobs intersect, that came across."

"What about on the personal front? Exes?"

"We started seeing each other shortly after she transferred here from Atlanta. And while we were taking it slow, letting it all . . . unfold, neither of us was seeing anyone else. She had a serious relationship in college. It lasted over two years. She was involved with another cop for a while, but said she preferred the casual dating scene as a rule. That I was breaking her rule. I know there was someone else, someone serious, and that ended before she transferred to New York."

"Any complaints about any neighbors, anyone in the building hassling her?"

"No. She loved that little apartment of hers. Dallas, she has family back in Atlanta."

"I know. I'll notify them. Can I contact anyone for you?"

"No. Thank you."

"I didn't bring a grief counselor because—"

"I don't want a grief counselor." He pressed his fingers to his eyes. "I have a key for her apartment. You'll want that."

"Yeah."

She waited while he went up the silver stairs, and paced around his living space until he came back with a key card. "Did she have one to this place?"

"Yes."

"Change your codes."

He drew a breath. "Yes, all right. I need you to keep me informed. I need to be involved in this."

"I'll keep you informed."

"I need to be part of it. I need that."

"Let me work on that. I'll contact you. If you need to talk to me, I'm available for you twenty-four seven. But I've got to get back to this, back to her."

"Tell Ty . . . Tell him to play Eric Clapton for her. Any of the discs in my collection. She particularly liked his music." He moved to the elevator, opened the grille.

"I wish sorry meant something. Peabody . . . she told me to tell you the same." She stepped in, kept her eyes on his as the grille closed and until the doors shut.

On the drive back, she tagged Peabody. "Did the sweepers find the weapon?"

"That's a negative."

"Damn it. I'm heading back to the scene. Contact the morgue. Chief Medical Examiner Morris assigns ME Ty Clipper to this matter. He requests the ME play Eric Clapton during autopsy."

"Oh, man. How is he? How—"

"He's holding up. Make sure they understand these are Morris's directives. I'm on my way back. You and I are going to go through her apartment, inch by inch."

"I was about to start on that. I talked to Burnbaum and his kid. Nothing more there. The knock-on-doors hasn't turned up anything. Security—"

"Fill me in when I get there. Ten minutes."

She clicked off. She wanted silence. Just silence until the emotional knots loosened. She'd be no good to Amaryllis Coltraine if she let herself stay twisted up over the grief in a friend's eyes.

At the apartment, she waited until the morgue team carried the body out. "She goes straight to ME Clipper," Eve snapped. "She's a cop. She gets priority."

"We know who she is." One of the team turned after the body was loaded in the wagon. "She's not only a cop, she was Morris's lady. We'll take good care of her, Lieutenant."

Satisfied, she went inside, took the stairs to Coltraine's apartment. Using the key card Morris had given her, she found Peabody inside.

"It was hard," Peabody said after one look. "It shows."

"Then I'd better get over it. Security?"

"I took a quick scan. Nothing on the rear door. He had to come in that way, jam the camera. EDD's on it. Front door cam ran the whole time. I've got her coming in about sixteen hundred, carrying a file bag—which is still here—and a take-out bag. She didn't go out again, not by the front. Stairway has cams, and they were

26

compromised. Both the rear and stairway cams shut down from about twenty-two thirty to about twenty-four hundred. Elevator has cams, and they ran through. She didn't take the elevator. Neighbor confirms she used the stairs, habitually."

"The killer had to know her, know her routine. Had to take her in the stairway."

"I've got a team of sweepers in there now, going top to bottom."

"Taking her that quick, that clean, the killer had to know she was going out. So either that was another habit, or he lured her out. We'll check her transmissions, but if that's how it went down, he used her pocket 'link, then took it with him. Someone she knew. A friend, an ex, one of her weasels, someone in the building or close by. Someone she'd let get the drop on her."

Eve glanced around the apartment. "Impressions?"

"I don't think she left under any kind of duress. Everything's just too tidy for that, and that droid kitten?" When Peabody gestured, Eve frowned at the snoozing ball of fur. "I checked its readout. She set it to sleep mode at twenty-three eighteen. It doesn't seem like something you'd do if you were in trouble."

Eve studied the room as she wandered it. It had a female feel, a fussy woman's order to it. "The killer contacts her, via her pocket 'link. Come out, meet me for a drink, or I had a terrible fight with my boyfriend, come over so I can boo-hoo all over you. No, no." Eve shook her head, wandered into the small bedroom with its mountain of pillows on its neatly made bed. "She had her clutch piece. Most cops are going to carry a weapon, but I don't see her strapping on a clutch to go have a drink."

"One of her weasels. Meet me here, at such and such time. I got some good shit."

"Yeah, yeah, that could work. We'll talk to her boss, her partner, her unit, see what she was into. She could've been meeting another kind of source, or just meeting someone she didn't completely trust. A little extra insurance with the clutch piece. And still he got the drop on her, took her down without a struggle."

"She wouldn't have been expecting to see him in her stairway. Her guard's down, and that's that."

Eve said nothing. She needed to turn it over awhile, walk it through. "Let's see what we can find here."

They got to work, searching through drawers, in closets, through clothes, in pockets. The dead had no privacy, and Eve thought as a cop; Coltraine would have known and accepted that.

She found the goodie drawer in the bedside table— body oils, a few toys—and had to block the image that kept trying to lodge in her head of Morris and Coltraine rolling around naked on the bed.

"She liked pretty underwear," Peabody commented as she went through other drawers. "All her stuff's in the lingerie level. Sexy, girlie. She liked pretty things. The little bottles, the lamps, the pillows. Her drawers are neat and organized, nothing like mine. She doesn't have a lot of *stuff*, you know. No clutter. And what's here doesn't match-match, but it all works together. It's just a really pretty place, to keep dogging the same word."

Eve stepped to a clever little corner table that held a

compact data-and-communication system. In the single slim drawer she found a memo book. But when she tried to bring up data, it denied her access.

"She's a cop. She'd've passcoded it," Eve said. "We'll want this tagged for EDD. I want in."

She learned more about the victim on the search. Peabody was right, she'd liked pretty things. Not overly fussy and frilly, just female. But no clutter, not crowded, and everything in its place. The roses in the living area were real, and fresh.

She found a trinket box that held florist cards, all from Morris. He'd said they'd been exclusive for months. At least as far as flowers went, Eve thought, he was right.

That didn't mean she hadn't had something on the side. When a woman went out that time of night, it could be a booty call.

Yet, it just didn't strike right. She'd seen Coltraine with Morris. She'd felt the zing between them.

"Secure building," Eve said out loud. "A nice, compact apartment, droid pet. Nice furniture, nice clothes. Not a lot of either. She's selective. Not much jewelry, but again, what she has is good quality."

"Same with the hair products, the enhancers," Peabody put in. "She knew what she liked, what worked for her, and stuck with it. Me, I've got a drawer full of cast-off lip dyes, eye gunk, hair crap. Perfume. One scent. There's leftover Chinese in the fridge, vac-sealed, some health food, bottled water and juices. Two bottles of wine."

"She's got a lover, but lives alone. The men's toiletry

kit is probably Morris's. We'll check with him rather than sending it straight to the lab. The man's shirt, boxers, socks, pants, they look like him. Not a lot of him in here, though. They probably spent more time at his place. It's about four times as big as this, and the location's prime for cafés, clubs, restaurants, galleries. How'd the killer know she was in last night? Stalking her? I should've asked Morris how often they were together, if they had a routine."

"Dallas, you gave him a break. Gave him a little time. We'll follow up."

"The killer didn't come in here. Too risky. Why chance being seen? No, no, he tagged her on her pocket 'link."

"They could've set up a meet prior."

"Why risk that? She might tell somebody—Morris, her partner, her boss. I'm meeting X tonight, and then we'd be talking to X instead of wondering who the hell he is. Morris was working, she'd have known that. So she's not going to tag him at that hour and tell him she's headed out for something. She just gets her stuff, turns off her cat, and goes. She knew her killer, or whoever set it up.

"Let's get the sweepers in here, and have EDD pick up her electronics." She checked her wrist unit. "We'll go by the morgue before notifying next of kin."

"I'll do that. You told Morris," Peabody added. "I'll tell her family."

"Okay. Then we'll both talk to her partner, her squad, her boss."

In the car, Peabody sat slumped in the seat, staring

30

out the side window. "Dallas? I got this thing eating at me, and I just want to get it out."

"You felt bitchy and resentful because she hooked up with Morris."

"Yeah." Peabody let out the word, like relief. "I didn't even know her, hardly at all, and I let myself think, like, who the hell is she, sashaying—I even thought the word *sashay*, because she was from the South—in here and getting all smoochy with our Morris? Stupid, because I'm with McNab and never had a thing with Morris anyway, except the occasional perfectly permissible and healthy fantasy. But I decided I didn't like her, just for that. And now she's dead and I feel like crap about it."

"I know. I've got the same thing going. Except for the fantasy part."

"I guess that makes me feel a little better." She scooted up again, studied Eve's profile. "You really never had the teeniest fantasy about Morris?"

"No. Jeez."

"Just a little one. Like you'd go to the morgue one night, and it's strangely empty, so you go into the main cutting room and Morris is there. Naked."

"No! Stop filling my head with that crap." But oddly, some of the sick weight in Eve's belly eased. "Don't you and McNab bang often enough to keep you from having prurient fantasies about a colleague? In the freaking dead house?"

"I don't know why. The morgue's creepy, but Morris is severely sexy. McNab and I bang plenty. Just last night we—"

31

"I don't want to hear about you and McNab banging."

"You brought it up."

"Which illustrates how your sick Morris fantasies screwed up my mental health."

Peabody shrugged that off. "Who did Morris put on Coltraine, specifically?"

"Clipper."

"Die-For-Ty? Talk about the sex. How come so many death doctors are wholly iced?"

"A mystery I've pondered throughout my career."

"No, seriously. Clipper's like *ummm*. He's gay and has a partner, but a yummy treat for the eyes. His partner's an artist. He paints people, literally I mean. Body painting. They've been together about six years."

"How do you know all this stuff?"

"Unlike you, I enjoy hearing about people's personal lives, especially when it involves sex."

"At least since Clipper's not into women, you won't be troubled by sexual fantasies."

Peabody pursed her lips in thought. "I can work with it. Two naked guys, body paints, me. Oh yeah, endless possibilities."

Eve let Peabody have her moment. Easier, she knew, to think about crazy sex than the murder of another cop, than the grief of a colleague and friend.

The moment passed soon enough. Once they arrived at the morgue, started down the long white-tiled tunnel, the mood shifted. It wasn't just death, it wasn't just murder. Nipping and gnawing at objectivity were the keen teeth of personal loss.

32

They crossed paths with a tech who stopped, slid her hands into the pockets of her long, white coat. "Ah, Clipper's using Morris's suite. I don't know if he—if Morris is going to check in or anything, so maybe when you talk to him you could tell him . . . We're all here."

"Okay."

"Whatever we can do." The tech shrugged helplessly, said, "Hell," and strode away.

Eve moved on to the autopsy room where Morris habitually did his work. In his place stood ME Ty Clipper, a solid six feet with a muscular body clad in a pale blue shirt and khaki pants. He'd rolled up his sleeves neatly to the elbow, donned a clear cape.

He wore his hair in a close-cropped skullcap. A short, neat goatee added a hint of edge to his conservative attire, and interest to his angular face. But with Clipper it was all about the eyes. Huge, heavy-lidded, they were the color of crystallized amber and a jolt of contrast to his dark skin.

"I haven't finished. I'm sorry." His voice held a hint of his native Cuba.

"What can you tell me?"

"She wasn't raped. There's no evidence of sexual assault, or sexual activity. That would matter to Morris."

"Yes, it will." Like a murmur in the background a man sang a plea to someone named Layla. "Is that Eric Clapton?"

"Yes."

"That'll matter to him, too." Eve set it aside, stepped forward.

Coltraine lay on the slab. "No defensive wounds."

33

Eve studied the body now as she would any piece of evidence. "No signs of violence other than the throat burns."

"There are minor bruises on her shoulder blades, and the back of her head." Clipper gestured to the comp screen, called up the scan. "Of the sort you'd incur by knocking back against a wall."

"She was shoved, pushed."

"Possibly. Death ensued soon after. The burns on the throat are consistent with a stunner pressed to the area. Contact burns. Have you found her weapon?"

"No."

"Until you do, I can't confirm it was the murder weapon, or if another was used. Only that the wounds are consistent with contact burns from a police-issue."

"If her own weapon was used, how the hell did he disarm her? Shoves her back, she hits the wall. It's not enough, not for a cop. There aren't any cuts, no evidence of restraints." Because he didn't offer, as Morris would have, Eve picked up a pair of microgoggles herself, leaned over Coltraine to examine. "No abrasions on her wrists, her ankles. Here. Right here. On her biceps. Pressure syringe?"

"I believe so."

"How did he get close enough to her, without her putting up a fight, to drug her?"

"I have the tox screen flagged priority. You're right that there are no signs of violence outside the body. But there are, in."

Eve glanced up at Clipper, then shifted to study what the precise Y-cut revealed. "What am I looking for?"

34

"Her internal organs show signs of distress."

"Dying will do that." But she followed him, looked closer. "She took a hit?"

"I need to complete more tests before I can be sure. I understand you want quick answers," he added at Eve's hiss of impatience. "But—"

She shook her head, willed herself to throttle back. "Morris wanted you because, I'd say, you're thorough and you're precise. Give me best guess. I won't hold you to it."

"A high-range stun, frontal assault. No more than three- to five-feet distance. A body shot."

"Which would have taken her down, down and out. She takes a hit, it knocks her back against the wall—in the stairwell, and she goes down. He has to get her down to the basement. No signs she was dragged. So he has to carry her. Or there could have been more than one assailant. Carry her down. Why not just finish her off in the stairwell and be done with it?

"Because there was something they wanted, something to say, something they needed her to say, to tell them," Eve continued. "So he/they cart her down, and they bring her back with a jolt—a hit of amphetamine, adrenaline." Pain, Eve thought, they'd brought her back to pain. Helpless. Body paralyzed from the stun, mind aware. "To tell her something, to ask her something. And when they finished, they shut her down. She'd have known it was coming. When they pressed the stunner to her throat, she'd have known."

She pulled off the goggles, tossed them aside. "They used her weapon. They used it to kill her because it's more insulting, more demeaning. Ambushed her in the stairway, dropped her. Carried her down, jolted her back, took her out. In somewhere around twenty minutes. That's quick. Took her weapon, ID, badge, 'link, jewelry. Why the jewelry? The rest makes sense. It's professional, but the jewelry's amateur hour. So why? Just because you can? Just because you want? Souvenirs, mementos?"

"Because it left her with nothing?" Peabody voiced the question. "It strips her. They leave her dressed, maybe because it's not about that kind of power or violence, even that kind of humiliation. But they take what's important to her, and leave her on the floor. With nothing."

"Maybe." Eve nodded. "Maybe so. I don't think Morris will come in today," Eve said to Clipper. "But if he does, do whatever you have to do, whatever it takes, to keep him away from her until she's . . ."

"I will."

3

Eve moved quickly through Central. She took the glides rather than the elevator to avoid getting into a box with other cops. She passed enough of them—uniforms, soft-clothes, detectives, brass—to know word had spread.

When she turned into her own bullpen, all movement, all chatter ceased. And, she knew, it had to be addressed.

"At twenty-three forty last night, Detective Amaryllis Coltraine was murdered by person or persons unknown. Every member of this division is hereby notified, or will be notified, that any scheduled leave may, and likely will, be cancelled until this case is closed. I will clear overtime for any and all who are tapped to join the investigative team. Any of you who require personal or hardship leave in the interim will have to clear it with me, and will have to make it damn good.

"There will be no statements to the media, offically or unoffically, on this matter unless cleared through me. You can all consider this part of your current caseload. She's ours now."

She walked to her office, straight to the AutoChef for coffee. She'd no more than taken the steaming mug out when Detective Baxter came in behind her. "Lieutenant."

"Make it quick, Baxter."

"I wanted to say Trueheart and I are cleaning up a few loose ends on a case. We should have it tied up pretty soon. You need grunt work, legwork, shit work, whatever on this, my boy and I," he continued speaking of his stalwart aide, "we're up for it. Screw the overtime, Dallas. We're not putting in for any of that, not for this."

"Okay." She'd expected no less, but it was satisfying to have her expectations met. "I'm going to be talking to her boss, her partner, whoever she worked with back in Atlanta. I'm going to require copies of her case files, opened and closed, her notes. And I'm going to want fresh eyes going over them. I'm going to need runs on everyone in her apartment building. Everyone she came into contact with routinely. Her neighbors, the guy she bought her food from, who delivered her pizza. Any previous relationships, any current. Her friends, the bartender where she drank. I want to know her inside and out."

"Morris—"

"I'll be going back there, but he needs some time. By the time you tie up those ends, I'll have plenty for you and Trueheart."

"Okay. I, ah, made half a play for her a few months back."

"Baxter, you make half a play for anything female."

He smiled a little, appreciating her attempt to keep it light. "What can I say? Women are the best thing going. She gave me half a flirt back, you know? But she was all about Morris. There's nobody out there who wouldn't jump to work this case, because she was a cop. But every one of them will jump higher, jump faster because of Morris. Just wanted to say."

"Let me know when you close your case."

"Yes, sir."

She took her coffee to her desk, noted she had multiple incoming transmissions. Some would be from the media, she thought, and those she'd dump on the liaison, until ordered otherwise.

Eve picked through, passed, discarded, held. And played the one from her commander. Whitney's administrative assistant relayed his orders. She was to report the minute she was in her office.

She set her coffee aside, rose, and walked back to the bullpen. "Peabody, contact Coltraine's lieutenant and request a meet with him at his earliest convenience. Also request he arrange same with her partner or partners. I'm with Whitney."

She could wish for more time, Eve thought as she traveled the labyrinth of Cop Central to Commander Whitney's domain. Time to put her thoughts together, to start her murder book, to refine her notes, to begin her cold and intrusive search through the life of a dead cop. But when Whitney pushed the bell, you answered the door.

He didn't keep her waiting, either. The minute she walked into the outer office, the admin directed her into the inner sanctum.

He rose from behind his desk and filled the room with his presence. He wore command the way a man wore a suit perfectly tailored for his height, his girth. It belonged to him, Eve had always thought, because he'd earned it—with every step.

Though he rode a desk rather than the streets, that suit of command had been tailored for a cop.

"Lieutenant."

"Sir."

He didn't gesture for her to sit. They would do this standing. He studied her for a moment, his wide, dark face solemn, his eyes cold.

"Report."

She gave it quickly, straight out, every detail even as she laid disc copies of her on-scene on his desk. "I'm arranging to meet with her lieutenant, her partner, anyone from her house who may be able to provide insight or details."

"Morris is covered."

"Yes, sir. He was working, and there are witnesses, as well as security discs and his log to support. There's no need to spend time ascertaining his whereabouts. He's clear."

"Good. That's good. Play it out for me, Dallas. Your view."

"She was home. She either received a call on her pocket 'link or had a previous meet—personal or official is not possible to confirm at this time—previously arranged. Her weapon box was unlocked and empty. There are compartments for her standard issue, and a smaller clutch piece, as well as holsters for both. She used a hip holster for her standard."

For herself, Eve preferred the harness—the feel and the weight of it.

"She went out armed."

"Yes, sir. I'm more inclined to think she went out on the job than socially. Because of the clutch piece. But I don't know her yet. I don't know what kind of a cop she was yet."

He nodded. "Continue."

"She left the apartment sometime after twenty-three eighteen. She had a droid pet and switched it to sleep mode at that time. She set her security, and took the stairs. Wits state this was her habit. The ambush came in the stairway, frontal assault. She took the hit, which knocked her back against the wall. The assailant transported her to the basement of the building, administered an as-yet-unknown stimulant to bring her to. At twenty-three forty, a weapon, possibly her own, was held to her throat and fired. I have EDD checking the security. We know that the rear door cam was jammed. He came in that way, and from my examination, the lock looked clean. So he had a key card and code, or he's very skilled. He knew her habits, and knew she'd be coming down the stairs. He contacted her, and she went out to meet him. That's how I see it. She knew her killer."

"For the time being, any media will be funneled through the department liaison. The death of one cop won't stir up the juices in any case. If that changes, I'll let you know. You're free to assign as many men to your investigative team as you feel necessary. Again, if that changes, you'll be informed. This is now flagged priority, for every department involved. I want copies of all reports as they come in, or as they're completed."

"Yes, sir."

"Whatever you need on this one, Lieutenant."

"Understood."

"I'll be speaking with her family shortly, as will her lieutenant. I assume they'll want a funeral or memorial in Atlanta, but we will be holding a memorial here. I'll let you know when it's arranged."

"I'll see my division is informed of the details."

"I've kept you from it long enough. But before you go, I want to ask you something from a personal level. Does Morris have all he needs?"

"I wish I knew. I don't know what else can be done for him, at this time. They were, I think, becoming very serious."

Whitney nodded. "Then we'll do what we do, and find the answers for him."

"Yes, sir."

She went back to it, closed herself in her office to review her notes, to open her murder book, to start her board.

"Dallas?"

"Lab reports are already coming in," Eve said as Peabody stepped inside. "I didn't have to threaten or bribe anybody to get them this fast. It's not just because a cop went down. It's because the cop was Morris's lady. They shot her up with a stimulant—enough so she was conscious and aware, but unable to move, to fight. No trace on her. No prints on the outside, rear door. Sealed up, and had to wipe it down for good measure. No prints, at all. Her internal organs showed extreme trauma, from a stun. If she'd lived, she'd have been in bad shape. He didn't take any chances, but was careful, and knowledgeable enough to know what setting to use so she'd go down hard, stay down, but live. Until he was finished."

"I spoke with the locals in Atlanta. I arranged for a grief counselor for her parents and her brother."

"Good. That's good."

"Her lieutenant can and will speak with us anytime. They worked squad-style, so she partnered or teamed with everyone in her unit."

"Then we'll talk to everyone in her unit. Let's go get started."

Peabody glanced at the board, and Coltraine's ID shot. "She was really beautiful." She turned away, followed Eve. "I started runs on the other tenants, and Jenkinson said he had some time, so he's helping on that. I checked in with EDD. McNab said they're on top of it. And they've already sent somebody down to pick up her unit at her house. Her cop house."

"I know what you mean."

"He told me she'd saved, on her home unit, she kept e-mails from Morris. Funny ones, romantic ones, sexy ones." She let out a sigh as they went down the glides. "And some from her parents, her brother, some from friends back in Atlanta. She had them all in different files. There was job stuff on there, too. He's sorting it out. Her last transmission on her home 'link was about eight last night. From Morris. He talked to her while he took a dinner break. Nothing else on her home unit yesterday. She worked an eight-to-four shift."

"We need to know when she got the Chinese, if it was pickup or delivery."

"Chinese?"

"Leftovers in her kitchen. She had a take-out bag with her when she came in, security discs. When did she order it, did she stop on the way home, bring it from work? Start checking take-out and delivery places near her building."

"Okay."

"ME's report said she ate about seven-thirty, drank a glass of wine. She ran the recycler, so there's not much left for the crime lab. Let's find out if she ate alone. We're going to put together every step she took, from the time she got up yesterday morning."

"Did you ask Morris if they were together the night before she died?"

"No. Shit. No. I should have. Damn it." She stopped in the garage, took out her pocket 'link. "Give me some room, Peabody." She keyed in Morris's number. She didn't expect him to answer, and was dumped straight to voice mail. "Morris, it's Dallas. I'm very sorry to disturb you. I need to put a time line together for yesterday. When you can, if you can let me know if you and Detective Coltraine were together yesterday morning, it would—"

"Yes." His face came on-screen. His eyes were dull, dark, and empty. "She stayed here the night before. We had dinner around the corner, a bistro. Jaq's. About eight, I think. And we came back here. She left yesterday morning, about seven. A little after seven. She had an eight-to-four shift."

"Okay. Thanks."

"I spoke with her twice yesterday. She called me

sometime in the afternoon, and I called her, at home, on my dinner break. She was fine. I can't remember the last thing I said to her, or her to me. I've tried, but I can't."

"It doesn't matter what the last thing was. Everything else you said to each other over these past months, that's what adds up. That's what counts. I'll come by later if you—"

"No, but thank you. I'm better off alone for a while."

"That was a good thing you said to him," Peabody commented when Eve shoved the 'link back in her pocket. "About all the things they said to each other."

"I don't know if it was right, or bullshit. I'm winging it."

Coltraine's cop shop squatted between a Korean market and a Jewish deli in post–Urban Wars ugliness. The concrete box would probably withstand a bomb, but it wouldn't win any beauty prizes.

Inside, it smelled of cop. Foul coffee, sweat, starch, and cheap soap. Uniforms milled around in their hard shoes, coming in from details or heading out again while civilians shuffled their way through security. Eve held her badge to a scanner, had it and her prints verified with Peabody's, and passed through.

She moved straight to the sergeant's desk, badged him. He was a hard-eyed, craggy-faced vet who looked like he enjoyed a nice bowl of nails for breakfast.

"Lieutenant Dallas and Detective Peabody, out of Central, to see Lieutenant Delong."

Those hard eyes trained on Eve's face. "You the ones who caught the case?"

He didn't have to specify which case—not for Eve, or for the cops within hearing distance. "That's right."

"Eighteenth squad's one floor up. Stairs there, elevator there. You got any juice on it?"

"We've just started to squeeze. Has anyone off been in to see her, anyone we might want to talk to, the last few days?"

"Nobody comes to mind. If you need to see my log, I'll make sure you get it. The rest of the desk shift's, too."

"Appreciate that, Sergeant."

"I don't know what kinda cop she was, but she never passed this desk without saying good morning. It says something about a person, they take a minute to say good morning."

"Yeah, I guess it does."

They took the open, metal stairs, and Eve felt cop eyes follow her to the second floor. The squad room was smaller than her bullpen—and quieter. Six desks jammed into the room, four of them manned. Two detectives worked their comps, two others their 'links. The Public Administrative Assistant sat at a short counter. His eyes were red, Eve noted, his white, white skin blotchy as if from a recent crying jag. He looked, to her, very young.

"Lieutenant Dallas and Detective Peabody to see Lieutenant Delong."

"Yes, we're—he's expecting you."

Once again, Eve felt cop eyes on her. This time she shifted, met them, one by one as the routine activity in the squad room stopped. She saw anger, resentment, grief, and a measurement. Are you good enough to stand for one of ours?

46

And through a glass wall she saw the man she assumed was Delong rise from his desk and start out.

He stood a little under average height, looked mid-forties and fit—strong through the shoulders. He wore a suit, dark gray with a white shirt, gray tie. A crop of wavy black hair swept back from a thin face that showed strain around the eyes and mouth.

"Lieutenant, Detective." He offered a handshake to both. "Please come back."

Silence followed them into the glass-walled room. Delong shut the door. "First, let me say you'll have complete cooperation from me and the squad. Anything you need, any time you need it."

"Thank you."

"I've already copied all of Detective Coltraine's case files, and cleared EDD to take her electronics. I also have copies of her personnel file, and my evaluations." He picked up a pouch. Peabody took it, slipped it into her file bag. "You can use my office to talk to the squad, or one of our boxes. There's a small conference room upstairs, if that works better."

"I don't want to put you out of your office, Lieutenant, or cause your men to feel they're being interrogated by another cop. The conference room would be fine. I'm sorry for your loss, Lieutenant. I know it's hard to lose a cop under your command."

"Hard enough if she'd gone down in the line. At least then, you know. But this . . . Is there anything you can tell me?"

"We believe she was ambushed in the stairwell of her building, taken down to the basement. We haven't found her weapon. It may have been used to kill her. What was she working on?"

"A robbery in Chinatown, a break-in, electronics store—a couple cases of pocket 'links and PPCs were taken, a carjack—armed. It's all in the files."

"Did she report any threats against her?"

"No. No, she didn't. I have an open-door policy. We're a small squad. If something's up, I usually hear about it."

"Who was she partnered with?"

"We work as a squad. She'd have worked with everyone at some time. I usually paired her with Cleo. Detective Grady. They had a good rhythm. But she was on with O'Brian for the break-in."

"How'd she get along with the rest of the squad?"

"She slid right in. We had some ribbing going on. Southern transplant, and her looks. But she held her own, and earned respect. I'm going to say my squad runs pretty damn smooth. Ammy fit it."

"What kind of cop was she?"

He sighed a little. "She was solid. A detail cop. Organized, good eye. She'd work a case through, no bitching about OT, no griping over paperwork. She was an asset. She cleared her share of cases. She wasn't flashy, didn't need the big collar. She was steady. Did her job."

"And her personal life?"

"She wasn't flashy there, either. Everybody knew she was involved with Morris. We got a squad of four here. It's hard to keep secrets. She was happy. If she had trouble, she didn't share it, she didn't show it."

"Why did she transfer out of Atlanta?"

"I asked her, the way you would. She told me she'd started to feel as if she'd gotten into a rut, that she needed a change of scene, of routine. I wish I had answers. I wish I had something clear-cut to give you. I know your reputation, Lieutenant. Detective," he added with a nod to Peabody. "While part of me wants my team on this case, I know Ammy's in good hands."

"Thank you. If you'd direct us to the conference room, we'll set up. If her most usual partner, Detective Grady's available, we can talk to her first."

"I'll take you up."

The room boasted a single long table, a lot of creaky chairs, two wall screens, a wide whiteboard, and an aged AutoChef.

Peabody tried the coffee, blanched. "It's worse than ours. I didn't think that was possible. I'm going to hit Vending for a soft drink. You want one?"

"Yeah, thanks."

While she waited, Eve thought of Delong. She understood. If Coltraine had gone down in the line, under his command, there would be guilt and grief and anger. But he'd know why. The bad guy got the edge that day. He'd know who, and even if that bad guy needed to be chased down, he'd know.

She set her recorder and her notebook on the table. Took out her PPC to refresh herself on Detective Cleo Grady.

Thirty-two, Eve mused. Detective third grade with eight years in. New York transplant from Jersey. No marriages, no cohabs, no children. Several commendations, and a handful of disciplinary slaps. Part of Delong's squad for three years, transferring at her own request from SVU. Parents retired to Florida. No sibs.

She glanced up when Cleo rapped on the doorjamb. "Detective Grady, Lieutenant."

"Have a seat."

It showed in the eyes, Eve thought. The anger and the resentment. And in the tight line of the mouth. Cleo wore her streaked blond hair short, straight, sleek, and showed off a couple of winking blue studs in her earlobes. The eyes, a deep, almost navy blue, stayed level with Eve as she crossed the room.

She hit five-five, with a body both solid and curvy. She wore simple brown trousers, a white shirt, and a thin tan jacket over it. Like Eve, she preferred the shoulder harness.

"The boss wants us to cooperate, so we will." She had a quick, clipped voice, a little raw at the edges. "But this should be our case."

"If it was my partner or a member of my squad, I'd probably feel the same. But it's not your case. We're on record here, Detective." She paused as Peabody came in, shut the door.

"I picked up some water and Pepsis," Peabody said, and set bottles on the table.

Cleo shook her head. "The least you can do is tell me what you've got."

"You can talk to your lieutenant about that. We brought him up to date. You can play the hard-ass with us, but that's not helping Detective Coltraine."

"If you're looking to dig up dirt on her—"

"Why would we be? We're not IAB. We're homicide.

Your squadmate was murdered, Detective. So cut the crap. You and Coltraine were often partnered."

"Yeah, the boss thought we complemented each other."

"Did you also interact on a personal level? Socially?"

"Sure we did. Why wouldn't . . ." She shook her head again, held up a hand. She picked up a bottle of the water she'd initially rejected, twisted it open, drank. "Look, maybe I'm sorry for the attitude, but this is hard. She was part of my team, and we got to be friends. We worked damn well together, you can look at our case files and see that. And we got so we'd hang out sometimes. Have a drink after shift or a meal. Maybe just the two of us, or maybe with some of the other guys. It wasn't always about the job, either. We'd talk about regular stuff. Hair and weight and men."

"You were close," Peabody commented.

"Yeah. We each had our own life, but we hit it off. You've got to know how it is. When you're working with another female, there are things you can get into, things you can say that you wouldn't with a man."

"Did she tell you about any old lovers, boyfriends, guys that wanted to be with her?"

"She was seeing a couple guys casually back in Atlanta before she transferred. One was another cop, and that was basically a booty buddy she'd been tight with awhile before. The other was a lawyer. She said it just wasn't a good fit, and both of them got to just drifting along in the relationship. One of the reasons she transferred was because she felt her personal life got stale, and she felt she was losing her edge professionally. She wanted something new."

"Nobody serious?" Eve pressed, thinking of what Morris had told her. And saw Cleo hesitate.

"She mentioned there'd been somebody, pretty intense for a while. But it hadn't worked out."

"Name?"

"No. But it bruised her up some—emotionally. She said they broke it off, and she'd done the casual thing for a couple months with the lawyer. But she wanted a change—a new place, new faces. Like that."

"And once she'd transferred—on that personal level."

"The thing with the ME started pretty quick. She hadn't been here long when they met. Ammy said there was this instant spark. They took their time. I mean, they didn't jump in the sack right off. When they did . . . like I said, you tell a woman partner things. She was crazy about him, and it came off mutual. I went out with them—like a double date deal—a few times. They gave it off—that spark. She wasn't seeing anyone else."

"She never mentioned anyone pushing her, on that personal front."

"No."

"Did she take meets on her own? With weasels, other informants, or arrange to deal with suspects solo?"

"Not generally. I mean, she might hook up with one of her weasels solo. But she'd been working this area less than a year. She didn't have that many."

"Names?"

Cleo's back went up, Eve could see it. No cop liked to share weasels. "She mostly used this guy who runs a pawnshop on Spring. Stu Bollimer. He's originally from Georgia, so she played the connection."

"Were you using him on anything currently?"

"I know she gave him a bump on the Chinatown robbery we're working, and he said he'd keep his ear to the ground."

"Anything you worked on generate trouble, somebody who'd want to hurt her?"

"You bring in bad guys, they're not going to be happy with you. Nothing stands out. I've been going over and over it since I heard. We're a small squad, and most of what we handle just isn't that juicy. She liked doing the small jobs. The mom-and-pop whose market gets ripped off, the kid who gets knocked off his airboard so some asshole can steal it. The truth is, she was thinking, maybe down the road, about marriage and having a family, taking the professional mother deal. She liked her job, and she was good at it—don't get me wrong. But she was thinking, especially since Morris, that down the road . . ."

"All right, Detective. If you'd send Detective O'Brian up, I'd appreciate it. If he's not available, your lieutenant can send up whoever he can spare."

"O'Brian's working his desk. I'll send him." Cleo got to her feet. "I don't think it's too much to ask that you come to us if you need more manpower on this. Not every cop works out of Central."

"I'll keep that in mind. Thank you, Detective." After Cleo went out, Eve sat back. "Does she just not get it? Is it just a blind spot?"

"That every cop in that squad is currently a suspect?" Peabody shook her head. "I guess you don't look at your own family first."

"Civilians don't. Cops do—or should." Eve made a couple of notes, then reviewed her data on O'Brian.

"Next up has twenty-three years in. He made first grade five years back. He's been with this squad for a dozen years. Second marriage, fifteen years in. No kids from marriage one, two from marriage two. Commendations, and two valorous conduct citations. Worked Major Case until he transferred here. That's a big shift."

Eve finally cracked her tube of Pepsi, took a hit. "He's been here the longest, longer than his current lieutenant."

"Guys like that can be the touchstone of a squad. The one the others go to when they don't want to go to the brass."

"We're going to be here awhile yet. Check in, will you? See if there's anything new we can use here."

O'Brian, beefy, long-jawed, sharp-eyed, stepped in as Peabody moved to the far end of the table. "Lieutenant. Detective."

"Detective O'Brian. We're splitting duties here, to try to keep ahead of the curve. We can talk while my partner makes some contacts."

"Fine." He sat. "Let me save you some time. Detective Coltraine was a good, steady cop. Dependable. She liked to dig into the pieces for the little details. When she first joined the squad, I had my doubts she'd make the cut. That was my own prejudice, because she looked like someone who should be making beauty vids. After a couple of shifts, I saw what was under her. She knew how to be part of a team, how to handle herself in the field, and with the rest of the squad.

"If she got taken down in the stairwell of her own place, it wasn't a stranger."

"How do you know how she was taken down?"

His eyes never shifted from Eve's. "I've got connections. I used them. I haven't shared what I dug up with the rest of the squad. What gets shared there's up to the boss. But I'm telling you here, if she left her place last night carrying both her weapons, she was on the job. She went down in the line. And I'm going to be pushing for her to have that honor."

"Who could have gotten into her building?"

"Fuck if I know. We don't work that much heat here. She didn't have anything going for somebody to swing out and kill a cop. We got a break-in, electronics. Inside job, no question. We'd've had the guy sewed before noon today. I'll still have him sewed before end-of-shift. He's an idiot, a screwup. He's not a cop killer. I know Delong gave you the case file. You'll see for yourself."

"Could she have, when picking at the pieces for the little details, on this, on something else, have scraped up something hot? Something that came back at her?"

"If she did, she didn't tell me. We had a—I guess I want to say a kind of relationship where she'd talk a case through with me." The grief showed now. He stared down at the table, but Eve saw it working over his face. "She had dinner at my place a few times. My wife liked her, a lot. We all did. Maybe it was Morris."

"Excuse me?"

"Something he was working on, or had. Somebody who wanted to pay him back. Where do you hit? She was in love with the guy. It showed. The few times he

55

came in, to hook up with her at end-of-shift? It was all over both of them. I don't know. I'm reaching. I can't see anything she was on, anything she was connected to that she'd die for."

"Would you mind telling me why you transferred out of Major Case?"

He shrugged. "The job's a good part of the reason my first marriage went south. I got another chance. Got married, and had this kid. A little girl. I figure, I'm not going to risk it again, so I transferred. It's a good squad. We do good work here, and plenty of it. But I don't get many calls in the middle of the night, and most nights, I'm home for dinner with my family. So you don't have to ask, that's where I was last night. My kid—the oldest—she's fourteen now. She had a friend over for a study date. Mostly bullshit," he said with a hint of a smile. "Around midnight, I was giving them both a raft of grief for giggling like a couple of mental patients when they should've been asleep."

"Detective Grady mentioned a weasel, Stu Bollimer."

"Yeah, Ammy cultivated him. He's from Macon so she used the old home connect. The guy was born a weasel. I can't see him setting her up, not for this. He's small change."

"All right. I appreciate it, Detective."

"Are you going to keep the boss in the loop?"

"That's my intention."

"He's a good boss." He pushed back from the table. "If she'd felt anything coming, anything to worry about, she'd have gone to him, or to me."

"How were her instincts?"

For the first time, he hesitated. "Maybe not as tuned as they could've been. She was still feeling her way here, a little bit. Like I said, she was hell on details, and she was good with people. Put wits and vics at ease. But I guess I wouldn't say she had the gut. The head, yeah, but maybe not the gut. Doesn't make her less of a cop."

"No, it doesn't. She's going to get our best, Detective O'Brian."

"Can't ask for more."

"Who should we talk to next?"

"Newman maybe. He's not going to get dick done today anyway."

"Would you send him up?"

Peabody waited until the door shut. "Touchstone," she said again. "He'll take this the hardest. The boss is the boss, but he's the team leader."

"She didn't have a cop's gut. He didn't want to say it because it seems disrespectful. But he knew it might help the investigation. She didn't have the gut. Got the call, went out. Probably never felt any twinge. She'd been set up—and it doesn't feel like impulse, but something planned out. But she didn't feel it. It's good to know."

She reviewed her data on Detective Josh Newman.

4

Eve found Josh Newman sad, steady, and talkative. The easygoing type, she decided. The sort that did his job, did it competently, then went home after shift and left the job on the job.

Average, was how she thought of him. The family man who just happened to be a cop, who would unlikely make it to detective second grade. And who gave her no new insights on Coltraine.

She moved on and took Dak Clifton. Though he was the squad's youngest member at twenty-nine, he'd been a cop for eight years, and held his detective's shield for nearly four of them. She thought of him, within minutes, as the Hot Shot.

His strong, good looks—the warm gold skin, the steel blue eyes and tumbling sun-tipped brown hair—probably served him well with female wits. Just as his aggressive, kick-your-ass interview style might have given some suspects the shakes.

Eve didn't care to have it directed at her.

He leaned in, pushing into her space, with his eyes hot and bright. "We don't need outside brass on this. This investigation needs to be handled in this house, in this squad. We take care of our own here."

"It's not up to you to say who handles this investigation.

It's done. If you're going to take care of your own, Detective, you can start by easing back."

"We worked with her. You didn't. She's just another case to you."

Since his words echoed Cleo Grady's, Eve gave him the same response. "You don't know what she is to me. You want to bitch, bitch to somebody else. Now you'll answer my questions."

"Or what? You'll haul me down to Central? Big fucking deal. You're in here jacking us up when you should be out there hunting down the one who killed her."

"I'll tell you what the big fucking deal is, Clifton. Detective Coltraine is dead. You're here wasting my time and pissing me off when you should be doing everything you can to aid the investigation of a fellow officer."

Now Eve pushed into his space. "And that makes me wonder. Are you just an asshole? Or is there some reason you don't want to answer my questions? Let's assume you're just an asshole, and start with your whereabouts yesterday from twenty-two hundred to twenty-four hundred hours."

The gold skin went hot as he showed his teeth. "You're no better than the IAB rats."

"Consider me worse. Whereabouts, Detective, or yeah, we will continue this at Central, in a box."

"I was home, with a woman I'm seeing." Sneering, he sat back, deliberately rubbed his crotch. "Want to know what we were doing, and how many times we did it?"

"Peabody?" she said with her eyes on Clifton's. "Are

either of us interested in what this asshole did or didn't do with his cock between the hours of twenty-two and twenty-four hundred last night?"

"We couldn't be less."

"Name the woman, Clifton, and consider yourself lucky I have more important things to do right now than write you up."

"Kiss my ass."

"I'm no more interested in your ass than I am your dick. Name, Clifton, or I'll find the time to write you up, and you'll take a thirty-day rip for it. You'll start the rip sweating in a box in my house if you don't stop screwing with me. Name."

"Sherri Loper. She's upstairs in Communications."

"Tell me about your relationship with Detective Coltraine."

"We worked together."

"I'm aware of that. Were you friendly, unfriendly?"

"We got along fine."

"And occasionally worked cases together?"

He shrugged, stared up at the ceiling. "Some of us actually do the job."

Eve sat back. "If you keep trying to bust my balls here, Clifton, I'm going to bust yours. Believe me, I'm better at it. I'm rank, and don't you forget it. Now show some respect for the rank and for your dead squadmate."

"I said we got along fine, and we did. Hell, Ammy got along fine with everybody. She had that way. She was good with people. You think I don't want to know who took her down? We all want to know. It doesn't make any sense." Some of the bravado cracked as he dragged his fingers through his hair. "Why the hell aren't you hammering at the people in her building? It had to be somebody in there. She lived in a secure building, and she was careful."

"Have you been to her building, her apartment?"

He closed up again. "Sure, a couple of times. Picked her up, dropped her off when we worked a case together. I have a ride, she doesn't. So what?"

"Did you and Detective Coltraine have a personal relationship?"

"You mean did I screw her. Look, bitch—"

Eve leaned in again. "I am a ranking officer. If you call me a bitch, you'd better damn well put *Lieutenant* in front of it. Answer the question."

"No. Not like you mean. We had a drink now and then, like everybody else in the squad. Maybe we grabbed a meal. She was tied up with the death doctor. You ought to be talking to him. He had access to her building, her apartment, he'd know how to take her out fast, leave a clean scene."

"Do you have any knowledge that there was any friction between her and Dr Morris?"

He shrugged, scowled off toward the window. "People have sex, they have friction. First person you eyeball with murder is the spouse or lover. But you're here, grinding us through it."

"So noted. You're done, Detective."

Eve sat, watched as he strode out, gave the door a slam behind him. "He made a play for her, that's my take. Too much heat there. He made a play and she brushed him back, and then she goes for Morris. He's the type used to having women go for him, not somebody else."

"He'd be stupid to give us an alibi we can break," Peabody said.

"Yeah, but we'll check it anyway. In fact, you do that now. I'll go thank Delong."

"If there was something between him and Coltraine—or tension between them because she didn't let there be—wouldn't the rest of the squad know?"

"Cops are good at keeping secrets."

They met outside, where, at Peabody's insistence, they grabbed a quick to-go lunch from the deli. Eve wasn't sure what was inside the roll she ate while they leaned against her vehicle, but it was pretty damn good.

"So, Clifton's alibi checks out." Peabody chomped into her own sandwich with obvious enjoyment. "But she was pretty pissy about it. 'Yeah, we spent the night together, so what.' Snarly, defensive. She and Clifton deserve each other."

Eve ate, watched cops come and go. Busy little house, she thought. And little meant more interaction, more internal relationships. Cops tended to stand for each other, it was part of the code. She'd taken down wrong cops before, and it was a hard and ugly process.

She hoped she wouldn't have to take one down for this.

"Clifton's had a lot of disciplinary slaps, and a few marks for using undue force. He's got a temper. This

62

murder doesn't feel like heat. But we need to dig into him, and his alibi, a little deeper."

"I hate that. I hate looking at us for this."

"Then we hope it's a straight bad guy, one without a badge. But we look. We'll take the weasel next, then I want to go back to the scene, go through it again." She walked around to get in the car, leaving Peabody no choice but to hop in.

They found the pawnshop and its proprietor easily enough. The guy looked a little like a weasel, Eve thought—or what she figured a weasel looked like. He sat in back of his security glass, making a deal with a guy sweating for his next fix.

Bollimer's long, sharp nose twitched in the center of his long, thin face. Scenting cop, Eve decided, as the man's bright, black eyes darted over toward her and Peabody.

"You got fifty."

"Come on, man." The junkie's body twitched, his voice piped with desperation. "I need the hundred. It's worth more'n that. Worth two-fifty easy. Have a heart, man. I need the one."

Bollimer sniffed through his nose, pretended to examine the wrist unit more carefully. "Seventy-five. That's the best I can do."

"How about ninety, maybe? How about ninety? It's a nice piece."

"Seventy-five's the limit."

"Okay, okay. I'll take it."

Bollimer tapped some keys on his minicomp, and it

spat out a form. He slid it through the chute. "You know the drill."

The junkie scrawled his name on both parts, tore off his tab, slid the other end back to Bollimer. After keying in another code, Bollimer sent the seventy-five jingling down a tube. "You got thirty days to reclaim," he said, and only shook his head as the man rushed out of the shop.

"He'll be back, but not to claim this." Bollimer tagged the wrist unit, set it aside. Then he ran a hand over the near-mirror gloss of his slicked-back hair. "What can I do for you officers today?"

"Regular customer?" Eve asked.

"Binks? Sure. This is his property." Bollinger tapped the wrist unit. "I've seen him wearing it before."

"Sooner or later, he's going to get a jones on without anything to hock. Then he's going to start stealing, end up mugging somebody."

Bollimer nodded sagely. "It's the way of this sad, sad world. I run a straight place. Licensed. I check the hot sheet for stolen merchandise every day, and cooperate with the authorities. You looking for something hot maybe hasn't hit the sheets, you can take a look around."

"We're Homicide." Eve pulled out her badge, held it up to the security screen. "We're investigating the murder of Detective Coltraine."

His mouth dropped open while his black weaselly eyes popped wide. "What did you say? Ammy? You're telling me Ammy got killed?"

"The media's reported it. Her name was released to

them a couple hours ago. Don't you listen to the screen, Stu?"

"What the fuck I want to hear that shit for? Hold on. Just hold on."

He pushed a button, had the screen coming down on his front door. Eve heard the lock click. Though his shock and distress rang true, she set a hand on her hip closer to her weapon when he pushed back on his rolling stool, got up, and hurried to unlock his cage door.

When he came out, she saw the gleam of tears in his eyes. "What happened? What happened to that girl?"

"Somebody killed her last night. Her body was discovered in the basement of her apartment building this morning." That much the media had.

"That's not right. That's just not right." He pressed his fingers to his eyes for a moment. "You got she used me as a confidential informant?"

"Yeah. Did you feed her anything recently that might've pissed someone off enough to take her out?"

"No. No. Petty shit, just petty shit. I used to be higher level. Got busted. Did time. You know all that, too. Since then, I've kept it straight, mostly. I didn't like the slam, and don't want to go back. Ammy came in one day, with the blond cop. They're looking for some jewelry got taken in a mugging. Turns out I had one of the pieces—a ring. I did the transaction like an hour before. Son of a bitch. I usually got a nose for the hot."

He tapped his finger to the side of his bladelike beak. "The blonde, she comes down hard—but the thing is, it wasn't on the hot sheet yet. What am I, I says, a fucking mind reader? I give them the ring, the ticket, the ID copy. Full cooperation. Me, I'm out the two hundred I paid, but that's the way of it."

"They get the guy?"

"Yeah. Ammy, she comes back alone the next day, to thank me. How about that?" he added with a slow, sappy smile. "She comes in to thank me, and to tell me the guy who rolled the couple for the jewelry and shit gave the ring to his girlfriend. And she turned right around and comes in here to hock it. So they got her to flip on the boyfriend, recovered all the shit. Hardly ever happens that way. We got to talking, 'cause we're both from Georgia. I haven't been south of Jersey for about twenty years, but still. She'd come back in, by herself, bring me coffee. How about that? And I sort of fell into passing her information if I had any. She was a sweet-heart. A goddamn sweetheart." Those tears gleamed again. "They hurt her?"

"Not as much as they could have." Eve took a chance. "They took her piece. Do you have a weapons business on the side, Stu?"

"I won't even take knives, much less stunners or blasters. But I know people who know people who maybe do. I'll check around." He cleared his throat. "Is there going to be a service for her, anything like that? I'd want to come. I'd want to pay my respects. She was a sweetheart."

"I'll make sure you know when I have the details of that." She drew out a card, passed it to him. "If you find out anything, hear anything, think of anything, contact me."

"You got that."

Eve started out, turned. "You said she came back, alone. Did she always come in here or meet you solo?"

"Almost always. You know how it is when you're courting a weasel. It's one on one."

"Yeah. Yeah, it is. Thanks."

Peabody sniffled when they stepped outside. "God, he nearly had me dripping. I think he loved her—sincerely. Not like I want to roll with you in chocolate sauce, but like a daughter or something."

"She's coming across as having that effect on people. Maybe she was going out to meet another weasel. One she was courting."

"I like that better than thinking somebody in her own squad did her."

"There has to be something in her notes, or on her comps. Something, somewhere, if she was working with another informant—or working on cultivating one." Eve got in the car, sat, considered. "She could have stepped into something bigger than she knew. Or courted somebody who strung her along for a while. She said the wrong thing, asked the wrong question. The weasel, or somebody higher up the chain, has to take her out."

"She worked a lot of robberies, burglaries. Whoever it was got into her building, slick and smooth. So, somebody who's into more than petty stuff."

Still considering, Eve pulled out to head back to the scene. "We'll get Feeney, nobody does a search and cross faster. Well, except maybe Roarke. Feeney can check with Robbery, Robbery Homicide, Major Case.

Whatever might link up. Cross with her case files. Maybe something will pop."

"Even with Feeney, and McNab—and maybe the magic of Roarke—that's going to take a lot of man-hours. Feeney would spring Callendar into it, if you asked. She's fast."

Before she could respond, Eve spotted the Chinese restaurant. Less than two blocks from Coltraine's apartment, she thought as she pulled over. "Did you get that list of restaurants?"

"Yeah." Peabody pulled out her PPC. "This one has to be on it as we're nearly to her place. China Garden. It's the closest coming from this direction. There's another, the other side of her building, that's a little closer. Plenty of others in a five-block radius."

"She took the stairs. I bet she walked to work when she could. It's close to a mile, but she needed to learn the streets, and she used the stairs. She'd walk right by here. Even if she took the subway, she'd get off a block down, and still walk by here. Let's check it out."

The narrow dining room sparkled red and gold. Despite the recent consumption of sandwiches, Eve realized it was past the usual lunch hour, still too early for dinner. Still, several tables were occupied by people drinking from small cups or nibbling on mini eggrolls. When they entered, a woman with a short, spiky crown of hair slid out from a corner booth to come forward.

"Good afternoon. Would you like a table?"

"No, thanks." Eve palmed her badge, held it down at her side.

"Ah." The woman glanced down, then up again. Her

eyes, a sea green in her exotic face, showed both understanding and sadness. "You're here about Detective
Coltraine. Please, come sit. You'll have tea."

She turned, called out a quiet order in musical
Chinese as she walked back to the booth. The young
woman who'd been sitting with her rose quickly and
hurried into the back. "I'm Mary Hon." She gestured
Eve and Peabody to sit. "My family and I were very
sorry, very sad, to hear about what happened."

"You knew Detective Coltraine."

"She was a good customer, a lovely lady. We're all
praying for her safe passage, and praying that her killer is
brought to justice."

"Did she come in yesterday?"

"I served her myself." Mary nodded as the fresh pot
of tea, the cups arrived. She poured from the squat
white pot. "I thought back after we heard, in case it was
important. It was early, before six. Maybe close to six.
She told me she'd window-shopped on her way home,
and tried on shoes she couldn't afford. We joked a little
about shoes. She didn't know what she wanted to eat,
and asked me to surprise her. Sometimes she did that. I
gave her the moo-shu chicken—it was very good last
night—and two spring rolls, because I knew she was
fond of them."

"She came in alone?"

"Yes. She said she wanted takeout as she'd be eating at
home, alone, and doing some work. It was early, as I
said, and we weren't very busy yet. So we talked while
the kitchen put her food together. I asked why she
didn't have a date. She told me she had to work, and her

boyfriend was also working. Putting in extra time because they were going on a long weekend together soon. She seemed very happy. She took the order and paid, without even looking at what we'd given her. She said goodbye, and she would see me soon. I think she was only here for fifteen minutes. Not long. Not very long."

"Did she usually come in alone?"

"Most always." Mary lifted her teacup with her elegant hands. She wore a wide gold ring, and her nails were long, painted a glossy rich red. "Once or twice she came with the man she was seeing. She called him Li. They had love all around them. I hope you won't tell me he's the one who hurt her."

"No, he's not the one who hurt her. Thank you, Mrs. Hon. You've been very helpful."

"I'll miss seeing her."

"Sadder and sadder," Peabody said when they were back on the sidewalk. "I guess you don't think of how many people you brush up against, or how they might remember you. The guy at your corner deli, or the owner of your favorite take-out spot. The clerk where you usually shop for clothes. Not to sound too Free-Agey, but it matters. It all matters, what we leave behind with the people we brush up against."

"Someone she brushed up against wanted her dead. Let's walk from here. Follow her steps."

Somewhere around six, Eve calculated, Amaryllis Coltraine walked this way, carrying take-out Chinese for one. Nice day, nicer than today when the sky couldn't make up its mind if it wanted to rain or just stay gloomy.

Had she strolled, or had she picked up the New York pace and clipped right along?

Strolled, Eve decided. What was the hurry? She wasn't especially hungry, wouldn't eat for an hour or so. By all appearances, she'd planned to spend the evening in, catching up on a little work.

"Even if she took her time, less than five minutes to walk it." Eve went in the front, as Coltraine would have, using her master where Coltraine would have used her key card. "Check her snail-mail drop."

Peabody used her master on the narrow box, as she had that morning. And as it had been that morning, the box was empty.

"She'd take the stairs."

They walked past the elevators, cut to the right. They passed through the fire door, and Eve paused to study the layout again. Back door straight across, stairs going up and down to the right.

"Which way was she going, out the front or the back? She didn't have a ride, so was someone picking her up, or was she getting wherever she thought she was going on foot, subway, cab? They didn't ambush her here. It doesn't make sense, not if they were inside, to take her this close to the lobby fire door. Someone's more likely to walk in from this level than any of the others."

"Maybe she went out the back, or started to. They were lying in wait, dropped her. They wouldn't have had to gain access that way. She'd have opened the door."

"Possible. Yeah, possible. But when you hang around the rear of a building, you're exposed. You look suspicious. Still, if you were quick enough . . . possible."

They started up. "The stairs are clean. No litter, no graffiti, no hand smudges on the rail or the walls—the kind you'd get from long, regular use. Most people probably take the elevator." Eve paused on the next landing. "Here's where I'd have taken her. Keep behind the stairs. You'd hear her coming down, be able to judge her speed. She turns here, to round for the next level, you're facing her. Close. Blast. Done. You haul her up, or you and your accomplice haul her up, carry her down two levels. It's not likely you'd run into anybody that time of night, but if you do, you're armed. You just take them down, too."

Eve narrowed her eyes, studied Peabody. "You weigh more than she did."

"Thanks for reminding me of the eight pounds I can't get off my ass."

"She was more my weight," Eve continued, ignoring the sulk. "Shorter, but we weighed in close to the same. You've got a strong back. Haul me down to the basement."

"Huh?"

"Over the shoulder. Firefighter's carry. That's the way he'd have done it. Leave his weapon hand free if he needs it." Eve pressed back against the wall, imagining slapping against it from a hard stun. And let herself slide to the floor. "Haul me up, cart me down."

"Man." Peabody rolled her shoulders. She squatted, grunted. It took her two tries to get Eve's deadweight over her shoulder. And another long grunt to straighten back up.

"I feel stupid," she muttered as she trudged to the stairs. "Plus you're heavier than you look."

"She wouldn't've been a feather." Eve lay limp over Peabody's shoulder. "Unconscious, carrying two weapons, her 'link, her communicator, restraints. Whatever else she took out with her. You're making good time," she added, as Peabody turned on the last landing. "Even bitching about it. If the killer was male, he probably had more muscle, more height than you. Plus he's got purpose. Get her down, through the door fast. He wants to get it done."

"Okay." Puffing only a little, Peabody stopped at the basement door. "What now? Door's sealed."

"Break the seal, use your master. He'd have used his, or her key card to open the door." Eve scowled as Peabody bumped her up, shifting the weight to dig out what she needed. When they were in, she closed the door with her self-maligned butt.

"Okay, you're going to kill me shortly. What do you do first?"

"I dump you on the floor."

"But he didn't. She'd have had more bumps and bruises if he'd just dumped her. He laid her down. Lay me down."

"Jeez."

She managed it, then just crouched, bent forward with her elbows on her thighs.

"You need more gym time, pal." Eve lay where she was. "He disarms her. I'll break your fingers if you try it," she warned Peabody. "Takes her badge, her 'link. Takes it all. Brings her around with a stimulant." Frowning again, Eve checked the time. "She left the apartment—

we've got to estimate about twenty-three twenty-two. Maybe she fooled around after she turned the droid off, but we've got to estimate that. No more than a minute or two to get down the stairs. Ambush, cart her down. Less than three minutes with you hauling me. Make it twenty-three-twenty-five to get to this point. Even adding time in to take the weapons, the badge, jewelry, add more for the stimulant—which would've jumped her right back—that leaves ten minutes or so before TOD. That's a long time."

"He had things to say."

"Yeah, or things he wanted her to say. A conversation? Emotional torture? He does her, but he doesn't rush the leaving. He didn't unjam the cameras for another ten minutes."

"Maybe he didn't take her weapon and the rest until after he killed her?"

"Disarm first. SOP. You'd be stupid to leave her weapons on her—just in case. He was checking his tracks after he'd finished her. Making sure, I'd say. Making sure he didn't leave any trace, make any mistakes." Eve sat up, studied the room from her vantage point. "So far as we can tell, he didn't. Unless he's idiot enough to try to hock her ring, her weapon, he left nothing behind."

She got to her feet. "Let's take another pass through her place, then we'll go back to Central, hook Feeney into it, and put together what we have."

She wished it was more, Eve thought as she sat back at her desk at Central. A full day's work, and most of what she had was impressions—how people saw the victim, felt about her. She had her own image of Coltraine to add to it. She could walk in her footprints, create what she believed was a fairly accurate time line of events. But she couldn't know who or what had drawn the dead cop out of her apartment.

The hour she and Peabody had spent searching, hoping to find an answer, or a hidey-hole where Coltraine had stashed some secret, hadn't given her any more.

She had Feeney and some of his best e-geeks on research and cross-check. She had several of her own men pouring over Coltraine's cases, past and present. She had Coltraine's backup date book, with no entry on the night she died.

It just wasn't enough.

She copied all data to Dr Mira, the department's top profiler, and requested a meet at the doctor's earliest convenience. She copied all data to her commander, then to her home unit.

She started to rise. One more cup of coffee, one more pass before she took it all home and tried a fresh approach on it there.

Baxter came in, carrying a sealed box. "This came for you, special messenger. They scanned it downstairs. There are weapons inside. Police issue."

"Where's the messenger?"

"In holding. It's been scanned for prints. The messenger's are on it, and two more sets—both employees of the mail drop where it was left. No explosives scanned."

Peabody crowded in behind Baxter. "They've got to be hers. What else could they be?"

"Let's find out. Record on. Package, addressed to Lieutenant Eve Dallas, Homicide Division, Cop Central, delivered by special messenger. Scanned and cleared." She took out a knife, cut through the seal.

Inside were two police-issues, Coltraine's badge, and her ID. A single disc snugged into a protective case. Eve shoved down impatience. "Let's get the contents checked for prints, and this disc cleared."

"I've got a minikit in my desk." Peabody rushed out.

"It's a slap in the face," Baxter said, his fury barely held under the surface. "We already know that. Here, I took this off a cop, killed her. See what you can do about it."

"Yeah. But if you're cocky enough to take the slap, you're cocky enough to start making mistakes." She took the print kit Peabody brought in, used it herself. "Wiped down. Contents, interior of the box, all clean. No hair, no fiber, no nothing."

She ran the disc through a hand analyzer. "Text disc. No video, no audio. No viruses detected. Let's see what the bastard has to say."

She plugged it into her machine, ordered it to display. The text was bold font, all caps.

I TOOK THESE OFF THE CUNT COP, AND KILLED HER WITH HER OWN WEAPON. SHE WAS EASY. YOU CAN HAVE THEM BACK. MAYBE SOMEDAY SOON, I'LL BE SENDING YOURS TO SOMEBODY ELSE.

"Let's log them in," Eve said coolly. "And have a little chat with the messenger. Baxter, you and Trueheart take the mail drop."

"I'll grab the boy and go."

"Peabody, with me."

5

As Eve drove home, she wondered if Coltraine's killer understood the full import of having the weapons and the badge back in official hands. Despite the insult of the message, and its implicit threat, their return meant a great deal.

A cop's weapon wouldn't be used to do harm.

An in-your-face gesture, sure, Eve reflected, and with a smirk. *I took it, I used it, here you go.*

The messenger wasn't connected. The kid had just been doing his job. She'd leaned on him pretty hard, Eve admitted, pushed, prodded, maybe scared a few weeks off his life. But now she was sure he wasn't in on it.

The mail drop led nowhere. Bogus name and address on the receipt, prepaid, comp-generated form the killer could have picked up at any of hundreds of locations at any time, or, in fact, downloaded on his own unit or at any cyber-café.

All she had there was the location of the drop, and the time the package was retrieved and logged in.

Same-day drop, expedited delivery ordered and paid for.

He'd been prepared, she thought now. Prepared to move on it as soon as the media ran with the story and reported the murder—and the name of the primary investigating officer. Fill in her name, dump the package, go.

That told her it had always been part of the plan. Not just the in-your-face shipment to Cop Central, but the use of Coltraine's weapon against her. The entire setup was all planned in steps and stages.

And that was something to chew on.

She thought of Morris, what he was doing, how he was coping, when she turned through the gates toward home. The spring she'd nearly forgotten about during the long day, exploded here. White and pink blossoms shimmered on the trees, glowing like chains of pastel jewels against the twilight.

Cheerful heads of daffodils danced with the more elegant cups of tulips in cheerfully elaborate sweeps. It seemed to her as if some happy artist had dabbed and stroked and twirled all his joy across this one secluded slice of the city, spilling it out here so the grand house could rise through it.

The towers and turrets speared up into the deepening sky, the terraces and strong lines jutted out. The lights in the many windows welcomed her, and sent the rich stone to a sparkle as evening shifted toward night.

She left her humble vehicle at the foot of grandeur, walked between the pansies Roarke had planted for her—that blooming welcome home—and into the house.

Summerset wasn't lurking in the foyer like a black cloud over a sunny spring day. It threw her off-stride for an instant not to immediately confront Roarke's major-domo and her personal nemesis. But she heard the

voices from the main parlor and realized he was probably serving somebody something.

And instantly thought: *Crap. Who's here?*

She considered skulking up the stairs, closing herself
in her office. But security would have already registered
her coming through the gates. Stuck, she crossed the
foyer to the parlor.

She saw Roarke first—it occurred to her she almost
always did. He sat in one of the rich-toned, high-backed
chairs looking relaxed, amused. At home.

Despite, she realized with a jolt, the baby in his lap.

Several things tumbled into her brain at once. Her
friend Mavis's happy giggle, Leonardo's contented smile
as he lifted his wife's hand to kiss her fingers.
Summerset's skinny, black-clad presence, and the big
grin—scary, she thought—on his bony face as the fat cat
squatted at his feet.

And the baby, Bella Eve, all pink and white and gold.

Lastly, the memory struck that they'd made plans to
have Mavis and her family over for dinner.

Crap again.

"Hey." She stepped in. "Sorry I'm late."

"Dallas!" A bundle of color and cheer with her artfully tangled pink-tipped blond curls, Mavis bounced
up.

She tended to bounce, Eve thought, as Mavis hurried
over in towering, triangular-shaped heels covered with
rainbow zigzags. The bounce sent the green-and-pink
diamond pattern of her microskirt fluttering. She
wrapped Eve in a hug, then just beamed pleasure out of
eyes currently the same sharp green as her skirt.

Thank God Mavis hadn't gone for the pink there, too.

"You missed the *best* time. We ate like oinkers, and Belle showed everybody how she can roll over, and shake her rattle."

"Wow," was all Eve could think of.

Leonardo started over. He was big where Mavis was tiny, copper-skinned where his wife was rosy pale. And together, Eve had to admit, they looked pretty damn perfect.

He leaned down, kissed Eve's cheek. The sausage twists of hair in the style he was currently sporting brushed her skin like silk. "We missed you."

"Yeah. Sorry."

"Not a thing." Mavis gave Eve's arm a squeeze. "We know how complete the job is. Come see the baby!"

Mavis dragged her across the room. It wasn't that she was reluctant to see Belle, Eve told herself. Exactly. It was just that the baby looked so perfect—like a doll. And dolls were just freaky.

She looked at Roarke first, saw his amusement had increased. "Welcome home, Lieutenant."

"Yeah." She might have kissed him—more as apology than greeting—but that meant leaning over the perfect pink-and-gold doll with its big, bright staring eyes.

"You haven't greeted all our guests." Smoothly, so smoothly she didn't see it coming, he rose and plunked the baby into her arms.

Eve managed to choke back a curse so the sound she made was more of a raw-throated squeak. She held Belle

81

at arm's length, much as she might a potential incendiary device. "Ah, hi. Nice dress."

The fact that it was pink and full and fluffy had hidden the tiny reality under it. How could anything that small be human? And what went on inside its brain when it stared that way? Stared until a thin line of sweat crept down your back?

Not sure what to do next, Eve started to turn—very slowly—to pass the baby to Mavis, Leonardo. Even Summerset. Possibly the cat. When Belle blinked those big baby-doll eyes, and shot out a huge, gummy grin.

She kicked her legs, waved her pink rattle, and made some sort of gooing, cooing sound.

Slightly less scary that way, especially with the drool sliding down her chin. And damned if she wasn't ridiculously cute. Eve bent her elbows a fraction, gave the baby a small, experimental bounce. And something white bubbled out of her grinning mouth.

"What is that? What did I do? Did I push something?"

"It's just a little milk puke." Laughing, Mavis dabbed Belle's mouth with a tiny pink cloth. "She ate like an oinker, too."

"Okay. Well. Here you go." She held the baby out to Mavis.

As Mavis took Belle, Leonardo whipped out a larger pink cloth—like a magician—and draped it over Mavis's shoulder.

"Lieutenant."

Summerset's voice had Eve's shoulders tightening. Here it comes, she thought. He'd ooze his disapproval all over her—like milk puke—because she'd forgotten they were having company and missed dinner.

She braced for it, ran several snarling responses through her brain, and turned. He simply handed her a glass of wine. "I'll bring your meal in here."

Her eyes stayed narrowed as she watched him leave the room. "That's it? That's all? Is he sick or something?"

"He knows why you're late," Roarke said. "That you're investigating the murder of a fellow officer. Give him some credit."

She frowned into her wine, drank some. "Do I have to?"

Since it was obvious she couldn't head straight up to work, she sat on the arm of Roarke's chair. "Anyway, I left you a message about being late. I remembered to do that. I get credit, too."

"So noted." Roarke rubbed a hand on her thigh. "Progress?"

"Not much. It's hard enough when it's another cop. But having to tell Morris, seeing his face . . ."

"Morris?"

"They had a thing, Morris and Coltraine—the vic. A serious thing."

"Oh. No." Mavis clutched Belle tighter. "This was Ammy? The woman he's been seeing? We never turned the screen on today, never heard. Roarke just told us you'd caught a case, a cop killer. We didn't know it was . . . Oh, Leonardo."

He put his arm around her, drew both his girls closer. "This is . . . horrible. We ran into them at a club one night, sat down with them. You could see how much they . . . It was there between them," Leonardo said with sorrow in his gilted eyes. "I'm so sorry, so sorry. Is there anything we can do for him?"

"I honestly don't know."

"We only met her that one time." A tear slid down Mavis's cheek before she pressed it to the top of Belle's head. "She seemed so up, and they were so into each other. Total vibe, total sparkage. Remember, honeypot, how I said after they were just gone squared over each other."

"I remember."

"It's good it's you." Mavis firmed her chin, patted Belle's back. "You'll find the bastard who did it. Morris knows that. We're going to leave so you can do the cop stuff. If there's anything—you know, stuff I know how to do—you just tag me. I'm there."

They began to transfer Belle into her carrier as Summerset walked in with a tray. "You're leaving."

"Bellissimo needs to go night-night." Mavis rose on her rainbow tiptoes to kiss Summerset's cheek. "We'll be back—us girls—for the big bash. A bridal shower and all that girl stuff's just what we all need. And you guys." She elbowed her husband. "Zipping off to Vegas for the man party."

"Vegas?" Eve blinked. "Huh?"

"My duties as best man," Roarke told her. "I'm looking forward to it."

When she was alone with Roarke, the wine, and an elegantly arranged plate of food, she frowned. "Why do you have to go all the way to Las Vegas—shit, you do

84

mean Las Vegas, right? You're not going off planet to Vegas II."

"No, we're going to the original."

"But, what if I need help with all those women? I don't even know what they're planning because Peabody and Nadine are doing all that, so what if—"

"You could easily find out the plans instead of pretending it won't actually happen. And you'll be just fine. They're your friends." He tapped her chin with a fingertip. "Eat your dinner before it gets cold."

"I'm going to take it up, eat at my desk."

"Fine. Then you can tell me what happened to Morris's lady, and what I can do to help you find her killer. He's my friend, too," Roarke added.

"Yeah, yeah, I know." She gave in for a moment, moved into him, dropped her forehead on his shoulder. "God. Oh, God, it was horrible. The hardest thing I've ever had to do. It made me sick inside, just sick to knock on his door. To know I was about to break a friend in two. I have to find the answers for him. It's more than the job."

"It is, yes." He held her close and tight, and as Mavis had with Belle, rested his cheek on her head. Battled back his own fears. "Whatever you need from me."

She nodded, drew back. "Let's take it upstairs. It always helps me see things clearer, or from other angles, when I run the case by you."

They started up. "Tell me a little about her first. Did you know her well?"

"No. I ran into her a couple of times at the morgue. She transferred here a few months ago. From Atlanta.

Mavis had it—the vibe thing. He was in love with her, Roarke, and with everything I've learned since this morning, she felt the same about him. I get that she was a good cop, detail-oriented. She didn't live the job." She glanced over at him. "I guess you get what I mean by that."

He smiled a little. "I do."

"Organized, feminine. She had eight years on the job. No big flash in her jacket, no big lows. Steady. People liked her, a lot. Her squad, her main weasel, hell, the woman who owns the Chinese place where she ordered her takeout. I can't figure out what she did, who she twisted, to be targeted like this."

"It was target specific?"

"Yeah." In her office, she sat behind her desk, told him the details while she ate.

"The locks were checked for tampering?"

"Yeah, and they say no. Could've used a master, could be another tenant in the same building. Could have managed to dupe her key card, or someone else's in the building. Or he could be as good as you, and didn't leave a trace."

"She was taken down with a stunner," Roarke mused. "They're not easy to come by, and very pricey. Could he have disarmed her first and used her own weapon both times?"

"It doesn't play. No defensive wounds, and other than the kill burns, and the bumps on the back of her head, her shoulder blades, no offensive wounds. No cop turns over her weapon like that, not even to someone she knows."

"You'd give yours to me," he pointed out. "If I asked to see it for a moment, you'd give it to me."

Eve considered that. "Okay, maybe she would, to someone she was really tight with. But it still doesn't stream that way for me. She was heading out, sidearm and clutch piece. Taking the stairs, because she always did. That's a setup. And it had to be done fast and smooth. No time to ask her nice if she'd let you hold her stunner."

She pushed up, began to pace. After, Roarke noted, she'd eaten only half her meal. "We ran all the tenants. Got a few criminal pops, but nothing major. We'll interview everyone again who came up with any sort of a sheet, but I have to ask myself why she'd be going out, armed, to meet one of her neighbors."

"She might have been using the stairs simply to get to one of the other floors rather than the exit."

Eve stopped, frowned. "Okay, that's a thought. She arms herself first, though, so it's not a neighborly visit. It wouldn't be smart, going to another apartment for a meet when it's on the shady. Then why did the killer, if he's inside, need to jam the rear door security camera? Maybe to throw us off," she said, answering herself. "So we're looking outside the building."

She paced again. "Unnecessary complication. But we'll interview the tenants again. It just feels like an extra step to take, when SOP would be to run and interview everyone anyway."

"I can help with the electronics."

"That's Feeney's call. He's always happy to have the uber e-geek on board, but he may have it well under

87

control. I've got a lot of case files to wade through. I need to study her currents, her closed, her open, and what I got from Atlanta. You can—yeah, yeah, it's an insult to you—but you can think like a cop. Maybe you can take a look at Atlanta while I do New York. Plus, they need to be cross-referenced. I need to know if anything from before connects with now."

"And I can do that faster than you."

"Yeah, you can." She angled her head. "You can also think like a criminal, which is handy. Would you have sent her weapons to the primary? Why or why not?"

"I wouldn't have taken them in the first place. A smart criminal takes nothing—unless it's straight thievery, which this wasn't—and leaves nothing of himself behind. Otherwise, there's that connection."

"But he did take them. And I don't think he's stupid."

"They must have served a purpose. Leaving them—especially if he used one to kill her—would be, in my opinion, more of an insult to her. And you, or whoever caught the case. So taking them served another purpose, even if it was just the jab to you by sending them back. He's not a pro."

"Because?"

"A pro does the job, walks away, moves on. He doesn't taunt the police."

"Agreed. He might be a professional criminal, but it wasn't a professional hit. It looks simple, on the surface, but it was actually much too elaborate—and too personal—for a straight hit. A straight hit, you don't take her in a populated building, but lure her out of it, maybe to a meet. Take her there, or along the way. He wanted something, information or something she might have taken with her we can't know about. Or he wanted to give her a message before he finished her. And he wanted her found without much delay.

"I want to set up my board here, and run some probabilities before I start on the case files." She dug out a disc. "Here's Atlanta. All data's on my office unit, which I know you can access."

"Then I'll get started."

"Roarke." It had niggled at her all day, and still she hadn't meant to ask. Hadn't meant to bring it up. "Morris . . . when I was with him today, he said that being involved with a cop, being in a relationship with one . . . He said every day you have to block out the worry. Fear," she corrected. "He said fear. Is that how it is?"

He slipped the disc into his pocket to take her hands, and rubbed his thumb along her wedding ring. The design he'd had etched into it was an ancient charm. For protection. "I fell in love with who you are, with what you are. I took on the whole package."

"That's not answering the question. Or, I guess, it is."

His gaze lifted from her ring, met hers. Held hers. "How can I love you and not be afraid? You're my life, Eve, my heart. You're asking, you're wondering if I ever worry, if I ever fear, that one day Peabody or Feeney, your commander—a cop who's become a friend—will knock on my door? Of course I do."

"I'm sorry. I wish—"

He cut her off by brushing his mouth over hers—

once, then twice. "I wouldn't change a thing. Morris is right, you have to block it out, and live your life. If I didn't, couldn't, I'd never let you leave the house." He brought her hands to his lips now. "Then where would we be?"

"I'm careful."

He gave her a look filled with a mix of amusement and frustration. "You're smart," he corrected, "you're skilled. But not always as careful as you might be. I married a cop."

"I told you not to."

Now he laughed, and kissed her again where her brow had furrowed. "And would I listen? I'm damn good at being married to a cop."

"Best I ever saw."

His eyebrows shot up. "Well now, that's quite the compliment."

"I don't take it for granted. I know it seems maybe like I do, but I don't. I don't take for granted that when I walk in two hours—or maybe it was three—late like tonight, forget we had plans, you don't get mad. Or all the other things. I don't take it for granted."

"That's good to know." Odd, he realized, that she would need reassurance here. Or not so odd, really. The death of another cop, and one a friend had loved, brought it home. "We made promises to each other, nearly two years ago now. I'd say we've done a damn fine job at keeping them so far."

"I guess we have. Listen, if sometimes you can't block it, you should say it. Even if we fight about it, you've got a right to say it."

He traced his finger down the dent in her chin. "Go to work, Lieutenant. There's no worries tonight."

Sure there were, she thought when he went into his office. But it seemed like they were handling them okay.

She had told him not to marry her, she remembered. Thank God he hadn't listened.

She set up her board, pinning up Coltraine, her squad, the names of any tenant in her building with a sheet, the names of the particulars in her most current cases. She added a photo of the shipping box, the weapons, the note, the badge. Lab reports, the established time line. She had a description of the ring the victim should have been wearing, and a close-up of it she'd extracted from a photo in Coltraine's apartment.

Why had the killer returned the gun, but kept the ring?

She studied the board, angled it so she could study it from her desk. Armed with a fresh cup of coffee, she sat to run a series of probabilities.

The computer calculated an eighty-two-point-six percent that the victim and her killer had known each other or had some previous contact. A ninety-eight-point-eight percent that the victim was a specific target.

So far, she thought, she and the machine were in accord.

She decided to leave it there, and start on the case files.

Neither case contained any actual violence, she noted. The threat of it in the Chinatown case, but no execution of violence. Two males, wearing masks, rush into a market at closing, grabbing the female owner as she wheeled in one of the sidewalk carts, and holding a knife to her throat. Demand all cash and credits on the premises, and the security discs. Get both. Order both the owners—husband and wife—to lie on the floor. Apparently grab a few snack packs and book.

Less than three hundred netted—small change for armed robbery, she mused.

The vics had been shaken up, but unharmed. Though they'd turned over the discs, the husband had noticed a tattoo on the wrist of the knifeman—a small red dragon—and both had stated they believed the robbers had been young. Teens to early twenties.

The snack pack snitch told Eve the same.

They'd given the police a very decent—and unusually consistent—idea of height, weight, build, coloring, clothing. Two witnesses saw two young men matching the description running away from the direction of the market.

Penny ante, Eve mused. A couple of stupid kids. Confirmed, as the investigating officers had tracked down the tattoo parlor, and were ready to hunt up and pick up one seventeen-year-old Denny Su who'd had the ink on his right wrist.

No idiot teenager, and his as-yet-unidentified dumb friend, had the smarts to access Coltraine's building and get the drop on a cop.

The break-in—literally, as a window had been smashed to access—netted a bigger profit. But a guy who could finesse the solid security at Coltraine's building had the skills to finesse the less solid on the electronics shop. Plus, the glass had been broken from the inside, leading the investigators to conclude—ta-da—inside job. They'd begun to lean on one of the employees. From the notes Eve read, she'd say they were leaning in the right direction.

In this case, the suspect was again young, fairly stupid, and had a short sheet of shoplifting charges. Guy liked to steal, simple as that, Eve mused. He didn't score for her as a cop killer.

She took the time to run both through probability, and in each case the machine agreed with her, with both percentages under eighteen percent.

Eve sat back, studied the board. "Do I run your squad through my comp, Coltraine? It's an ugly business, cops running cops. The comp's going to favor them. Nothing in their data to hint at the dirty. Why does a clean cop, at least clean on record, kill another cop? The machine's not going to find that logical.

"Neither do I. But I have to run it."

"Eve."

"What?" She glanced over, saw Roarke in the doorway that adjoined their home offices. "Sorry, talking to myself. You found something interesting in Atlanta."

"I found something. A case she worked about three years ago. You haven't gone through these files yet?"

"No. I just got them in this afternoon. What about the case she worked three years ago?"

"A robbery. An upscale antique shop. The manager was beaten, several thousand dollars' worth of merchandise taken, nearly that much destroyed. They also forced him to open the safe and turn over all the cash, credits, and receipts—which carried the credit and debit card

93

data. One of the other employees found him when he went in to work, notified the police and the MTs. Coltraine was assigned."

"Okay. So?"

"During the investigation she interviewed the owner of the shop, and according to her case file, spoke with him on the matter several times. His name's Ricker. Alex Ricker."

6

"Ricker." The name rammed into Eve like a bare-knuckled jab. Sucker punch. "Max Ricker's son?"

"Yes. I checked to be sure."

She took one long breath to regain her balance. "So Alex Ricker has property and business in Atlanta. Wasn't he in Germany or something?"

"He was raised there, and his father kept him insulated. When Ricker and I had . . . business together, Alex was kept back. I never met him. I'm not sure any of Ricker's associates did—not then."

Yes, she had her balance back now, and walked it through. "You worked with Ricker, back in the bad old days. Went out on your own, did a hell of a lot better. Years later, you help me take Ricker down, way down, so he's spending the rest of his miserable life in a concrete cage off-planet. I wonder what his baby boy thinks of that."

"I don't know anything of their relationship, but I do know that Ricker's connected to me—to my father, to yours. I know he went to a lot of trouble to take me down, and failed. And to end you, and failed. Now his son may very well be connected to your victim."

Eve sat back, tapped her fingers on her thighs. Thinking, thinking. "Max Ricker had a lot of cops in his pocket. A lot of officials, a lot of politicians. We dug some of them out last year, but it's unlikely we dug them all. Would Ricker have passed them to his son?"

"I can't say for sure—yet. But who else?"

"Yeah. And his *businesses*, too—what we didn't find and shut down. Certainly, his contacts, his power points, and there'd be finances. Coltraine meets the son of a notorious criminal, now doing life—well, several terms of life—she'd have run him. She'd run the owner of the business that got hit. It's routine. Make sure it doesn't come up an insurance fraud, at the very least. When she did, she'd have made the connection to his father. She'd ask him about it. Have to."

She pushed up, walked to her board to study Coltraine's ID shot. "She'd have to ask. Three years ago Ricker was still at large, still slithering through the loopholes, but any standing background check on the son would have coughed out the data on the father."

"I don't know if it has any bearing on your case, but . . ."

"Yeah, but." She looked back at Roarke. "Did she close it? The case?"

"In a manner of speaking. She narrowed it down to three suspects. In each case when she secured a search warrant and went to serve it, she found the suspects gone and several items from the antique shop on the premises. Within two days, the bodies of the three men were found floating in the Chattahoochee River—chained together."

"The what river? Did you make that up?"

"I suppose I could have, but no. I suspect some Native Americans did that a few centuries ago."

"I think it'd be embarrassing to be dead in the Hoochie-Coochie River."

"Chattahoochee."

"What's the difference?"

"Quite a bit, I'd think, to Atlantans." He moved to her, laid a hand on her cheek. "And now that you've finished lightening the mood until you can get a handle on this . . ."

After a while, Eve thought, marriage turned walls into clear glass so both of you could see right through each other. "Okay. Okay, so maybe it's like father, like son? Ricker's a killer. He didn't think twice about snapping necks or slitting them. The son gets ripped off, hunts down the ripper-offers—or follows Coltraine's dots to same—and does them. Or has them done. She'd have to look there."

"According to the file, Alex Ricker was attending a charity event, in Miami, with a few hundred witnesses at the time of death of the three suspects."

"Didn't want to get his hands dirty, ordered the hit when he was covered."

"Possibly. If so, he proved as elusive as his father did. Oh, and I accessed the ME reports on the dead thieves." He watched her start to speak—to object, no doubt— then swallow it. "They'd been beaten over the course of several hours, incurred numerous broken bones before their throats were slit. That's the Ricker touch, in my opinion."

"She had to know it." Eve studied Coltraine again,

tried to see into her head. "Everyone says she was thorough, detail-oriented. She wouldn't have missed the link."

"The files note a follow-up interview with Alex after the bodies were recovered, and the verification of his alibi. While the homicide case went cold, all of Ricker's property was recovered."

Eve rubbed the back of her neck. "Three years ago. She didn't put in for transfer here until just under a year ago. As much as I'd like to burn another Ricker for pretty much anything, I can't see the connection between her murder and a trio of payback homicides three years ago."

"Maybe there isn't. But Alex Ricker is in New York, and has been for the last week."

"Is that so?" Eve stuck her hands in her pockets, rocked on her heels. "Now, see, that's just too much coincidence. Where is he?"

"He has a pied-à-terre on Park Avenue."

"Convenient. I'll have to pay him a visit in the morning."

"I'll be going with you." He held up a hand before she could speak. "Anything that involves Ricker, his son, his second cousin, his bloody pet poodle, I'm in it, too."

"They don't allow dogs on the Omega Penal Colony. Okay. I'm not going to argue about Ricker—either of them. We did enough of that a year ago."

"A year ago," Roarke pointed out. "A kind of anniversary. And here we have another dead cop—and you were littered with them last spring—as well as another Ricker. Oh, aye, far too many coincidences here."

She'd already followed that path. "We need to do a deep background on Alex Ricker. When did he buy the Park Avenue property, what other businesses does he have, and how many of them are in New York? How often does his name pop up in conjunction with an investigation? And what has he been doing for the past year? Has he contacted his father? A lot of questions."

"You won't find the answers to all of them on these units. Not with the privacy laws and CompuGuard. Believe me, he'll be protected under several layers."

"Then we'll use your unregistered."

He angled his head. "That's a quick leap for you, Lieutenant."

"Maybe." She stood as she was, hands in pockets, and stared into Coltraine's face. "And maybe she found out more about Alex Ricker three years ago than she noted in her files."

"You think he, like his father, had cops in his pocket? Including her?"

"I don't know." Inside her belly knots twisted. "God, I hope not, for Morris's sake. But if she was dirty, I need to find out. If she was clean, and if Alex Ricker had something to do with her death, I need to find out."

In Roarke's secured office, the privacy-screened windows opened to the lights of the city. The slick U-shaped console held the sharpest of cutting-edge equipment—shielded as well—from the vigilant eye of CompuGuard.

Illegal, Eve thought, so whatever they found here

couldn't leave the room. But she'd know. For Morris, she needed to know.

Roarke, his hair pulled back in a short tail, his sleeves rolled up, stepped behind the console. He laid his hand on the palm plate. "Roarke. Power on."

The console flashed on, a sea of jeweled lights and controls.

Roarke acknowledged. Power on.

"We'll want coffee," he said to Eve.

"I'll get it." She programmed a full pot from the office AutoChef, poured two tall mugs. When she turned, Roarke stood where he was, watched her. Waited.

"All right." She crossed over, set his mug down, placed hers on the jut that held the auxiliary computer.

For Morris, yes, she thought. But not only.

"My father worked for Ricker. Your father worked for him, and we've established before that they met, and were working on the same job before the night in Dallas. Before I killed my father."

"Before you, an eight-year-old girl, stopped him from raping you again."

"Okay." Truth could still dry the throat and chill the blood. "The fact is, he's still dead. So's your father. And your father pulled a double-cross, on Ricker, on a weapons deal. About twenty-four years ago."

"In Atlanta."

"Yeah. In Atlanta. Down the line, you worked for Ricker."

Roarke's tone turned very cool. "In a manner of speaking."

"Were associated with him. Jump further down the line, Ricker shows up in New York, and he's hell-bent on destroying you."

"And you."

"Three years ago, when Ricker was probably dreaming about eating your liver, Coltraine connects with Ricker's son. In Atlanta. Between that point and this point, we brought Max Ricker down. One year ago. And a couple months after that Coltraine requests a transfer to New York. She gets cozy with the chief medical examiner. A man I have a close work relationship with, and who we both consider a friend. Alex Ricker comes to New York; she dies. I think when you've got that many intersections, you have to take a real hard look at the road."

"And how will this be, for you, if this somehow tracks back to your father and mine?"

"I don't know. I guess we'll have to find out." She took a breath. "I don't know how it'll be for either of us, but we need to find out."

"We do, yes."

"The killer sent her weapons, her badge back to me. Personally. Maybe he's got a mole in Dispatch, and arranged for me to be assigned. But the fact is, it doesn't take a brain trust to figure out that even if someone else had caught this case, I'd have been involved. Because of Morris. That package was always going to come to me."

"Then we're on the same page. And the note inside the package becomes more a threat than bravado."

"Possibly. She wasn't a street cop, Roarke. She was a

puzzle solver, a detail chaser. But she wasn't street, sure as hell wasn't New York street. Nobody's going to take me with my own weapon. Damn if I'll have that in my jacket at the end of the day."

He nearly smiled. "So pride will keep you safe?"

"Among other things. If I'm a target, why take her down? Why put every cop in the city on alert, *then* go for me?" She faced Roarke over the wink of jeweled lights. "I'm better than she was. That's not bragging, that's just fact. So it's smarter to try to take me out cold than to try it when I'm already looking for a cop killer. And when, within the first twenty-four hours, I'll find Alex Ricker in her files."

"Logical. And somewhat comforting."

"In any case, that's all speculation. We need data."

"It'll take some time, to get under the layers."

"I'll use the auxiliary and keep going through her case files."

Roarke sat, and began to peel at the first layers.

Ricker, he thought. The name was like a virus in his life, springing out, spreading, then crawling back into hiding only to slither out again. And again.

He had reason to wonder if Ricker had been responsible for jamming the knife in Patrick Roarke's throat in that alley in Dublin years ago. And that, Roarke admitted, was the single thing he'd have to be grateful to Ricker for.

Not true, he corrected, not entirely true.

He could be grateful for what he'd learned during his association with Ricker. He'd learned how far he would go, and where he wouldn't go. He knew it had both amused and annoyed Max Ricker that he wouldn't deal in the sex trade when it involved minors or the unwilling. That he wouldn't kill on command, or for the sake of spilling blood.

He'd taken lives in his time, Roarke admitted. He'd spilled blood. But always for purpose. Never for profit. Never for sport.

He supposed, in some oddly twisted way, he'd learned more of his own lines, his own moralities from Max Ricker than he had from his own unlamented father.

What, he wondered, had Alex Ricker learned from *his* father?

German boarding schools, Roarke noted. Military type. Very strict, very costly. Private tutors on holidays, then private university. Studied in business, finance, languages, politics, and international law. Played football—soccer to the Yanks.

Covering many bases there.

No marriages, no children on record.

Alex Maximum Ricker, age thirty-three, residences in Atlanta, Berlin, Paris, and most recently, New York. Financier and entrepreneur listed as occupations of record.

Also covering a lot of bases. Current net worth: 18.3 million.

Oh, no, there'll be more than that. So, Roarke thought. Let's get down to it.

He worked steadily for an hour, ordering multiple runs and chipping away manually.

"Covering asses, too, aren't you now?" Roarke

mumbled to himself when he hit a block, shoved and tunneled around and under it. "Not so quick to toot your own horn as your father was. Smarter. All that posturing and preening helped bring him down, didn't it? Ah, now, there's a start."

"What? What have you got?"

"Hmmm?"

"I've got nothing." Eve swiveled around to him. "Zip. You've got something. What?"

"Apparently, it's not coffee," he said with a glance at his empty mug.

"What am I, a domestic droid?"

"If so, why aren't you wearing your frilly white apron and little white cap, and nothing else?"

She sent him a pained look of sincere bafflement. "Why do men think that kind of getup is sexy?"

"Hmm, let me think. Mostly naked women wearing only symbols of servitude. No, I can't understand it myself."

"Perverts, your entire species. What have you got?"

"Besides a very clear picture of you in my head wearing a frilly white apron and little white cap?"

"Jesus, I'll get the damn coffee if you'll cut it out."

"What I've found is the reason Alex Ricker hasn't blipped on my radar, not that I've given him much thought. But from a purely business standpoint, why he hasn't blipped."

"Why?"

Roarke gestured to the wall screen when he ordered data to transfer there. "He's scattered and spread himself out, with numerous small to mid-size companies.

None of them with holdings that cross the line into interesting."

"What's the line where they become interesting?"

"Oh, for me? Eight to ten million, unless I'm looking to acquire small, individual properties or businesses."

"Oh yeah, anything under ten mil's boring." She rose to get the coffee. "Is he laundering or hiding income?"

"Not that I've found so far. He's bought or established companies. Some he owns outright, others a controlling interest. Still others a small percentage. Some of his companies are arms of his other companies."

He took the coffee she brought him, patted his knee in invitation, and laughed at her sour look. "Some of his companies own property—homes in Athens, Tokyo, Tuscany. He holds some of these interests through an Atlanta-based operation called—logically enough—Varied Interests. Others are held by the Morandi Corporation, which was his mother's name."

"Dead mother, as I remember."

"Very dead. He was six when she ingested an unhealthy number of tranqs and supposedly fell or leaped from her bedroom window, twenty-two stories above the streets of Rome."

"Where was Max Ricker?"

"Excellent question. According to statements in the very thin police file on her death, he was in Amsterdam when she jumped, or fell. Alex also has a company he called Maximum Exports, which owns—among other things—the antique store in Atlanta that was hit. There's no criminal on him. He's been questioned on various accounts by various authorities on various continents. But never charged.

"All of these business activities and the structuring are perfectly legal," he told her. "Close to the edge on some, but never over. I've no doubt, unless he's a complete bint, he's got a second set of books on every one of his enterprises, and considerable funds sheltered in coded accounts."

Roarke sat back, sipping coffee. "He stays under the radar, you see. Very carefully under. No splash, no flash. Quietly successful businesses that make no real noise. Until you dig down, put them together and see there's really one entity that's worth about ten times what his official data lists for him."

"And there's probably more."

"Oh, very likely. I can find it, now that I've got his pattern. I could find those coded accounts, with enough time."

"Those would probably still be on the legal side. What about the illegal side?"

"Some of these may be fronts. Or I'll find smaller, more obsure businesses that serve as fronts. An antiques business—of which he has several worldwide—is always a handy way to smuggle all manner of things. There's an easier way for me to find out if he's taken over some of his father's trade. I can ask people who know people."

"Not yet. For one, I don't want the people who know people to signal him we're coming to see him. For another, I don't want to get so bogged down in Alex Ricker, when there's no clear evidence he's involved. Coltraine's the priority. I'm going to run her financials.

I'm going to run them from here because I don't want to set up any flags there either. I'm hoping she was clean, and if she was clean, I don't want to be responsible for even a whisper she might've been dirty."

"I'll run them. I'll do it," he said when she started to protest. "I can do it faster, as we both know. And it'll be easier for you if you don't have to do it yourself. I know it troubles you to look at one of your own this way."

"It's worse. She's dead. I can't ask her. She can't defend herself. She can't say, 'Fuck you, bitch, for even thinking it.'"

She dragged a hand through her hair, then crossed the room to stand and look out the window. "And here I am, using illegal means to try to find out if *she* was tangled in something wrong. If she was on the take, or Alex Ricker's weasel."

"As chief medical examiner, Morris could access this case file?"

"Yeah, he could find a way to get it. So by making sure this area of investigation isn't in that file, am I protecting him or myself?"

"Darling Eve, I see nothing wrong with doing either, and both. If you find the worst, he'll have to know. If you don't, what good would it do you or him for him to know you felt compelled to look?"

"You're right. You do it. You'll be faster."

She stayed at the window, staring out at dark and light. Had Morris taken a soother, given himself a chance to sleep, to put it away for a few hours? Or was he staring out at the dark and the light?

She promised she'd find the answers for him. But what if those answers were the woman he loved was a bad cop, a liar, that she'd used him? What if the answers were as painful as the questions?

"Eve."

She turned, braced. "What?"

"I can do another level or two, try some tricks, but what I'm seeing here is a woman who lived within her means. You may be interested to know a New York City detective third grade makes a bit more than an Atlanta detective. But the cost of living balances that out. She paid her bills on time, and now and then went a little over budget on her credit card and carried a balance for a month or two. There aren't any unusual deposits or withdrawals, no major purchases.

"I've tried the most usual mix of names—hers, her family's, Atlanta, and other key words that make sense to me and the computer to search for a second account. I haven't found one."

Most of the tension eased. "So, at this point, it doesn't look like she was on the take."

"You were in her apartment. Was there any art, any jewelry?"

"Nothing that rings the bells. Framed posters, street art, a couple of good pieces of jewelry, the rest tasteful costume. Let's let this alone until we talk to Alex Ricker. I don't want to do this to her any more until I have to."

"All right." He ordered all data saved, then laid his hand over the palm plate again. "Roarke. Power down."

When the console winked off, he crossed to her, put

his hands on her shoulders. "It's harder when it's personal."

She closed her eyes a moment. "I can't stop thinking about him. How he's dealing, or not dealing. What I might find, and how whatever that is will affect him. I should take myself off the case, for all the same reasons I can't and won't take myself off the case. Because a friend's life has been turned inside out."

With a nod of understanding, he stepped back to take her hand, to walk her to the elevator. "Tell me your instincts about her—your feelings. No filters," he added as they stepped into the car. "Master bedroom," he ordered.

Eve hesitated, then shrugged. "I was a little bitchy about her, I guess."

"Because?"

"Well, it sounds stupid. But because of Morris. Because he's . . . He's Morris, and I didn't see her coming until she was already there and he's gooey-eyed. It's not like I have—ever had—that kind of *thing* with Morris. Or wanted one, or even thought about him. Not like Peabody and her sexual fantasies. I mean, Jesus."

"Why that slut. I thought I was her sexual fantasy."

Relieved with how he'd played it, she gave him a bland stare as they stepped into the bedroom. "You lead the charge, but apparently Peabody's got the capacity for lots of fantasy partners. Probably all at the same time."

"Hmm. Interesting."

"And I probably just violated some girl code by saying that, which doesn't apply to your question anyway." She pushed her hands through her hair. "I don't know what I thought of her, exactly, because it was all filtered through that 'Wait a damn minute, this is Morris' attitude. Which is embarrassing now that I really think about it."

"You have a connection. An intimacy. Not all intimacies are sexual. She was an interloper."

"That's it." Eve pointed a finger at him. "That's exactly it. And she didn't deserve that from me. She made him happy. Anybody could see it. I'd say, now that I think about it, her apartment didn't surprise me. The look of it, the neatness of it, because that's how she struck me. A woman who had things in place, and knew what she liked. Dressed well—not flashy, but well. Sexual. She gave off the sexual and the female more than the cop, but the cop was there. Under it. She took her time, in how she talked, how she moved. That's a Southern thing, isn't it? Nothing New York about her. I don't know." She shrugged again. "It's not much."

"Your instincts on a very brief acquaintance told you she was a woman of subtlety—not flashy. Comfortable with her sexuality, who took her time and who liked order, respected her own tastes, and who was willing to try something new. A new city, a new man. That's considerable, I'd say. Your instincts and what you've learned since confirm that her work was just that to her. Work. It didn't drive her life. Given that, it's very possible, isn't it, that a sexual woman of taste could find herself attracted to a man like Alex Ricker. And he to her. Wouldn't that relationship, if one developed, have

110

eventually conflicted with her work, or become somewhat problematic?"

"A cop hooking up with a guy with a shady rep?"
She arched her eyebrows. "Gee, why should that be a
problem?"

He laughed. "We're different, you and I." He put his
arms around her. "But it's interesting, isn't it, to speculate how a similiar situation might go very, very badly."

"We could've taken a turn, ended up—"

He shook his head, touched his lips to hers to stop
the words. "No. We were always meant to end up here."
He pressed the release on her weapon harness. "Always
meant to find each other. Save each other. Be with each
other."

She laid her hands on his cheeks. "That's the
Irish. But I like the thought of it. Those weird intersects
in the past—your father, mine, Ricker. They didn't stop
us from getting here. Roarke." She lowered her hands,
removed her harness. "When Ricker intersected with us
again, it screwed us up for a while. I don't want that to
happen again. I don't want wherever this investigation
may lead to cause a rift between us again."

"I wouldn't want to see you take this investigation
into an area that causes a rift. Same goal," he said at her
frown. "Different angles of approach. Do you want me
to promise, Eve, that I won't get pissed off if you put
yourself in Alex Ricker's sights, as you did with his
father? I can't. The name Ricker makes it personal.
There's no way around that."

"You have to trust me to do my job, to handle
myself."

"I do. Every day of my life."

She understood then it was his trust in her, his belief in her that held his fear for her at bay. "Then I'll promise something. That I'll try to tell you beforehand whenever I have to deal with Alex Ricker during this investigation."

"Try?"

"If something comes up, if I can't take the time, or hell, don't *know* ahead of time, then I can't tell you. I can't make a promise to you I might have to break."

"All right. That's fair enough. I'll promise to try not to get pissed off."

She smiled now. "I'll probably have to do something, and you'll probably get pissed off."

"But we'll have tried."

"Yeah. So in case trying doesn't turn out to be enough, let me say this now. I love you."

The pleasure rose warm in him, circled his heart. Again his arms went around her, again his mouth lowered to hers. "No one but you," he murmured. "Always."

She wrapped around him, hard and tight, giving what he needed before he asked. All. Everything. It undid him, this love, for her and from her. The depth and breadth of it left him weak and wanting, desperate and staggered.

She poured herself into the kiss and filled him. And still, he thought, there would always be more.

However many times they'd loved each other, how many ways, it was always now, and always new. The taste of her, familiar and fresh, stirred him like the first time. Those strong arms around him, that mouth both pliant and avid. Yes, this was everything. This was all.

His murmur came from the core of his heart, in the language of his blood. "*A grha*."

He lifted her. That quick, careless strength, the sensation of being taken made her head spin. His power, hers, combined so she felt just a little drunk when he laid her on the bed, when his body covered hers. The weight, the shape, the *feel* of him. How could she ever get enough?

Had all the years they'd both starved for love caused this bottomless need for each other? His scent—she turned her face into his throat, breathing him in. His touch—and arched under the stroke of his hands. His taste—that punch of sensation whenever their mouths met.

No one else had ever brought her here. No one else had ever compelled her to take him with her.

Slow, dreamy, drugging, hands and lips, sighs and movement. His shirt and hers peeled away so flesh could meet flesh, so hands could roam over curves, over planes to entice and delight.

The long lines of her never failed to fascinate and arouse him. The shape of her—the subtle curves captivated him with those seductive contrasts. Skin so soft, so smooth over rigidly toned muscle.

A warrior's body, he often thought. One who gave herself to him and brought him endless thrill, and impossible peace. She trembled for him, rose up and over. Lost as he was lost. And when he slipped inside her, she said his name. Said his name as her body arched up to his, as she twined around him, as their eyes met.

He was inside there, too, he thought. In those eyes, in that gilted brown. Lost, and found. And it was her name on his lips as they took each other.

7

Eve contacted Peabody with orders to return to Central and follow up with EDD. She'd keep her partner in reserve regarding interviews with Alex Ricker. It seemed good strategy for her and Roarke to meet the son of the man who'd enjoy seeing the pair of them slow-roasted over an open fire without additional cop presence.

As she maneuvered through morning traffic to the Park Avenue condo, she hoped it wasn't a mistake.

"I need information from him," Eve began. "More, I need to get a sense of what his relationship was with Coltraine—if they had a relationship."

"All right." As she drove, Roarke continued to work with his PPC.

"He's not going to like us, or appreciate finding us on his doorstep. His father's locked in a cage. We turned the key."

"One of my fondest memories."

"Which is exactly what we can't push in his face if we want any kind of cooperation."

"And you think I'll go in with a neener-neener?"

She'd have laughed at the term if she hadn't been concerned he'd go in with the Roarke equivalent. The ice-cold fuck-you look. "I'm saying we either distance ourselves from past history, or use it. Depending on his reaction. His reaction may tell us if Coltraine's murder was, in any way, connected to us. I need something from him, to approach matters."

Roarke smiled a little, spoke blandly. "And, of course, I know nothing about the art of negotiation and inter-view."

"I've seen you work, pal. I don't want him squealing for a lawyer because you put on Scary Roarke."

"I've seen *you* work, pal. So I'd advise you to keep Lieutenant Kick-Ass under wraps."

She scowled before swinging over to the curb in front of the dignified old building. "I need to set the tone, the pace."

"You need to remember I've been on interviews with you before."

Roarke got out. The doorman halted his quick march mid-stride. The sour expression the dingy police-issue brought to his face transformed into polite welcome.

Irritating, Eve thought. One look at Roarke wearing his power the same way he wore the perfectly cut suit and Italian shoes, and it went from "Get that piece of shit away from my building" to "What can I do for you, sir?"

"Good morning, sir. What can I do for you?"

Eve nearly snorted. Roarke merely angled his head and sent her a very subtle smirk. "Lieutenant?"

She thought, *Showoff.* But said, "NYPSD." Eve held up her badge for the doorman. "Here to see Alex Ricker. My ride stays where it is."

The doorman's eyes shifted from Eve to Roarke, and back again. The puzzlement was clear, but obviously he knew a man didn't keep a primo gig on a door like this one by asking the wrong questions of the wrong people. "I'll call up, see if Mr Ricker is in and available. If you'd like to step into the lobby?"

He moved briskly to the door, held it open for them.

The outer dignity continued inside with the black-veined marble floor, the rich tones of wood that had likely been in place for a couple of centuries. The seating was red and plush, the tables topped by antique lamps with touches of gilt, all set off under a multitiered chandelier of dripping crystal.

The doorman opened a panel to reveal a wall 'link. After entering a code, he cleared his throat, squared his shoulders.

Eve studied the face that came on-screen. Not Ricker, she mused, but a man about the same age. What she'd call a slick character with an expensive haircut styled so the dark waves curved around a smooth, even-featured face.

"Sorry to disturb you, Mr Sandy. I have the police in the lobby asking to speak to Mr Ricker."

Nothing registered on Sandy's face, and his tone was very cool, very authoritative, faintly European. And, Eve thought, just a little prissy.

"Verify their identification, please."

Eve simply held up her badge again, waiting while the doorman ran his scanner over it, read the display. "Dallas, Lieutenant Eve, verified." He turned to Roarke.

"Expert consultant, civilian. Roarke," Eve said briskly. "With me."

"Send them up, please." Sandy ordered. "I'll inform Mr Ricker."

"Yes, sir."

The doorman started for an elevator as its dull gold door slid open. "Two passengers cleared for Ricker penthouse."

Eve and Roarke stepped inside. The doors closed without a sound.

"Nice building," she said conversationally. "Yours?"

"No." Knowing, as he was sure Eve did, the elevator's security likely ran to audio as well as video, he leaned back casually against the wall. "I doubt he'd feel . . . comfortable living in a building I owned."

"Guess not. Bet it's a nice view from the penthouse."

"No doubt."

The elevator opened directly inside a foyer that smelled of roses from the forest of them madly blooming out of a Chinese urn on a pond-sized table. Slick Character stood beside it.

"Lieutenant Dallas, Mr Roarke, I'm Rod Sandy, Mr Ricker's personal assistant. If you'd come with me?"

He led the way into a wide living space.

She'd been right about the view, it was a killer. The wall of windows and glass doors opened to a bricked terrace that jutted out toward the spires and towers of New York. Inside, the sunny, open space murmured with European dignity. Antiques mixed with deeply cushioned chairs and sofas, all in deep hues that translated wealth without flash.

A room, Eve mused, Amaryllis Coltraine would have approved of.

More flowers sat in the hearth in lieu of a fire, framed in marble. Paneled walls concealed such mundane matters, she thought, as entertainment and mood screens, room security, data-and-communication centers.

All that showed was comfort, style, and the money required to maintain both.

"Mr Ricker's just finishing up a 'link transmission. He'll join you as soon as he's free." The tenor of the statement indicated Mr Ricker was a very busy, very important man, and would make time for his lessers when it suited him. "Meanwhile, please sit, be comfortable. May I offer you coffee?"

"No, thanks." Eve remained standing. "Have you worked for Mr Ricker long?"

"Several years."

"Several years as his PA. And you don't ask the nature of our business here?"

Sandy's lips curved, very slightly. "I doubt you'd tell me if I did. In any case, there's no need." Something smug came into the polite smile. "Mr Ricker's been expecting you."

"Is that so? Where were you night before last from twenty-one to twenty-four hundred?"

"Here. Mr Ricker had dinner in, as did I. We remained in that evening."

"You live here?"

"When we're in New York, yes."

"Plan to be here long?"

"Our plans are flexible at the moment." He looked past Eve. "Should I stay?"

"No, that's all right."

Alex Ricker stood in the wide archway off the living area. His eyes, a dark, steady brown, skimmed over Eve to settle, to hold, on Roarke. He owned the sort of face, Eve thought, that seemed to have been chiseled, painstakingly, into angles and planes. Dark, bronzed hair with a hint of curl brushed back from his forehead. Like Roarke, he wore a suit, perfectly cut. She thought they looked like the dark and the light.

He stepped forward, a smooth gait, a slim build, with every appearance of ease. But he wasn't at ease, Eve decided. Not quite at ease.

"Lieutenant Dallas." He offered a hand, and a firm, businesslike handshake. "Roarke. I wondered if we'd ever meet. Face-to-face. Why don't we sit down?"

He chose a chair, relaxed back into it. And again, Eve thought, not quite relaxed.

"Your assistant said you've been expecting us."

"You," Alex said to Eve. "Obviously I've followed your . . . work."

"Is that so?"

"I think it's natural enough to be interested in the police officer responsible for my father's current situation."

"I'd say your father's responsible for his current situation."

"Of course." After the polite agreement, he glanced back at Roarke. "Even without that connection, I'd have had some curiosity about your wife."

"And I make a habit out of taking a personal interest in those who take one in mine."

Scary Roarke, Eve thought, but Alex smiled and continued before she could speak.

"I'm sure you do. In any case, I understand the two of you often work together, or I suppose it's more accurate to say you engage Roarke as a civilian expert on occasion. I didn't realize this would be one of those occasions."

The pause wasn't a hesitation but more of a beat, as Eve interpreted it. One that separated one tone and topic from another.

"You're here about Amaryllis. I heard what happened to her yesterday, so I've been expecting you. You'd study her files, from Atlanta as well as from here. Once you saw my name, you'd have to wonder."

"What was your relationship with Detective Coltraine?"

"We were involved." His gaze stayed level with Eve's. "Intimately involved, for nearly two years."

"Lovers?"

"Yes, we were lovers."

"Were?"

"That's right. We haven't been together for about a year now."

"Why?"

He lifted his hands. "It didn't work out."

"Who decided it wasn't working out?"

"It was mutual. And amicable."

Eve kept her eyes sharp, her voice pleasant. "I've found when people are intimately involved, for nearly two years, say, the breaking it off part is rarely amicable. Somebody's usually pissed."

Alex crossed his feet at the ankles and his shoulders moved in the faintest of shrugs. "We enjoyed each other while it lasted, and parted friends."

"Her work, your . . . background. That would have been a problematic mix for her."

"We enjoyed each other," he repeated, "and largely left work—hers and mine—out of the mix."

"For nearly two years? That's a strange kind of intimacy."

"Not everyone needs to blend every area of their lives. We didn't."

Getting under his skin now, Eve noted, just a little prick under the skin. She dug deeper. "Apparently not. I spoke with her former partner, her former lieutenant, and we've contacted her family. No one mentioned you, her lover of close to two years. That just makes me wonder. Were you really so intimate and amicable, or did you have something to hide?"

Something hardened in his eyes. "We kept it low-key, for the very reasons you named. My familial connections would have been difficult for her professionally, so there was no reason to include them in our relationship—or to involve others. This was our personal life. Our personal business. I'd think you'd understand that very well."

Eve lifted her eyebrows.

"The lieutenant and I were open about our relationship from its beginning," Roarke pointed out.

"Everyone makes their own choices."

"Your father wouldn't have approved, any more than her superiors," Roarke speculated as he studied Alex's face. "No, he wouldn't have liked his son and heir sleeping with the enemy, unless it was for the purpose of recruiting. That he would have approved of, quite well."

"If you're looking to use our relationship to stain Ammy's reputation, you're—" He broke off, settled back, but the temper had whipped out, left the sting in the air. "We kept business out of our relationship. And there comes a time when a father's approval isn't the driving force in a man's life."

"Did Max know?"

"You'll have to ask him," Alex said coolly. "You know where to find him."

"Yeah." Changing tack, Eve drew his attention back to her. "A concrete cage on Omega. Crappy place, isn't it?"

"Is this about my relationship with Amaryllis or with my father?"

"Depends. When's the last time you saw Detective Coltraine?"

"The day before she was killed. I got in touch with her when I got into town. She came here. We had drinks, caught up with each other. She was here for a couple of hours."

"Alone? Just the two of you?"

"Rod was here. Up in the office."

"What did you talk about?"

"How she liked New York, how she was settling in to her new home, her new job. What I'd done in Paris. I'd come in from there. She told me she was involved with someone. Seriously involved, and that he made her happy. It was easy to see that was true. She looked happy."

"And on the night she was murdered?"

"I had dinner in. About eight, I think. Rod would

know. Caught up with some work. He went to his room about ten, and I went out shortly after that."

"You went out? Where?"

"I was restless. I thought I'd take a walk, as I don't get to New York often. I like the city. I walked over to Broadway."

"You walked from Park to Broadway?"

"That's right." The faint edge of annoyance crept in. "It was a nice night, a little on the cool side. I wanted the lights, the noise, the crowds, so I ended up wandering around Times Square."

"Alone."

"Yes. I hit a couple of video arcades. I like to play. I stopped in a bar. Crowded, noisy. They had the game on-screen. American baseball. I prefer football. Not what you people call football. Real football. But I had a beer and watched some of the game. Then I walked back here. I'm not sure of the time. Not very late. Before one, I'd say."

"What's the name of the bar?"

"I have no idea. I was walking around; I wanted a beer."

"Got a receipt?"

"No. It was one bloody beer. I paid cash. If I'd known I'd need an alibi, I'd've done considerably better."

Temper, temper, Eve thought. "A man in your position, a businessman with international interests—and considering, again, your background—might find it necessary to own a licensed weapon."

"You know I do. You'd have checked already."

"You're licensed for a civilian stunner, which is

registered in your name. Maybe, since you're being so cooperative, you'd allow me to take it with me, have it tested and examined. Since you were having a beer and watching the game when Detective Coltraine was killed."

Resentment lay cold on his face. "If my father was anyone else but Max Ricker?"

"I'd still be asking for it. I can get a warrant, if you'd prefer."

He said nothing, only rose. He walked to a table, unlocked a drawer. It was smaller, sleeker, and less powerful a weapon than hers. One that stunned only. He offered it to her, along with its license.

"Handy," she said.

"As I said, I was expecting you. I'm not my father." He clipped out the words as Eve put the weapon and paperwork in an evidence bag, labeled it, sealed it. "I don't kill women."

"Just men?"

"I cared about her, or we wouldn't be having this conversation. Now we're done." He accepted the receipt Eve printed out of her PPC. "I expect the cop who put Max Ricker in that cage will catch the person who killed Amaryllis."

He walked back to the foyer, called the elevator.

"You know the routine, don't leave town, stay available, blah blah." Eve stepped onto the elevator with Roarke.

"Yes, I know the routine. I also know if our backgrounds made us who we are, we'd all be fucked."

He walked away as the doors closed.

When they hit the sidewalk, Eve stopped, turned to speak. Roarke simply shook his head, then took her arm and led her to the car.

"What?" she said, and repeated when they were inside, "What?"

"Drive. If I were a man who'd been expecting a visit from a cop who'd be looking at me for killing another cop, I'd have myself a plant on the street, with eyes and ears. And then I'd know just what that cop thought about me and our conversation."

Eve frowned as she drove. "You actually have people who walk around listening to other people?"

He patted her hand. "We're not talking about me, are we?"

"Privacy laws—"

"There, there." He patted her hand again. "He was in love with her, and still is. To some extent, still is."

"People often kill the ones they love."

"Well, if he did, he's either amazingly stupid about it, or damned clever. Pathetic alibi like that. You'll be getting a warrant for his building's security discs, to verify his coming and going."

"First on the list. He'd have to know that, so he'll have come and gone pretty much as stated. He's wide open for the time in question. Wide. And he was nervous when we got there. He lost some of the nerves as we went along because he got mad. The stunner's not going to play out. He gave it up too easily. He could have another, unregistered, unlicensed. Hell, he could have a freaking arsenal."

"Max did love the weapons' trade. He's smoother

126

than his father," Roarke commented. "And yet not so smooth. Odd, really. Max wouldn't have shown those nerves, wouldn't have felt them come to that. Yet the son has a polish the father lacked. He doesn't seem the type to use the word *cunt* when referring to Amaryllis. It's too vulgar."

"Maybe he hires vulgar underlings."

"Very possibly. Or it was a deliberate choice because it seems off. Because it seems more like his father."

"Maybe. He's interested in us, has been interested in us. But—"

"No more, it seems, than reasonable. Given the circumstances."

"It seems," she agreed. "There's either some tension between him and his father, or he wanted us to think there is. I wonder which. Anyway, are you going to midtown? To your office?"

"I suppose I am."

"I'll dump you there."

"Shows me what I'm worth to you. Now I'm dumped."

"I mean drop you off there, take you. Whatever. But speaking of dumping. She breaks things off back in Atlanta. He's pissy about it—amicable, my ass—but maybe it's like, sure, screw it, who needs you. Or maybe he keeps at her some, and that's why she decides to transfer."

"The timing would indicate she wanted distance."

"What did he say? He doesn't get to New York often. Then he comes here, contacts her. Here we go again, she thinks, and just when she's gotten into this romance with Morris. When things are smoothed out. She goes to see him, tries to convince him it's over and done. He could play that out. Like you said, he's smooth, he's polished. But it burns his guts. This bitch can't dump me. She's not going to get away with it. Works himself up. Really gets up the steam. Contacts her that night, demands she come meet him, or he's going to make it sticky for her with Morris, with the department."

"She might argue with him, or try to reason," Roarke continued her thought. "Or simply go along. But she'd take the precaution of strapping on her weapons."

"Yeah, but he's waiting for her. Already in. Could be he managed to get her key card when she came to visit, or his pal Sandy did—clone it, get it back without her realizing it. Takes her out on the stairs, carries her down, brings her back so he can tell her no woman tells him it's over. Maybe he lets her plead with him, promise him, tell him she loves him—whatever she thinks will save her life. But he knows she's lying, and that just makes it worse, so zap. Lights out."

She shook her head. "And it just doesn't ring all the bells for me."

"He'd have hurt her more. That's what you're thinking."

"Wouldn't you? Bitch dumped you, now she's spreading them for some other man. Gotta pay."

"He loved her. Maybe enough to kill her, and too much to hurt her."

Since she understood exactly what he meant, she shook her head. "People are so screwy. It wasn't impulse,

128

that's the other thing. It wasn't like: I'm going over there and deal with that bitch. It was too organized for that. So, you take it back, figure he'd planned it awhile. Before he even got to New York. He'd have known about Morris. He could have had her shadowed, and then he'd have known about Morris. Plays nearly the same way then, except he invites her over, makes nice. So good to see you again, glad you're happy. Aren't we mature adults? Then he calls her, tells her he needs to see her, or he's in trouble, needs her help, whatever it takes. And she goes."

She shoved her way across town. "Or, and here's one I don't like because it could work. They were still screwing around. She was in his pocket. Things went south, and he did her or had her done. I hate that it's the one that works the best."

"It only works best with the current data," Roarke pointed out. "Is there anything I can do to help with Morris?"

"No, there's really not. I called, straight to his voice mail this morning. I didn't want to . . . you know. Just said I wanted him to know we're working on it, and he could tag me whenever he needed. I've got to ask him if he knew she'd been tangled up with Alex Ricker. I have to ask, and I don't think he did. He'd have told me yesterday. However much shock he was in, he'd have told me that, given me the lead. So I'm going to be the one to kick him in the gut again."

Harder for her, Roarke knew, than facing down an armed psychopath. "I can reschedule some things, go with you. We can go see him now."

The offer made her throat burn. He would do that. He would always do that. She had that. "I can't. I have to get back, get all this down in the book, get the stunner to the lab. I need to fill Peabody in. And other stuff. I'm hoping I'll have something more solid when I talk to Morris."

She got as close to the big black tower that housed Roarke Industries as the madness of New York allowed. "Thanks."

"Actions speak louder." He cupped her neck, and leaning to her took her mouth in a kiss that made her swear she could see little red hearts dancing over her head. "Take care of my cop."

"I try to make a habit of it."

"If only you did." He stepped out, shot her a last look with those blue laser eyes, then strode down the sidewalk to the black spire he'd created.

She went by the lab first, hand-delivered the stunner. On her way to Homicide, she made a mental list of what had to be done. Get the Alex Ricker interview into the file, along with her impressions. Check, for her own curiosity, how often father and son communicated. Run probabilities on all the scenarios she'd run through with Roarke. Meet with Mira to get a solid profile on both vic and killer. Update Peabody, study EDD results.

Then, because it couldn't be put off, she'd deal with the "other stuff" she hadn't explained to Roarke.

She'd contact Don Webster in IAB.

Because, goddamn it, if anybody'd had a whiff of Coltraine and Max Ricker's son, it would've been IAB.

If they'd known, the info on that relationship would've been passed along from Atlanta to New York.

Webster would know.

The idea of having to wheedle information out of Internal Affairs—and out of a former one-night stand—just burned her ass. Stewing about it, she strode into the bullpen, annoyed.

"Dallas! Hey! Wait!"

Scowling, she waved off Peabody's shout. "I need five."

"But—"

"Five!" Eve shouted back, and stomped into her office.

Morris sat in her visitor's chair.

"Oh, hey." The next time Peabody told her to wait, Eve promised herself, she'd wait.

"I know better." He got to his feet. She could see the long, sleepless night on him—the shadowed eyes, the pallor. "Better than to get in your way, better than to ask questions, to push at you when you push yourself harder than anyone could. I know better. But it doesn't matter."

"It's okay." She shut the door. "It's okay."

"I'm going to see her. I needed to come here first, needed you to tell me whatever you could before I went to see her."

Eve's 'link beeped, and she ignored it. "A little milk in your coffee, right?"

"Yes, a little. Thanks."

She programmed coffee, using the time to organize her thoughts. "I spoke with her family."

"I know. So have I now."

She gave him the coffee, took her own seat, swiveling it to face him. "And I spoke with her lieutenant here and in Atlanta. With her partner there, with her squad here. She was very well liked."

He nodded. "You're trying to comfort me, and I'm grateful. I need more. I need facts. Theories if that's all you have. I need to know what you think happened. And why. I need you to promise you'll tell me the truth. If you give me your word, you won't break it. Will you promise me the truth?"

"Okay." She nodded. "The truth. I give you my word. I need the same from you. I have to ask you something, and I need the truth."

"Lies won't help her."

"No, they won't. Morris, did you know that Detective—that Amaryllis had had an intimate relationship with Max Ricker's son, with Alex Ricker, before she transferred to New York?"

8

She knew the answer instantly. His eyes widened; his lips trembled open. He said nothing for a moment or two while she watched him drink coffee and compose himself. He sat, not in one of his sharp, stylish suits, but in a lightweight black sweater and jeans, with his hair pulled back in a simple tail with none of the usual ornamentation.

As he sat, in silence, she knew just as she'd told Roarke, she'd kicked a friend in the gut a second time.

"Morris—"

He held up a hand asking for another minute. "You've confirmed this?"

"Yes."

"I knew there had been someone, that she'd been involved with someone before she left Atlanta." He lifted a hand to rub at his temple. "They'd broken it off, and it left her upset, at loose ends. It was one of the reasons she decided to transfer. Just a fresh start, a clean slate—some distance between what had been and what could be. That's how she put it. I should've told you yesterday. I didn't think of it. I couldn't think—"

"It's okay."

"She mentioned it, the way you do when you're

getting to know someone. She said . . . What did she say? I'm trying to remember. Just that they couldn't make it work, couldn't be what each other needed them to be. She never mentioned his name. I never asked. Why would I?"

"Can you tell me, did you get a sense she was worried about him, about how they'd ended it?"

"No. I only remember thinking what kind of fool had let her get away. She didn't bring it up again, and neither did I. It was the past. We were both focused on now, on where we were going. On what could be, I suppose. Did he do this?"

"I don't know. It's a lead, and I'll follow it. But I don't know, Morris. I'll tell you what I know, if you trust me to handle it."

"There's no one I trust more. That's the truth."

"Alex Ricker is in New York."

The color that came into his face was rage, barely controlled. "Hear me out," she demanded. "He contacted her, and she went to see him the day before she died. He volunteered this information to me this morning when I went to see him."

Morris set his coffee aside and, rising, walked to Eve's skinny window. "They weren't still involved. I would have known."

"He said they weren't, and that they broke off their relationship amicably. They met as friends. They had a drink and a catch-up conversation during which she told him she'd met someone, was involved. He stated that she looked happy."

"Did you believe him?"

134

Hell, she thought, how did she dance around her suspicions and keep her word? "I believe he might have been telling the truth, or part of the truth. If she'd felt threatened or worried, would she have told you?"

"I want to think so. I want to think even if she hadn't I would have seen it, felt it. She didn't tell me she was meeting him, and now I can't ask her why she didn't. What it means that she didn't."

She didn't have to see his face to know there was pain. "It could be it meant so little to her she didn't feel it was worth mentioning."

He turned back. "But you don't think so."

"Morris, I know people in relationships do strange things. They say too much, don't say enough." Take me, she thought. Had she told Roarke she intended to contact Webster?

"Or it could be, especially since our relationship had become very serious, I might have asked questions. Ones she didn't want to answer. It's not that she'd been involved with someone before, neither of us were children. But she'd been involved with Alex Ricker."

"Yes."

"The son of a known criminal, a known killer. One who, when they were involved, was still at large. Still in power. How likely is it that Alex Ricker is uninvolved, unconnected to his father's activities? But she, a police official, became involved with him."

"He's never been arrested or charged with any crime."

"Dallas."

"Okay, yeah, it's dicey, it's tricky. It's sticky. I'm a police official, Morris, and I not only got involved with a man cops all over the planet—and off it—gave the hard eye to, I married him."

"One forgets," he murmured. He came back to sit, to pick up his coffee again. "It would've caused some friction for her on the job. As it did for you." When she said nothing, Morris lowered the mug. "Was she investigated?"

"I'm going to find that out. But . . ." Truth, she reminded herself. That was the deal here. "She kept it to herself. From Ricker's statement, from what I've gotten out of Atlanta, and out of her squad here, nobody knew she'd had a personal relationship with him."

"I see."

Worse, Eve realized, worse for him that the relationship with Alex had been *important* enough for her to have kept it a secret.

"It could've been for a lot of reasons. The simplest is she wanted to keep her personal life off the job."

"No, you're trying to comfort me again, to spare me. I know how the grapevine works. Everyone in my house, in hers, I'd wager nearly every cop, clerk, drone, and tech in Central knows Ammy and I were involved. Keeping it quiet had to be deliberate, and because of who he was. And to keep it quiet for that long? That's serious."

He paused a moment, and his brows drew together. "You're going to find out. You mean you're going to talk to IAB?"

"It's necessary."

"If they didn't know, they will now. After you talk to them."

"I can't go around it. I'll be as careful as I can, but—"

"Give me a minute." He stared down into his coffee. "Max Ricker carried cops in his pockets like other men carry loose credits. You're wondering now if his son had Ammy in his."

"I have to ask. I have to look at it. If I factor it out, push it off to spare her rep, maybe her killer slips through the gap. That's not going to happen. Not even for you."

"I *knew* her. I know how she thought, how she felt, how she slept and ate and lived. I'd have known if she was dirty. I know how she defined her work and how she felt about doing it."

"You didn't know about Alex Ricker."

He stared. She watched the shutter come down, the one that shut her out as a friend, as a cop, as a colleague. "No, I didn't." He got back up onto his feet, spoke stiffly. "Thank you for keeping me informed."

She got to hers before he could get to the door of her office. "Morris, I can't and won't apologize for doing my job, but I can be sorry that the way I need to do it causes you pain. Just like I'm sorry to have to say this. Stay away from Alex Ricker. If I don't have your word you'll keep clear, make no contact with him, I'll put a tail on you. I won't let you impede the investigation."

"You have my word." He went out and closed the door behind him.

Alone, Eve sat at her desk, dropped her head into her

hands. Friendships, she thought, were so damn compli-
cated, so bound with sharp edges that could jab a hole
through you at any given point.

Why did people always get tangled up with other
people? Why put ourselves through this *shit*?

She *had* to consider the possibility Coltraine had been
dirty. Wasn't that hard enough? Did she have to carry
the guilt for hurting Morris along with it?

Crap. Yeah, she did. No way out of it.

She wanted to ignore the knock on her door, really
wanted just to wallow for a while in a little stew of self-
pity. But duty won.

"What? What the fuck do you want?"

The door eased open a few inches, and Peabody
peered in. "Ah. Are you okay?"

There it was, Eve supposed. There was the answer to
why people got tangled with people. Because when you
were down, when you were wallowing, someone you
mattered to would ask if you were okay.

"No. Really not. Come in. Shut the door." When
she had, Eve blew out a breath and shook it off.
"EDD?"

"There's nothing off on her home or work units.
Nothing off on her house or office 'links. Nothing ref-
erencing an appointment or meet for the night she died.
Her date books check out. The only one we haven't
been able to pin down, so far, is a notation for AR, the
day before her murder. It's listed under personal. No
address, no number, with the additional notation of a-
slash-s, which corresponds with 'after shift' in her other
notes."

"I've got that one. Sit down. AR is Alex Ricker."

"Alex . . . as in Max Ricker?"

"As in his only son. Here's the deal."

Though she kept silent during Eve's recap, various expressions raced over Peabody's face, and Eve could read them perfectly. They ranged from Holy Shit to Poor Morris to What Now.

"You told him?"

"Yeah."

Peabody nodded. "Well, you had to."

"I didn't tell him about Ricker's lame alibi, because he didn't ask. I didn't tell him it was pretty damn clear to me Ricker still has feelings for Coltraine. Even without that, it was bad enough. I need you to get a warrant to search Alex Ricker's penthouse, and to confiscate and search his electronics. He'll be expecting it. He'll have covered himself, if need be. But we're pretty damn smart around here. We can see what's under the covers if we look hard enough. We've got to check his idiot alibi. See who's clear to sweep around Times Square with a picture. Sports bars are the focus. We'll take over there once I'm finished up and able to get back out in the field."

Eve rubbed her eyes. "Now I've got to twist Webster into meeting me somewhere away from here, where we're not going to run into other cops or anybody else."

"Lets you see how it was for her. I mean different reasons and all, but it's stressful trying to arrange to see somebody on the down-low. I can't imagine doing it for almost two years. Either she really loved him or the sex was, like, stupendously mag."

"Or she liked the thrill, and the profit."

"Oh, right." Peabody's face fell. "It's hard to go there."

"Tell me. But I'm going, and . . . I've just thought of the perfect place." She swiveled to her 'link. "Shut the door on your way out. No point in advertising I'm calling the Rat Squad."

The Down and Dirty was a sex and strip joint where the patrons downed the throat-searing, stomach-burning adult beverages, and liked it. For those who could pay the freight, private rooms offered a cot and a lock, and an area in which to perform whatever natural or unnatural acts they chose.

Privacy booths were often choked with smoke while illegals were passed around like candy corn. At night, the stage generally held a band of some sort, in various stages of undress and with questionable talents. Dancers with the same qualifications usually joined them—as did patrons who might be influenced by those adult beverages and/or illegals.

Violence was known to break out—suddenly and gleefully—which was part of the appeal to some. Odd and unattractive substances stuck to the floor, and the food was utter crap.

Eve's bachelor party had been held there, during which she'd caught a murderer. Good times.

The man behind the bar towered up to about six and a half feet of muscle. His black skin gleamed against an open leather vest and body ink. His shaven head shone like a dark moon as he mopped the bartop and the holoband beat out a jungle rhythm for a trio of impressively built and talentless dancers.

Crowds didn't pack into the club this time of day, but a few men huddled at tables sucking brews, apparently content to watch the clumsy footwork since it was attached to naked tits.

Two of them scanned her as she strode by, then hunched down to make themselves, she supposed, disappear. The guy behind the bar gave her a good, long stare. Bared his teeth.

"Hey, skinny white girl."

"Hey, big black guy."

His wide, homely face broke into a grin. He reached across the bar with arms as long as Fifth Avenue, lifted her off her feet, and slapped his mouth noisily to hers.

"Come on," was all she could say.

"Can't help it. I missed seeing your face, plus I thought about you just this morning. How about that?"

"Yeah, how about that. How's it going, Crack?"

"Be up, be down. Mostly be up these days. I went by the park this morning, like I do once in a while, to take a look at the tree you had planted for my baby girl. My baby sister. It's greening up. Makes me feel good to see how it's getting green."

His expression changed from pleasant to dangerous, like a flick of a switch, when someone dared to approach the bar for service while he was otherwise engaged.

The customer slunk away.

They called him Crack, it was well known, for his

141

habit of cracking skulls together—be they employee or patron—if their behavior displeased him.

"Whatchu doing in my place?"

"I've got a meet, and I wanted to have it in private."

"You want a room?"

"Not that kind of private."

"Good to hear. I like your man. I hope he be up."

"Roarke being up is never a problem."

Crack's laughter was like a thunderclap.

"Anyway, I thought I could take the meet here, and not run into another cop. If that's not a problem for you."

"You want, I'll kick these assholes out of here, close the place down, and you can have it to yourself as long as you want."

"Just a table, thanks."

"Drink?"

"Do I look suicidal?"

"Got some bottled water in the back." His gaze tracked away from her. "You don't wanna see other cops, you got a problem, 'cause one of your kind just came in."

She nodded, spotting Webster. "It's okay. That's my meet."

"Take any table you want."

"Thanks." She walked toward Webster, then gestured toward a corner table, and kept walking.

It was always a little awkward, dealing with him, she admitted. Not because she'd bounced with him once, when they'd both been detectives working Homicide. But because he'd taken the bounce a lot more seriously than she had.

More awkward yet as, years after, he'd lost his mind apparently and put a move on her. One Roarke had walked in on even as she'd been deflecting it. The two of them had gone at each other like a couple of crazed wolves, wrecked her home office and caused each other considerable bodily damage before Roarke had knocked Webster unconscious.

They'd come to terms, she reminded herself. She and Roarke, Roarke and Webster, she and Webster, whatever.

Still. Awkward. And that was before you added the sticky layer of Internal Affairs.

Webster, a good-looking man with sharp eyes, scanned the room, then sat—like Eve—with his back to the wall. "Interesting choice of venue."

"Works for me. I appreciate you meeting me."

"Aren't we polite?"

"Don't start with me."

He shrugged, leaned back. "Can we get coffee in this place?"

"Sure. If you've got a death wish."

He smiled at her. "Does Roarke know you're meeting me in a sex joint?"

"Webster, I'd as soon nobody knows I'm meeting IAB anywhere, anytime."

And leaning against the wall, his back went up. "We've all got a job to do, Dallas. If you didn't need IAB, we wouldn't be here."

Since he had a point, she didn't argue. "I need to know if IAB has any connection to or any interest in my investigation of Detective Amaryllis Coltraine's murder."

"Why would you ask?"

"Yes or no, Webster."

"Have you uncovered any evidence or are you pursuing any line of investigation that indicates there is or should be IAB involvement?"

She leaned forward. "Fuck that. A cop's dead. Try to care a little."

He mirrored her move. "Fuck that. If I didn't care I wouldn't be IAB."

"Give me a yes or no to my question, I'll give you a yes or no to yours."

He leaned back again, studying her. Calculating, she knew, how to handle it. "Yes."

The knot in her belly twisted, but she nodded. "Yes. I need to know if she was dirty, Webster."

"Can't tell you. Can't tell you," he repeated, pointing a warning finger when her eyes fired, "because I don't know."

"Tell me what you do know. Quid pro quo," she added. "I'll reciprocate, with the stipulation we both keep this conversation off our records, unless both agree otherwise."

"I can do that. You wouldn't be here if you hadn't already made the connection between Coltraine and Alex Ricker. Is he a suspect?"

"He is. I don't have enough, or much of anything on him. But I'm looking. IAB's been on her since Atlanta, then?"

"The bureau down there got a tip she was involved with Ricker."

"A tip?" Eve prompted.

"Some photos of Coltraine and Ricker—hand-holding, lip-locking—landed on IAB's desk."

"Handy. Somebody wanted her roasted."

"Probably. It doesn't change the picture. IAB got the package about nine months before she requested transfer. They followed through on it, confirmed. While each maintained a separate residence, they essentially lived together in a third—a condo in Atlanta in a building owned by Max Ricker. Private entrance, private elevator, private garage. She could come and go with little risk of being seen. They also spent time together when she was off the roll. She traveled with him to Paris, London, Rome. He bought her jewelry, high-ticket items."

"No high-ticket items in her place," Eve put in. "No evidence she kept a lockbox anywhere."

"She gave it all back when they split."

"How do you know? You had her surveilled? You had the place wired?"

"I can't confirm or deny. I'm telling you what I know."

"If all this was going on, why didn't IAB pull her in?"

"Contrary to popular belief, we don't go after cops for the fun of it. Alex Ricker? No criminal, no evidence of criminal. No evidence Coltraine was on the take or passing police info to him. Hypothetically, if the place was wired, Alex Ricker and his old man are the types who have places swept regularly."

"And who are smart enough not to discuss anything incriminating unless they're sure it's safe."

"They got bits and pieces."

"Did she meet Ricker?" Eve demanded. "Max Ricker? Have any dealings with him?"

"Nothing came up. Then again, like I said, she and Ricker's boy, Alex, traveled. So they could have. But those bits and pieces included the boy making it clear he didn't want to discuss Daddy. So they didn't. Upshot is, things got rocky in paradise, seriously rocky after Daddy went down."

"When we took him down," Eve murmured.

"Yeah. She started spending more time at her own place. They argued a few times when there were eyes on them. Then it shut down. Few weeks later, she put in for the transfer to New York."

"That's when you guys took over."

"We kept an eye on her. Nothing close. Maybe if we had, she'd be alive. The fact is, we looked, couldn't find, and put her on the outer rung. Nothing we picked up since she transferred indicates any contact with Ricker—Max or Alex."

"Alex Ricker's in New York. She met with him the day before she was murdered."

"Fuck me."

"You didn't know."

"I just said we'd bumped her down." Frustration pumped out of him. "We don't crucify cops, goddamn it. She'd screwed around with the son of a known bad guy, but nobody can pin anything on the son. It smelled, sure, but nobody found anything to pin on her either. She came here, by all appearances kept her nose clean. We weren't dogging her. I wish we had been. I

146

don't like dirty cops, Dallas, but I sure as hell hate dead ones."

"Okay, fine. Throttle back, Webster."

"Fuck that, too. Are you looking at jealous former lover here? He does her or has her done because she walked away, and she's heating sheets with Morris?"

Eve lifted her eyebrows.

"Christ, everyfuckingbody knows Morris had a thing going with her. I'm goddamn sorry for him."

"Okay. Okay." She did her own throttling back because she knew that as truth. "Yeah, it could play that way. The problem is, he has a really crappy alibi. If he's a bad guy, he's a really smart one, so why doesn't he have a solid alibi?"

"Sometimes the crappy ones are more believable."

"Yeah, I've gone there, too. He was still in love with her, at least part of the way. Still stuck on her."

Webster twisted his lips into a pained smile. "I know how that goes."

Eve eased back, cursed herself for walking straight into it. "Come on."

"I've recovered," he said easily. "But I do know how it goes. It pisses you off, and pushes at you. I never wanted to kill you though."

"Whoever did her wanted it. Planned it. You can't tell me either way, if she was dirty or not."

"No. You can't tell me either. You can't give her the benefit of the doubt. Whatever you want to say about IAB, you know you have to look at her for being on the take, or at least under the influence of her feelings for the guy. You have to follow the line."

"I don't have to like it."

Heat leapt back into his eyes. "You think I do?"

"Why do it otherwise?"

"Because we're sworn to uphold the law, not use it. Protect and serve, not grab whatever you want along the way. Not do whatever you want. We're supposed to stand for something."

She couldn't argue. "Did IAB look at me when I hooked up with Roarke?"

"Yeah, some. You knew it, in your gut. Your rep, your record held up. Plus," he added with a quick grin, "nobody's ever pinned anything on him either. The fact is, I know from personal experience, he could be the baddest of the badasses out there, and he'd never use you."

He hesitated, then seemed to come to a decision. "You may never see captain. They may never pull the bars out of their tight asses for you."

"I know. It doesn't matter."

"It should."

It surprised her to hear the resentment—for her sake—in his voice. And left her without a clue what to say.

"Anyway." Webster shrugged. "I'll take a look at things, on my own time. So we don't put a smear on her if she didn't earn it. If you get any more on Ricker, either way it leans, I'd appreciate if you'd pass it on."

"Okay. I can do that."

"How much does Morris know?"

"I told him about Ricker before I tagged you. I'm not going around him on this."

"So he knows you were going to run this up with IAB."

"He put the dots together, yeah."

"If you talk to him again, tell him I'll be keeping a lid on it."

"I will. He'll appreciate it."

"Yeah, unless I find something. Then he'll want to eat my heart with cranberry sauce. I have to get back." He got to his feet. "Be careful around Ricker. You put his father over. Odds are he'd be happy to eat *your* heart raw."

Eve waited until Webster walked out, then went over to say her goodbyes to Crack.

Eve supposed it would be weird to most, and just another day in the life of a cop, to go from a meeting in a sex club to a consultation in the pretty, cool-aired office of Dr Charlotte Mira.

As the department's top profiler and head shrink, Mira claimed a roomy space, decorated to her own liking. Which edged toward female and class.

Just like the doctor herself.

Mira sat, her legs crossed and shown to advantage in a pale pink suit. Her deep brown hair curled softly around her calm, lovely face as she sipped tea.

"I sent a card of condolence to Morris," she told Eve. "It seems such a small thing to do for a friend at such a time. You've seen him, of course."

"Yeah. He's holding on. It's wrecked him, you can see it, but he's holding. You were able to read the files, the updates? Everything?"

"Yes. One of our own goes down, it's a priority. She had an affair with Max Ricker's son. A dangerous business. A professional risk. Yet I wouldn't characterize her as a risk taker."

"She was a cop."

"Yes, which always involves risks. But according to her files, she never once in her career discharged her weapon. She solved puzzles. She was a thinker. An organized, detail-oriented thinker. She came from a good background, upper-middle-class, single-marriage family. She excelled in school. Her job evaluations were always solid and steady. No black marks, no shiny stars. This was a careful woman. Alex Ricker was the exception."

"Love, lust, or gain?"

"If gain, or only gain, why risk the connection, the closeness? To continue in the relationship for more than a year, to go to the trouble to hide it from her colleagues, her family? Lust can start the fire, but it rarely keeps it burning for long. It may have been all three."

"The attraction first—the lust. Hot guy, interesting guy, classy. Dangerous. The good girl gets a tingle from the bad boy."

Mira smiled a little. "Are you projecting?"

"I didn't get a tingle. I got hit with a brick. Yeah, I see some parallels, but the way she played it . . ."

"Wasn't the way you did," Mira finished, "or ever would. It's possible the clandestine nature added some excitement. Everything I've studied about it indicates she followed the rules. Except here. That's another form of excitement."

"So she leads with lust, and there's all those tingles—the excitement. Come away with me to Paris tonight. Hotdog. And yeah, she jumped through a lot of hoops to be with him," Eve considered, "and to stay with him, so love—or what she thought was—had to play a part. She's in love, and he says, maybe you could do me this little favor. Not a big thing. Stars in the eyes, you do the little favor. What does it hurt?"

"And the next favor's bigger. You're in deeper." Mira nodded. "It's a logical pattern."

"Maybe he starts to ask too much. There's more risk for a woman not wired for them, and it starts going south. It went south, according to my source, right around the time Ricker went down. She sees what happened, wonders if that's going to happen to the son *and* to her."

"It changes the pattern," Mira agreed. "Alex is now, with his father's defeat, in charge."

"She can't handle it, breaks it off. Puts distance between them. Clean slate, that's what she told Morris. Fresh start. Alex Ricker loses a lover and a resource. Bad break for him."

"His father is a violent, unstable man. A known criminal, a man of power and no conscience. His mother died when he was very young. Accident, suicide."

"Or murder," Eve added.

"Yes, or. While he was given a superior education, and raised with the advantages money can buy, he was placed in confined institutions, regimented schools. As his only acknowledged blood kin—as only son—Max

151

Ricker would have expected a great deal. Demanded it. He'd be expected to excel, and expected—when his father was ready—to step up and take the helm. He, too, from what I've studied, is a careful man. While he may be in the business of risk, he's certainly minimized it by covering himself with layers of protection. His public persona is much more polished than his father's. He has, with careful, even meticulous PR, evaded the scandal of having a parent convicted of all the crimes Max Ricker was convicted of."

"It stings him anyway."

"Oh, it would have to. His only surviving parent, and the one who saw to his needs for most of his life, is locked away. Much of his wealth confiscated. And as you said, his father's arrest, the repercussion of that, closely coincided with the breakup with Detective Coltraine."

"He had a real bad week, I bet."

"He'd have to be angry, feel betrayed, deserted. Again. His mother left him, now his father's taken, and the woman he loves—or is intimately connected to—leaves."

"A careful man could bide his time."

"Yes, a careful man could. But—"

"Damn it. I knew it."

"There's no intimacy in the killing. No passion, no retribution. It's cold, calculated, distant. She belonged to him, in a very real sense. Either just as a woman or as a woman and as a resource. If that sense of betrayal and that anger—even cold and controlled—led him to kill her, I'd expect to see some sign."

Mira sipped her tea, shifted. "Could he resist hurting

her, taking more time? Certainly a man with his profile would be much more apt to choose a safer place for the kill. Still, using her own weapon is personal, even intimate. It's insulting."

"He hired it out."

"Much more likely, in my opinion. A careful man, used to protecting himself and his interests. A hired kill staged to look like a personal one. Sending the weapon back, to you, with a personal message? Again conflicting meanings. A careful man would have left, or ordered the weapon left on the scene. If not, then would have disposed of it. Sending it back, that's a taunt."

"It's an I-dare-your-ass. The killer was proud of his work, and wanted to get that last lick in."

"Yes. Tell me, was she in love with Morris? You'd know."

"Yeah. I think she was."

Mira sighed. "Only more painful for him. But if she was in love with Morris, I don't believe she'd have betrayed him. It doesn't fit her. If she'd ended the relationship with Alex Ricker, and found someone else, she wouldn't betray it."

"Which gives Ricker another motive. If their personal relationship was dead, how about their business one? If they'd had one."

"I'd say, if there was one, they were tied together. Why would she risk it?"

"Maybe he didn't give her a choice. I want her to be clean."

Mira reached out to touch Eve's arm. "Yes, I know you do. So do I. It's painful to see a friend in pain."

"He trusts me to do the job, but I don't know if he'll ever forgive me if doing it proves her dirty. It pisses me off I have to care about that. I wouldn't have to care if . . ."

"You didn't care."

"That's the bitch." She pushed up. "Thanks."

"Anything you need on this, anytime. I've cleared it."

Eve stepped out, started back to Homicide. To do whatever the job demanded.

9

The problem with being the son of a notorious criminal was that it was a lot easier for cops to obtain search warrants. With one in hand, and a small battalion of cops behind her, Eve entered Alex Ricker's penthouse for the second time.

The fact that he had a trio of lawyers with him didn't surprise her.

The head guy, who identified himself as Henry Proctor, gave off the impression of elder statesman with his flow of white hair, craggy face, conservative dark suit. She imagined his rich, baritone voice had echoed through many courtrooms, sculpting the law like a chisel on marble to defend his high-collar clients.

"My client is fully prepared to cooperate with the police in this matter, to the letter of the law."

"You can read this letter of the law." Eve offered the warrant. "We're authorized to search the premises, and to confiscate and examine all data and communication devices, including portables and personals."

"One of Mr Ricker's legal counsel or staff will observe every level of the execution of the warrant. Which will be conducted on record. Mr Ricker will also exercise his right to record the search and confiscation. He will make no statement, and will not be questioned at this time."

"Fine by me. Captain Feeney."

It wasn't usual for the head of EDD to assist in the execution of a warrant. But Eve wanted no mistakes—and Feeney had wanted in. She nodded to her former partner, her trainer.

His basset-hound face remained sober. She wondered if she were the only one in the room who knew how much he was enjoying himself. Any slap at a Ricker gave the day a little shine.

"Okay, boys and girls, you know the drill." He stepped forward, a contrast to the slick and polished in his rumpled suit and worn-in shoes. "Receipts will be issued for any equipment and devices removed."

"An estimated time of return would be appreciated. This causes considerable inconvenience."

Feeney scratched his head through his wiry thatch of ginger and silver hair. "Depends, don't it?"

"Detective Baxter, you and your team will begin the search on the third floor. Officer Carmichael, take this level. Peabody," Eve added, "we'll take the second floor."

She wanted the bedrooms, the private spaces, the areas of intimacy. Even people who knew better generally felt safest in the place they slept, had sex, dressed, undressed. It was, in Eve's mind, the most likely spot for Alex to have made a mistake, to have forgotten something that could tie him to Coltraine's murder.

They didn't speak. She'd already informed the team, down to the lowest uniformed drone, that everything they said, everything they did, every expression, gesture, and sneeze could and would be on record. And could and would be used by the lawyers to question both the procedure and the intent of the search and seize.

"We'll start with Mr Ricker's bedroom," she told Rod Sandy.

He stood behind them, disapproval in every line of his face and body. He turned out of the airy, second-floor parlor and into the spacious master suite.

Alex knew how to live, Eve mused. The parlor spilled into a tidy office/sitting room with a black glass work counter holding mini-units. A matching wet bar, a couple of club chairs, and an entertainment screen filled in the blanks. Knowing Roarke's fondness for panels, she ran her fingers over the walls.

"This is what you're looking for." Sandy stepped behind the wet bar, opened a panel. Inside, a cabinet held wine and liquor. "We'll cooperate, Lieutenant," he said, disdain dripping, "so you'll finish this invasion and get out."

"So noted." Eve mirrored Sandy's tone, and with her eyes on his, added to the team, "Check for others."

She moved on with Peabody.

The man liked space, she decided. The bedroom sprawled, one wall fully glassed to open to the terrace and the city beyond. Alex could enjoy his morning coffee or evening brandy while sitting at the bistro table or reclining on the gel-sofa. An antique desk held another mini d and c. Mirrors reflected back the watered silk walls, and the enormous four-poster bed.

In silence, Sandy moved around the room, opening panels for another bar, an AutoChef, screens. Eve wandered, scanned the dressing area with its racks and drawers and counter—and thought she might, finally, have hit on someone with as many clothes as Roarke. And into the luxury of the marble and stone bath.

This was going to take a while.

"Roll up your sleeves, Peabody. Let's get started."

It took a man with brains and some experience to carefully, even meticulously remove anything remotely incriminating from his domain and leave the personal.

She found condoms and sex toys, various lotions billed to enhance the sexual experience. Nothing that crossed the legal lines. She found an army of grooming and hygiene products that told her Alex gave a great deal of thought and time to his appearance.

But vanity wasn't a crime.

His wardrobe told her he preferred and could afford natural fibers and personal tailoring, that even his casual dress was meticulous in style. She found he liked soothing colors and comfort, preferred boxers over briefs—and unless his bedtime reading was a plant for her benefit, he liked spy novels.

What she didn't find in his bedroom was a personal pocket computer.

"I'm not finding a PPC, Rod."

He stood, soldier-straight, arms folded. "I'd assume Mr Ricker would have his on his person."

"And not have one at his bedside? Strikes me as odd. Doesn't it strike you as odd, Peabody, that Mr Ricker wouldn't have a handy PPC at his bedside, where he could work in bed when the mood struck, check the box scores, send an e-mail, whatever?"

"It does strike the odd note, Lieutenant."

"Would it be against the laws of this state not to own two personal computers?" Sandy said coolly.

"Nope, just that odd note."

She walked out, through the parlor, opened a door. Inside she found what looked to be a small guest room. Bed, screen, tiny kitchenette. She crossed over to another black glass counter. On it sat a vase of fresh flowers and a decorative bowl.

"Another odd note. This looks like a work counter, like the one in the master suite. The kind that usually holds equipment. And instead, we've got flowers."

She took a deliberate sniff. "Pretty."

"I don't believe flowers are against the law, either."

"No, but we're racking up the odd notes, Rod. Like why there's a palm plate on this door. Extra security on this room."

"Mr Ricker initially considered making it his office, then decided against it."

"Uh-huh." She stepped up to a narrow chest of drawers, began opening it. "And this looks brand, spanking new. Like it's never been used. Like maybe it was just put in here. Don't get much company?"

His smile hit a perfect middle between sour and smug. "We're redecorating."

"Yeah, I bet." She gestured Peabody to the single closet while she stepped into the adjoining bath.

Compact, efficient, scrupulously clean. But she'd bet it had been used. Just as she'd bet the equipment once housed in the "guest room" had been transferred to another location very, very recently.

"Oh, hey, Rod? There's this other odd note. The one

where you told me you and Alex spent the night in—that would be the night Detective Coltraine was murdered—and Alex told me he went out."

"I assumed Alex was in."

"Don't keep very good tabs on your boss for a PA, do you, Rod?"

He bristled; she enjoyed it. "I don't *keep tabs* on Alex. We had dinner in, as I stated. I went upstairs about ten. I wasn't aware, until he told me this afternoon, that he'd gone out that night. I believe it's still legal in this country for a man to take a walk and have a beer."

"Last I checked. So, how'd you get along with Detective Coltraine?"

"We got along very well, though I hadn't seen her in about a year. I'm sorry for what happened to her and sorry it upsets Alex."

"You didn't see her when she came to see him a couple days ago?"

"No. Alex wanted to see her alone. I was up here."

"You seem to spend a lot of time up here." She sent him an overly cheerful smile. "Since you do, why don't we take a look at your quarters, Rod?"

She went through the motions—as much for procedure as to needle the annoying PA—but knew there would be nothing to find. Alex was smart, he had experience, and he'd anticipated the search.

Once it was done, and they were outside, she conferred with Feeney. "Did you see the small bedroom off the big, second-floor parlor?"

"Yeah. Palm plate and voice code on the door. Unless he uses it to hold his sex slaves against their will, I'd say the equipment in there was moved out in the last day or two. And that equipment's probably unregistered."

"Funny, I was thinking the same. Except about the possible sex slaves."

"Guys think about sex slaves more than women do. Probably."

"I can only suppose. He'd have wiped anything on his equipment."

"Unless he's stupid, sure." Feeney took out the bag of nuts in his pocket, rattled it. Offered it to Eve. "We'll be able to tell if he wiped, maybe find the echoes."

Because they were there, she took a couple of sugared almonds, crunched. "But if he had unregistered, he'd have kept anything incriminating on that."

"Unless, again, stupid."

"I guess it was too much to hope we'd find Coltraine's ring tucked into a box in his sock drawer."

"Worth a shot. Guy's got the shady on him." Feeney jutted a chin toward the building. "Slicked over more than his old man, but he's got the shady on him."

"Yeah, he does. But shady's a leap away from cop killer. I'm going to work from home. You get anything, I want to hear about it."

"Back at you. I didn't know the lady, but she was a badge. And there's Morris. You got EDD, and me, round the clock until we put this one away."

She walked over to Peabody, who was in a huddle with her cohab, McNab, and his EDD pal, Callendar.

McNab stood jingling whatever would jingle in two of the pockets of his maxicargo fire-red pants. His blond hair was braided back from his thin, pretty face to hang down the back of his lightweight daffodil-yellow jacket. Beside him, Callendar was a busty explosion of color in a zigzag-patterned T-shirt, floppy overshirt, and glossy pants.

"Pizza hits all the notes." Callendar chomped on gum so her jaw movements sent the huge triangles dangling from her ears jumping. "You buy."

"I'm on for pizza, but the tab's a grab." McNab held out a fist, and Eve's eyes narrowed as the two e-detectives went through the first round of Rock Paper Scissors.

"Gee, I'm sorry to interrupt playtime, but there's this pesky chore of hunting down a cop killer."

"We're on it." McNab turned earnest green eyes to hers. "We're going to hunker down in the pen. We're just settling on the fuel and the buy."

"I cleared the night for it, Lieutenant," Callendar told her. "But you gotta prime the pump. We took eight desk units, twelve wall, and sixteen portables out of those digs. Anything on there bouncing to Detective Coltraine, we're going to find it."

But pumps had to be primed. Eve dug into her own pockets. "Pizza's on me. Peabody, I'm working from home. You can coordinate the search-and-seizure results, log it all in. Cross all the t's. After that, choose where you're most useful."

"Got that. One thing." She quick-stepped with Eve toward Eve's vehicle. "If Ricker and company hauled equipment or anything out of there, it should be on the building's security discs. So we should—"

"I've got them. I'm going to scan them at home."

"Oh." Peabody's face registered mild disappointment. "I guess I should've figured you'd think of it. I just didn't want to say anything about it while we were inside, and on record."

"It's good you thought of it."

"Well. Oh, and one more thing. If you think we should reschedule Louise's bridal shower and all, I can take care of it."

"Crap." Eve pushed a hand through her hair. "I forgot about it." Again. "No, just leave it. We'll see. If you talk to Nadine about that, and she uses it to try to pump you—"

"The investigation is active and ongoing. We're pursuing all leads. Blah, blah."

"Okay then." Eve climbed into her car.

She made the tail within three blocks. In fact, it was so sloppy a shadow, she felt insulted.

Late-model, nondescript black sedan. Tinted windows. New York plates. She noted the plate numbers, turned to add a few blocks to her drive home. The sedan made the turn, huddled back two car lengths. She considered pulling over, seeing if her tail would follow suit to drive past, then scramble to double back.

Instead, she allowed herself to be caught at the next light while the river of pedestrians flowed in front of her. Why would Ricker hire such a shitty tail? she wondered. A man with his connections, his reach ought to be able to put someone with more skill, and more technology on her.

A homer on her car—or at the least a three-point tail

that could mix it up. In this traffic, she might've missed it. Stupid, amateur move, she decided. Maybe she'd drive around awhile, waste their time, see if they'd swing up close enough so she could use her car to barricade then roust them.

Meanwhile, she might as well find out who owned the sedan.

She engaged her dash comp. "Run vehicle registration, New York. Eight, six, three, Zulu, Bravo, Echo."

Acknowledged. Working . . .

When the light turned, she eased across the crosswalk, flicked a glance in the rearview.

She caught the van out of the corner of her eye. Pinned by cross traffic, she had nowhere to turn. As it barrelled down on her, she punched the accelerator and hit vertical.

"Come on, you piece of shit. Come *on*." For an instant, she thought she might make it, but the speeding van caught her sluggishly-lifting rear wheels. The impact slapped her back in the seat. As the car spun, executed a clumsy nosedive toward Madison Avenue, it filled with safety gel.

She thought: *Fuck.* And crashed.

She heard it—sounds muffled by the gel—the smash, crunch, screech. She went into another sloping three-sixty as the car that had been directly behind her at the light slammed her front fender. Or more accurately, she slammed it. Despite the gel, she felt the jolt slap through her whole body.

Dizzy, disoriented, she shoved out of the car, fumbled for her weapon. People thronged around her, with everyone talking at once through the bells gonging in her head.

"Get back, stay back. I'm a cop." She rushed toward the wrecked van. Her quick scan showed her the sedan, streaming sedately up Madison.

Gone, baby. Gone.

Blood in her eye, literally and figuratively, she approached the door of the van, leading with her weapon. And found the cab empty.

"They ran!" One of the eager witnesses shouted it at her. "Two men. I saw them run that way." The witness pointed east, toward Park.

"I think one was a woman," another witness weighed in. "God, they just *rammed* you, then took off."

"They were white guys."

"One was Hispanic."

"They had dark hair."

"One was blond."

Eve carved through the helpful crowd, yanked open the rear doors. In disgust, she studied the surveillance equipment.

The tail hadn't been stupid and sloppy. She had.

She yanked out her communicator. "Dallas, Lieutenant Eve, officer-involved vehicular, Madison and . . . Seventy-fourth. Require assistance." She elbowed her way back to the car that had hit her after she'd crashed. A woman sat inside, blinking.

"Ma'am? Ma'am? Are you injured?"

"I don't know. I don't think." With glassy eyes and

pinprick pupils, the woman stared at her. "What happened?"

"Require medical assistance for civilian," she added, then turned to look at her crunched, mangled vehicle.

"Goddamn it," she muttered. "Requisitions is going to take out a contract on me."

The information he'd gotten claimed she wasn't hurt. But Roarke took no one's word when it came to his wife—not even hers. Of course, he thought, with a simmering anger he used to cover fear, she hadn't been the one to contact him. Nor did she answer on her pocket 'link, as he'd been trying it since he'd started across town.

When he reached the barricade, he simply left his car where it was. They could bloody well tow it, he thought. And bill him.

He covered the rest of the ground on foot, moving fast.

He saw the wreck first—the accordion pleats of metal, the shattered glass, bitten chunks of fiberglass.

Fear rolled over the anger like lava.

Then he saw her, on her feet. Standing. Whole. And arguing, by the look of it, with one of the medical technicians in front of an ambulance.

"I'm not hurt. I don't need to be examined, and I'm sure as hell not getting in that bus. The safety gel discharged. Can you *see* how much I'm wearing? How's the civilian? How's the woman?"

"Shaken up is all," the MT told her. "But we're taking her in, getting her looked over. You ought to come in. Your eyes look shocky to me."

"My eyes are *not* shocky. My eyes are pissed. Now go away and . . ." She trailed off when she spotted Roarke, and he noted her eyes went from pissed to baffled.

He walked straight to her, controlled the terrible urge to simply sweep her up and away. He skimmed his finger beside the shallow cut, and the blueing around it that marred her forehead.

"Is this the worst of it then?" he asked her.

"Yeah. How did you—"

"I'll see to her," he told the MT. "If she needs to go in for treatment or exam, I'll see to that."

"Yeah? How?"

"She's my wife."

"Yeah?" the MT repeated. "Good luck, buddy."

"Did you have to—"

"Yes. My car's behind the barricade. Let's go."

"I can't leave the scene yet. I haven't cleared everything, and I need to make sure the responding officers have—"

He rounded on her, slowly, very slowly. "Could you leave the scene if you were unconscious and being transported to the nearest hospital or health center?"

The narrowed glare she aimed at him didn't penetrate. "Let's go," he repeated.

"A minute. Officer Laney, I appreciate your prompt response."

"Wish it could've been sooner, Lieutenant, and we'd busted the assholes." Laney, a hawk-eyed black female, glowered at the van currently being loaded on a flatbed. "The sweepers'll go over every inch of it, and the sedan, too. You ought to go with the MTs, sir. You took a hell of a ride."

"I'm just going to go home. Thanks." She turned back to Roarke, walked with him. "I'm not hurt."

"Most people who aren't hurt aren't bleeding."

"I banged my head, that's all. Jeez, if I'd known you were driving home this way and would see that, I'd have tagged you first." She glanced back, winced at the unholy mess in the intersection. "It looks worse than it is. Personal injurywise. Let me get them to clear us through here."

She walked to one of the uniforms at the barricade, had a short conversation. When she turned back, saw Roarke opening the door of his rich-guy's car for her, she winced again.

"Don't, ah, pet or pat me or anything until we're out of here. It makes me look weenie."

"Far be it from me." He got behind the wheel, threaded through the opening the uniform made for him. He headed up Madison to circle the great park, and head home.

"What happened?"

"I was an idiot. Fell for it. Stupid. Goddamn it."

"Other than that, what happened?"

"Did a search and seize on Ricker's place, which he was expecting. Still, it had to be done. I split off after, to head home, work from there. Spotted a tail. I should've *known*. It was sloppy, obvious, and I got smug. Had my attention on the tail, and verifying the registration, start to cross at the light, and wham."

She slapped her hands together for emphasis, and the

movement had the wound on her head throbbing in double time. She hunched, and resisted poking at it since Roarke would notice.

"Then this van comes out of nowhere, laying for me. I punched it, over and up, but a vehicle like that, it doesn't respond like the freaking wind. So he caught my rear wheels, sent me into a dive. I crash, wreck my ride. The woman behind me at the light catches my fender, sends me into another spin. I'm padded in there, but Jesus, round and round. Meanwhile, the guys—or guy and a woman—who may be white, or Hispanic, may be goddamn aliens from the planet Vulcan according to witnesses—are out and gone before I can get out of the car. The sedan's shooting up Madison and was dumped on Eighty-sixth and Third. No wits forthcoming there, so far."

Since he seemed to be watching traffic, she did a cautious little poke at her throbbing forehead. And, of course, pushed the throb to triple time.

"Leave it be," Roarke said mildly.

Annoyed, embarrassed, she dropped her hand. "The van was reported stolen by some delivery company in the Bronx this morning," she continued. "The sedan is registered to a guy in Queens, and according to his wife and his boss, he's in Cleveland on business, and has been for two days. The vehicle was boosted from long-term parking at the transpo center in Queens."

She slumped down in her seat. "Damn it."

"It's a stupid way to try to kill you," Roarke said after a few moments.

"They weren't trying to kill me. Just mess me up,

169

shake me up, screw me up. Good job. But what's the *point?*" She pushed up in her seat again. "Even if you mess me up, the investigation's ongoing. We've got the electronics from Ricker's. I've got the security discs. It's not like we're going to say, oooh, somebody wrecked Dallas's ride, so we've got to shut down our investigation and hide."

"Why didn't you answer your 'link?"

"My 'link? It didn't signal." She dug it out of her pocket, scowled at it. "It's dead. Must've gotten gunked up. Nature of the crash. The gel just exploded. Not just cushy bags, but the gunk. Everywhere." She scratched her head and rained little specks of blue gel out of her hair. "See?"

"I'm grateful for it."

She gave herself the indulgence of a sulk. "They'll never put that vehicle back together. It's the best one I've ever had. Now it's trashed."

"A worry for another day."

He drove through the gates, stopped. "I'm afraid you'll have to be a weenie now, as I intend to pat and pet."

"I'm really okay."

He drew her in, held her, breathed her. "I'm not, so you'll have to give me the next bloody minute or two."

He turned his lips to her cheek, then touched them lightly to her injured forehead. Then found her mouth, and gave way to some of the fear.

"I'm sorry." She cupped his face, moved him back. "I'm sorry. I didn't think about you coming that way, coming in on that. Getting scared that way. I'd've been scared if it'd been vice versa."

"Peabody contacted me." He pressed his finger to her lips now before she could curse. "To assure me you were all right, not seriously hurt. She was afraid they'd flash it on the media reports, on traffic, on something, and I'd hear about it that way. She didn't want me to worry."

"And I didn't think of it. Sorry again."

"You were a little preoccupied. You'll tell me the truth now. Is the bump on the head all of it?"

"Pretty sure. I'm a little sore from being jostled around. Got a little queasy and dizzy from the dive and spin. That's passed."

"Well, then, we'll go in and fix you up."

"We being you, right? Not His Scariness."

"As long as there's nothing serious, we shouldn't need Summerset."

"That's what I say all the time, we shouldn't need Summerset. But do you listen?"

He smiled, kissed her hand, and drove to the house.

She was prepared for the once-over from the black crow of the foyer. Summerset didn't disappoint. "I see you've destroyed another police vehicle. Perhaps you now hold the record."

Because she was afraid she just might, Eve only curled her lip and started up the stairs. Beside her, Roarke caught the inquiry in Summerset's eyes, shook his head.

Summerset crouched to stroke the cat. "She's all right. Just a bump or two. He'll see to her. You stay with me until she's more herself. Not one nasty comment from her." Summerset tsked as he and Galahad walked back toward the kitchen. "I'm sure she'll be more herself tomorrow."

Upstairs, Eve took the blocker Roarke gave her without protest, and sat through his ministrations of her head wound. There had been a time, they both knew, she'd have fought him on both. So when he offered her a soother, and she refused, he simply nodded.

"You'll feel better for a soak in the tub."

"You want to see me naked."

"At every moment of every day." He went into the bathroom, ordered the tub to fill at the boiling temperature she preferred. He added salts of some sort to the water, then turned where she waited and began to undress her himself.

"Getting in with me?"

"I'm not, no. Though, tempting. You'll soak, use the VR for a relaxation program. Then you'll eat something soothing." Every inch he undressed he studied for bruises, swelling, and was relieved to find none. "As it's the alternative to a trip to the hospital, you'll obey orders like a good girl."

"I'd rather you soak with me, and maybe try out a dual VR. Something sexy. And I could be a bad girl."

He arched a brow. "You're trying to take my mind off the fact you've been hurt. It's a damn good attempt." He gave her a light, almost paternal kiss. "In you go, Lieutenant. Alone."

"You're turning down sex. Maybe you're the one who got knocked on the head." But she stepped into the frothy, swirling water of the wide tub, and couldn't stop the moan of pleasure. "Okay, yeah, this is good."

He took VR goggles out of a drawer, set a program. "Relax."

"Am."

He slid the goggles on her, heard her sigh. He got himself a glass of wine, as good as a soother, he thought. And leaning against the door, he sipped it slowly, and watched her while she soaked away the aches.

Home, he told himself. She was home and whole and safe.

10

Relaxed, rested, Eve bundled into a robe. She stepped to the mirror, scooping her hair back to examine the cut on her forehead. Not bad, she decided, and pulled her bangs over it. You could hardly see it.

Which was bullshit, she admitted, blowing those bangs with an irritable exhale, because *he'd* see it. He knew it was there. She'd scared him, pulled him away from his own work—with a side dish of worry—and for no good reason. If she'd taken two seconds to think, to contact him, to tell him she'd banged up her vehicle, but she was okay, he wouldn't have worried.

Big black mark in the Good Wife column. She tended to rack those up.

Worse, he hears she's been in a crash while she's investigating the murder of another cop. Just not good.

Guilt smeared over relaxation as she walked back into the bedroom. "Listen, I want to say . . ." She trailed off. She scented the red sauce first, then spotted the plates of spaghetti and meatballs on the table of the sitting area. "Damn it."

"Not in the mood for pasta?" He narrowed those bold blue eyes to give her a critical study. "You must've hit your head harder than we thought."

"I was going to do it—get dinner, I mean. One of

the fancy things you like, because— Hell." She gave up, hurried to him to wrap her arms around him. "I'm sorry. I'm sorry. I was so pissed off at what happened, at myself, I didn't think."

He stroked a hand down her hair first, then gave the choppy ends a quick tug. "I'm not angry with you."

"I know. You could be, but you're not. So I have to be even sorrier."

"Your logic is fascinating, and elusive."

"I can't pay you back with sex or salt-crusted sea bass or whatever because you're too busy taking care of me. So now I've got this black mark in my column against the bright shiny star in yours, and—"

He tipped her head up. "Are we keeping score?"

"No. Maybe. Shit."

"How am I doing?"

"Undisputed champ."

"Good. I like to win." He brushed her bangs back to study the injury himself. "You'll do. Let's eat."

Just like that, she thought. Then, no. No, not just like that. She shifted her grip on him so her arms linked around his neck. "I love you." And kissed him, soft, slow, deep. "I love you. I love you. I'm just going to keep saying it," she told him as she pressed her body to his. "Racking them up, so I have a supply built up for when I forget to say it. I love who you are, what you are, how you talk, how you look at me."

Her lips roamed over his face, down his throat, along his jaw, coming back to his with soft, sumptuous seduction. "I love your body, how you make me feel. I love your face, your mouth, your hands. Put your hands on me, Roarke. Put your hands on me."

He'd planned to see she ate, rested a bit. To keep his eye on her in case . . . in case. Now she was taking him under. Drawing him down to drown in her.

He nudged the robe off her shoulders, so it slithered to the floor. And put his hands on her.

"More. More. I love you." Her lips skimmed over his ear; her teeth scraped along his neck to add a shock of lust. "I want more. I want you." She tugged at his jacket, and her laugh was a low, arousing purr. "Too many clothes. Like the first time, you're wearing too many clothes. I have to fix that."

To solve the problem, she ripped his shirt open, and laughed again. "Yeah, that's better. Oh God, I love you." Her breath hitched from the skill of his hands, his mouth, even as her fingers got busy on the hook of his trousers. Even when she found him, hot, hard.

"In me, I want you in me. I want you crazy and inside me. I want to see what it does to you, while I feel what it does to me."

He would have lifted her, swept her up and to the bed. Driven himself, driven her beyond reason. But her mouth came back to his, so tenderly. Sweet, so sweet. He fell helplessly into the warm liquid mists of love.

"Come to bed," he murmured. "Come to bed with me."

"Too far." In a lightning change of mood she hooked her foot behind his, shifted her weight. He landed under his hot-eyed naked wife on the couch.

Before he could catch his breath, her mouth was on his, tongue teasing, teeth nipping. His body quivered as he tried to find his balance.

"I'm going to take you." Her breathless threat pounded through his blood. "I won't stop till I'm finished, and you won't finish until you're in me. Until I let you in me."

She demanded, she took, she dragged him to the heady brink of control, only to leave him quaking while she soothed and smoothed tenderness over greed.

He thought he might have begged her, or cursed her. And still she had her relentless way with his body, his heart.

His eyes were wild, and those strong, toned muscles trembled under her hands, her lips. He said her name, again and again, mixed and jumbled with words in English and Gaelic. Prayers, pleas, curses, she couldn't know. Didn't care. His fingers dug into her, a bruising testament to his loss of control. When she offered, he feasted on her breasts like a man starving. Even when those fingers, that mouth shot her to orgasm, she held on. Held on.

She would take him.

Her breath screamed in her lungs; her heart beat to bursting. But she watched what she did to him, watched his eyes go molten with what she could do to him.

She gripped his hands, a vise of fingers. "Now," she said. "Now, now, now." And taking him in, rode him like a demon.

His vision blurred, and through the haze she was white and gold, slim and strong. His body bucked beneath hers, lashed to fury by pleasure. And striking, the dark blade of that pleasure carved him hollow.

He didn't move, wasn't sure he was capable. Reason, reality crept in slowly so he realized they lay tangled together on the sofa, a sweaty, sticky mess of still-quivering limbs and gasping breaths.

Christ Jesus, was there a luckier man in the universe?

Her skin was still hot, almost feverish. Her head lay like a stone on his chest. He considered, seriously, simply closing his eyes and sleeping just as they were for the next day or two.

Then she moaned, and she sighed. He searched for, and found, the connection between his brain and his arm so he could lift it and stroke her back.

And she purred.

"Bet you didn't see that coming," she murmured.

"I didn't, no. If I'd realized rapping your head would turn you into an insatiable sexual maniac who'd use me so brutally, I'd have coldcocked you long before this."

She snickered against the side of his neck, then sighed again. "It wasn't the head rap, it was the spaghetti. Or the spaghetti was the last in the line."

"We'll be eating it for the rest of our lives. Every bloody meal."

She shifted a little, snuggled a little. "It just, it all just made me go all gooey—and I was going to be all gooey and romantic and seduce you." She lifted her head, smiled down at him. "Then I got really hungry."

"I'm happy to be on the menu, anytime."

"I screwed your brains out."

"And then some."

"And now we're really disgusting."

"No question about it."

"I guess we should grab a shower before we eat cold spaghetti."

"We can heat it up."

"I like it cold."

"Only you," he muttered. "All right then, a shower. But you'll keep your hands to yourself, you pervert. You've used me up."

She gave a snorting laugh. "Boy, when the tables turn, they really turn. Come on, pal, I'll give you a hand."

They ate cold spaghetti, and since she'd proven herself quite healthy enough, Roarke poured her a glass of wine to go with it.

"Tell me about Alex Ricker, the search and so on. I'm interested."

"I think he's got as many clothes and shoes as you."

"Well now, that's not right. I'll have to make a note to add to my wardrobe straightaway."

"The thing is . . ." She wagged her fork at him, "I know you're not joking."

"Why would I?"

"Anyway." She twirled pasta. "He was expecting us, and prepared. Trio of lawyers on-site to make sure we were good little cops. Full cooperation and all that. Place is perfect and pretty much what you'd expect. But there were off notes. Especially the guest room that had so obviously never been used, with a couple of pieces of furniture in it that looked like they'd just been plucked from the showroom floor. Not a crime to buy new furniture or have an unused room, and palm plate and voice security."

"Ah, his private office. He probably had the unregistered equipment in it removed before we spoke to him this morning."

"That'd be my take. Feeney's on board with that, too. I've got the building's security discs, but even if we see him personally carrying out boxes, or hauling in a dresser, he's clear. Fully within his rights. I've got nothing on him but suspicion, and knowing he's wrong." She scowled, loaded her fork again. "He's just wrong."

"Wrong enough to have killed her, or had her killed?"

"I don't know. Yet. PA Sandy covers his big fat lie of this morning by saying he *assumed* Alex was home all evening. Bullshit."

"I tend to agree, but because?"

"Because they live in the same space, because they know each other and have since college. Because that little prick knows exactly what goes on when, where, and how."

"Why lie when Alex was going to say he'd gone out?"

"Good question. Could be he'd advised Alex to say he'd been home, told him he'd corroborate, then Alex changed his mind. Anyway, we're checking on the alibi, but haven't hit either way there. He's smart," Eve muttered. "Alex is smart and fairly cool-headed. So why would he pull something so ham-handed and useless as wrecking my ride?"

"You could've been much more seriously hurt. Yes, you could've been," Roarke said before she could protest. "If you'd taken a full broadside, I'd be eating cold pasta beside your hospital bed this evening. Those police-issues are like bloody tin cans."

"They're reinforced," she began, then shrugged at his steely stare. "Okay, they're crap. But I kinda liked that one, damn it. It had some moves, and wasn't completely ugly. I was used to it. And now I'm going to spend a couple of headachy hours on paperwork. Sucks sideways."

"That may be your answer. You're injured—minor or serious—your vehicle is wrecked, and you're required to spend time on routine paperwork rather than the investigation."

"A lot of risk, small benny. You have to steal two vehicles, tag mine, hire people willing to ram into another vehicle in broad daylight on a busy street. I don't know why it would be worth it to him."

"You're responsible for his father's imprisonment, and you're mine. Anything he could do to hurt you may be worth it to him."

"Maybe. Maybe. Could've been the little prick's idea, and execution. He doesn't like me."

"And I'll bet you were so friendly and polite in your dealings with him."

"Nah, I liked pinching at his tight ass. Either way, I mean if it was either of them that set up that stupid ambush, it'll trip them up. And Alex will be taking up residence in a cage next to his old man's. I'm working with Mira. In some ways he fits her profile, in others, it's not quite the right fit. I have to keep looking at her. There's a connection between Coltraine and her killer, and looking at her may be how to find him. Find him, wrap him up, put him down."

"Do you want it to be Alex because of his father?"

She took time to drink a little wine, consider it. "I hope not, but I can't discount that element. I know— who'd know better?—that who and what we come from go a long way to forming who we are. Would I be a cop if it wasn't for what was done to me? What he did to me? Would you be who you are without what was done to you?"

"It comes down to fate for me, I think. There are choices made, of course, along each step, but part of fate is what we make."

She frowned. "That only makes sense if you're Irish."

"Could be. You chose, Eve, the law, the order of it. You could've chosen to hide inside the victim instead of standing for others."

"I couldn't be the victim. It wasn't a choice. I *couldn't* be what they'd tried to make me, and live that way. Neither could you. You couldn't be the kind of man your father was, one who took orders from others, who beat young boys, who killed the innocent."

"And enjoyed it."

"Yeah, enjoyed it. Your father and mine." Everything inside her darkened. "And Max Ricker. They got off on the cruelty, and the power it gave them over someone smaller or weaker. So we know a lot about that, you and me—and him. And Alex. We know a lot about that, because it's in us. You and me, we took different roads, but we never took that one. We never took the cruel for the sake of it. But it's in us."

"And you have to wonder which road Alex took."

"He was trained to run his father's empire. That empire took a major hit last year. But the son developed his own interests, too. He's got those contacts, that backing, that foundation, and the smarts and know-how to absorb some of his father's holdings—some that slipped through. To restructure others. He's crooked, and a cop he used to sleep with is dead."

She stabbed a bite of meatball. "Maybe Coltraine was dirty, maybe she wasn't. But she was involved with him. And maybe, since she'd made her distance there, taken this fresh start, she was working up to some whistle-blowing on him. That's a good, strong motive to kill her."

"But?"

"But." She shook her head as she ate. "Where's her documentation? Feeney and his gang of geeks would've detected a wipe, or tampering. I damn well think I'd have detected somebody being in her place and doing that wiping or tampering. But her comps are clear. He's not as good as you."

"Why, thank you, darling."

"I'm serious. There's nothing in his background that leads me to believe he's that savvy with the e-work. That he's that damn good he could pull all this off. Get to her, get to her files, and leave nothing. No trace."

She stared into her wine as if she might find that trace, that one vital clue swimming in the deep red. "If she was going after him, or she was going to drop the dime there, she'd have documentation. She was a maniac

183

about documentation. Her reports and case notes are fucking textbook. It was her strength."

"Kept elsewhere."

"Yeah, yeah, shit, like I haven't thought of that?" Frustrated, she took another sip of wine. "I've got nothing that indicates she had a safe house, a bank box, a hidey-hole. Nothing that . . . Oh fuck me. Fuck me!"

"Again? Good God, Eve."

"Yeah, a riot of laughs." She pushed her glass into his hand, shoved up. "Morris. She hooks up, falls for Morris. Spends a lot of time with him, a lot of time at his place."

"Ah. And may have passcoded and hidden something on one of his units. Or stashed copies of said data among his data discs."

"I'm an idiot for not thinking of it."

"That would make me an idiot, as I didn't think of it either. And I'm a bloody genius about these things." He smiled when she stared at him. "So I'm told."

"I've got to check it out. I've got to—crap, he could be a target, too."

"I believe we're going out," Roarke said, and set his wine and hers aside.

From the sidewalk, Eve stared at the windows of Morris's loft while her stomach clenched. The privacy screens were engaged, and she could see only the faintest glow behind the glass.

"God, I hate this. He wants to be alone, just wants time and space to grieve, and I've got to go in there, pry in there."

"A lesser friend would have waited until tomorrow,

and sent an EDD contingent in. You're respecting him and his grief as much as you possibly can." Roarke took her hand. "I don't want to put myself in his place, but if I were? I'd want the same."

"I promised to tell him the truth, and keep him in the loop. Well, this is the damn loop." She bore down, walked over, and pressed his buzzer.

It took time, but she saw the security light go on. She faced the camera. "I'm sorry, Morris, really sorry to disturb you. We need to come up. We need to talk."

The only response was the green glow, and the mechanical thunk of the locks being released. They went in, but when she turned to the stairs, the elevator grate opened, and its light went green.

"Okay then." She took a breath, stepped in with Roarke.

When the grate opened again, Morris stood on the other side.

He looked as he had that afternoon. A little tired, Eve thought, a little more worn, but much the same. The lights of the loft were quiet, as was the music haunting the air.

"Have you made an arrest?"

"No. But I need to tug on another line of investigation."

He nodded, then seemed to focus on Roarke for the first time. "Please, come in. Both of you."

Roarke touched Morris's arm, just the lightest of contacts. "I wish there were more than words, because they're never enough, or they're simply too much. But I'm very sorry."

185

"I've been sitting here, in the dark—or near dark—alone, trying to come to terms. Death is my business. It's a reality, a finality I've made into my profession. But I can't come to terms."

"Death is your business," Roarke said before Eve could comment. "Eve often says the same. I'm on the outside, of course, but I've never seen it that way. The truth is your business. Seeking it for those who can't seek it for themselves is what you've made into your profession. She worries for you."

"Roarke."

"Quiet," he said to Eve, mildly. "Hurts for you. You mean a great deal to her. To both of us. We'll do whatever it takes to help find the truth for Amaryllis."

"I saw her today." Morris stepped away, sat—weariness in every movement. "Clip had done all he could. The people in my house, all they could. How many times have I stood there while someone looked on dead love? How many hundreds and hundreds of times? It doesn't prepare you for when it's yours. They'll release her soon. I've, ah, cleared it to have her memorial tomorrow, in one of Central's bereavement suites. At two. Her family will have one next week in Atlanta. I'll go. And still, it doesn't seem real."

Eve sat on the table in front of him, to face him. "Have you spoken with a grief counselor?"

"Not yet. I'm not ready for that yet. I should offer you a drink." When Eve started to shake her head, he continued. "I could use one. I've been careful not to, not to use that to block it out. But I think I could use a drink. There's brandy on the sideboard."

"I'll get it," Roarke told him.

"If not a counselor, would you speak with Mira? A friend?"

He waited until Roarke came back with a snifter. "Thanks. I don't know," he said to Eve. "I don't know yet. I've been thinking of dead love."

He drank some brandy, met her eyes. "But here you are," he murmured. "Did you know I had a brother?"

"No."

"I lost him when I was a boy. He was twelve, and I was ten. We were very close. There was an accident while we were on holiday one summer. He drowned. He wanted to go out, into the ocean early in the morning. We were forbidden, of course. Not without our parents, but we were just boys. He was a strong swimmer, and a daredevil. I worshipped him, as boys do."

He sat back, sipped his brandy. "I promised I wouldn't tell, swore an oath to him. So he let me go with him, and I was so excited and terrified." The memory brought a ghost of a smile to his lips, to his eyes. "There was little I liked more than when he'd let me in on an adventure. Our father would skin us if he found out, which made it only more thrilling. In we went—warm water, warm waves, with the sun barely up, and the gulls screaming."

He closed his eyes, and even that hint of smile vanished. "I wasn't as strong a swimmer, and couldn't keep up. He was laughing and teasing me as I thrashed my way back toward shore.

"Out of breath, eyes stinging from the salt, the sun starting to burn over the water. I remember all that. I

187

can still feel all that. I turned in the shallows, panting, to yell at him to come on, to come back before we got caught."

He opened his eyes, looked into Eve's again. She saw old pain in them.

"And he was gone. I couldn't swim back, couldn't save him. Couldn't see him. I suppose if I'd tried, if it had occurred to me to do anything but run for my father, I'd have drowned, too."

He let out a breath. "So. They said he may have gotten a cramp, or been swamped by a wave, simply tired out, or been caught in an undertow. I wanted to know how and why my brother was dead. I wanted the truth. But they couldn't tell me."

"So you look for it now," Roarke said.

"So I look for it now." He looked at Roarke. "You're right. The business of truth. I never found it with my brother. I'm not sure I can bear losing someone I love a second time and not know why. Not know the truth."

"What was his name?"

Morris looked up from the brandy, into Eve's face. For a moment his eyes swam with memories, tears, and gratitude. "Jin. His name was Jin." He sat forward, gripped Eve's hand. "I'm glad you came. I'm glad you're here. You . . . you've hurt your head," he said abruptly.

"It's nothing. Just banged it."

"You're not clumsy."

Truth, she remembered, and told him.

"You're not considering this may be someone who simply wants to kill or hurt cops?"

"It doesn't play that way. Neither incident was random."

"No." He pressed his fingers to his eyes. "You're right. You didn't come here to tell me about this. Why did you?"

"EDD's been combing her electronics. Nothing pops, Morris. The investigations she was working on just don't fit in with murder. There's nothing in her files, her notes, her personals to give any indication she was in trouble, felt uneasy, had been threatened. There's only one notation about Ricker—and that's a memo in her date book that she was meeting AR, at the time and the date he confirms. There's nothing to indicate she knew she was or had been under the watch of IAB. And she had been."

"IAB had investigated her."

"They got a tip about her relationship with Ricker, when they were in Atlanta. They had eyes on her, eyes and ears when they could manage it. They lived together, essentially, for well over a year."

He kept his eyes steady. "I knew she'd had a serious relationship. She never lied to me about it, or tried to play it down."

"Okay. She occasionally traveled with Ricker. Vacation type stuff. He bought her some jewelry. That's all they had. They never assembled any evidence that it was anything but a personal, a romantic relationship."

"And, of course, never just asked her."

"Not according to my source."

"Which would be Webster, Dallas, I'm not a fool. Have they had her under watch here?"

189

"Initially. The relationship with Ricker ended, appeared to end, a couple of months before she requested the transfer. Their contact was minimal after the breakup, and dribbled down to none. But the New York bureau was notified, and took a look at her. Webster said they bumped her down—just nothing there—and they weren't on her when Ricker contacted her, when he got to New York."

"He's your prime suspect."

"He's a suspect. Prime's pushing it with what I have. I know he's crooked. She would have known that, too. Webster's going to do some digging, and keep a lid on it. He'll be careful with her, Morris."

"IAB, now—it's—" He broke off, shook his head.

"I'm sorry. She may have been a source for Alex back in Atlanta. Morris, you know I have to consider that. If she was involved with him, in love with him, she might've stepped over the line for him. I have to look there as long as I'm looking at him. And I have to think, either way it was, maybe she took a good hard look at things. After she'd come here, after she had that distance, and you. Maybe she'd started to put things down, thought about putting down details and flipping on him."

Both the anger and the fatigue had cleared from his face as he heard her out. "If that's true, and he found out—"

"If and if. But there's nothing on her units. Nothing. She spent a lot of time here. A lot of time with you. Maybe time here when you weren't."

"Yes, depending on our shifts, or if either of us got

called in. You think she might have used my comps, tucked something in, because it felt safer. More secure."

"I'd like to have my expert consultant here take a look. And, I know it's weird, but if I could do a search. In case she hid discs or any kind of documentation."

"Yes. Please." He got to his feet. "I'll make coffee."

Morris helped with the search, and Eve thought he seemed more himself—precise, focused—for the doing. She took the kitchen, the living area, leaving him to the bedroom while Roarke concentrated on the office.

She dug through containers and clear jars, in drawers and behind them. Under tables, cushions, behind art, and through Morris's extensive music disc collection. She examined every stair tread before going up.

In the bedroom Morris stood in front of the closet, a filmy white robe in his hands.

"It smells of her," he said quietly. "It smells of her." And hung it up again. "I can't find anything."

"Maybe Roarke'll have better luck. Can you think of anywhere else she might put something? Hide something?"

"I can't. She was friendly but distant with her neighbors. You know how it is. She was closest with her squad. But if she'd given one of them anything, they'd have come to you, or certainly to their lieutenant, with it by now."

"Yeah."

She blew out a breath. "Maybe there's nothing here because there's nothing anywhere."

"It feels as though it's the first thing I've done of any

consequence, the first I've done to help her. Even if it was to find nothing. You believe she crossed the line."

"IAB couldn't prove it."

"That's evasion. You think it."

"Truth, Morris? I don't know."

"What did she do with the jewelry he bought her?"

"She gave it back when they split."

He smiled, really smiled, for the first time since she'd come to his door the day before. "That's who she was, Dallas."

She brooded about it on the drive home. "Waste of three hours. Nothing. Nothing there. If we couldn't find anything between us, there's nothing there. Wasted time."

"It wasn't, and far from it. He looked alive again when we left. In pain, in sorrow, but alive." Roarke reached out to cover her hand. "Not wasted time."

11

Back in her home office, she ran the security discs. She watched Rod Sandy, carrying a briefcase, exit the elevator, cross the lobby, exit the building at eleven-twenty-six the morning after Coltraine's murder.

He looked grim.

"Favor," she said to Roarke, "do a search on the time the first media reports of Coltraine's murder hit."

While Roarke obliged, she continued the run, watched people come and go. None exited—according to the elevator readout—on the penthouse levels until Sandy returned at twelve-oh-eight.

"The first bulletin hit at ten-fifty-three on ANN," Roarke said, referring to All News Network. "Broad sweep reports followed on every major station by eleven."

"Quick work," Eve muttered. "That's quick work if Sandy carried discs and anything incriminating or questionable out with him—which he damn well did—to another location."

"He wouldn't have taken his unregistered out across a public lobby."

"No." She switched to elevator security. Again she saw Sandy step in, ride down, get off. Others took the car to other floors. Then the screen went blank and black. "What the—is that the disc or my equipment?"

"Neither. The security cam shut down. Was shut down," Roarke corrected. "No blip, no static, no jump such as you'd get if there was a malfunction. The building would have a basement, utility areas, a delivery entrance."

"Delivery entrance on the cross street." Eve shifted to that disc. "Son of a bitch, coordinated shutdown. Smooth. Even if I dig up a wit from the building, or the buildings across the street that saw loading and unloading, it proves nothing. Still . . ."

"He'd need a vehicle—truck or . . . a van to move the equipment."

"And to carry the new furniture in. He wouldn't have used a stolen van," she added, in response to Roarke's unspoken question. "Furniture delivery truck maybe. He owns an antique store on Madison, and another downtown. Maybe I get somebody to ID it, and say, 'Yeah, I saw these guys carting out boxes, carting in a dresser', it's not evidence. But this tells me he took care of business the morning after Coltraine was killed. He covered his ass."

"Devil's advocate, darling, but under the same circumstances, I'd have been covering mine hours earlier if I'd done murder. By the time the body was discovered, there'd be nothing on the premises I didn't want the cops to see."

"He's not as good as you. I said that before."

"I never tire of hearing it."

"On the night she died we've got him on the cam, coming and going at the times he gave us. Or close enough not to argue with. But he shuts it down to remove his unregistered and take a furniture delivery. No, not as good as you."

She gave Roarke a thoughtful look. "You'd've doctored the discs if you felt you needed to. But most likely, you'd have let it all go on record. What the fuck do you care if the cops see packages leaving your place? Something new coming in. No crime in it. The cops hadn't had the first word with you. You'd've let it stand and said prove it. With the 'fuck you' implied."

"How comforting to be so well understood. He's given you just what you wanted to know, hasn't he? He's—as you put it—on the shady side, and he had something to hide."

"Which doesn't make him a killer," Eve admitted. "But if the shady side included cops on the payroll, why stop at one? I've got to take another look at her squad, which probably means reaching out to IAB again. Crap."

"Again. Yes, I gleaned that when you talked to Morris."

Realizing she'd yet to mention her meet with Webster, she glanced over. "If a lead indicates the vic may have been a dirty cop, I've got to tap that resource."

"Define tap."

Even though she realized it was his intent, Eve nearly squirmed. "I had a meet with Webster. I used the Down and Dirty—Crack says hey. We're both keeping it off the log, for now."

"Interesting venue."

"The connection with Crack makes it my turf. We're sharing data."

Roarke tapped her chin. "Isn't it lucky I'm not the jealous type?"

She simply stared at him. "Oh yeah, that's lucky."

When he laughed, she shook her head, then walked over to study her murder board one last time. "The killer's on here. The trigger or the one who cocked it. Nothing else makes sense. But what did she do? What did she do, what did she know, who did she threaten to bring it down on her?"

She slept on it, and didn't sleep well.

In the dream, Eve sat on a slab in the morgue, with Coltraine sitting on her own. They faced each other while the mournful sounds of a saxophone played through the chilled air.

"You're not telling me enough," Eve said.

"Maybe you're not listening."

"That's bullshit, Detective."

"You can't think of me as Ammy, or even Amaryllis. You're having a hard time seeing me as just a woman."

"You're not just a woman."

"Because of the badge." Coltraine held hers in her hand, turning it over, studying it. "I liked having it. But I didn't need it. Not like you. For some, the job is just *a* job. You know that about me, you know that much. It's one of the reasons you can think, can believe, I used the badge for personal gain."

"Did you?"

With her free hand, Coltraine brushed back her blond, glossy hair. "Don't we all? Don't you? I don't mean the pitiful pay. You gain, personally, every day, by being in charge, in control, doing the work. Pushing, pushing, pushing what you were aside for what you are."

"It's not about me."

"It's always about you. Victim, killer, investigator. The triad, always connected. Each one links the other, each one brings what they bring to the table. One can't be without the other two in this game." Coltraine puffed out a breath, a soft sound of annoyance. "I never expected to die for it, and that—let me tell you—is a total bitch. You do."

"I expect to die?"

"Sitting on a slab, aren't you? Just like me. But expect's the wrong word. You're prepared." As if pleased, she nodded. "Yes, that's better. You're prepared to die, for the badge. I wasn't. I was prepared to do the work until it was time to step away from it and get married, start a family. You're still surprised you've managed to be a cop and a wife. You can't figure how it's possible to be one and have a family, so you don't think about it."

"Kids are scary. They're foreign and—"

"What you were when he hurt you. When he beat you and terrorized you and raped you. How can you have a child until you fully understand, accept, forgive the child you were?"

"Did getting murdered give you a license to shrink?"

"It's your subconscious, Lieutenant. I'm just one of your dead now." She looked over to the wall, and all those cold, steel drawers. "One of the many. You and Morris, both so oddly comfortable here. Did you really never think about tapping that?"

Even in the dream, Eve felt heat rise into her face. "Jesus, this is *not* my subconscious."

"It sure as hell isn't mine." With a laugh, Coltraine shook back her hair. "But loving someone without the sex, even the sexual buzz? That's special. I'm glad he has you now, glad he has that with you. It was different for him and me. That sexual buzz?" She snapped her fingers. "Almost that quick. And from there, a lot more. He was the one, I think he would've been the one to be with, to believe in, have a family with."

"What about Alex Ricker? Sexual buzz?"

"And then some. You know that. You know exactly the kind of sexual buzz a man like that throws off."

"He's not like Roarke."

"Not that different, not all that different." Coltraine pointed at Eve, smiled easily. "That bothers you. We're not that different either. We fell for it, we wanted it. We just handled it differently. Would you, could you, have walked away from him if he hadn't shed the shady?"

"I don't know. Can't be sure. But I know if he had asked me to be with him, to make a life with him and to look the other way while he broke the law, he wouldn't be Roarke. Roarke's who I stayed with."

Now Coltraine wagged that finger back and forth. "But he does break the law."

"Hard to explain, even to me. He doesn't break it for his own profit, for his own gain. Not now, not anymore. If he does, it's because he believes in right, in justice. Not always the same right, the same justice as I do. But he believes. Ricker didn't shed for you. I got that much, too."

"They come from harsh fathers and dead mothers, these men. Isn't that part of what makes them, and part of our attraction to them? They're dangerous and compelling. They want us, and want to give us things."

"I don't care about the things. But you did. You did or you wouldn't have given them back. Huh. Subconscious scores. You gave them back because they did matter, and because they mattered you couldn't keep them. It wouldn't have been a break then, not a clean one. You wore the ring your parents gave you instead, a reminder of who and where you'd come from. Solid middle-class family."

"Maybe you are listening."

"Maybe you looked the other way when you were with him. Maybe you even told him things you shouldn't have—because the badge was just a job, and secondary. But you weren't dirty. You weren't on the take. That's not what you wanted from him, and not what you'd have given him. If it was, you'd have given the badge back, too. You could lie to yourself when you were with him that it was nobody's business what you did on your own time, nobody's business who you loved."

Coltraine's smile warmed and spread. "Now who's the shrink?"

Ignoring the comment, Eve went on. "But even when the job's secondary, it gets in the way. It got in the way, and he wasn't going to change. You couldn't keep loving him when he couldn't love you enough to see that. So you gave back the things, and you walked away. But you kept the badge."

Coltraine studied it again. "A lot of good it did me." She looked up at Eve then, and her eyes, so bold and green, filled with sorrow. "I don't want to stay here."

"They're going to let you go soon."

"Do you think any of us go anywhere until we have the truth? Do you think there's peace without justice?"

"No, I don't," Eve admitted, knowing it would always drive her. Would always make her push. "You won't stay here. You've got my word. I promise you, you won't stay here."

Could you make a promise to a dead woman in a dream? Eve wondered. And what did it mean that she had, that she'd needed to?

As she dressed, she glanced over at Roarke, who sat with his coffee, his stock reports, his cat. Didn't look so dangerous now, she mused. Not such a bad boy. Just an absurdly handsome man starting the daily routine.

Except, of course, he'd probably started the routine a good hour or two before, with some international 'link transmission or holo-meeting. But still, didn't look so dangerous.

Which, she supposed, was only one of the reasons he was. Very.

"You were already giving it up."

He turned his attention from the scrolling codes and figures on-screen to Eve. "Giving what up?"

"The allegedly criminal activities. When we met, you were already shedding. I just sped up the process."

"Considerably." He sat back with his coffee. "And with finality. Otherwise, I'd have, most likely, kept my finger tipped into a few tasty pies. Habits are hard to break, especially fun ones."

"You knew we'd never have this otherwise. We'll always slip and slide some on that line that shifts for us, but that? That would've been a wall, and we'd never have had this with a wall between us. You wanted this, wanted me more."

"Than anything ever before or since."

She walked over, and as she had with Morris the night before, sat on the table to face him. Galahad flopped over on Roarke's lap to lay a paw on her knee. An oddly sweet gesture.

There were all kinds of families, Eve supposed.

"I didn't want this, because I didn't know what this was. But I wanted you more than anything before or since. I couldn't have looked the other way, but I couldn't have wanted you more than anything if you'd asked me to. I might've tried, but it wouldn't have held between us."

"No."

"The habit, the . . . hobbies—that's exactly what they'd become for you. They weren't the driving force, not the way they'd been when you started. Not survival, not your identity. Success, positions, wealth, power, security, yeah, all that's essential. But you don't have to cheat to get them or keep them. Besides me, your own pride played a part. Sure, it's fun to cheat, but after, it's just not as satisfying as doing it the hard way."

"Sometimes cheating's the hard way."

She smiled. "Maybe so. Here's the thing. He—Alex Ricker—he didn't give it up for her. He expected her to look the other way, and she did, for close to two years.

But it couldn't hold. He didn't or wouldn't give it up because he didn't want her more than anything. She was secondary to him, just as the job was secondary to her. Maybe they had the heat, and maybe they loved each other."

"But it wasn't enough."

"I wondered if we were connected to her murder. I don't know that yet, but we're connected to her. We took Max Ricker down, and when we did, the dynamics shifted. The son climbs up a few rungs on the power chain, doesn't he? Or is free to—"

"Shed the shady," Roarke finished. "And he didn't. He didn't choose that."

"She had to know, at that crossroads, he never would. She made her choice, because of that. Or it had to play out. The timing just fits too well for the other."

"He didn't choose her, she couldn't choose him."

"Yeah." She thought of Coltraine sitting on the slab in the morgue—her badge in her hand, and tears in her eyes. "He didn't kill her. If she was secondary, what's the point? He made a choice, she made hers. If he was that miffed about it—because it couldn't have been about pride and ego—you get crime of passion. Why wait a year, then fuss around with it?"

"Maybe he changed his mind."

"Yeah, I think he might've. At least changed it enough to come here to see her, to gauge the ground. He'd've known she was in another relationship. Maybe pride again, with vanity tossed it. He's got plenty of both. He sees she's happy, that she's moved on. That had to sting some, but enough to take her out?"

She shook her head again. It just didn't play through for her. "He let her go in the first place. And under it, he still doesn't want her more than he does the life he leads. He's a businessman—a crooked businessman, but enough of one to know when a deal's not on the table. There just isn't enough love there for murder, not cold, premeditated murder."

"Not for love, or for passion then." Since she hadn't gotten any for herself, Roarke offered her his coffee. "If she had something on him, was working for him? Or had been?"

"If she had anything, she kept it to herself during their breakup, after it, and for a year."

"Why hit her now?" he said as she drank his coffee, passed him back the empty mug.

"I kept pushing there because I was thinking like me, I mean, seeing her as a cop. Not as a woman who'd been in love. If she'd wanted to punish him, she'd have gone after him when her info was hot, when she was hurt or pissed. She was never dirty. She gave back the jewelry."

"So you said before, but you went back to that possibility."

"Yeah, because I missed a step, and I guess that's what nagged at me. It's not just that she gave back the jewelry, but that she kept the badge. It was just a job, but it was *her* job. And she kept it. That's what I missed."

She pushed up now to think on her feet, to think on the move. "If she wasn't dirty, wasn't out for him—and goddamn it, her type would've had that documentation we can't find—and he let her go, all we've got between the two of them is a couple of people who decided it didn't work out, and cut their losses. Not everybody kills over a broken affair."

She turned back. "The alibi's too lame. I've been fighting that one. If he'd done it or had it done, he'd be covered. It's not one of those psych things—the smug 'if I'd known I'd need an alibi, don't you think I'd have one'. He's too neat and tidy *not* to have one. I kept looking at him and looking at him because his name is Ricker. I've wasted time."

"You haven't, no. No more than you did last night at Morris's. You've clarified. How could you not look at him, go through all the steps, pick at the pieces? He's the most logical suspect."

"Yeah, and that's . . . Son of a bitch."

"And just a half step behind you, I'll ask who'd gain by putting Ricker in your sites as a murder suspect?"

"A competitor. Plenty of bad guys wouldn't scratch their ass over killing a cop."

"You're such a comfort to me," Roarke murmured.

"I'm smarter than the bad guys. Wasn't I a half step ahead of you?"

"Only because I gave you the nudge. Still, it isn't what I'd call an expert frame job."

"Doesn't have to be, obviously. I've had Ricker on the hot seat since. He had to break down his penthouse, relocate docs, equipment. Cost him time and trouble. You could probably find out if he's got any hot deals cooking, something this inconvenience is going to tangle up."

"I probably could."

"And I'm right back to being focused on him." She

pinched the bridge of her nose. "But he's the only thing that makes sense—that connection is *it*. She didn't have any cases with the kind of heat that turns to murder. Nobody in her building had anything going with her, anything against her we can find. And she was going out—that's how it plays no matter how many times I run it through, turn it around. She was going out, armed. Whoever was on that stairwell was a bad guy or a cop. And a wrong cop's worse than a bad guy."

"Someone besides Alex with a cop in his pocket."

"Could be. Yeah, it really could be. And if that's how it goes, the cop has to be in her squad."

"Back to IAB."

"I'm thinking yes."

"Well, have some breakfast first."

"I'll grab something. I should get in and . . . Crap. Damn it. My ride."

"Have some breakfast," Roarke repeated, "then we'll deal with your transportation."

Scowling, she jammed her hands in her pockets. "I lost my appetite thinking about those bastards in Requisitions."

Roarke simply walked over and programmed her a ham-and-egg pocket. "Here, quick and easy."

"I guess." She took a sulky bite where she stood. "I'd get Peabody to offer personal sexual favors again, but they're not going to buy that a second time. They'll make me beg, then they'll still give me the crappiest piece of junk in the junk pile. I could bribe Baxter to do it," she considered.

"The personal sexual favors?"

"No, but . . . maybe. Requisition a new vehicle. Like he needs one. They like him. Except they already know it's my ride." Her tone turned bitter as cop coffee. "They have their spies everywhere."

"This is a very thorny problem, Lieutenant. I think I can help you with it."

"They'd give me the pick of the fleet if you offered them personal sexual favors. But I'm not going there. There have to be lines, there have to be limits. Besides, I'm a goddamn lieutenant." She stuffed her mouth with ham and eggs and thin, warm bread. "I shouldn't have to beg," she muttered around the food. "I'm a boss."

"You're absolutely right. The bastards." He slung an arm around her shoulders. "Let's go downstairs. I think I may have a way around all this."

"It's not like I did anything. It's wrecked, sure, but it was wrecked in the line. Fuckers."

"I agree. Fuckers."

The amusement in his tone was lost on her as she wallowed and stewed. "I hate playing it this way. It just gripes me. But I can't get bogged down in this during an investigation. So, maybe you could come up with a couple of cases of prime brew, or VIP seats for the ball game. A really shiny bribe."

"I could, no doubt. But let's try this instead."

He opened the front door.

In the drive sat a vehicle of dull and somber gray. Its lines were too practical, too ordinary for ugly—so the best it could claim was drab. It did boast some shiny bits of chrome that glinted hopefully in the morning sun.

"Peabody already took care of it?"

"No."

She'd started to walk to it, struggling against the personal disappointment that it was much more humble in appearance than her old one—*a lot* more humble, so the shiny bits came off as pitiful as cheap lip dye on a homely woman. Then she stopped, frowned.

"Don't tell me it's yours. You don't have anything this ordinary in your toy box."

"It's not mine. It's yours."

"You said Peabody hadn't . . ." Now who was a half step behind? "You can't buy my official vehicle."

"There are no rules or regulations restricting you from driving your own vehicle on your official duties. I checked."

"Yeah. I mean no. I mean you can't just give me a ride."

"Of course I can, and fully intended to. It was going to be your anniversary gift. And now I'll have to come up with something else there."

"You were going to give me a cop ride for our anniversary in July. What, you're a sensitive now and foretold my ride would get trashed?"

"It was only a matter of time. But no. I thought it was a gift you'd appreciate. Now, it's not a gift. Now, it's a request. You'll do a favor for me and take it, use it."

"I don't get why you'd—"

"It's loaded," he interrupted. "The internal data and communication, both primary and secondary, are state of the art. Its vertical and air are comparable to the new XS-6000."

"The XS . . . you've got to be kidding me."

"As with much else, it's what's inside that counts here. It'll go from zero to sixty—ground or air—in under one-point-three seconds."

"Sweet."

"It can achieve a fifteen-foot vertical lift within that same amount of time." He smiled as she began to circle it, study it. Smile widened to grin as she opened the hood. She knew next to nothing about engines.

"It's really big and shiny under here."

"It's programmed for solar, noncombustible, and combustible fuel. Its body is blast-proof, as are its windows. It's a bloody tank that'll move like a rocket. Auto-nav, of course, holo-map, voice or manual controls. It has an electronics detector that will notify you if anyone has rigged it—or attempted to. There's an in-dash camera with a reach of a hundred and fifty yards in any direction."

"Jesus."

"Memory seats. Alarms, lights, and sirens as required by the department. A blast screen that can be activated between the front and back sections if you have a need to transport any suspicious characters. Let's see, have I forgotten anything?"

"Yeah, the twelve-disc tutorial that tells me how to run it. Roarke, I can't—"

"It's programmed for your voice and print, no codes necessary." She wouldn't, he'd determined, get out of it that way. "For now, you just tell it what to do. It's programmed for Peabody as well, as I know you very occasionally allow her to take the wheel. And for me. If at any time you want someone else to drive, you can authorize them."

"Okay, now hold on. This is worth five times— maybe ten times—what a department ride is. I've never actually bought a vehicle, so I'm ballparking here. I can't drive around in something that costs more than all the rides in my department put together. Pretty much."

He thought she could be as skittish as a virgin when it came to money. "But I can bribe your fuckers and bastards with cases of brew and sports tickets."

"Yes. Not logical, but yes."

He just brushed a finger on the healing cut on her forehead. "Think of this. If you'd been driving this yesterday, you'd not only have avoided the accident, you'd have apprehended those in the van. You may very well have closed your case by now."

"Oh, that's not—"

"But more, I'll say again. This isn't a gift. It's a favor to me. I'll know when you're in it, you're safe. So I'm asking you to do this for me."

"It's sneaky of you." She hissed out a breath. "Damn sneaky of you not to get pissed or demand. Make it a favor. That you're doing it as much for yourself as me."

With the soft spring morning around them, the homely ride beside them, his eyes met hers. "That would be the truth."

"Yeah," she said after a moment. "Yeah, it would be. I can do you a favor."

"Thanks." He touched his lips to hers.

"Hey." And she grabbed his lapels, dragged him back for a long one. "Pretty damn smart, aren't you? You made it just ugly enough. Inconspicuous. Nobody looks twice."

"I have to admit, that was a hard one for me. I think one of the designers had a breakdown. Cried for an hour."

She laughed. "It's good. It's really good. You had it built for me. Jeez, it's my first actually owned-by-me vehicle, and you had it built for me."

"It's the DLE Urban—and one of a kind."

"DLE? What—oh." It took her a minute, and pleased her absurdly. "Dallas, Lieutenant Eve."

"And, as I said, there's only one. We're manufacturing others with the body type—for the economical range—but none will have the unique capabilities of this one."

"What'll it do?"

"I had it up to two-ten on the straight—road and air. But I'm a better driver than you, so don't be pushing it."

"Man, it almost makes me jones for a vehicular chase. Well, one day."

"No doubt."

"I can tell the bastards in Requisitions to get screwed." The mere thought of it had her doing a hip-wiggling dance in the drive. "Hot *damn!* I've got to try it out, got to get to work, got to give Requisitions the finger." She grabbed him again, kissed him again. "Thanks. It's probably the best favor I've ever done for anybody. Catch you later."

"Yes, you will."

He watched her climb in, grin when her butt hit the seat. She pressed her thumb to the pad, and the engine rumbled to life.

"Hot *damn!*" she shouted again, flashed him that grin.

And shot off down the drive as if in pursuit of speeding felons.

"Oh well, Christ. She could hit a brick wall in that and walk away whistling."

"I see the lieutenant likes her new vehicle," Summerset said from the doorway.

"She does. Ah, God." He held his breath while she did a trio of 360s, obviously testing the maneuverability. Then went in sharp vertical to drive over the gates instead of through them. "She's never had her own before. I don't know why I forget things like that. For a bit, it'll be like a new toy. Then she'll settle down with it."

"Your first, boosted at about the age of twelve, ended up nose down in a ditch outside of Dublin."

Roarke turned around. "I didn't think you knew about that."

Summerset only smiled. "Or that you'd managed to hide it in Mick's uncle's garage for the two weeks or so you had it before you got cocky and wrecked? You learned a lesson, didn't you, and were more careful with the next one you boosted."

"It was a thrill. The stealing as much as the driving."

"Do you miss it?"

"The stealing? Now and then," he admitted, knowing Summerset would understand. "Not as much as I thought I might."

"It would be more, I'd say, if your life lacked other thrills." When Roarke's face broke into a grin, Summerset huffed. "Take your mind out of the gutter, boy. I'm speaking of the work you do, of your own and with the

211

police. And this may pertain to one or the other, or both, but while you were showing the lieutenant her new toy, Alex Ricker called. I didn't want to interrupt, and told him you'd get back to him."

"That's interesting, isn't it?"

"Have a care. Ricker would have enjoyed bathing in your blood. His son may have the same sentiments."

"Then he'll be just as disappointed."

Roarke went in to return the call, and wondered what sort of thrill the day might bring.

12

It was hard, but Eve resisted hitting lights and sirens and smoking it all the way downtown. She didn't resist doing a seat dance while she threaded through traffic, skimmed around maxibuses, beat out the competitive Rapid Cabs at lights.

Schooling the elation out of her voice, she contacted Webster. She knew the minute he came on the sweet new dash screen of her sweet new ride, she'd rousted him from sleep.

"IAB's got choice hours."

He shoved the heel of his hand in his eye. "I'm not on the damn roll today."

"Like I said. Are you alone?"

"No, I've got six strippers and a couple of porn stars in here with me."

"I'm not interested in your pitiful dreams. I'm pursuing another line. I need to know if any of Coltraine's squad's under, or was under, IAB watch."

"You want me to violate the privacy of an entire squad so you can pursue a line?"

Eve nearly made a snide comment about IAB and privacy, but decided against it. "I have to consider the victim didn't leave the house with her weapon and clutch piece to have a drink with friends. I have to consider she considered herself on duty at that time. I have to consider, from her profile, she wasn't going on duty alone."

"Consider's just a fancier word for guess."

"She was a team player, Webster. She was part of a squad. I have to consider one or more members of that squad killed her, or set her up for it. If so, I have to consider that individual or individuals may have caught the interest of IAB in the past."

"You could go through channels on this, Dallas. It's a legitimate line of inquiry."

"I'm not even going to dignify that one."

"Shit. I'll have to get back to you."

"Use privacy mode if and when," she told him, then cut him off. Her next move was to contact Whitney's office and request an appointment to brief and update her commander.

Once she arrived at Central, she went straight to her office, intending to pick her way through new theories. She wanted to run several probabilities—hopefully with information pried out of Webster—before her meeting with Whitney. A second consult with Mira, she thought, pushing on the in-squad connection could add weight.

She got coffee first, then saw the report disc from Baxter on her desk.

She plugged it in, ran it while she drank her coffee. And weighing the information, sat back and mulled it over with more coffee.

She'd started the probabilities without Webster when Peabody came in.

"They announced Coltraine's memorial," Peabody told her. "Today at fourteen hundred, in Central's bereavement facilities."

"Yeah, I got that from Morris. Get a divisional memo out, will you? Anyone not actively in the field or prevented from attending by duty needs to put in an appearance. No time lost. Dress blues preferred."

"Sure. I'll just—"

"Hold on. Question. What would you say to the fact that Alex Ricker paid one visit, and one only, to his father on Omega eight months ago. And there's been no correspondence of any kind recorded between them during the father's incarceration?"

"Well . . . It could lean a couple of directions. Ricker might not want his son to go there, to see him in prison, powerless. He may have forbidden it after the first visit, and told his son to move on, not to contact him, but to focus on his own life."

"Do little pink fairies sing and dance in your world, Peabody?"

"Sometimes, when it's very quiet and no one else can see. But, I was going to say it's more likely that the father–son relationship here isn't a close one. May in fact be strained, even antagonistic."

"Yeah, if what Baxter dug up from the supervisors at Omega is fact, I'd go with option two—with the addendum being Alex Ricker's chosen to distance himself from his father. For his own reasons. Wonder what they are."

"Bad for business."

"Why? Your old man's a renowned, successful, badass

bad guy. Yeah, he got that badass handed to him, but he had one hell of a run first. Built his criminal empire, and so on. People in that business are going to respect and fear the Ricker name," Eve concluded, "the Ricker connection. The blood tie."

"Okay, maybe. Let's back up a minute. You think maybe the data Baxter got is wrong?"

"I think it's very odd that there are virtually no communications listed to or from Max Ricker since he took up residence at Omega."

"None? As in zero? I know they're strict up there, but inmates get a certain amount of communication allowance each month, right?"

"They do," Eve confirmed. "But with Ricker? Nobody calls, nobody writes. Bullshit. No visitors other than the single one documented from Alex. No, even in a world with dancing fairies, I don't buy it."

Frowning, Peabody leaned on the doorjamb. "Then you'd have to ask why he—Max Ricker—would want to hide communications and visitors, keep them off the record. And how the hell he'd manage it at a place like Omega."

"Tune out those fairies, Peabody. Bribes are universal. He could manage it, and we'll be looking into that. As to why? To conceal communication and connections with the aforesaid criminal empire. Maybe the son's covering for the father, or happy to take the top spot in a figure-head mode, while Dad continues to pull the strings."

"The name stays strong," Peabody calculated, "and the son gets the glory while Daddy still gets to play. It's good."

"It might be. Bringing it back to business at hand, maybe Coltraine knew more about that than made either father or son happy once the relationship ended. I vote for Dad if it moves that way. Alex didn't know Coltraine was going to be hit. He's too smart to put himself on the suspect list for a cop killing."

"But see, you're thinking he's too smart, so it makes it a solid."

"People come up with the lame when they think cops are idiots. He doesn't. They come up with the lame when they're smug and want to play games. He's careful. Everything I've got on him says he's careful."

She swiveled around to face her murder board. "The only incautious step I see him making anywhere, any-time, is becoming personally involved with a cop. He padded layers on that, but it was still incautious. Coming to New York days before the hit, staying on through that hit? That's just brainless."

She glanced at the time, cursed Webster. "I have to go brief the commander. Keep going on these probabil-ities. And start files on each individual member of Coltraine's squad, including her lieutenant."

"Man."

"It gets worse. I'm expecting a return from Webster, privacy mode. Beep me if it comes through while I'm out."

Eve pulled out her communicator as she strode out of Homicide and to the glides. Feeney answered with a "Yo."

"What's the best way to find out if someone on Omega is blocking or altering visitation and communi-cation records?"

217

"Go there, run it through on-site." He gave her a long, hard stare. "Not doing it, kid, not even for you."

"Okay, what's the second best way?"

"Get somebody young enough to think it's exciting, smart enough to do the dig, and shoot them off to that godforsaken rock."

"Who can you spare that fits those requirements, and can go now?"

Feeney blew out a breath that vibrated his lips. "Since this is gonna be connected to Coltraine's murder, you'd want young, smart, and already familiar with the investigation. I can pull Callendar off, send her."

"What kind of authorization do you need to—"

"Hey. Captain's bars here."

"Right. Can you send her asap? I can see she gets fully briefed while en route. Don't send her alone, Feeney. Send some muscle with her, just in case. Do you have any muscle up here?"

"Geeks have muscle, too." He flexed his own biceps as if to prove it. "Get me the why we need to dig, and I'll put it through."

"Thanks." She switched to Peabody. "Get Feeney the data from Baxter, and write up my take on why it's bull-shit. He'll be sending Callendar and geek muscle to Omega to check this out."

"Jeez, not McNab."

"Would you characterize McNab as geek muscle?"

"He's . . . okay, no."

"Push it, Peabody. I want her on her way quick, fast, and in a hurry."

"On it. Privacy-coded message just came through."

"Okay." She shoved her communicator away, pulled out her pocket 'link. It took her a few minutes to remember how to transfer a keyed transmission from her desk unit to a portable device, so she had to slow her pace.

She scanned the readout on the move, scrolling through for the highlights. She saved it, rekeyed it, then put her 'link away before going into Whitney's office.

She gave her report on her feet while Whitney sat at his desk.

"Detective Peabody is continuing the probabilities. Further—"

"You don't believe Alex Ricker's presence in New York, his reconnection with Coltraine the night before her death, is a coincidence?"

"No, sir. I fully intend to interview him formally, here, at Central. I believe that reconnection may have been part of the motive, and the timing. I don't believe he himself murdered Coltraine, or ordered it done. In fact, I believe had he known about the hit, he'd have taken steps to stop it, or would have warned her."

She paused a moment, working out the wording. "I believe she was important to him, just not the most important. He took steps to keep his connection to her quiet, as much for himself, his reputation as for hers. Her death brought that connection to the surface. He knew it would. He expected cops at his door once he learned she'd been killed."

"Why would he care if his connection to her became known, while they had their affair or after?"

"Pride and caution. It's just not good business for a

man in his position, with his interests, to have a cop as his lover. For him, business comes first, and his reputation is an essential element of that business. Her murder may have been an attempt to frame him, to cast suspicion on him, thereby damaging his reputation. His public businessman rep, and his underground rep."

"Using her as a weapon against him."

"Yes, sir. Because of who he is—maybe more because of who his father is—his prior affair with Coltraine puts him at the top of the suspect list on her murder. Bad for business," Eve added.

"You're leaning toward a competitor?"

"Possibly. She may have been killed because she was viewed as a weakness in him. She was, essentially, the only misstep he's made professionally. Whether she was in his pocket or not—and I don't think she was, given her profile and record, her background and personality. If she was, then he, in turn, was foolish to develop and maintain an intimate relationship with one of his tools."

She hesitated a moment, then decided to speak frankly. "I'm aware there is speculation in some corners that I'm Roarke's tool. Or vice versa. In point of fact, me being a cop is more problematic for him than not. And, well, vice versa. For Alex Ricker, living with a cop, maintaining an intimate relationship and a professional one? It's asking for trouble, and he doesn't."

"So you've concluded Coltraine may have been killed because of Alex Ricker, but not by or for him."

"Yes, sir."

"A competitor, an underling. That's a wide field, Lieutenant."

"I think it may be more narrow, Commander. According to the record, Alex Ricker visited his father on Omega only once in the last eight months. There have been no communications between them, or, in fact, between Max Ricker and anyone since he began his multiple life sentences."

"No communications, whatsoever, to or from the penal colony?"

"According to the records, no, sir."

Whitney's smile was tight and hard. "How stupid does he think we are?"

"Max Ricker has nothing but disdain for cops, and in the last few years his ego far overshadowed his judgment. That's one of the reasons he's in a cage. Since we're not stupid, I've asked Captain Feeney to send a couple of e-men to Omega to check the veracity of those records."

"When do they leave?"

"Today, sir. I hope within the hour. We could speed the process by requesting the civilian consultant make transportation available to the department for this purpose."

The faintest glint of humor lit Whitney's eyes. "I'll leave the arrangements to you, Lieutenant. I have some connections on Omega. I'll use them to speed the process once they're on colony."

He sat back, humor gone, drummed his fingers. "Not a competitor. Not an underling. You believe Max Ricker ordered the hit on Detective Coltraine."

"Yes, sir. I do."

"To strike at his son, or to protect him?"

"That's a question I hope to answer when I get Alex Ricker in the box."

While Eve reported to her commander, Roarke stepped out of the car, nodded to his driver. Alex Ricker did the same. The steel blue water lapped the sand of Coney Island as the men approached each other.

Neutral ground, Roarke mused, didn't have to be somber, staid, and serious. Business of this nature didn't require the ambience of dank back rooms or vacant lots. He enjoyed the idea of having this meeting on the grounds of the revitalized amusement center. The reconstructed Ferris wheel symbolized something to his mind.

Life was full of circles.

Though it was far too early in the day for that ride or any of the others to spin and play, people walked the beach, slurped flavored coffees or sugar drinks as they strolled the boardwalk.

At sea, both pleasure boats and busy ferries sailed.

The ocean breeze flipped at the hem of his light-weight overcoat while he lifted his arms and allowed Alex's man to scan him for weapons and bugs. And his performed the same task on Alex.

"I want to thank you for agreeing to meet me," Alex began when they were both cleared. "Even if it is a strange choice of location."

"Do you think so? A spring morning, out of doors, sea breezes."

Alex glanced around. "Carousels."

"And more. A New York landmark, a tradition that fell into disuse and disrepair—and shut down. A pity that. After the Urbans there was a push to revitalize, renew, and this place benefited from that. It's hopeful, isn't it, that fun has a place in the world?"

"How much of it do you own?"

Roarke only smiled. "Well then, you could find that out for yourself, couldn't you? What do you have to say to me, Alex?"

"Can we walk?"

"Of course." Roarke gestured, and they began to walk over the wooden slats, with their drivers several paces behind.

"You were my nemesis when we were young," Alex told him.

"Was I?"

"My father pushed you into my face, at least initially. This is what you need to be. Ruthless, cold, always thinking ahead of the others. Until he decided you weren't ruthless enough, cold enough, and worried you thought too far ahead of him. Still, you were shoved at me. I'd have to do better than you, by his measure, or I'd be a failure."

"That's a pisser, isn't it?"

"It was. When he came to fear and detest you, it was worse. He ordered three hits on you that I know of."

Roarke continued to stroll. "There were five, actually."

"Why didn't you ever retaliate?"

"I don't need the blood of my competitors. Or even

223

my enemies. He was, for some years, nothing to me. But he should never have touched my wife. I'd have done him for that, if you're interested. For putting a mark on her."

"You didn't, and he lives."

"Because doing so would've put another mark on her, as that's who she is."

"You let him live to protect your wife?"

Roarke paused, looked Alex in the face. "If you think the lieutenant needs protection, mine or anyone's, you've severely misjudged her. I let him live out of respect to her. And I became convinced living, as he is condemned to live now, was worse than death."

"It is, for him. He'll never admit it, not even to himself. A part of him will always believe, needs to believe, he'll fight his way back. Not just off Omega, but back to the top of his game. He'll live for that, and live a long time, I think, dreaming of your blood. And your cop's."

"I sincerely hope you're right." In the smile he sent Alex, Eve would have seen the dangerous man who lived inside the polish. "I do wish him a very long life."

"I hate him more than you ever could."

Yes, Roarke thought. He'd heard the hate in every word, and between each one as well. "Why is that?"

"He killed my mother." Alex stopped now, turned to the rail, looked out to sea. "All of my life I believed she'd fallen. That it had been a terrible accident. While part of me wondered if she'd given up, and jumped. But neither of those were true."

Roarke said nothing, simply waited.

"He'd been losing control bit by bit over the last years. Becoming more and more unstable. He'd always been violent, quick to violence, easily enraged. I never knew what to make of him as a child. One minute I'd be treated like a prince, his most treasured son. The next I'd be picking myself up off the floor with a split lip or bloodied nose. So I grew up fearing and worshipping him, and desperate to please him."

"Many, if not most, who worked for him felt the same."

"Not you. In any case, over the last dozen years, we'll say, some of his demands, his decisions were dangerous. Unnecessary and dangerous. We argued. We started arguing about the time I went to university. We'd gotten to a point where I wouldn't tolerate being knocked down, so he didn't have that weapon to use. So, when he realized he couldn't knock me down physically, he used another means.

"He should have done to me what he'd done to the bitch who bore me. That's how he put it to me." On the rail, Alex's knuckles went white. "He should have gotten rid of me the way he had her. Watched me fall, watched my brains splatter on the street."

Alex took a minute, just breathed in the sea air. "I asked him why he would have done it. He said she'd passed her usefulness, and she annoyed him. I should be careful not to do the same. Later he recanted. He'd only said it because I'd made him angry, because I'd disrespected him. But I knew he'd told me the absolute truth. So, you can believe me when I say I wish him a long, long life as much as you."

"I'm very sorry. You can believe that as well."

"I do. One of the reasons he hated you, hates you, is because you have a code. A moral code of your own that he couldn't shake."

He turned from the sea now to face Roarke. "You've no reason to believe I have one of my own, but I'm telling you, I didn't kill Amaryllis. I didn't order her killed. I'd never hurt her, or wish her harm. I loved her once. I cared about her still, very much. Whoever did it is using me as a shield. A diversion. And that infuriates me."

"Why tell me?"

"Who else?" Alex demanded with some heat. "Your cop? In my place, would you strip out your guts to a cop? A cop who has every reason to suspect you of killing one?"

"I wouldn't, no. Are you looking at me for putting in a good word for you?"

"Your sense of fair play disgusted my father. I suppose I'm counting on it. I don't know who killed her, or even why. I've tried every resource I can think of to find out, and I've got nothing."

The sea spread at Alex's back, and the sun poured over him. In its strong light, Roarke saw pain, and the struggle to suppress it.

"I'm going to tell you that I came to New York hoping to convince her to come back to me. Because no one else in my life has ever made a difference. And I could see in a moment it would never happen. She was happy, and she was in love. And we were still who we were in Atlanta, still who we were when we went our separate ways. She could never accept me, what I am, what I do, and be happy. She'd faced that, and walked away. After seeing her again, I faced it."

"Did you think she would change what she was in Atlanta, or now?"

"Yes. Yes, I did. Or that she'd just ignore my business dealings. They had nothing to do with her, or with us. But she couldn't resolve it. And after a while, couldn't live with it. Or me."

"Did it never occur to you to adjust your business dealings?"

"No. It's what I do. If I have my father in me, it's that. I hope to God that's all of him I have. I've never killed, or ordered a kill. It's not . . . practical."

"The men who hit your antique store in Atlanta died very badly, I'm told."

"They did. I didn't order it."

"Max did?"

"They insulted him—by his way of thinking—by making a fool out of me. Out of his blood. So he dealt with it, his way. And his way put me and my interests under a great deal more scrutiny than necessary. I don't kill, it's simply not good business."

He shrugged that off as a man might when discussing his preference for mutual funds over individual stocks as an investor. "I'd be impractical, and the hell with good business, if I knew who killed Ammy. Because I loved her once, and because I never had the goddamn balls to kill my father for what he did to my mother."

When Alex went silent, when he turned back to the

water, Roarke stepped to the rail beside him. "What are you looking for, from me?"

"I want—I need to know who killed her, and why. You have resources beyond mine. I don't know how many you might be using in your connection with the police, or what I can offer you to use more for this. For her. But you've only to name your price."

"You don't know my wife. You know of her, but you don't know her. You'd do well to put your trust in her to find those answers. Added to that? You don't have to pay for my resources, Alex, when my wife has only to ask for them."

Alex studied Roarke's face, then nodded and looked back out over the water. "All right. I promise you if I learn anything, anything at all that could help, I'll tell you."

"I'll take your promise, but I can't give you the same. That would be up to the lieutenant. But I'll give you this: When she finds who did this—and she will—should that person meet with a bad end, I'll keep your part in that to myself."

Alex let out a half laugh. "That's something." He turned, offered Roarke his hand. "Thank you."

They were close to the same age, Roarke mused, and both started their lives with men who enjoyed spilling blood. Alex as the prince, and himself as the pauper.

Despite some of the basic similarities, and for all of Alex's polish and his background of privilege, Roarke sensed the naive.

"Something your father wouldn't have told you," he began. "Taking blood, it leaves a mark on you. No matter how it's done, or how it's justified, it leaves a mark that goes in deep. Be sure you're willing to wear that mark before you take the blood."

Back in the car, Roarke deactivated the recorder built into his cufflink. He considered removing the micros-tunner inside his boot, then left it where it was. You just never knew.

Both were prototypes currently in development, made of materials undetectable by even the most sensitive scanners currently available. He knew, as his company was also developing the scanner that would detect them.

Always cover both ends of the game, he thought.

Part of him regretted he couldn't tell Alex that he wasn't Eve's prime suspect. Or even a suspect in her mind at this point. But that, too, was up to the lieutenant. But he could regret. He'd had a mother, too. A mother who'd loved him, and who his father had killed. Outlived her usefulness, hadn't she? Become an annoyance. Yes, he could feel for Alex there.

He could feel even as he wondered at the man's lack of awareness. A man who'd let love walk away rather than give ground, or try at least to find the middle of it. And now, Roarke mused, couldn't see what was staring him square in the face.

His 'link signaled. His lips curved when he read *Darling Eve* on the display. "Hello, Lieutenant."

"Hey. I've got a favor. Can—where are you?"

"I'm in transit at the moment. I had a meeting."

"Is that . . . you had a meeting on Coney Island?"

"I did. A pity it was so early in the day and I couldn't treat myself to the roller coaster. We'll have to come back, you and I, and make up for it."

"Sure, when I've lost my mind and want to rush screaming through the air in a little car. Never mind. Favor. I need to—"

"Answer a question first, and I promise to grant whatever the favor might be."

Suspicion narrowed her eyes. He loved that look.

"What kind of question?"

"A yes or no for now. Question, Lieutenant. Is Max Ricker behind Detective Coltraine's murder?"

"What, do you have me wired? Have Whitney's office bugged?"

Roarke glanced at his cufflink. "Not at the moment. I take that as a yes."

"It's not yes or no. I suspect, strongly, that Max Ricker is behind it."

"That's good enough for me. What's the favor?"

"I need your fastest off-planet transpo. New York to Omega Colony."

"We're going to Omega?"

"No, Callendar and another e-detective will be. I think Ricker's pulling some strings up there, believe his communication and visitation records have been wiped or doctored. I want to know who he's been talking to. It can take twenty-six hours or more to get to Omega by regular means."

"I can cut that by more than a third. I'll arrange it, and get back to you with the details."

"Okay. I owe you."

"A roller-coaster ride, at least."

"No, I don't owe you that much."

He laughed when she clicked off. After arranging the flight, passing the information back, Roarke settled down and thought of Max Ricker.

Time had to stop, Eve thought, as she changed into dress blues. The dead deserved their moment, she supposed that was true enough. But in her mind, memorials were for the living left behind. So time had to stop, for Morris. She might do Coltraine a hell of a lot more good in the field, or working her way to getting Alex Ricker in the box. But there were other duties.

She pulled on the hard black shoes, stood and squared her uniform cap on her head.

She walked out of the locker room to take the glides down to the bereavement center.

She thought of Callendar and some bulky e-geek named Sisto, preparing to be flung like a couple of stones from a slingshot toward the cold rock of Omega. Callendar, Eve recalled, had appeared seriously juiced at the prospect of her first off-planet assignment.

It took all kinds.

This time tomorrow they'd be there, be digging in. They'd mine those logs and find what she needed. They'd damn well better find what she needed. Because every inch of her gut said Max Ricker had ordered the hit. She'd get to the why; she'd get to the how. But the e-team had to get her Ricker and his contact.

Max Ricker wouldn't pay for killing a cop. What more could be done to a man who would live the rest of his miserable life in a cage? But others could and would pay, and that would have to be enough.

She hoped it would be enough.

The doors of the room Morris had chosen stood open so the music flowed through them. The bluesy sort he and the woman he'd loved had enjoyed. She caught the scent of flowers—the roses—before she stepped into the room crowded with cops.

Red roses, Eve noted, and photographs of the dead. Casual, candid shots of Coltraine smiling mixed with formal ones. Coltraine in uniform looking polished and serious, in a summer dress on some beach laughing. Small white candles burned a soft, soothing light.

With some relief she saw no casket—either closed or open—no clear-sided box currently in vogue that displayed the body. The photographs were enough to bring her into the room.

She saw Morris through the crowd standing with a man in his late twenties. Coltraine's brother, Eve realized. The resemblance was too strong for anything else.

Peabody broke away from a group and moved to Eve's side. "It's a big turnout. That's a good thing, if there can be a good thing. It feels weird being in blues again, but you were right about that." She tugged her stiff jacket more perfectly into place. "It's more respectful."

"Not all her squad thought so." Eve's gaze tracked over. Coltraine's lieutenant and Detective O'Brian wore the blue, but the others in her squad elected to remain in soft clothes.

"A lot of the cops stopped in from the field, or came

in before they had to head out again. There's not always time to change."

"Yeah."

"It's hard seeing Morris like this. Seeing him hurt."

"Watch the cops instead," Eve suggested. "Watch her squad. Make sure you speak to every one of them. I want impressions. I'll be doing the same."

But for now, Eve thought, she had to take the hard, and speak to Morris.

13

Eve brushed by O'Brian first, deliberately, then stopped. "Detective."

"Lieutenant." He met her eyes, then looked away to the roses and candles. "Morris did right here. It's the right way. For her, for us. It's the right way."

"The cop way?"

He smiled, just a little. "Some of that. But the rest? It shows who she was. You can see her here."

"It's hard for you, losing one of your squad."

"I see her desk every day. Somebody else'll be sitting there before much longer, and you'll get used to it. But it's hard not seeing her there. Harder knowing why. My wife just came in. Excuse me."

He moved off, working his way toward a woman who stood just inside the doors. She held out a hand, and O'Brian took it.

Eve turned away. She waited until a group of people speaking to Morris stepped off. Then went to him.

"Dallas." Now it was Morris who held out a hand, and she who took it.

"You did right here," she said, echoing O'Brian.

Morris's fingers tightened on hers briefly. "It's all I could do. Lieutenant Dallas, this is July Coltraine, Ammy's brother."

Concentration narrowed in July's gaze. "You're the one in charge of . . ."

"Yes. I'm very sorry for your loss, for your family's loss."

"Li says there's no one better. Can you tell me . . . Is there anything you can tell me?"

"All I can tell you now is your sister has all my attention, and that of every officer assigned."

Shock and grief dulled eyes the same deep blue as his sister's. Eve saw his chest move as he struggled to breathe his way to composure. "Thank you. I'm taking her home tonight. We felt, my family and I, we felt someone should be here for this memorial, and to bring her home. So many people here. So many came. It matters. It means a great deal."

"She was a good cop."

"She wanted to help people."

"She did. She helped a lot of people."

"It's not the time to ask, not the place, but I'm taking her home tonight. When my parents—I need to tell them. I need that. You're going to find who took her away?"

"Yes."

He nodded. "Excuse me."

Morris took Eve's hand again as July hurried off. "Thank you. For the dress blues, for what you said to him."

"I told him the truth as I know it. She was a good cop, everything I find confirms that. And I will find who killed her."

"I know you will. It helps me get from moment to moment."

He wore a simple and elegant black suit, with a black cord winding through his long, meticulous braid. And she thought his face looked thinner than it had even the day before. As if some of the flesh had been carved away.

It worried her.

"Her brother was right," she told him. "It matters that so many people are here." She glanced over, spotted Bollimer, and the owner of the Chinese restaurant where Coltraine had ordered her last meal. "She mattered to a lot of people."

"I know. They'll cremate her tomorrow, and hold a memorial in a few days. I'll go to Atlanta for that, where there will be more people she mattered to. I know, in the odd way of these things, I'll find some comfort. But knowing you'll find who killed her gets me from moment to moment. Will you speak to me later, tell me what you know?"

"Yes."

Morris squeezed her hand again, then his gaze shifted over her shoulder. Eve turned to see Mira and her husband.

Mira moved naturally, simply put her arms around Morris and held him. When he dropped his head on Mira's shoulder, Eve looked away.

Dennis Mira rubbed Eve's arm, and made her throat burn. "When death strikes home," he said in his quiet way, "it's harder, I think, for those who face it every day."

"I guess maybe it is."

Something about him, Eve thought—his gangly frame in his oddly formal black suit—was as comforting as she imagined Mira's hug would be. "It's the knowing how it works, and what it leaves behind."

He studied one of the photographs. "She was very lovely, very young." And looked at Eve. "I don't think I've ever seen you in uniform before. Have I?" His eyes took on that vague, distracted look that appealed to her. "In any case, you look formidable."

"I guess I am."

He smiled at her, then stepped up to Morris. Eve slipped away.

She took Clifton next, winding her way toward the detective where he stood with a group of cops. She caught a snippet of conversation, centering around baseball.

Meant nothing, Eve admitted. People talked about all manner of things at memorials.

"Detective."

It took him a half a beat, Eve noted. The uniform threw him, she thought. "Lieutenant." He shifted away from the others. "Any word?"

"We've got a couple of leads. We're on them. Any thoughts of your own?"

"I told you what I know, and from what I hear you should be watching your back."

"Should I?"

"Heard the killer sent you her badge and weapon, then tried to take you out. Smells like a cop killer who targets female officers."

"Well. You'd be safe then."

She watched temper kindle in his eyes. "I didn't pick up a badge to be safe."

"No? Did you pick it up so you could tune up suspects?"

"I get the job done."

"You've got some interesting rips in your jacket, Detective."

"What's it to you?"

"Just making conversation."

"You homicide cops. You come in after it's over. We're the ones out in it every day, trying to keep assholes from killing each other."

"Gee, I guess if you did a better job, I'd be out of one."

He edged in on her with a little tough guy move—quick roll of the shoulders, curl of the lip. "Look, bitch, you don't have a clue what a real cop does."

"Oh? Then why don't you educate me?"

The lip curl went to a sneer.

"Dak." Cleo Grady strode up. "Newman's looking for you. He got a bang on the Jane Street case."

Clifton gave Eve the hard eye for another few seconds. "School's out. I've got to go do some real cop work."

"Good luck with that," Eve said pleasantly, then turned to Cleo. "Was that true, or a way to keep your squadmate from taking a shot at a superior officer?"

"It's true, the other part's just good luck. We're all wound a little tight these days, Lieutenant."

"My impression is Clifton's always wound a little tight."

Cleo only shrugged. "We feel shut out some, on top of the rest. We come in here, and it hits us in the face. Somebody took her out, and we're not part of the investigation. We don't know you, but we know you're looking at us. You don't expect some resentment?"

"Resentment doesn't bother me, Detective Grady. Murder? That just pisses me off. If Newman got a bang, why didn't he tag Clifton instead of looking for him in the crowd?"

"You'd have to ask him," Cleo said coolly. "But maybe to show some respect."

"When one of you gets a bang on an ongoing when you're off shift or separated, how do you tag each other?"

"Depends on the circumstances."

"I'd say communicator if you're soloing in the field. But if one of you was, say, at home, a 'link tag makes more sense. A lot of cops stash their communicators along with their weapon, their badge, and so on."

"That's what I'd do. If you're asking."

"Me, too. But I'd try the house 'link first. Hanging at home, why have your pocket on you? Except then that tag would be on the 'link. You tag the pocket, well, all you have to do is take it with you."

"Goddamn it," Cleo said under her breath. "You *are* looking at us."

"I'm looking at everybody."

"Look all you want, while whoever did this to Ammy walks away. What kind of cop drags other cops through the blood?"

Cleo spun around, stormed away.

"And here you are, making friends as always."

Eve glanced over her shoulder, into Roarke's eyes. "I've got a couple more to go."

"I'll leave you to it, and pay my condolences to Morris." He trailed a finger over the shoulder of her uniform jacket. "We need to have a conversation."

"Okay. As soon as I can. Crowd's starting to thin out, so I've got to piss off a couple more people before this is over."

"If anyone can," Roarke said, and left her to it.

She found Delong just outside the doors in conversation with ME Clipper. Delong broke off as Eve approached.

"Lieutenant Dallas."

"Lieutenant Delong."

"If you'll excuse me," Clipper said, "I haven't yet paid my respects."

Delong waited a moment, then gave Eve a come-with-me signal and moved another couple of feet away from the entrance. "I know you've got a job to do," he began, "and nobody, *nobody* wants you to do that job successfully more than I do. But I'm telling you, here and now, I resent you pushing at my squad. I particularly resent you pushing at my squad here when we're mourning one of our own."

"So noted."

"I hope it is. I'll also tell you I fully intend to make my feelings known on this to Commander Whitney."

"You're free to do so. Meanwhile, I'll tell you that I believe Detective Coltraine left her apartment that night to go on the job. She left her apartment to go on the job because someone contacted her and lured her out.

Someone who knew her habits, someone she trusted. Someone she worked with. Or for."

Color flooded Delong's face. "You don't know that. A cop goes out, she straps it on. For the job, or to go pick up some goddamn milk."

"Not this cop. If you knew your detective, you know that."

He didn't have Clifton's tough-guy move, but he edged in on Eve just the same. "Do you think you can try digging up dirt on my men? Say one of them killed their fellow officer and not pay a price for it?"

"No, I don't. If someone did the same to my men, I'd kick some ass. I'd also be asking myself some hard questions. I'd be looking harder and deeper than anyone."

"I'm not you."

"No, you're not."

"Be careful where you push, and how hard."

He might have stormed off then, but Whitney and his wife stepped off the glide. Instead, Delong walked stiffly up to them. Hands were shaken, Eve noted, condolences certainly offered. Then she saw Whitney nod before Delong strode onto the upward glide.

The Whitneys crossed the distance to Eve.

"Commander, Mrs Whitney."

Mrs Whitney, trim in her stark black suit, took Eve's hand in both of hers. The gesture, so out of character, had Eve blinking. "You have a difficult job. More difficult today."

"Yes, ma'am."

"I'll be right in," Whitney said, and patted his wife's

arm. He blew out a breath when she went into the bereavement room. "A cop goes down, those with the bad luck to be married to one feel it. Well. Lieutenant Delong wants to speak with me, at my earliest convenience. You wouldn't know what that may be about, would you, Lieutenant?"

"I couldn't say, sir."

"Won't say. You're cutting close to the bone, I expect. As squad boss, he'd want to defend and protect his men."

"Yes, sir. Or he's protecting himself."

"If you connect him, or any of his squad to Ricker, make it solid. If we aim to put a cop in a cage, I don't want any room for error."

Though she wanted to get back upstairs, Eve took the time to corner Clipper. "What did Delong want?" she demanded. When Clipper merely looked pained, she hissed out a breath. "I'm investigating a cop murder. If it applies to my case, I want to know what he said."

"He just asked if there was anything I could tell him, and why he's blocked from receiving any reports on the case. He's upset and frustrated, Dallas. Who wouldn't be?"

"What did you tell him?"

"That my hands are tied. You're in charge. That's the way it is, and that's the way my boss wants it. So my hands are tied." Clipper used one of them to rub the back of his neck. "He's steaming over you. I figure you know that already."

"Yeah, I got a sense."

"Every one of his men have contacted or come down to the morgue, hoping for information. I've got it locked down."

"I appreciate that. Any of them give you grief?"

Clipper gave his trim goatee a slow, thoughtful stroke. "We'll say Detective Clifton suggested I make love to myself, and suggested I'd already done so with my mother, on several occasions."

"You're a card, Clip. Did he get physical?"

"I was holding a laser scalpel at the time of our conversation. I can say I had the impression he might have wanted to dance otherwise."

"Okay."

"There's really nothing I can tell any of them."

"Yeah, but they don't know that. Let's keep it that way."

Eve caught Roarke's eye as he spoke with the Whitneys. She angled her head toward the door, then signaled to Peabody.

Roarke, she thought, knew where to find her.

"Impressions," Eve said as she started up with Peabody.

"That's a very unhappy squad, with some anger just under the line. Word's circulating that we're spending more time and energy looking for dirt on them than on pursuing alternate leads."

"Where did the word originate?"

"You know how it is, Dallas. This one says he heard that from this one who said that. Cops are gossip whores. I will say I haven't been pumped so many times in such a short span since McNab and I moved into the apartment and felt honor bound to do it in every room. Twice."

"Yes, my day wouldn't have been complete without hearing that."

"Various techniques," Peabody continued, "which also bring back fond memories of that night. Delong's straight out, with an authoritative snap. Like I'm required to answer his questions because he's rank. The Newman guy sort of circles around, trying to get you to trip up and spill. O'Brian's got the sad eyes and fatherly demeanor going for him. Grady tries the solidarity between us girl detectives. And Clifton goes direct to bully."

"Did he put hands on you?"

"Not quite. I think that was going to be next, but O'Brian drew him off. Before that, Clifton got pissy I wasn't telling him whatever he wanted to know and accused me of being an ass kisser. I responded that I have yet to have the privilege of kissing your ass, which I rate as the best—female variety—in the department."

"That sounds like a pucker-up to me."

Peabody snorted. "It was worth it. He went all puce. Or is it fuchsia? Which is the weird name that means hot pink?"

"I have no idea, nor want one."

"Anyway, he went that color, and I'm pretty sure he was going to give me a shove. Then O'Brian came up, got in front of him."

"That was enough?"

"He said, 'Remember where you are, Dak. Don't shame our Ammy, or the rest of your squad.' Clifton said it was a couple of homicide bitches trying to shame the squad. But he backed off, walked away. Then O'Brian apologized for him, with the sad eyes and father demeanor."

Eve grunted, and walked straight into the locker room. "Interesting. Interesting dynamics over there." She thought it through as she undressed.

"O'Brian's the father figure. The oldest, the most experienced. The rest of them look to him, even before they look to the lieutenant. He has them over for barbecues and—what do you call them—potluck dinners."

Eve sat to remove the hard black shoes. "Newman, he's the average joe, just your roll-with-it guy. The one you have a brew with after shift. Keeps his head down, and his mouth mostly shut. Direct opposite of Clifton. Hothead, short fuse, bad attitude. He likes using the badge or his fists to push people around."

"Well, so do you. Kind of."

"Yeah, so do I. But for me it's a nice by-product. With him it's the priority. Rules and regs, screw that. If you're going through a door, he's the one who's got to go first. His control button's faulty. The rest of them keep an eye on him, talk him down. But sooner or later . . ." She shook her head. "That short fuse is going to blow."

Eve hung up her uniform, stowed the shoes, then began to dress. "Grady? She's smart enough to use the fact she's got tits when it works for her, and to forget them when it won't. She's ambitious, and you can bet she knows how to work everyone else in the squad."

"She wants the boss's chair?"

Eve glanced around. "Maybe, but she's not working as hard for it as I'd expect. But she seems to like being in the small pond. As for the lieutenant, he's a steady-as-it-goes type. Sticks mostly with the paperwork. Stands for his men, and I can't fault him there, but Jesus, he's going to complain to Whitney about how I'm doing my job. That's weak. It's fucking weak to go to command like that. You don't have a strong squad if the helm's weak."

Peabody sighed as she buttoned her shirt. "It's going to be one of them, isn't it?"

"That's my money. Maybe more than one of them." Eve checked her wrist unit. "Callendar and Sisto should dock in about twelve hours. I put Webster's report on your unit. Read it. Roarke's got something, so I'm going to talk to him. Then maybe we'll see if we can invite Alex Ricker down for some conversation."

"He'll be neck-deep in lawyers."

"And won't that be fun?"

"Like a barrel of rabid monkeys. Oh, Nadine came by. She didn't bring a crew," Peabody said quickly. "It was a sympathy call. Genuine. She couldn't stay, and you were busy, so she said she'd see you tomorrow."

"About what?"

"Dallas. The shower's tomorrow. Louise's shower."

"Oh." Crap. "Right."

"We'll be by around two to set things up."

"What things?"

"Stuff."

"If I can light a fire under . . ." Peabody's face turned kicked-puppy pitiful. "All right, all right." No point in pulling out her hair, Eve thought. Just no point. "You set up whatever, and let me know when it's done. I can work until."

Maybe longer than until, Eve thought as she headed out, if Callendar came through. It was probably too much to hope for, but it helped to think she might be slapping restraints on Ricker's contact instead of watching a bunch of women coo over some stupid shower present. Besides . . .

"Oh shit, oh shit, stupid shower present!"

Now she did pull her hair as she made the dash to her office.

Roarke sat in her visitor's chair, comfortably involved with his PPC. He glanced up, let loose a regretful sigh. "You changed. And I didn't have any time to ogle you in uniform."

"I have to go shopping!"

Staring at her, Roarke pressed his fingertips to his temple. "I'm sorry, I believe I must have had a small stroke. What did you say?"

"This isn't funny." She bent down, gripped him by the lapels. "I forgot to get a thing for the thing, and I don't even know what the thing is supposed to *be*. Now I have to go out and hunt something down. Except—" Her eyes went from slightly mad to speculative. "We have all kinds of things around the house. Couldn't I just wrap something up and—"

"No."

"Crap!"

Roarke sat calmly while she dropped into her desk chair and buried her head in her hands. "Do I correctly interpret the thing for the thing as a gift for Louise's bridal shower?"

"What other thing is currently being shoved down my throat?"

"Mmm-hmm. Give me a moment." Eve muttered, but her head shot up when she heard him say, "Caro."

"Yes! Genius. Caro can get the thing."

"No," Roarke said it firmly and had Eve slumping again. "Caro," he repeated. "If you were hostessing a bridal shower for a good friend, what would be the appropriate sort of gift?"

Eve swiveled so she could bang her head on the desk. Roarke and Caro talked—questions, answers—but she didn't take it in. They might have been speaking Greek.

"Thanks. Something's come up here, so I'll likely be working from home later. Let me know if you need me for anything. Have a nice weekend."

He clicked off, and Eve opened one eye to peer at him. "What did—"

He held up a finger, and continued to work on the PPC. "All right then," he said after a moment. "Caro believes, given your relationship and the occasion, you should get Louise something both personal and romantic."

"What, a sex toy?"

"No. Not exactly," he amended. "Lingerie. A nightgown, or as she delicately put it, an ensemble."

Eve straightened. "I'm supposed to buy Louise fuckwear?"

"Which is how to indelicately put it."

"I can't do that. It's . . . Even if I wanted to, which—who would—I don't know her size or anything."

"I do. I just hacked into her account and have all her sizes. Now, I'm afraid you're going to have to go into an actual store as you've left this too late to purchase anything appropriate online."

"Oh God. Just kill me."

"Don't worry. I know just the place."

"Of course you do. I wanted to pick up Alex Ricker, sweat him in the box for a while."

"I thought you weren't looking at him for Coltraine's murder."

"I'm not. But I can't tell what he knows until I know. He may not know what he knows until I pry it out of him. If Max Ricker ordered the hit, his son's the reason. One way or the other. He's running the businesses now. He's got to know something."

"I don't think so. Which is what I wanted to speak to you about before we drifted off to lingerie."

She grimaced as she glanced at her open door. "Don't keep saying lingerie in here. It's a cop shop."

"I met Alex this morning. In fact, had just finished the meeting when you contacted me about transportation to Omega."

"You—Jesus. You can't just—on Coney Island."

"My choice, the venue." Roarke made himself as comfortable as possible in her saggy visitor's chair. "He asked for a meeting."

"It could've been a trap. It could've—"

"It wasn't. And as I said, my choice of venue. Believe me, I was well secured."

She held up her hands. It was a waste of time to argue, since it was already done. And a waste of energy not to believe he'd been, as he claimed, well secured. "What did he want?"

Roarke handed her a disc. "You can listen to it while I drive. You'll be working, you see, and we'll visit this charming shop I know. They gift wrap."

Eve frowned at the disc. "You got a recorder past him?"

Roarke only smiled.

14

Eve listened to the recording straight through, let it stew in her mind, then replayed it. She sat back, considered—and noticed vaguely that Roarke was having a fine time weaving through uptown traffic like a snake through high grass.

"You believe him? You believe he's telling it straight about his feelings and loyalty—or lack thereof—to his father?"

Roarke cut east, went vertical over a double-parked delivery truck, then waited sedately at the light. "I do, yes. I should have tried out the video element, then you'd have a better sense. It was in his eyes. I recognize that in-the-bone hate, as I have it myself for my own."

"For the same reason," Eve pointed out. "Maybe he knows. Maybe he played that card *because* he knows you'd relate."

"It's not impossible, but it would be smart work on his part as I only found out myself last year. Do you think he's lying about his mother?"

"When I read the file, my first thought was Ricker did her. First thoughts aren't always the right ones. But my second thought, and my third thought came back to that. No, I don't think he's lying about Ricker tossing

251

his mother out the window. I'm working on whether it matters to him."

"You're trying out the mirror again, to see if it reflects. He and I—both with violent fathers—murderous bastards both. If mine didn't beat the hell out of me by sundown, well now, that was a lost day for him. His, or so he claims, embraced him one moment and cuffed him the next. If true, he had the worst deal to my thinking. At least I always expected the boot."

"He had a mother—he indicates—loved him for the first years of his life."

"And I didn't. I think he got the short end there as well. I never knew what I missed. He says he grew up trying to please his father. I never gave a damn about pleasing mine, except to avoid that boot. I hated him from my first memory, so it becomes just the way of it. I'd think coming to that hate later in life boils it hotter, so to speak.

"You'll want to run it by Mira, I expect," Roarke added as he cruised up Madison. "But he wasn't lying."

"Okay." If she couldn't take Roarke's word on that, Eve thought, then whose? "Okay, it fits. One visit from him to Omega, then nothing. No contact. And if you angle it toward his relationship with Coltraine, the timing . . ."

"You take Max down, and some of that splashes on Alex. He spins, restructures, reevaluates. And his lady realizes he's not going to take this chance to step away, to become fully legitimate. He's never going to do that."

"She makes her decision, breaks it off. He makes his.

252

He gives her up rather than give up the shady. He's not a mirror of you," Eve stated.

Roarke glanced at her. "And he got the short end of the deal again, didn't he? For here I am with my wife, about to shop for lingerie. And he has no one."

"He came here hoping to change that. That's the trigger. That's why Ricker pushed the button. To give his son the boot."

"I'm sure you're right. That's at least part of it."

"So he knows what his son's up to," Eve calculated. "Which means someone in Alex's organization is feeding Ricker. Someone close enough to know Alex intended to contact Coltraine, what he hoped. And when. I vote for—"

"Rod Sandy."

"I was voting," Eve complained. "Damn it."

"There now." Roarke patted her hand, shifted to her. "Alex's PA, his friend—longtime friend. Certainly a confidant. He'd know, as you've concluded, that Coltraine was never on the take. That she wouldn't turn that way. He'd have known when they met here in New York how it went between them."

"And the next day, she's dead. Sandy didn't call her. She went armed, and that still says one of her squad to me. But he might have been on the stairs. If he managed to doctor the security, or find another way out—knowing Alex was out of the place, then—"

"An interesting theory. Hold that thought. Or rather, put it on hold and think lingerie."

"Why would I—oh." She focused on her surroundings and noted they were parked. How the man

253

managed to find a street-level spot in midtown on a Friday evening baffled her. "Where is this place?"

"Just around the corner, on Madison." He joined her on the sidewalk, took her hand. "We should take advantage of luck—with the parking and the evening, and polish off the shopping with dinner. There's a nice place just across the street. We can sit outside, share a bottle of wine and a meal."

"I really ought to—"

"Work, yes." He brought her hand up to kiss her knuckles.

He'd sit and eat with her in her office while she did just that, she thought. Because it was the natural order for her.

She stopped at the corner, looked at him. "Maybe if it was a date."

"Sorry?"

She angled her head, lifted her eyebrows. And watched his smile spread. "Ah. Darling, would you go out to dinner with me tonight?"

"She won't, I will," a woman said as she passed them. "I'll even buy."

"Yeah, I'll go out to dinner with you tonight." She kept her hand in his as they walked half a block.

In the place called Secrets, the window displayed human replicas lounging in silky robes, posing in fanciful bits of lace and satin, flirting in tit-enhancing corsets. Rose petals littered the floor. Eve studied the window, concluded that under normal circumstances she'd have to have a stunner pressed to her head to get her in the door.

She supposed friendship often amounted to the same.

"Is this yours?"

"The shop? I have a small interest. Twenty percent," he added when she frowned at him.

"Why only twenty?"

"The couple who run it—and own the rest—used to work for me. They came to me with their idea, their concept, proposal, and business plan. I liked it. So I gave them the backing. About five years ago. There's a second one downtown now, in the Village. But it's a bit funkier. This one's more Louise, I think."

"Then I could've just ordered something, had it delivered. Not have to actually . . . shop."

"Be brave, little soldier," he said and opened the door.

He'd have gotten an elbow in the ribs for the crack, but he knew her well enough to evade.

The place smelled . . . sexy, she decided. Like smoldering candles and subtle whiffs of perfume. Select items spread like exotic butterflies over displays where others floated like suspended jewels. A woman sat in a gilt and velvet chair perusing a selection of minuscule bras and panties as if they were indeed jewels.

Another stood across the room, carefully wrapping something red and silky in tissue for a customer.

"It doesn't even show," Eve muttered. "What's the big deal when you're just going to cover it up with clothes?"

"Let me count the ways."

"See?" She bumped his hip with hers. "That's just fuckwear, like I said. I'm not sure I want to—"

She broke off when the tissue lady spotted Roarke

and shot out a megawatt smile. "So good to see you again," she said to the customer. "Enjoy."

"Oh, I will. *He* will." With a laugh, the customer started out, swinging her tiny, shiny silver bag.

"What a wonderful surprise." The owner, Eve concluded, crossed over in her skinny pink heels to hold out both hands for Roarke's.

"Adrian. You look lovely."

"Oh." She fluffed at the soft sunny waves of her hair. "It's been a busy day. If you could just give me another moment?"

"Take your time." As she went over to Bra-and-Panties, Roarke turned to Eve. "See anything you like?"

"Is this where my underwear comes from? The stuff, I mean, that appears like magic in my drawers? And the robes that mysteriously find their way to my closet or the hook in the bathroom?"

"Sometimes." He wandered a couple of steps away to study a short gown as pale as water, and nearly as transparent. "Adrian and Liv have exquisite taste. Being women, they have a sense of what makes a woman feel sexy or romantic, confident, desirable. And being women who are attracted to women, they know what catches the eye and makes a woman sexy and so on to another."

"So it's a lesbian fuckwear shop?" She rolled her eyes when Roarke aimed his at her. "Just saying. And yeah, okay, it's classy stuff in a classy atmosphere. Sex but no skank."

"That should be their slogan."

She grinned. "That's what you get for taking me out of my element."

He caught her face in his hands, surprised her with a cheerful kiss. "I wouldn't have you any other way."

"You go for skank as well as the next guy."

"Darling Eve, only when the skank is you."

She laughed, poked him in the chest. "Keep it that way, pal."

"Sorry to keep you waiting." Adrian hurried over to them as Bra-and-Panties left the shop—with a bag. "I let Wendy, our clerk, go about an hour ago. Hot date. Of course, when you're on your own, that's when you get three and four customers at once. Lieutenant Dallas."

She took Eve's hand, shook it enthusiastically. "It's so good to finally meet you. Roarke says you're not one for shopping."

"No. Really not. But you've got a really nice place here."

"We love it, thanks. My partner and I."

"How is Liv?" Roarke asked her.

"She's great. She's pregnant," Adrian told Eve. "Thirty-two weeks."

"Congratulations."

"We're over the moon about it. She was just so tired today, so I made her go home at noon. She'll hate knowing she missed you. Both of you. What can I help you with? Something special?"

"For me? No. No. I'm good. More than."

"That one." Roarke gestured to the waterlike gown. "But we'll get to that after. Eve?"

"Oh, yeah. Well. I have this thing, and the word is this kind of stuff would work for it."

Adrian narrowed her eyes—serenely blue—in thought. "A thing, but not for you. You need a gift."

"Yes." Thank God. "Yes, I need a gift."

"The occasion?"

"Like pulling teeth, isn't it?" Roarke commented.

"Shut up." Eve blew out a breath. "Okay. It's a shower thing. Bridal shower thing."

"Oh, yes, we'll find just the thing. What's your relationship with the bride? I mean," she added, correctly assuming Eve was about to panic again. "Is she a good friend, a relative, an acquaintance?"

"A friend."

"Eve's standing up for her at the wedding," Roarke put in.

"A very good friend then. Tell me about her. What she looks like to start."

"She's blonde."

Roarke sighed. "Describe the subject, Lieutenant."

"Right." That she could do. "Caucasian female, early thirties, blonde and gray. About five-five, approximately one-fifteen. Slim build, even features."

"All right then." Pleased, Adrian gave a decisive nod. "Would you say she's traditional, edgy, artistic, flamboyant—"

"Classic."

"Excellent. Now then." Adrian tapped a finger to her lips as she strolled around the shop. "What does she do?"

"She's a doctor."

"Is this her first marriage?"

"Yes."

"Is she madly in love?"

"I guess. Sure. Why else?"

"She may have bought something for her wedding night already. But . . . as her matron of honor, that's where I'd advise you to aim. Classic. Romantic." Adrian opened the door of a tall, narrow cupboard. "Like this."

It was a long sheer robe open over a long shimmering gown. Not quite gray, Eve mused, not really silver. But the color of . . . moonlight, she decided. "That could work."

"Silk, with satin accents at the bodice, the straps. And the back——" Adrian turned it to display the low back with its wisps of crisscrossing satin. "I love the back."

"Yeah, that could work," Eve repeated.

"I wish you had a picture of her. It's an important gift. It should be perfect."

"You want a picture?" Puzzled, but game, Eve pulled out her PPC. She ordered a standard run on Louise Dimatto, then turned the screen around to Adrian to display the photo ID. "That's Louise."

"Oh, that's mag! Isn't she pretty? Can you bring it over here? If I can just scan it—the photo?"

"Well——"

"You'll like this," Roarke said, and took Eve's arm to lead her through the open doorway. As Adrian stationed herself at a computer, Roarke took Eve's PPC, made some adjustment, and printed out Louise's photo. "Use this."

"Perfect. We're the only intimate apparel shop in the city to have this system. Which we would never have been able to afford without Roarke's backing. I scan her photo, and input the data you gave me on her height

259

and weight. Now let's add the Latecht boudoir ensemble—Moonlight Elegance. And have a look."

The computer sent out a beam over the small table, and the beam sent out a swirl of light dots. The light dots shifted, connected.

"A miniholo," Eve murmured.

"In a sense, yes. It takes the data and reconstructs. And . . . There. What do you think?"

Eve bent down for an eye-level study as the hologram of Louise circled inches off the table in the moonlight gown. "I've gotta say, that is seriously iced. It's really close. Maybe she doesn't have quite that much—" Eve wiggled her fingers in front of her own breasts.

"More delicate there?" Adrian made a slight adjustment.

"Okay, yeah. Very frosty. If I had one of these in my department . . . I'm not sure what I'd do with it, but I'd find a use. We can do holos, but not right off a comp station. They use them more in the lab, for forensics. Reconstructing a DB."

"DB?"

"Dead body."

"Oh."

"Sorry." Eve shook her head, straightened. "It's bull's-eye. Thanks."

"I love when it works! The computer says size six, which is also my opinion from the data, but—"

"That's my information," Roarke assured her.

"Excellent. Still, if for any reason it doesn't work for her, she can bring it back. I'll box and wrap it for you. But in the meantime. Mini Waterfall, wasn't it? We have

260

your data on here already, so this will just take a moment."

Eve barely blinked before Louise disappeared and she saw her own form wearing the short, nearly transparent gown. "Holy shit."

Adrian laughed. "It looks delicious on you. You're never wrong," she said to Roarke.

"We'll have that as well."

Eve swallowed, ordered herself to look away from herself and couldn't. "Would you turn that off? It's strangely disturbing."

"Of course." Still beaming at Eve, Adrian ordered the image off. "Is there anything else while you're here? Do you have enough tanks?"

"Enough what?"

"Support tanks. You prefer them to a bra for work."

Eve opened her mouth, but couldn't quite choke out a word.

"She could probably use a half dozen," Roarke said.

"I'll take care of it."

"I know you will." Roarke leaned over to kiss Adrian's cheek. "We're going out to dinner. Why don't you wrap all that up, put it on the account, and have it sent?"

"My pleasure. Sincerely, Lieutenant."

"Thanks."

"Our best to Liv," Roarke added as he led Eve out.

"She knows what I'm wearing under my clothes. She knows what I look like naked. Yes, this is very disturbing."

"It's her business to know," Roarke pointed out.

"And however attractive she may find you, she's devoted to Liv."

"That's not the point. That is not the point. And people wonder why I hate shopping. I want that wine. A really big glass of it."

"I can take care of that." He put an arm around her shoulders, kissed the side of her head as they walked across Madison.

It was good and it was right, Eve thought later, to remember her actual life now and again. To step away from the work, even just for a few hours, and enjoy sitting at a sidewalk table on a balmy May evening in the city, drinking good wine and eating good food with the man she loved.

She leaned across the table toward him. "Consider this the wine talking."

He leaned toward her so their foreheads nearly touched. "All right."

"You're never wrong, just like she said."

"About the nightgown?"

"That's for you, and we both know it. About dinner. Here. Us. It's a good thing."

"It is a good thing."

"I don't remember to give you the good things enough."

"Eve." He closed his hand over hers on the table. "I think you remember exactly the right amount."

"That's the wine talking."

"Maybe. Or my calculating getting you in—and out—of that nightgown tonight."

"Slick operator." She sat back, took a long breath as she watched people, watched traffic. Hurry, hurry by. "It's a good city," she said quietly. "It's not pure and it's not perfect. It has some nasty edges, some hard lines. But it's a good city. We both chose it."

"I've never asked you why, exactly. Why you did choose it."

"Escape." Her brows lifted as she frowned into her wine. "Maybe it is the wine for that to be the first thought. I guess it was a part of the motivation. It was big enough to swallow me if I needed it to. It's fast, and I wanted fast, and the crowds. The work. I needed the work more than I needed to breathe back then."

"That hasn't changed overmuch."

"Maybe not, but I'm breathing now." She lifted her wine, sipped.

"So you are."

"When I came here, I knew. I can't explain why, but I knew. This is my place. Then there was Feeney. He saw something in me, and he lifted me out. He made me more than I ever thought I could be. This was my place, but if he'd transferred to Bumfuck, Idaho, I'd have gone with him."

Had she ever thought of that before? Eve wondered. Ever realized or admitted that? She wasn't sure.

"Why did you choose it?" she asked Roarke.

"I dreamed of New York when I was a boy. It seemed like a shiny gold ring, and I wanted my fingers around it. I wanted a lot of places, and did what I did to get them. But here's where I wanted my base. That shiny gold ring. I didn't want to be swallowed; I wanted to own. To own here."

He looked around, as Eve had, to the crowds, the traffic, the rush. "Well, that's saying something, isn't it? Then I fell for it, like a man might fall for a fascinating and dangerous woman. And it became more than the owning—the proving to myself, and I suppose, a dead man—and became more about being."

"And you brought Summerset here."

"I did."

She sipped her wine. "Fathers make a difference, and they don't have to be blood to do it. We both found fathers, or they found us, however it worked. It made a difference."

"And you're thinking Alex Ricker lost his, the day he learned his father murdered his mother. And that made a difference."

"You read me pretty well."

"I do indeed. Let's go home, get to work."

She waited while he paid the check, then rose with him. "Thanks for dinner."

"You're welcome."

"Roarke?" On the sidewalk she stopped, studied his face, then shrugged. "What the hell, it's New York." And threw her arms around him, took his mouth in a long, shimmering kiss. "For reading me well," she said when she released him.

"I'm buying a bloody case of that wine."

She laughed all the way to the car.

*

At home, she peeled off her jacket, tossed it on the sleep chair. In shirtsleeves, she circled her murder board.

"You said you were going to work from home, too. To Caro," Eve reminded him.

"So I am. But not before you tell me what you plan to do."

"I'm thinking about asking you to contact your new best friend before getting started on your own stuff."

"And why would I be doing that?"

It *had* to be the wine, she thought, because sometimes when he talked—just the way that hint of Celtic music wove through the words—she wanted to drool. "Um." She shook it off. "To tell him it's important that both he and his PA stay in New York. And that I'd like to talk with each of them tomorrow."

"On a Saturday. When you're hosting a party."

"I can do it in the morning. Peabody and Nadine are invading with God knows what stuff. I don't have to do any of that. They said."

"Easy, darling. And I'd be telling my new best friend this because?"

"Show of good faith. I'm inclined to believe him, blah, blah. I want to discuss some details tomorrow morning that may help me with a current line of investigation."

"And put the heat on Sandy. Could work. I'll do that. I'll be a couple hours, I expect, after. You do remember I'm off to Vegas tomorrow?"

"I . . ." Now she did. "Yeah, yeah, male debauchery."

"I could probably juggle things and go with you in the morning, as Peabody's occupied."

"No. No. You've juggled enough." She could take it alone, but he'd get pissy about that. And he'd have a point, she admitted. "I'll get Baxter."

"All right then."

Armed with coffee, Eve sat down to write up her notes. She ordered a secondary run on Rod Sandy, including his financials. The man had been in the Ricker stew since college, Eve thought. A long time.

He'd know how to tuck money away here and there. Maybe money paid by the father to betray the son.

She scanned the EDD reports on the data mined from the 'links and comps confiscated from the Ricker penthouse. Nothing to Omega, of course. It wouldn't be that easy. Nothing to Coltraine but the single contact from Alex asking her over for a drink. Nothing to Coltraine's precinct or any member of her squad.

But a smart guy like Sandy? He wouldn't leave that clear a trace—one, in fact, his pal Alex might stumble on and question.

Second pocket 'link somewhere. Stashed, hidden, already ditched?

She checked her wrist unit. Hours, she thought, still hours before Callendar docked, much less started digging. Eve told herself to consider it time to refine her theory, to check for wrong turns.

She poured more coffee, had barely begun when Roarke stepped back in. "You reach Alex?"

"Yes, that's done and he's expecting you about nine. Eve, Morris was at the gate. I had Summerset let him through."

"Morris?"

"On foot."

"Oh, shit." She pushed away from her desk, and started downstairs. "What condition is he in? Is he—"

"I didn't ask. I thought it best to get him here. Summerset sent a cart down to him."

"A cart?"

"God, how long have you lived here? One of the autocarts. It'll bring him straight here."

"How am I supposed to know we have autocarts? Do I ever use an autocart? What's your take?" she demanded of Summerset as she came down the last flight of stairs. "His condition?"

"Lost. Not geographically. Sober. In pain."

Eve stood, dragging her hands through her hair. "Do some coffee thing," she told Summerset. "Or . . . maybe we should let him get drunk. I don't know. What should we do here? I don't know what to do for him."

"Then figure it out." Summerset moved to the door. Then he paused, turned back to her. "A drunk only clouds the pain for a time, so it comes back sharper. Coffee's best when you listen to him as that's what he'll need. Someone who cares who'll listen to him."

He opened the door. "Go on, go on. He'll do better if you go to him."

"Don't kick at me," she muttered, but went out.

The cart was nearly silent as he cruised sedately down the drive, made a graceful turn. It stopped at the base of the steps.

"I'm sorry." Morris rubbed his hands over his face like a man coming out of sleep. "I'm so sorry. I don't know why I came. I shouldn't have." He got off the cart

267

as she went down the stairs. "I wasn't thinking. I'm sorry."

She held out a hand. "Come inside, Li."

He shuddered, as if fighting a terrible pain, and only shook his head. She knew pain, and the fight against it, so moved to him, and took his weight, some of the grief when his arms came around her.

"There," Summerset murmured. "She's figured it out, hasn't she?"

Roarke put a hand on Summerset's shoulder. "Coffee would be good, I think. And something . . . I doubt he's eaten."

"I'll see to it."

"Come inside," Eve repeated.

"I didn't know where to go, what to do. I couldn't go home after . . . Her brother took her. I went and I watched them . . . They loaded her on the transpo. In a box. She's not there. Who knows that better? But I couldn't stand it. I couldn't go home. I don't even know how I got here."

"It doesn't matter. Come on." She kept an arm around him, walked him up the stairs where Roarke waited.

15

"I'm intruding, interrupting."

"You're not." Eve steered him toward the parlor. "Let's go sit down. We're going to have some coffee." His hands were cold, she thought, and his body felt fragile. There were always more victims than the dead.

Who knew better?

She led him to a chair by the fire, relieved she didn't have to ask Roarke to light one. Anticipating her, he already was, so she pulled a chair around, angling it so she sat facing Morris.

"It was easier, somehow," Morris began, "when there were details to see to. Easier somehow to go through the steps. The memorial, it centered me. Somehow. Her brother—helping him—it was something that had to be done. Then she was gone. She's gone. And it's final, and there's nothing for me to do."

"Tell me about her. Some small thing, something not important. Just something."

"She liked to walk in the city. She'd rather walk than take a cab, even when it was cold."

"She liked to see what was going on, be part of it," Eve prompted.

"Yes. She liked the night, walking at night. Finding some new place to have a drink or listen to music. She wanted me to teach her how to play the saxophone. She had no talent for it whatsoever. God." A shudder ran through him. Racked him. "Oh, God."

"But you tried to teach her."

"She'd be so serious about it, but the noise—you'd never call it music—that came out would make her laugh. She'd push the sax at me, and tell me to play something. She liked to stretch out on the couch and ask me to play."

"You can see her there?"

"Yes. Candlelight on her face, that half smile of hers. She'd relax and watch me play."

"You can see her there," Eve repeated. "She's not gone."

He pressed the heels of his hands to his eyes.

Panicked, Eve looked over at Roarke. And he nodded, centered her. So she kept talking.

"I've never lost anyone who mattered," Eve told Morris. "Not like this. For a long time, I didn't have anyone who mattered. So I don't know. Not all the way. But I feel, because of what I do. I feel. I don't know how people get through it, Morris, I swear to Christ I don't know how they put one foot in front of the other. I think they need something to hold on to. You can see her, and you can hold on to that."

Morris dropped his hands, stared down at them. Empty. "I can. Yes, I can. I'm grateful, to both of you. I keep leaning on you. And here, I've turned up on your doorstep, pushing this into your evening."

"Stop. Death's a bastard," Eve said. "When the bastard comes, the ones left need family. We're family."

Summerset wheeled in a small table. Businesslike and efficient, he moved it between Eve and Morris. "Dr Morris, you'll have some soup now."

"I—"

"It's what you need. This is what you need."

"Would you see the blue suite on the third floor's prepared." Roarke moved forward now to sit on the arm of Eve's chair. "Dr Morris will be staying tonight."

Morris started to speak, then just closed his eyes, took a breath. "Thank you."

"I'll take care of it." When Summerset started out, Eve slid out of the chair and went after him. She caught him at the doorway, spoke quietly.

"You didn't tranq that soup, did you?"

"Certainly not."

"Okay, don't get huffy."

"I am never *huffy*."

"Fine. Whatever." She had more important things to do than wrangle with Summerset.

"Lieutenant," he said as she turned away. "It will likely be a very long while before I ever repeat this, if that day should ever come. But I'll say now, at this precise moment, I'm proud of you."

Her jaw very nearly slammed into the toes of her boots. She goggled at his stiff, skinny back as he walked away. "Weird," she muttered. "Very, very weird."

She went back inside, took her seat. It relieved her that Morris ate, that his voice was back to steady as he and Roarke talked. "Some part of my brain must have been functioning, because it brought me here."

"You'll talk to Mira, when you're ready?"

Morris considered Roarke's question. "I suppose I will. I know what she'll offer. I know it's right. We deal with it every day. As you said, Dallas, we feel."

"I don't know what you think about this sort of thing," Eve began. "But I know this priest."

A faintest ghost of a smile touched Morris's mouth. "A priest."

"A Catholic guy, from this case I worked."

"Oh yes, Father Lopez, from Spanish Harlem. I spoke with him during that business."

"Sure. Right. Well, anyway . . . There's something about him. Something solid, I guess. Maybe, if you wanted someone outside of the circle, outside of the job, you know, you could talk to him."

"I was raised Buddhist."

"Oh, well . . ."

That ghost of a smile remained. "And as I grew up, I experimented and toyed with a variety of faiths. The organized sort, I found, didn't stick with me. But it might be helpful to talk with this priest. Do you believe there's more, after death?"

"Yes," Eve answered without hesitation. "No way we go through all this crap, then that's it. If it is, I'm going to be seriously pissed off."

"Exactly. I feel them, and I'm sure you do, too. Sometimes when they come to me, it's done. They've gone, and all I have is the shell of what they were. Others, there's more. It lingers awhile. You know?"

"Yeah." It wasn't something she easily expressed, or shared. But she knew. "It's harder to take when it lingers."

"For me, it's hopeful. She was gone when I saw her. I wanted, selfishly, to feel her. But she'd gone, wherever she needed to go. I needed to be reminded of that, I think. That she's not gone, not from me, because I can see her. And that she's somewhere she needs to be. Yes, Father Lopez may help me come to terms. But so can you."

"What do you need?"

"Bring me in. Tell me what you know, all of it, everything. Not just what you think I should know, but everything. And give me something to do, some part of it. However mundane. Fact-checking or follow-ups, buying fucking doughnuts for the team. I need to be involved. I need to have some part in finding the person who did this."

She studied his face. Yes, the need was there. The intensity of it nearly burned a hole in her heart. "You have to tell me this, tell me straight. Respect her, respect me, and tell me the truth."

"I will."

"What do you want when we find him? What do you want done?"

"You're asking if I want to kill him, to take his life?"

"That's what I'm asking."

"I thought of it, even imagined it. There are so many ways, and in my position a lot of avenues to take. I did think of it. It would be for me, and not for her. It wouldn't be what she wanted. I would . . . disappoint her. How could I do that? I want what she would want."

"What is that?"

"Justice. There are a lot of colors there, though, a lot

of degrees and levels. We know that, too." His gaze skimmed to Roarke. "All of us know that. I want his pain, and I want his pain to last a very long time. Death ends—at least this part of us. I don't want his death, and I'll promise you on hers that I'll do nothing to end him. I want him in a cage, years, decades in a cage. Then I want him in whatever hell might exist when death ends that. I want a part of making that happen."

He reached across the table now, gripped her hand. "Eve. I won't betray her, or you. I swear to you."

"Okay. You're in." She picked up her coffee. "I'm going to start by telling you she was clean. There's no evidence that she was on the take or in anybody's pocket. All evidence is to the contrary. She ended her relationship with Alex Ricker in Atlanta. Her only connection to him was friendship."

"Did he kill her?"

"It's not tipping that way. It's reading like she was killed because of him, but not by him, and not with his knowledge, not through his orders, his wishes. I think Max Ricker ordered it done to punish the son, to screw with him."

"He killed her to . . . Yes, I can see that." When he picked up his coffee, Morris's hand remained steady. "I can easily see that now."

"To do it, he'd need someone close to Alex, and someone close to Col—to Ammy," she corrected. "I have two e-detectives on their way to Omega now. I think Ricker's got someone up there covering his visitor and communication log. I think he's been in touch, and he's been orchestrating this—maybe more than this. I'm

274

going to see Alex in the morning—but more, I'm going to see his personal assistant. That's the guy I'm looking at. Nobody's closer to Alex than this guy, this Rod Sandy. On the other part, I'm looking at her squad."

"One of her squad?" Morris set his cup down again. "Jesus. Jesus."

"It was an inside hit—inside her world, inside Alex Ricker's. I know it."

For a long moment, he stared at the fire. Stared in silence.

"I didn't think you were so close. I didn't believe you'd gotten this far. I should've known better. What can I do?"

"You can spend some time tonight thinking about anything she told you about the people she worked with. Little things: comments, observations, complaints, jokes. Anything you remember. Anything you observed personally when you went to see her at work, when you joined her for a drink, for a meal with anyone in her squad. Note it down."

"I will. I can do that."

"And try to sleep. You're no good to me if your brain's fuzzed up with exhaustion. Think, note, sleep. I'm heading out in the morning to interview Alex and his PA. Send anything to my unit here, and I'll review. I can talk to you more about it when I get back."

His eyes held hers, and they were sharp again—the dullness honed away by purpose. "All right. I'll start right away."

"Why don't I take you up?" Roarke rose.

"I was just coming to do so." Summerset walked in.

"Let me show you your room, Dr Morris, and you can tell me if there's anything else you need."

"Thank you." Morris looked back at Eve. "I have what I need."

As Morris left with Summerset, Roarke skimmed a hand over Eve's hair. "You're no good to me if your brain's fuzzed up with exhaustion. I don't know how you could choke those words out without them burning off your tongue. Nicely done, though. He'll will himself to sleep because of it."

"That's the plan. I need to finish up, and stow the murder board. I won't have him wander into my office and see that." She smiled at him as she rose. "It was nice what you did, seeing that he stayed here tonight."

Roarke took her hand. "We're family."

Somewhere in the dim hours of the morning, Eve felt herself being lifted. She managed to focus about the time Roarke carried her into the elevator from her office.

"Damn it, I conked. What time is it?"

"Around two, fuzzy-brain."

"Sorry. Sorry."

"It happens I got caught up myself, and the work took longer than I'd anticipated. I just surfaced myself."

"Oh." She yawned. "Maybe I should be carrying you."

"Easy to say now that I'm hauling you into the bedroom." Crossing it, he dumped her unceremoniously on the bed. "And I doubt either of us have the energy for a sexy new nightgown."

She managed to pull off a boot, toss it. "I don't know. I could fuel up if you put one on."

"Aren't you the funny one when you're asleep on your feet?"

She tossed the second boot. "I'm not on my feet." She dragged off her shirt, wriggled out of her pants. Then crawled up the bed. "Screw nightgowns," she muttered, then snuggled down in her underwear.

When Roarke slipped in beside her, she was already asleep again.

In the dream, Coltraine circled Eve's murder board. She wore a pale blue sweater and trimly tailored pants, and her weapon at her hip.

"I worked murder cases a couple of times," she said. "Not as primary, but part of a team. A break-in or mugging gone bad, that kind of thing. It always depressed me. I can't say I ever thought someone would be working my murder."

"Who does?"

Coltraine smiled over at Eve. "Good point. You know more about me now than you did when you started."

"That's usually the way it works."

"Some of it you're getting through Li's eyes. You can't trust that a hundred percent."

"No, but he won't lie."

"No, he won't." Coltraine moved over to where Eve sat at her desk, then leaned a hip on it. "I used to think you had to be cold to be a murder cop. Cold enough to walk in death every day, or nearly every day. To pick through lives, uncover all the secrets of people who couldn't hide them anymore. But I was wrong. You have to be able to control the heat, but there has to be heat. Otherwise, you wouldn't give a damn, not really. You wouldn't care enough to do what you have to do to chase murder."

"Sometimes it takes the cold."

"Maybe. I know more about you now, too, seeing as you've got me stuck in your head. You struggle with the law, because you have such intense and marrow-deep respect for it. Such strong belief. But it's the victim who pulls you, the victim who might have you question that line of law. More even than justice, and justice is your faith."

"This isn't about me."

"You know it is. We're as intimate as lovers now. Cop/victim. I'm one of the faces in your head now, in your dreams. You never forget them, no matter how many there are. That's your burden, and your gift. You let Li in, when the rules and regs come down against that. He's too close. But you've blurred the rules and regs because he's a victim, too. And he needed it. It's the cold part of you that's questioning that now, in the back of your mind. And it's the heat that knows it's right."

"Which part of you walked away from Alex Ricker?"

"That's a question, isn't it?" Coltraine rose, bent down to stroke Galahad as he bumped against her leg. "Nice cat."

"How about an answer?"

"You're wondering if I walked because he didn't love me enough to pull back from that line. To show me how much I mattered. Or if I walked because I remembered I was a cop, and I had a duty to that line of the law."

"It doesn't matter." Eve shrugged. "You walked, and that's what plays here."

"It matters to you, because of Li. It matters because of the badge. And it matters because you wonder what you would've done, if Roarke hadn't shown you how much you mattered."

"Not altogether. One and two, that's true. But the last? He shows me every day. I think I get how much you hurt when Alex didn't, because I don't have to wonder. I know. And I don't think it was the cop who walked. I think the cop came after. I think, maybe, you were a better cop once you came here."

"That's nice. Thanks. Still, I wasn't a good enough cop to keep myself from being taken out with my own damn weapon."

"Yeah, that's a bitch. But I'm looking at you, Detective. I'm looking at the way I think this set you up. And I'm thinking you didn't have a chance in hell."

"Well." Coltraine set her hands on her hips. "That's a real comfort to me now."

"Best I got."

A soft spring drizzle greeted Eve when she strode outside to meet Baxter. She watched him whip his snazzy two-seater down the drive and jerked a thumb at the unsnazzy body of her own vehicle.

"Aw, come on, Dallas, why take your latest hunk of junk when I've got my primo?"

"Official business, and I'm driving."

"A man's gotta haul his ass out of bed on a rainy Saturday, and he can't even set it down in a decent ride." He grumbled all the way, but transferred his ass from one car to the other. "Well, nice seats, I gotta say."

"Is your ass all comfy now?"

"Actually it is. Surprising how . . . what, whoa." He leaned forward to goggle at the dash. "Look at this! Sizzling Jesus, this heap is loaded. It's—"

He broke off, flung back against the seat as she poured it on down the drive. "And she fucking moves, baby! This is not departmental issue. I am not a fool."

"Depends on who you're asking. And I have the option, per regs, of using my personal ride if it meets code. Just like you use that toy back there."

"Dallas, you have depths I've never plumbed."

"You never plumbed any of my depths."

"That's your loss, sister. And Peabody never said a word about this ride."

Eve actually winced as she remembered. "She hasn't seen it yet. So you'll keep it zipped about it. Otherwise, she'll get all whiny about not seeing it first, or some such shit. Partners can be ass pains."

"Not mine. Boy's a jewel. So, you figure Ricker Junior's PA and bestest pal fucked him over and killed Coltraine."

"Killed her or helped set her up for it. And set up Alex Ricker for good measure."

"Bestest pals can be ass pains."

She had to laugh. "You can't begin to know. We'll work them separate. Start out straight interview. Just going over details. Then I'm going to peel Sandy off, leave you on Ricker. I want to heat him up, and I don't want his bestest pal getting in the way."

"Works for me. You really don't figure Junior's in it? Motive's there, opportunity, even with the alibi. All he had to do was snap his fingers."

"If he was going to snap them, he'd have snapped them long-distance. His old man set him up, it's just like him. Once we pin Sandy, he's going to flip. He's a turncoat, so he'll turn again. And we'll skewer whoever Ricker has in the Eighteenth Squad."

"I hate it's a cop. But yeah, I went through the files, your notes. It's gotta be."

Eve's in-dash beeped. "Dallas."

"Callendar reporting from Omega." Callendar's face, tired eyes, major grin, filled the screen. "There was some delay at docking, but Sisto and I are in. We're cleared and logged, and about to be escorted straight to Communications. The warden's authorized us access to . . . well, pretty much everything."

"Get me something, Callendar."

"If it's here, we'll get it. Man-o, this place is grim. You ever been here?"

"No."

"Good choice. Even the staff and admin areas are grim. I bet if you gave kids a mandatory tour of this place, they'd never so much as think about boosting somebody's airboard." She glanced away, signaled. "They're ready for us."

"I want to hear the minute you have anything. Even half of anything."

"Cha. Back when. Callendar out."

"Cha?" Eve repeated.

"As in 'gotcha'." Baxter rolled his eyes. "E-geeks."

Eve shook her head, in perfect accord. "E-geeks."

She swung to the curb at Ricker's building. "On duty," she said and preened a little when her light flashed on.

"Solid."

"If we wrap this, I'll show you how she verticals as we head back."

She badged her way in, moved straight to the elevator when the doorman said they were already cleared and expected by Mr Ricker.

He met them in the foyer. "Lieutenant."

"Mr Ricker. Detective Baxter. We appreciate you making time to answer a few more questions."

His tone was as polite and neutral as Eve's. "I want to cooperate in any way I can."

"As discussed, we'd also like to speak to Mr Sandy."

"Yes. He's probably in the kitchen, getting coffee. Please sit down. I'll get him."

"Prime digs," Baxter commented as he looked around. "And they say crime doesn't pay."

"Only idiots say that."

"The world's full of idiots."

Alex came back alone. "Sorry, he's generally an early riser, so I assumed . . . He must be upstairs. Excuse me."

As Alex started up, Eve and Baxter exchanged glances.

"You thinking what I'm thinking?" Baxter murmured.

"Somebody's gone rabbit. Goddamn it. Routine

follow-up, what spooked him? There's nothing here to make him bolt, risk his position, turn our suspicions. It's stupid."

"Lieutenant." Alex came to the top of the stairs, and she saw it in the pale set of his face. "Rod isn't here. His bed hasn't been slept in. I won't object if you want to look for yourself."

Damn right they would. Eve started up. "When did you last see him?"

"Last night, about eight. He had a date. But he knew you were expected this morning. It's not like him to miss an appointment. And he's not answering his 'link. I just tried it."

Eve walked to the doorway of Sandy's room. "Who's the date?"

"I don't know. I didn't ask."

She moved past Alex to check the closet, then frowned. "His things are still here. Anything missing, that you can tell?"

"Whatever he wore last night—ah, let me think. He had on a brown leather jacket, black pants, I think. I can't recall what color shirt. Casual. A casual date. His clothes are here, as far as I can tell. But why wouldn't they be? He had no reason to leave, and wouldn't leave without telling me."

"Maybe it was a sudden decision," Baxter suggested with just enough sarcasm to have Alex turn frigid eyes on him.

"He doesn't make sudden decisions, and he works for me. He's my oldest friend, and he works for me. Obviously, the date turned into something more than casual, and he stayed the night. He's overslept and doesn't hear his 'link. I'm perfectly willing to answer any questions you have for me now, and I'll see to it that Rod makes himself available to you as soon as he gets back."

He turned to Eve then. "I didn't contact my lawyers. They don't even know you're here. I'm not playing you. Rod just—"

"Got lucky?" Eve suggested. "Baxter, wait for me downstairs."

"Sure."

"Rod's done nothing but be careless about an appointment," Alex began.

"Stow it. Who was your driver yesterday?"

Biting and cold replaced polite and neutral. "And that's relevant because?"

"Because I want to know, Mr Cooperation. Who drove you to your meet with Roarke?"

"Carmine. Carmine Luca," he added when Eve simply stared. "He's downstairs, in an apartment I keep as staff quarters."

"Bring him up."

"I don't understand why you want to interview my driver."

"You'll understand after I do. Bring him up, or call your lawyers and tell them to meet you downtown."

Eyes, already cool, went to ice. "Maybe I misjudged the situation. I'll bring him up, and we'll see if you make me understand. Otherwise, unless you've got a warrant, you're gone."

Alex pulled out a 'link as he pointed Eve toward the door. "Carmine, I need you up here."

Within minutes, the big, burly Carmine lumbered in. He had, Eve thought, a face like stone that had been battered for decades by wind and water. Tough, pitted, and blank.

"These officers would like to ask you some questions, Carmine. Answer them, is that clear?"

"Yes, sir, Mr Ricker."

"When did Rod Sandy ask you about Mr Ricker's meeting with Roarke?"

"I don't know about any meeting."

Eve looked at Alex. "Would you like to make it clearer, or should I?"

"Carmine, I want you to answer the lieutenant's questions. I had a meeting with Roarke yesterday morning, on Coney Island. You drove me."

"Yes, sir, Mr Ricker, but I thought—"

"Don't think," Alex said, with a kindness in his tone Eve hadn't expected. "I appreciate it, Carmine, but we're just trying to clear something up. So you can answer the questions. Unless I say otherwise. All right?"

"Yes, sir, Mr Ricker."

"When did Rod Sandy ask you about Mr Ricker's meeting with Roarke."

"Which time?"

"All the times."

"Okay, well, he asked me about it before. Making sure and all that everything was set up. Mr Sandy makes sure things are set up for Mr Ricker. So I told him how it was all go, and we had the car ready, and the scanners—" He stopped, looked at Alex.

"It's all right."

"And the coffee in the mini-AC. And all like that."

"He asked you about it afterward, too?"

"He asked, after, how Mr Ricker was feeling. You know, his state of mind and stuff. And I said how it went okay, and maybe Mr Ricker seemed a little down on the drive back. But it went okay, and there wasn't no trouble or nothing. I said how it seemed like Mr Ricker and Roarke got along pretty good, and how they talked awhile. He worries about you, Mr Ricker. It's Mr Sandy, so I didn't figure it was talking out of turn or nothing."

"It's all right, Carmine."

"What else did you tell him?" Eve asked.

Carmine's gaze slid to Alex again, and again Alex gave the assent. "Not much to tell. We had a beer, and we were talking about the game some, and he was saying, sort of thinking out loud, like, that Mr Ricker and Roarke would do this business deal after all. So I said, I didn't think it was any kind of business deal. How I didn't catch much, 'cause you're not supposed to listen, but the breeze carried the voices sometimes. How it seemed they were mostly talking about Miss Coltraine and Mr Ricker's father, and how maybe—"

"Maybe?"

"Mr Ricker."

"Keep going," Alex demanded, not so kindly now.

"Well, it sounded like maybe Mr Ricker thought his father might've done something. I was just talking to Mr Sandy, Mr Ricker."

"Yes, you were," Eve said before Alex could speak. "Did you talk to him about anything else?"

"Not really. I didn't hear that much. I wasn't trying to hear, I swear. I guess, now that I think about it, Mr Sandy asked a lot of questions, and he wasn't exactly happy I didn't know more than I knew. I just said how at the end you and Roarke shook hands, and that was that."

"That's fine, Carmine, thank you," Alex said. "You can go back to your quarters now."

"Yes, sir, Mr Ricker. If I did anything—"

"You didn't. We're fine."

"One more thing," Eve said. "Did you drive Mr Sandy anywhere yesterday?"

"No. I drive Mr Ricker, unless Mr Ricker says different."

"Did you or anyone drive Mr Sandy anywhere this week?"

"No. We only got the one car here, and I drive it. Right, Mr Ricker?"

"That's right, Carmine. You can go."

Alex turned, walked into the living area, sat. "You think Rod's working for my father."

"And you don't?" Eve countered.

"We've known each other more than a dozen years. We're friends. Friends. He knows nearly everything there is to know about me. He knew what Ammy meant to me. You can't expect me to believe he's part of this."

"Why didn't you tell him the details of your meeting with Roarke?"

"It was private. Even friends don't share everything."

"I'd say, from the way Sandy pumped Carmine, he doesn't agree with that."

287

Alex pressed his fingers to his eyes. "So he was never really my friend. Just another tool. All these years."

"Maybe, or maybe one picked up and turned more recently."

"If he killed Ammy—"

"Could he have left the apartment that night, without security picking it up?"

"There are always ways," Alex said. "Yes. The son of a bitch. The son of a bitch said to me, that night, he said I should go out, take a long walk, hit Times Square, get some energy from the crowds. So I did."

"He indicated he thought you were in the apartment all night."

"We lie, Lieutenant." Alex clipped out the words. "You know that. I assumed he was covering me, so I did the same and told you I'd gone out when he was upstairs. That he didn't know I'd gone out. Just a couple of convenient lies. I hadn't hurt her. I would never have hurt her. So we covered each other. He set me up, my longtime friend, so I'm out walking New York, having a beer, just one more face in the crowd, while he's killing her. For what? For what?"

"Where would he go?"

"A thousand places. If I knew, I swear I'd tell you. He convinced me to come to New York," Alex explained. "To come now—for business, for her. Convinced me I needed to see her, talk with her. He knew how I felt, was feeling. I confided in him, like I would a brother. And he used it against me."

"I want all the data on his financials. All his financials. You understand me?"

"Yes. You'll have it."

"He takes trips, vacations, and so on without you. Time off where you wouldn't keep tabs on him."

"Of course."

Times he could've visited Omega, Eve thought. "Do you know who your father has in Coltraine's squad?"

"No. I don't know that he has anyone, not that I can confirm. He was always proprietary about that kind of thing."

"What did you and your father talk about when you visited him on Omega?"

"Nothing that applies to this."

"Everything applies to this."

Anger flashed across his face. "Understand I'm under no obligation to answer you, or to cooperate in this matter. But I'll tell you that I made it clear to my father I wouldn't be back, wouldn't communicate with him in any way. That I'd come to see him only because I wanted to look at him—this last time—and know he was exactly where I wanted him to be."

"And his response?"

"He didn't need me, or want me. He promised to bring me down, and when he was done with me I'd have nothing. As nothing was what I deserved. That was the gist."

Alex closed his eyes, fought for control. "What could he have offered Rod to have him do this? What could he have promised him he couldn't have asked me for?"

"You're going to tell me everything you know about Sandy, everything not on his official data. And you're going to get me those financials. While you do, Detective Baxter's going to turn his room inside out. Record on," she ordered. "Mr Ricker, do we have your permission to search the quarters of Rod Sandy on this premises, at this time?"

"Yes, you do. You have my permission to search his room, my permission to hunt him down like a dog. My permission to do whatever it takes to take him down. Is that enough?"

"It's a good start. Baxter."

"I'm on it."

Eve sat. "Tell me about Rod Sandy."

16

Eve pushed, shoved, and bullied her way through Saturday morning traffic. Beside her, Baxter worked furiously on the in-dash auxiliary computer.

"We need an e-man if we want to get into some of these accounts," he told her. "I can pull up the standard ones. No major activity over the last ten days. But the others are trickier. It's going to take me some time."

"I've got an e-man. Recheck the transportation."

"He didn't get on any public transpo out of the city, not using his legit ID. Private's going to take longer. And private's the way he'd go. He could've taken a cab or a car service out of New York and picked up a private any damn where with the lead he's got on us."

"He's got to tap one of his accounts." There was always a trail, Eve thought, and money was the biggest breadcrumb. "And he'll contact Ricker on Omega. He does what he's told. He's a drone, just a goddamn drone. He'll follow instructions, if not direct from Ricker, then from whoever Ricker's got working him."

"He panicked, left with the clothes on his back, whatever cash he had, probably some files. But the panic's working for him."

"Not for long. He may get out, get away, but he's already a dead man. Jesus, Baxter," she said when he turned to her. "Ricker's not going to let him run loose. His value just bottomed out. He's worthless. We find him first or Ricker's going to shut him down."

Too impatient to wait for the gates, Eve hit vertical and soared over them. Baxter said, "Yee-haw."

"We find which account he tapped." Eve tore down the drive. "When he tapped it, and backtrack to where he was when he tapped it. We search on private transpo, starting in the city, working out. And we call in the locals on all of Sandy's and all of Alex Ricker's residences. He'll want a place to catch his breath, to pick up more of his things. If he's got any brains, and he does, he'll be quick about that and he's already gone. But we find out where he was, and we'll start tracking where he goes from there."

She swung out of the car, strode up the steps.

"You." She jabbed a finger at the lurking Summerset. "Be useful. Contact Feeney and McNab, tell them I need them here. Now. Baxter, call in your boy," she added as she headed upstairs.

"You recall," Summerset called after her, "you're hostessing a bridal shower in approximately six hours."

The sound Eve made was perilously close to a scream.

"Bridal shower?" Baxter repeated.

"Shut up. Shut up. Never speak of it." She rounded toward her office and nearly ran into Morris.

Baxter pulled up short. "Ah, hey, Morris."

"You've got something," Morris said.

"Got someone, lost him, now we're going to find

him." She pushed past him, then let out an oath when she saw the connecting door between her office and Roarke's was closed. The red light over it indicated he was working.

She'd owe him, she told herself. Big-time.

She knocked.

When he opened the door, irritation sparked in his eyes. "Eve. Closed door. Red light."

"I'm sorry, I'll grovel later if you want it." Beyond him she could see several suited figures. Holo-meeting, she realized, and figured the groveling would be major. "I need your help, and I've got a ticking clock."

"Ten minutes," he said and shut the door in her face.

"Man, am I going to pay for that. Baxter, use the auxiliary to keep on the transpo. We need to start pushing through Sandy's friends, relatives, contacts, acquaintances, girlfriends, boyfriends, his fucking tailor. This guy's not a loner. He's tagged someone, somewhere."

"I can help." Morris stood in the center of the room. "Let me help."

She gave him a quick study. He looked rested, and that was a plus. Summerset must have dug up a shirt and pants for him—somewhere. "Morris, I'm going to have to bring my murder board back in here. Can you handle that? Don't say it if you don't mean it."

"Yes."

"I'll have to fill you in as we go. For now, go in there." She gestured toward the kitchen. "Program a whole buncha coffee. It's not just scut work. It's necessary."

"I don't mind scut work."

She went to her desk as he walked to the kitchen.

293

"Computer, all known data on Rod Sandy, on screen one. Priority run authorized, Dallas, Lieutenant Eve."

Acknowledged. Working . . .

"He gets worried," she began as the data began to scroll. "It sets off a little tingle when Alex tells him he's going to meet with Roarke. He's supportive, sure, that's his job. But he worries about it. He chews on it. Pumps the driver because he's not sure—not a hundred percent—that something in that conversation didn't set off a bell that rings too close to him. Can't pry too deep with Alex, and have that bell ringing any louder. The driver's not too bright. Loyal, but not too bright, and hey, it's Mr Sandy and he's got some prime brew."

She paced, studying the data as she worked it through.

"He gets enough from the driver to turn the worry up to some serious concern. What does he do next? He needs somebody to tell him what to do. Does he contact Ricker? No, no, he's a drone. He's a peg. There's a food chain. Drones don't go straight to the top. He contacts his keeper. Whoever worked with him on Coltraine. That's what he does."

She angled her head. "Computer stop scroll. Look at this, how about that? Never takes the lead. Tenth in his graduating class, and there's Alex in first. Cocaptains on the football team senior year, but look who gets MVP. Not our boy Rod, but Alex. And who has to take the VP spot to Alex's class president? Yeah, old runner-up

Rod Sandy again. Never grabs the ring, always second place. I bet he creamed his pants when Max Ricker offered him a chance to turn on his good pal Alex. I bet he wept tears of fucking joy.

"I bet there were women, too, women he wanted that never spared him a second glance because Alex got there first. I bet Coltraine was one of them. She probably knew it, too. Sure, she's smart, she's self-aware. She'd know he had a thing for her. Probably felt sorry for him. He'd have to hate her for that. Helping kill her would've been like a bonus."

She turned to pace again, and saw Morris watching her. "Shit. I'm sorry. I didn't—"

"Don't be." He came to her with coffee, held out the mug he'd poured for her. "I'll get your murder board for you if you tell me where it is. I see her as she was," he added.

"The panels over there open to a storage closet. Any time you need a break . . ."

"Don't worry about me. It's about her."

"No private air transpo out of the city fitting the time frame," Baxter announced. "Not with anyone using his ID, or anyone fitting his description. I'll widen the circle."

"Do that." She went back to her desk to work out a time line, and looked up and over when Roarke came in.

"Groveling can wait," he said before she could speak. "And I have specifics in mind there. But for now, what is it?"

"I've got Feeney and McNab on the way. I need a

detailed and deep search on Sandy's finances. I've got the hideaway accounts from Alex. The ones he knows of. I figure there's at least one more. Sandy's gone rabbit."

"And any self-respecting rabbit needs funds. All right, I'll see what I can find. But you'll be losing your e-team at four."

"But—"

"We'll be leaving, Lieutenant, as arranged, for Vegas. Charles's bachelor party."

"You guys are going to Vegas?" Baxter piped up, looking both sad and hopeful. "I know Charles."

Roarke smiled at him. "Would you like to go, Detective?"

Eve literally waved her hands in the air. "Hey, hey!"

"I'm already there. Can I bring my boy?"

"The more the merrier." Roarke poked a finger at Eve while she sputtered. "You'll be busy yourself. And what we can't find in the next few hours isn't to be found. But, in that unlikely event, I'll program an autosearch."

"I don't see why we couldn't just postpone the whole thing until—"

"Of course you don't. But you're out-voted."

"Life has to be." Morris stepped back from the board he'd set in the center of the room. "Or there's no point."

"Okay, wait. Wait." She had to think. "Until four. But if we pinpoint Sandy's location, or something equally relevant at three-fifty-freaking-nine—"

"We'll cross that bridge," Roarke finished. "Give me

what you have." He took the disc she gave him. "Feeney and McNab? We'll use the computer lab then. Send them along when they get here."

As impatience rubbed against guilt, Eve strode after him. "Listen, did I screw anything up—any important anything—by interrupting?"

"Oh, what's a few million lost now and then in the grand scheme? I'll try to win it back in Vegas."

"Oh God. Oh my God."

Laughing, he caught her horrified face in his hands. "I'm having you on, though I shouldn't let you off that hook so easily. It's fine. But annoying, so you'll be scheduling in that groveling. Now go away. I have other things to see to, besides your e-work, before I leave."

Sure. Fine. She went back to work.

"Nothing," Baxter told her. "I checked on the All-Points. We got a couple of hits, but neither of them turned out to be Sandy. Morris did a recheck on his accounts and cards."

"Still no activity. I can help Baxter with the search, the transportation."

She nodded, went back to her time line. When she completed it, as she posted it on her board, her e-team walked in.

She stared at Feeney. "What are you wearing? Not you," she said to McNab. "I never expect otherwise from you."

"This is my lucky shirt." Feeney jutted out his chin.

The lucky shirt was sea-sick green, and covered with maniacally grinning pink flamingos. On his explosion of hair he wore a black ball cap that had another flamingo leering from the bill.

"Jesus, Feeney, no man gets lucky dressed like that."

"Not that kind of lucky." He shot Baxter a steely glare when the detective hooted. "I got a wife, don't I? This shirt has a history. So far, it's won me eight hundred and a quarter."

"It can't be worth it. Never mind. Comp lab. Roarke's already there. In brief," she began, and gave them the bare bones.

"I think that shirt burned my corneas," she muttered when they left her office.

"E-geeks. What can you do?"

She glanced over at Baxter's comment, and saw Morris, stationed beside him, smile. "Run that auto for a minute. Take a look at the time line." She gestured to the board. "Alex Ricker contacts Roarke at seven-thirty. Summerset tells Alex Roarke will get back to him. Roarke contacts Alex at just after eight, and they set up the meet. Transmission runs eight minutes. Meet at Coney Island at ten. Meet lasts round about thirty minutes. According to Alex, he made two stops before returning to the penthouse. The first, his antique store in Tribeca, which is where I bet the unregistered was taken before our search. He left there approximately thirteen-thirty, and kept a business lunch appointment— verified—in midtown. He didn't return home until sixteen hundred. He states Sandy was in the penthouse at that time. They talked briefly, and during that conversation Alex mentioned that the driver was having the car washed and serviced."

"Bet he started sweating," Baxter said.

"He can't get to the driver until after seventeen hundred. He returns to the penthouse according to the time stamp on the security disc, at seventeen-forty-three. And yeah, he looks a little sweaty. He may have tagged his contact then, but he for damn sure did when Roarke contacted the penthouse and informed Alex that I'd be around the next morning with some follow-up questions. That's at nineteen-oh-five. It's too much. Too many things leaning in. Still, he doesn't leave for another hour. Time to get instructions, grab what he needs most."

"You can't know how much cash he might have had," Morris pointed out. "His own, or what Alex might have had in the place."

"It couldn't be much, couldn't be enough. Alex keeps funds in the penthouse, in a safe, but it's still there. Sandy couldn't open the safe without it signaling Alex. It's programmed. Enough, we'll say enough, for him to get out of the city. Maybe hole up until he can access more, make arrangements. It's all rushed, and he's methodical."

Panic, panic, Eve thought again. What do I do, where do I go?

"Maybe he has a credit account Alex didn't know about, and we haven't found yet. Maybe. Charge the transpo," she calculated, "and into the wind. But if so, we'll find it, and we'll track him. He can't function without funds."

"Reports have been coming in from the locals on some of the hot spots. No sign of him, no sign he's come and gone."

Eve nodded at Baxter. "And I'm betting he'd leave one. He's never had to run before, so he doesn't know how. He's lived a privileged life. He won't last without the privilege." She paused, frowned. "Where the hell is Trueheart?"

"Ah, he was en route, but you know, Vegas. He's making a quick detour. I've got to have proper attire, don't I?"

"You sent him to *pack* for you?"

"I don't need much. Anyway, Morris has it covered."

"Maybe you want to go to Vegas," she snapped at Morris, then instantly winced. "Shit, I—"

"It's almost tempting," he said easily. "That's how confident I am in you. But no, not this time."

She sat at her desk again and began to pick her way through Sandy's people. Parents, divorced, remarried—twice each. One sibling, one half sibling. According to Alex, Sandy wasn't close to any of his family. Still, family was the usual well, wasn't it, when you had to dip in for cash. She started the tedious process of contacting, questioning, intimidating, eliminating.

She barely glanced up when Trueheart came in, but noted Baxter's fresh, young apprentice had obviously dressed for the upcoming festivities. Pressed pants, casual shirt, good skids.

She tried not to think just how Baxter might corrupt sweet and hunky Troy Trueheart in Vegas.

She worked her way through family, current women, and out the other side of exes. She scowled when Summerset wheeled in a large table.

"What?"

300

"Lunch."

"Boy, I could eat." Baxter sat back, skimmed his fingers through his hair. "Got *nada*, Dallas. And my eyes are starting to bleed."

"I'll be using your kitchen," Summerset informed her, "to order up what I've prepared."

She continued to scowl as Summerset walked by her desk, the cat hopefully at his heels.

"When you find nothing," Morris said, "it means you're eliminating what surrounds the something."

"Is that a Zen thing?" Eve questioned.

"If not, it should be."

Eve got to her feet as Roarke, Feeney, and McNab came in. From the opposite end of the room, Summerset pushed in a double-shelved cart she didn't know she possessed.

"I'll give you a hand." McNab made a beeline.

"I have it, Detective. But there's a second cart in the kitchen. If you wouldn't mind."

"Anything I can do that leads to food." McNab all but danced his way on his knee-high purple airboots into the kitchen.

Feeney circled his head on his neck, rolled his shoulders. Eve heard the pops from across the room. "Getting creaky."

"I've arranged for a pair of masseuses on board," Roarke told him.

"You are the *man*." Baxter slapped his hands together.

"Twins."

"Oh, my aching heart."

"Could use a rub. Strictly therapeutic," Feeney added

when he caught Eve's beady eye. "We found the account. He buried it good. He's no dope. Got himself twelve mil and change. Went traditional and used Zurich. Hasn't touched it," he said before Eve could ask. "But we did a little finagle or two. He checked on it— or somebody did—via 'link. The 'link trans came from New York, and the time of the check stamps at sixteen-fifty-five, EST."

"Before he talked to the driver," Eve said, and rose to update her time line. "Starting to cover his bases. Worried."

"None of his accounts have been touched," Roarke put in. "He has bank boxes in four locations." He lifted his brows when Eve turned. "We finagled. He hasn't signed in for any."

"Friends," Feeney offered. "Family."

Eve shook her head. "It's not panning out."

Feeney glanced over at Morris, puffed out his cheeks. "We may have something that does, on Detective Col-traine. The 'link used to check the Zurich account. We dug in there and ID'd it. It's registered to Varied Interests."

"Alex Ricker's company."

"Yeah, company 'link—and we nailed it, and dumped the transes. We got them going to another 'link. Toss-away, can't trace it for ownership, but we got the ID and frequencies. There are transmissions between the 'links, from New York to New York, the day before the murder, the day of, the day after."

"Can you pin it down any closer?"

"Cheap toss-away, that's how it reads. No bells, no whistles. It's damn near impossible to get a read at all on

302

those bastards. It's got a filter on it. Had to be an add-on." Feeney scratched the back of his neck. "But we've got its print. Same as a fingerprint. Good as DNA."

"And if Callendar gets that print, coming into Omega?"

"We can match it."

"She'll get it if it's there." McNab watched Summerset arrange trays of deli meats, bread, cheeses, fruit, vegetables, salads, with the same intense devotion as the cat. "She's an arrow on that kind of thing. When she does, we may be able to put what she's got and what we've got together and make more."

"It's all there is to get with what we have," Roarke told her. "We're running an auto. If any of his accounts are opened—even for a check—or any of his bank boxes are called for, we'll know."

"Okay. It's good."

"So we eat." McNab made the first dive.

Cops, Eve thought, swarming like ants at a picnic. She started to go over to Morris, but saw Roarke move to him. It gave her heart a squeeze—a good one—to see him talking Morris over to the table.

She went back to her desk, and while the chaos reigned, ran a probability to see if the computer agreed with her instincts. Moments later, Roarke came up behind her, rubbed her shoulders.

"Morris okay?"

"Better, I think." Over her head, Roarke watched the activity at the table. "I'd say this is helping. Not just the work, the feeling of doing, but being here, with the others. You brought the murder board back in."

"I asked him first."

"No, I mean you brought it in. And he can see she's the center of it. Even when they're over there devouring sandwiches as if they're about to be outlawed, he can see she's the center of this. It would help."

"It won't help if the comp and I are right." She turned to face him. "I have to figure it two ways. Sandy's been off the scope for nearly seventeen hours. One, he's holed up somewhere, squeezed in a corner and sucking his thumb. Or two, he's already dead."

"And you and the probability scan you just ran favor dead. So do I. He's a liability alive. Ricker has no need to keep him breathing, and every reason to end him."

"Someone he trusted, like Coltraine trusted. It's gone back to the squad. It's one of them."

"You can't do more than you're doing. Let it sit, Eve, for just a while. Whoever it is feels safe, feels secure. He won't run like Sandy."

"No, he won't run. And as long as he's valuable to Ricker, he'll stay alive."

"Then let's get something to eat before your cops chew up even the tablecloth. I still have some things to see to before we leave."

"Yeah, you're right. Twins?" she added as they headed toward what was left of lunch.

"It seemed just the thing."

She built a sandwich, took the first bite. Through the thrum of guy talk and smacking lips, she caught the sound of female laughter.

Peabody and Nadine, both wearing girlie dresses, popped in the doorway.

"Mmmm, She-Body, look at you."

Love, Eve supposed, could cause even McNab to forget his stomach for a few seconds.

He bounced over to her, spun her around, then dipped her while she giggled—actually giggled—before he planted one on her.

"No! No! This is still a cop room. There is no dipping and kissing in a cop room."

Peabody simply sent her lieutenant a smile out of starry eyes. "Too late." For good measure, she gave McNab's ass a squeeze as he spun her back up.

"Doesn't this all look delicious?" Nadine fluttered her lashes. "And the food looks good, too." She gave Eve's cheek a pat as she passed, and brought a fiery blush to Trueheart's as she sidled up to him. "Are you on duty, Officer?"

"Give it up, darling." Roarke rubbed a hand over Eve's back. "Shift's over."

And that, she supposed, was that.

Peabody snagged a carrot stick. "I'm sticking with the rabbit food for now. We've got amazingly mag goodies for later. Ariel made them. I gained five pounds just carrying in the boxes. You can fill me in on all this."

"Later," Eve decided. "We're at a stop."

"Okay." Peabody gave the carrot a happy crunch. "Nadine and I brought most everything. Mavis and Leonardo should be here any minute, and they have more."

"Yippee."

"Trina and her consultants will be here by four to start setting up."

"Joy and—what? Who? Trina? *Why?* What have you done?"

"You said no silly games, and no strippers," Peabody reminded her. "We're doing the full-out girl party. Champagne, decadent food, body, hair, face treatments. Chick-vids, presents, gooey desserts. Big girl slumber party, followed by champagne brunch tomorrow."

"You mean . . ." The shock was sharp and cruel, a stunner blast against the heart. "Overnight? All night into tomorrow?"

"Yeah." Peabody grinned around her carrot. "Didn't I mention that?"

"I have to kill you now."

"Uh-uh. No games, no strippers. Those were your only rules."

"I'll find a way to hurt you for this."

"It's going to be fun!"

"Hurt you until you squeal like a pig."

Eve spotted Roarke moving to his office, and dashed after him. "Wait, wait!" She rushed in behind him, shut the door.

"You can't go to Vegas."

"Because?"

"Because you can't leave me here. We're married, and there are rules. I try to follow them. I don't know all of them, but God knows I try. And this *has* to be a rule. You can't leave me alone in a situation like this."

"What situation?"

"All these women. And Trina. Trina," she repeated, with considerable passion as she gripped his shirt.

"And gooey dessert and body things and chick-vids. All night. Slumber party. Do you know what that *means?*"

"I've had many dreams of them. Will there be pillow fights?"

She spun him around so his back hit the door. "Don't. Leave. Me."

"Darling." He kissed her brow. "I must. I must."

"No. You can bring Vegas here. Because . . . you're you. You can do that. We'll have Vegas here, and that'll be good. I'll buy you a lap dance."

"That's so sweet. But I'm going. I'll be back tomorrow, and lay a cool cloth on your fevered brow."

"*Tomorrow?*" She actually went light-headed. "You're not coming back tonight?"

"You wouldn't be in this state now if you paid attention. I'm taking a shuttle full of men to Las Vegas late this afternoon. There will be ribaldry, and a possible need to post bond. I've made arrangements. I'll bring back this same shuttle full of men—hopefully—tomorrow afternoon."

"Let me come with you."

"Let me see your penis."

"Oh, God! Can't I just use yours?"

"At any other time. Now pull yourself together, and remember that when all this is over, you'll very likely arrest a killer who's also a dirty cop. It's like a twofer."

"That doesn't make me feel better."

"Best I have."

She hissed out a breath. "I'm going to find someplace in this house where nobody is. And scream."

"That's a fine idea." He nudged her toward the hallway door. "I'll come find you before I go."

"It's not four o'clock yet," she said darkly. "Something could break."

"It may be your neck if you don't get out and let me finish my work." He gave her something closer to a shove, then for the second time that day, shut the door in her face.

17

She didn't consider it hiding. Maybe she was in a room she wasn't entirely sure she'd been in before with the door shut. And locked. But it wasn't hiding.

It was working, Eve told herself. In a quiet place, where she wouldn't be distracted. She could probably stay in here for the next twenty-four hours, no problem at all. She had a sleep chair, a work-station—a mini-unit, but very slick. She didn't see a wall screen, but when she booted up and requested one, the glass on the fancy mirror went black.

A little playing around with the control panel netted her a mini-AutoChef and friggie when the counter under the window opened, and up they came.

She poked into the attached bathroom and found all the necessities, including a shower designed like a little waterfall. Yes, she could be happy here. Maybe for years.

She got coffee, settled at the workstation. Callendar first, she thought.

"Yo," Callendar said when she came on-screen.

"Report."

"This place is a frigging hole, but it's got some serious hardware. You're caged here, you're seriously caged. Security's as tight as my uncle Fred on New Year's Eve. Even with the clearance and co-op, it's taken a while for us to get to the meat of the system. We've got our on-person communication devices because we're cops and got the authorization. Otherwise, they're held at docking."

"How far into the work are you?"

"I'm working the trans, Sisto's working the visitations. He's goose egg so far. I've got many a little ding, but it's a long way from a gong. It's going to take some time."

"What kind of ding?"

"It's really more of a burp. Do you really want me to explain it to you?"

Geek talk or party girls? Eve considered, decided they rated a toss-up. "I've got a minute."

"Let me put it this way. The burp may be a trans from here to New York, but I've got to go through half a zillion filters to nail that. I'm doing that because it's reading, so far, like it hit New York the afternoon of Coltraine's death—and it's not logged. Could be one of the techs here made it, off log, 'cause he was calling New York for some 'link sex. But I've got a suspicious mind."

"I've got a print—or whatever the hell—from a toss-away 'link here. I need to know if it matches."

"I nail this down, I can verify a match. Easy-peasy."

"Do you have Ricker's locations when the transmission was made?"

"It's still a burp, but the records have him in his cage. But the records also show that thirty minutes before the burp he was enjoying his daily hygiene privilege. Solitary shower, under full security. I've ordered A and V of that record, and the wheel's grinding slowly."

"He could've sent the trans on delay, or paid someone else to send it for him. Do you have the name of the guard or guards who took him from the cage to hygiene?"

"Yeah. We did a standard run—clear. I figured we'd go deeper if the burp turns into a really juicy belch." Callendar swigged down something pink from a clear bottle. "You want them?"

"Yeah." Eve noted down the names. "Good. Keep digging."

Eve signed off, sat back, and considered. It was the green light from Ricker to his New York hitter. It had to be. "Computer, full run, priority authorized." She read off the names and ID numbers of the guard and com officer. "Let's see what we've got."

An hour later, Roarke walked in. "Eve" was all he said.

"I've got something. Callendar heard a burp, and I've got something. Rouche, Cecil, cage guard on Omega—six years in. Assigned to max security wing. Ricker's wing. Divorced. But, oddly, his ex-wife's financials have had a serious increase in the last year. Well, not her financials so much as her insurance coverage. She's increased it to five mil. Now what does the ex-wife of an Omega guard, who also quit her mid-level drone job eight months ago, when she also relocated from a rental in Danville, Illinois, to a twenty-room villa in the south of France, have that's worth five mil?"

"Art, jewelry. Liquidating cash into solid invest-ments."

"You got it. Plus the real estate. She paid cash for the

house, which is in both her name and the ex's. Callendar's having him pulled in for interview once things click. And they will. I haven't been able to track the money yet. Can't track it back from the ex-wife to Ricker. You could probably—"

"No, I'm going to Vegas."

She goggled at him, jaw dropped, eyes bugging. "But, *Jesus.*"

"Callendar, who is more than qualified, has the guard, is on the search. You have your connection, your link to Ricker—who isn't going anywhere. The manhunt continues for Sandy, who you believe is probably dead anyway."

"But—"

Roarke didn't give an inch. "Knowing Ricker's methods, it's highly unlikely this guard has the names of the New York contact. You've narrowed it down to the squad, which was your instinct all along. And on Monday, you'll push forward on that. Whoever this cop is, you're smarter, and by God, more tenacious. But right now, you have a houseful of women, I have a limo waiting outside, and a group of men who are anxious to get very drunk and lose their money. It's life."

He took her face in his hands and kissed her. "It's our life. We're going to live it for the next twenty-four hours."

"When you put it like that," she muttered.

"Morris has gone home."

"Oh. Damn it."

"He said to tell you he wanted to think about you enjoying yourself for a few hours. That he felt lighter leaving here than he did when he came. I think he did, and I know he spoke to Mira for a short time before he left."

"I guess that's good. I guess that's something."

"Come on then, walk me out. Kiss me goodbye."

Trapped, she rose. "How'd you find me in here? House scan," she realized. "Didn't think about that. What's this room for anyway?"

"A guest office. You never know, obviously, when someone might need it. Good work, by the way, on the financials."

"I don't suppose, on the shuttle, you could—"

"No, I couldn't," he said, very firmly. "Tomorrow, after I get home and your guests have gone, is soon enough. We're going to enjoy ourselves."

"Easy for you to say."

"Yes." He gave her a full-out, and completely unsympathetic smile. "It is."

"There you are!" Mavis, in full party gear of a bride-white mini and knee-high skin-boots of screaming red, skipped down the hall. Her hair, the same screaming red as the boots, bounced as it tumbled to her waist. "Everyone's asking. I was just checking on Bella. You are the maggest of the mag! The little nursery's so cute!"

"We want Belle to be happy and comfortable whenever she visits," Roarke told her.

Eve's stride took yet another hitch. "You brought the baby?"

"I was going to bring a sitter, but Summerset said he'd rather be with Bellisimo than go to Vegas. The man is sugar. They're in there now, playing with Kissy Kitty and Puppy Poo."

Eve didn't want to know what Kissy Kitty and Puppy Poo might be, or imagine Summerset playing with them. Or anything. She did her best to scrub any and all imagery from her mind as Mavis bubbled on.

"We are going to have the abso-mega *best* time. Wait till you see the decorations, the *food*. And the salon is completely uptown. I'm going to plant a big wet one on my honey bear, so we can get this party started."

"What am I going to do?" Eve managed as Mavis bounded down the stairs.

"You're going to plant a big wet one on me. After that? I'm in an alternate reality."

There were so many of them, Eve thought, as everyone spilled outside where a limo the size of Long Island waited. She couldn't possibly know all these people. When her head stopped ringing, she realized she didn't. Strange faces mixed with the familiar.

The groom-to-be caught her in an enthusiastic hug. "Thank you," Charles told her. "For everything. Louise is so excited about all this."

Eve glanced over to see Louise with Dennis Mira. Good God, sweet Jesus, Eve thought, Roarke was taking Mr Mira to Vegas. Her world was inside out.

Somewhere in the chaos, men packed into the enormous limo. As it rolled down the drive, Baxter popped out of one of the moonroofs, shooting up the victory sign while the ladies cheered.

Then she was alone with them.

They squealed. Jumped around. They made inhuman noises and whirled in a blur of color and limbs. And ran for the house, still making them.

"Maybe it's all some strange dream."

Laughing, Mira stepped over to put an arm around Eve's shoulders.

"I didn't realize you were out here."

"It was quite a crowd and such an interesting dynamic. The men going off to their indulgence, and the women gathering here for theirs." Mira gave Eve's shoulder a little pat. "Celebrations, very defined, very traditional to prepare two individuals for becoming one unit."

"Mostly it seems like a lot of drinking and screaming."

"And at the very outer rim of your understanding, I know. But it's going to be fun."

"Okay." She noted Mira wore a dress—pale, pale blue and subtly elegant. "Do I have to change?"

"I think you should. It'll put you in the mood. In fact, I'd love to get a look at your closet and pick something for you."

"Fine, sure." The trade-off would give her time to pick Mira's brain. "Roarke said you talked to Morris before he left."

"Yes, and we'll talk again. He mentioned you suggested he see Father Lopez," Mira continued as they went inside, started upstairs. "I'm glad you thought of it. Morris is a spiritual man, and I believe Lopez can help him cope with all he has to cope with. The work you gave him helps, too, and it's good he's self-aware enough to have asked for it. It keeps his mind active, and more, makes him a part of finding the answers."

"I've got some questions."

"I imagined you did." Mira walked into the bedroom,

and at Eve's gesture, to the closet. She opened it, sighed. "Oh. Eve."

"He's always putting things in there."

"It's a fantasy. Like an eclectic little boutique." She glanced back. "See, I'm already having fun. Ask your questions. I'll multitask. Oh my God, the eveningwear alone!"

"I don't have to wear a formal thing, do I?"

"No, no, just a moment's distraction. Tell me what you've learned since the last report."

Eve told her about Alex Ricker's statements about his father, about Rod Sandy, Callendar's progress, the prison guard. From the nearly sexual sounds Mira made inside the depths of the closet, Eve figured she was talking to herself. Still, orals always refined her thinking.

"This." Mira stepped out with a flowing, thin-strapped dress the color of ripe plums. "It's simple, comfortable, gorgeous."

"Okay."

"It also has slit pockets, so you can keep your 'link and communicator on you." With an understanding smile, Mira passed the dress to Eve. "You're wondering if Ricker could and would kill Coltraine simply as a punishment for his son. To order the hit for no profit or gain. Just spite."

"I didn't think you were listening."

"I raised children. I know how to listen and do a myriad of other things at the same time. Yes. He could and he would. It's absolutely his pathology. More, his son is free, he is not. His son despises him. He would only need to despise his son more. Yes, again, he would use—

delight in using—a man his son considers his closest friend. He'd revel in it."

"It was coming to New York that was the kicker, wasn't it? Coltraine coming here to where I am, to where Roarke is. She signed her death warrant when she transferred here."

"It's not your doing, Eve."

"I know that. I'm asking, in your opinion, if he had her killed to get back at his son and at me. He used a cop to do it. He'd have other ways, other means. But he used a cop. I know it. That was for me. Sending her weapon to me. A direct threat, a little reminder that it could be me. That was for Roarke."

"At this time," Mira said after a moment, "with this data, with this history, yes. He manipulated this one act to strike at the three people who most obsess him."

"That's what I thought. It'll make taking his trigger down and shoving that in his face more satisfying."

"I know your mind's not on what's going on down-stairs."

"It's okay." Eve tugged at the skirt of the dress. "I'll multitask."

A short time later, she wasn't sure she had a mind. The pool house had been transformed into a female fantasy of gold, white, and silver canopies, lounge chairs, towering white candles. White tables held frothy pink drinks in crystal flutes, and silver trays of colorful food. Yet another held a tower of gifts with trailing ribbons.

To the far side of the deep blue water of the pool was the salon. Reclining chairs, massage tables, manicure and

317

pedicure stations—and the tables with all those tools and implements that always gave Eve a slightly queasy stomach.

"Bellinis!" Mavis pushed one into Eve's hand. "Mine are with the nonalchy bubbles since I'm nursing. But they're still delish. We're going to draw lots for services in a few minutes. After some lube."

"Don't put mine in."

Mavis grinned. "Too late," she said and danced off.

Eve thought: *What the hell.* And knocked back half the Bellini. It was pretty delish.

"What do you think?" Peabody asked, and gestured to encompass the whole space.

"I think it looks like a really classy bordello without any johns. In a good way."

"That was pretty much the idea. Listen, while it's all the chatter, we can slip out. You can fill me in on anything new."

Eve looked at Peabody, looked at the space, looked over to where Louise laughed with a group of women. "It's a party. The rest can wait. But since you asked, and meant it, the hurt downgrades from pig squeal to agonized moan."

"Really?"

"Really."

"Woot!"

As Mavis announced the first names for services, women shrieked. And Eve polished off the first Bellini.

Louise put another in her hand, tapped her own glass to it. "When I was a girl," she began, "I dreamed about getting married, and all that went around it. For a long time, after I grew up, I put those dreams aside. For the work, and because no one measured up to what I had dreamed as a girl. Now, with Charles and what we have, with all this, and what I have right this minute, it's so much more than I ever dreamed."

"You look stupid with happy, Louise."

"I am. I am stupid with happy. I know this is a bad time for you—and celebrating when Morris is going through so much—"

"We're not thinking about that now. So, how long before somebody gets drunk and falls in the pool?"

"Oh, no more than an hour."

It was an hour, almost to the minute, but nobody fell in. Mavis stripped off her boots, pulled her dress over her head and dived in, bare-ass naked. The gesture met with enthusiasm, so much so that dresses flew, shoes soared. Women, in a variety of sizes and shapes, joined her.

"My eyes," Eve moaned. "There aren't enough Bellinis in the world to save my eyes."

They swam naked, and when someone ordered music, they danced. They chattered like magpies and drank like fish. They reclined in the salon with their faces and bodies coated with strangely colored goo. They gathered in corners for intense discussions.

"It hits every note."

Eve glanced over at Nadine. "Does it?"

"Look at Peabody shaking it with Louise. And Mira over there chatting with Reo and—whoever that is, some friend of Louise's from the hospital. They're chatting like sisters while they get facials. I get caught up with work. You know how it is. And I forget to just hang with women. Just be with others of my species without any agenda. Then there's something like this, so completely female, and I like it. A lot. It hits the notes."

"I didn't see you jump naked in the pool."

"I haven't had enough to drink yet. But the night's young." Nadine gave her slow, feline smile. "Wanna dance, cutie?"

Eve laughed. "No, but thanks. Two things, then we'll get another drink. I might have a break on the Coltraine case, and I'll give you a heads up when it cracks open. Don't ask, not here. Second, I read the book. Your Icove book. You got it. I already knew the ending, but you pulled it off so I wanted to see how you played it out."

"It's been killing me not to ask you." Nadine closed her eyes, drank again. "Thanks. Serious and sincere thanks, Dallas."

"I didn't write it." Eve looked at her glass. "I'm empty."

"Let's go fix that."

It got stranger. The I-have-to-watch-my-figure food disappeared to be replaced by the gooey. Little frosted cakes, cookies, tarts gleaming with sugar, pastries oozing cream. Because she hoped to hear from Callendar, Eve switched to coffee. Nadine, having enough to drink, executed an impressive naked jackknife from the diving board. Several pairs of breasts bobbed in the swirling water of the corner jets. Eve worked hard to block out the fact that a pair of them belonged to Mira.

It just wasn't right.

"We're going to begin the open-the-gifts round," Peabody told her.

"Good, that should—What are you wearing?"

"My party pajamas." Peabody looked down at her bright yellow sleep tank and pants. The pants were covered with colorful drawings of shoes. "Cute."

"Why would anyone wear shoes on their pants? Shoes go on your feet."

"I like shoes. I love my pjs." Smiling sloppily, Peabody hugged herself and swayed. "They're fun."

"Peabody, you're completed wasted."

"I know. I had a gazillion belamies, belly buttons, biminis, whatever. And I ate much, too. So if I throw up, none of it counts! Didja know McNab called me from Vegas? He won a hundreds dollar."

Fuck it, Eve thought. A party was a party. "A hundreds dollar?"

"Uh-huh. He said if he wins a hundreds more, he's going to buy me a present. Oops! Presents! Time to open presents!"

Eve stayed out of the way as it seemed opening presents involved some ritual, and a change of venue from the pool house to the lounge beyond it. Following Peabody's lead, many of the guests also required a wardrobe change.

Mavis came in wearing a polka-dot tank and striped pants, and carrying the baby, who wore matching sleepwear.

Women flocked to them like cooing doves.

"She's hungry," Mavis explained. "Plus she didn't

want to miss the whole party." So saying, Mavis sat, plopped out a breast. Bella latched on enthusiastically.

Women sat or sprawled everywhere while Louise began the ritual of removing ribbons, bows, and paper. There were coos and ooohs, bawdy laughter at the gag gifts of sex toys. And the conversation around the openings turned to weddings, men, and sex.

Men, Eve thought, didn't have a clue what women said about them when they weren't around. Comparison studies, polls—discussions of length, thickness, duration, positions, quirks, preferences.

Mavis switched Bella to her other breast. "Leonardo can go all night. He's a—"

"Huggy bear," Eve said, and made Mavis giggle.

"Yeah, but that bear's got stamina."

"What's the record?" somebody asked her.

"Six in one night. Of course that was before Bellaloca here," she said through the round of applause. "We gotta squeeze in the hump and bump when and where we can these days. But the bear knows how to spring to attention."

"We hit five one night." Peabody waved her fresh glass. "And four is standard for special occasions. But mostly it's one—a nice long one, with maybe a short recap. McNab's more a puppy. Likes to play and play, then he's gotta curl up and sleep."

"I dated a guy once who was all buildup and no payoff. *Huge* cock," Nadine added, using her hands to demonstrate—to the hilarity of the women. "And he'd dock, and deflate. Like a turtle pulling back in the shell. He's The Turtle."

"I banged this guy once." Trina chomped down on an éclair, swallowed the pale gold pastry that nearly matched the color of her hair. "Not bad. We got together a couple times, then he says maybe I want to take it up a few notches. I figure toys, iced. But he wants a threesome. Gotta be open, right?" She chased the pastry with a pink Bellini. "But it turns out the third party was his fricking sister. He's The Snake," she said to the chorus of disgust.

"Dennis can still manage two."

"I can't hear this." Eve clamped her hands over her ears. "My head will explode."

"What? I have grandchildren so I don't have sex?" Mira asked.

"Yes. No. I don't know. That's the point."

Mira poked a finger at Eve's arm. "You have such a charming streak of prude. As I was saying, Dennis, given the right stimulation, can still go for two. When you've been married as long as we have, there are often stretches where warmth, comfort, the life rhythm stand in for sex. I wish that for you, Louise. The warmth and the comfort of a long life together, with the two rounds to surprise you both. Dennis is The Owl. Wise and quiet."

"What's Charles?" Nadine demanded. "The suave licensed companion turned sexual therapist. The sex has to be amazing."

"Isn't it just?" Louise gave a slow, satisfied smile that put a glow in her gray eyes. "He's The Leopard. Elegant, graceful, strong—and believe me, he can travel across the mesa. And back again."

"Leopards, puppies, owls—even snakes are sexy," Nadine complained. "I get a limp turtle. Your turn," she said to Eve, then wagged a finger when Eve shook her head. "Then I'll project. Panther. Sleek, mysterious, coiled, with an elegance and purpose of movement."

"Okay."

"Not fair! Okay, what's the record? How many times?"

"If you can count them, he didn't drop you out."

Nadine groaned, shuddered, grinned. "Bitch."

Amid the laughter, Louise opened the next gift. Eve sipped her coffee. "Wolf," she murmured, without thinking.

"Yes." Beside her, Mira patted her hand. "They mate for life."

When the last present was sighed over, Trina got to her feet. "Okay, girls, back to your stations. Next round of treatments." She turned, bared her teeth at Eve. "I pulled you."

"No. I'm not—"

"Yeah, you are. Everybody plays. Somebody get this woman a drink. The hair. It's mine."

She could handle a haircut. Probably. Particularly since there was no escape. "I don't want a body treatment," Eve began. "I don't want a face treatment. I don't want—"

"Yeah, yeah, blah, blah. Sit." Someone passed Trina a Bellini, which she pushed into Eve's hand. "I saved you for last, first round anyway. We're here for the duration if anybody wants to go again. It's nice what you're doing here."

324

Eve narrowed her eyes suspiciously as Trina arranged her torture tools. "What am I doing here?"

"Having everybody here like this. Louise is okay. Real okay. Got a solid base. Me, I don't have a lot of no-fucking-ways, but I couldn't've fallen for an LC and stuck. Not the big fall, you know? But she did, because he was the guy. And now she's got the whole piñata and all the candy inside. It's nice to have everybody here to get a bang out of it."

Just as Eve relaxed, as she considered there might be some skinny patch of common ground here, Trina turned, and her eyes went to slits. "Now what the fuck have you done to my hair? Hacked at it didn't you? Just couldn't let it alone or call me in to deal?"

"I didn't—I only. It's my hair."

"Not once I put the scissors to it, sister. You're lucky I'm a genius, and a humanitarian. I'll fix it, and I won't shave it bald down the center to make my point."

Trina grabbed a bottle and began to spray a mist on Eve's hair while she worked it with her fingers. "Plus you need a facial and an eye boost. You got some fatigue."

"It's not fatigue, it's alcohol. I've been drinking."

"I say you got fatigue, you got fatigue. I know about Morris's lady. Sick about it because that's one prime man—on all counts. You're going to get the bastard, but you're not going to do it with hacked-up hair and tired skin. I got standards."

"You want the hair? Take the hair, but leave the rest of me alone. I've got—"

Her 'link beeped. Eve struggled to get her hand

under the miles of cape, into the pocket of her dress. Trina just nipped in, pulled it out. "She's busy," she snapped even as Eve cursed her.

"Unrecognized voice print. Transmission for Dallas, Lieutenant Eve."

"Give me that, goddamn it." Eve grabbed, shoved. "Dallas."

"Dispatch, Dallas, Lieutenant Eve. Report to 509 Pearl Street. Officers on-scene. Body on second floor visually identified as Sandy, Rod, subject of your APB."

"Is the scene secured?"

"Affirmative."

"I'm on my way."

Before Eve finished the statement, Trina had the cape whipped away and the chair back in an upright position. "Should I find Peabody?"

"No, she can stay here. I can handle it. If anyone asks, just say I went to bed."

"You got it."

Eve slipped out of the room, started to make a dash.

"Hey, hey!" Spotting her, Peabody set off in staggering pursuit. "You can't run away. We're going to start the vids. You—you've got something," she said when she managed to focus.

"I've got it. Go on back. Go handle . . . whatever the hell it is down there."

"No, sir. I'm with you. I've got some Sober-Up with me. I can be level pretty quick. It's about Coltraine, so I'm with you."

"All right, but make it quick. I've got to go change. And so, by all that's holy, do you."

As Eve called for the elevator, Mira hurried over. "What's wrong?"

"DB ID'd as Sandy. I've got to go. She's got to sober up if she wants in."

"I want in."

"Go change," Mira ordered, and put an arm around Peabody's waist. "I'll take care of it. She'll meet you upstairs."

"Ten minutes," Eve snapped. She jumped on the elevator, thinking there was no way in hell her partner would be clean and sober in ten.

And, she thought as she rode up, no matter how hard she'd pushed that day, she'd never had a chance of taking Rod Sandy alive.

18

Eve peeled off the dress, yanked on pants, shirt, her weapon. She hunted up a short leather jacket and shrugged into it as she jogged downstairs. She realized she'd underestimated Peabody when her partner stepped off the foyer elevator with Mira and Mavis.

"I'm about halfway there," Peabody told her.

"You're all the way there when we get to the scene, or you stay in the car. Ah, do whatever you think works downstairs," she said to Mira.

"Don't worry. Everything's under control here."

"We're totally on top of it," Mavis assured her. "I told Summerset the what, so he brought your car around."

"Good thinking. We'll be back when we're back. Peabody."

Peabody went a little pale when the fresh air slapped her, but got into the car with the minimum of groans.

"If you even think about booting in here—"

"No, I'm past that. Where's the scene?"

"Building down on Pearl."

"I'll be leveled out by the time we . . . Where did you get this vehicle?"

"It's mine. We'll be using it from now on."

"Yours, like *yours?*" Peabody studied the dash. "Very frosty gadgetry."

"Use the very frosty gadgetry to map the fastest route to 509 Pearl and to ID the kind of building it is."

Peabody made the requests. "Three-level, multi-tenant, currently vacant. Rehab pending permits. Do you want the route in-dash or on audio?"

"In-dash. I hate when it talks to you. Inside a vacant building, second floor of. It sounds like the killer didn't want the body found so fast this time. That building's outside the Eighteenth's turf, but not far out. Coltraine's squad would know the terrain."

"How about Callendar and Sisto? I need to catch up."

Eve filled in the blanks, speeding her way downtown.

The building sat squat and sad, a gray slab generously coated with the indignity of graffiti. Windows gaped—mouths with the jagged edges of broken glass like bad teeth. A few were boarded, and more than a few of the boards tipped drunkenly. The bolt and chain on the front door had amused someone enough to take the time to hack it to pieces.

Had it been in perfect repair, it would still have been a joke.

Two black-and-whites nosed together at the curb. A couple of uniforms stood on the shallow concrete platform in front of the entrance, jawing. They broke it off when Peabody and Eve climbed out.

"Homicide," Eve said, taking out her badge and hooking it on her belt while Peabody got field kits out of the trunk.

"DB's on the second floor. We're backup. First-on-scene's inside. Place is empty—we did a sweep. Brought a coupla lights in, 'cause it's pitch in there."

Eve nodded, studied the chain and bolt. "These weren't compromised tonight."

"No, sir. We patrol here. It's been like that a couple months anyway. Funky-junkies flopped here. Owner complained, so we ran 'em off. They just find another hole."

It stank. Old piss, old vomit, a decade's worth of dust and grime.

The uniforms had set one of their field lights on the first level, so shadows danced over the piles of rags, papers, and assorted debris the junkies had left behind. She imagined the missing floorboards had been fed into the rusted metal can to burn for warmth. Same with the few missing stair treads, she thought as she stepped over the gaps on her way up.

The light from her field kit shone over a nest of mice in one of the holes, the babies like skinned blobs sucking on their mother's engorged belly. Behind her, Peabody said, "Eeuuww."

"Don't say 'eeuuww', for God's sake. We're murder cops."

"I don't like mice. Or maybe they were rats. They could be rats. And Daddy wasn't in there, so he's somewhere else." Peabody flashed her light left, right, up, down. "Waiting for a chance to run up my pants' legs and bite me on the ass."

"Should that occur, don't say eeuuww. Lieutenant Dallas and Detective Peabody," Eve called out. "Homicide."

On the second floor, in the glare of the field light, one of the uniforms moved toward the stairs. "Officer Guilder, Lieutenant. My partner's got the nine-one-one callers secured. You want them or the body first?"

"Body."

"He's over here. Couple of scavengers called it in. Nothing to scavenge in here. Whatever's left even the junkies didn't want, but they came in to pick through. Stated they found him when they were checking out a pile of old blankets. Thought he was sleeping at first, then figured out he was dead. Called it in."

"Civic-minded scavengers?"

"Yeah, what're the odds? But they come off straight to me. No weapons on them. Not even a sticker. When we responded, they directed us to the body. We recognized him from the APB, called it in."

Guilder gestured. "There he is."

Eve stood in the doorway of what in some dim past might have been an efficiency apartment. "Yeah, there he is."

He sat on the filthy floor, his back to the wall. He'd been stripped, leaving the small hole and dribble of heart blood on his naked chest exposed.

Nothing left to scavenge, Eve thought. That's the way the killer hoped it would read. She crouched down as much to study the angle of the body as what surrounded it.

"Got some prints in the dust here, probably from the scavengers. These? The smears? The killer sealed up, wore crime-scene booties from the look of it. Things had gone another way, few days, a week passes, more dust. You don't see the smears. Heart shot, dead-on. One blow, thin blade. Up close and personal. Verify ID and TOD, Peabody."

Eve sealed up, took out a pair of microgoggles and approached the body. "Probably a stiletto," Eve said as she examined the wound. "Don't want any spatter, any mess. Want it quick and done. Toss rags and useless tarps over him. You might walk right by this pile in the dark. Window's boarded. Somebody finds him, junkie, side-walk sleeper, scavenger, most of them aren't going to report it."

"Prints verify. Rod Sandy," Peabody said. "TOD one-fifteen this morning."

"Smart. Smart. Give him time to panic, to sweat, run him around some. Then lure him here when he's so knotted up he's not thinking straight. You need to take him somewhere inside, covered, off the track. You'd get here first, lure him up. He's got to be sweating. He doesn't want to stay in a place like this. He needs to get out, you have to help me get out. I can't stay in this rathole. And it's like, take it easy, it's all worked out. You might even put your hand on his shoulder. Holds him steady, gives you a target while you look in his eyes and stick him."

She pulled off the goggles. "Strip him down so it looks like he was killed for his clothes, what's in his pockets. But it's not so smart to cover him up. That's too much. Just like the single heart shot's too much. That's not mugging MO. Overthought it, that's what you did. Some showing off here, too."

"The killer should've messed him up some," Peabody put in. "Then left him on top of the rags instead of under them."

"That's right. The kill shot indicates skill. There's pride there. No postmortem wounds, like you'd see if he'd been flopped around while someone was yanking his clothes off. But he had to be careful, avoid leaving trace. All a waste of time anyway, because we're not idiots."

She straightened. "Let's get the sweepers in, and the morgue. I'll take the scavengers."

They looked typical, Eve mused. Two humanlike lumps so layered in clothing and grime it was next to impossible to judge gender or age. They sat on the floor, a wheeled basket between them. It held more clothes, shoes, what might have been broken toys and any number of damaged electronics.

They identified themselves as Kip and Bop.

"Legal names would be appreciated."

"We didn't keep them," Kip said. "We only keep what we want."

Bop clutched an enormous bag. "We keep it and we use it and we sell it. It doesn't hurt anybody."

"Okay. You came in here to look for things you could keep or use or sell?"

"Nobody else wants them." Kip shrugged. "Nobody lives here. Nobody cares."

"Did you see anyone else in here?"

"The man who's dead."

"Maybe you came in here last night, too."

"No. Last night we were on Bleecker. Lady there

333

leaves stuff out every Friday night, and it's good pickings if you get there quick."

"Okay. What time did you get in here tonight?"

Kip lifted his arm, tapped the broken face of his wrist unit. "It's always the same time. Here's what. We come in, go up to the top floor so's we can work it down. Not much up there, so we come on down, and work it. Maybe we'll find a good blanket or some socks in the pile. But we found the man who's dead."

"Did you take anything from him, or from the pile?"

"We found him pretty quick. Don't take from the dead."

"You go to hell other," Bop said with a wise nod.

"What did you do then?"

"We call the nine the one and the one. It's the right."

"Yeah, it's the right. You've got a 'link?" At Eve's question Bop clutched the bag tighter.

"It's mine!"

"That's right. It's yours. Thanks for using it. We can get you to a shelter if you want."

"Don't like shelters. Somebody'll take your stuff for sure."

Eve scratched her ear. "Okay. How about a flop for a couple of nights. A room, a bed. No shelter."

Kip and Bop exchanged looks. "Where at?" Kip demanded.

"Officer Guilder, is there a hotel nearby that will take them for a couple of nights? On the city."

"Sure. I know a place on Broad. The Metro Arms."

Another look passed between the scavengers. "We don't pay?"

"No, the city pays to show appreciation for your help." Though hers were still sealed, Eve stopped short of shaking hands.

"Don't need to kill for stuff," Kip said.

"People leave it all over anyway," Bop added.

Out on the street, Eve studied the building and those surrounding it while sweepers moved in and out. "If you live or work around here, you know buildings like this. Killer's turf, with the advantage of being way, way off the vic's."

"And without Kip and Bop, we're chasing our tails for Sandy for days, maybe more. All the arrows point to him for Coltraine. When we find him, it looks like he'd gone to ground, got rolled, got killed. You could construe he took off to avoid arrest—and that being tight with Alex, Alex remains a suspect on Coltraine."

"You could construe."

"Except for our motto." Peabody put on a serious look. "We're not idiots."

"Too bad for Sandy, he was. Let's go write it up."

"I was afraid you were going to say that."

There was plenty of action in Central in the dark hours. The whines of street LCs, the moans or giggles of junkies, the weeping of victims. Eve closed herself into her office to translate her record into a report.

When her 'link signaled, she pounced on it. "Callendar. Gimme."

Callendar grinned. "I got gimmes. Let me start with a big, juicy belch. Two, in fact. Transmissions from Omega to New York, confirmed. Both sending and receiving on

335

unregistered 'links. And yeah, baby, that would be the same 'link used on the home planet. They match."

"Oh yeah, baby," Eve echoed.

"Encrypted transmissions from here to there were not logged. Big no-nos on the party palace of Omega."

"Can you break them?"

"No encryption defeats me. But it's going to take a little time, and a couple hours' sleep. Meanwhile, Sisto had a little chat with our old friend Cecil Rouche's drinking buddy, who also just happened to be on communications at the time in question. Guy named Art Zeban. Zeban played it dumb at the jump, but smartened up when Sisto leaned on him. Which Sisto reports he enjoyed bunches. Zeban claims Rouche gave him a thousand a pop to keep the transes off log. Just a favor for a pal, with compensation."

"This is good."

"Better is that the Gs included wiping the record of Ricker's hygiene break."

"It's gone."

"Please." Callendar waved a hand in the air as if flicking off a gnat. "Nothing's ever gone when I'm around. I'll dig it out. Meanwhile in the meanwhile, I got authorization to search Rouche's quarters."

"Does he know?"

"Not yet. We're—"

"Keep him in the dark. Make sure he's unable to make any contact on planet—or off. No communications. Wrap him up, Callendar, and wrap him tight. Bring him and his drinking buddy home."

"All over that. This shit is fun!"

"While you're having fun, make goddamn sure none of it—not an inkling of it—leaks to Ricker. I want him closed down. If the warden has a problem, he can contact me. But Ricker is shut down tight until further notice."

"Total," Callendar said and signed off.

Eve added the new data, then rose to expand her murder board.

"I'm clear," Peabody said as she came in. "Unless you want to notify next of kin tonight, we . . ." She trailed off when she noticed the additions to the board. "You got something again."

"Callendar confirms Omega transmissions. They're encrypted, but she says she can break that. And she matched the on-planet send-and-receive to the 'link Feeney found. She's got the tech—" Eve tapped Zeban's photo. "The guard Ricker's bribing bribed him to keep them off the log, and to wipe the recording of Ricker's shower. But she says she can reconstruct."

"She's good. McNab says straight up. That's a lot of bribing."

"Yes, bribing on a penal colony. I was shocked. It's a food chain," Eve muttered. "Ricker at the top. You've got Sandy, and Rouche, Zeban, and probably more under that. But there's the link between Ricker and Sandy. That level. We need to fill that one in to make it all hold."

She turned around, frowned. "What time is it in France?"

"Um."

"I don't know either. I shouldn't have to know.

Roarke would know, but he's in Vegas. I don't know what time it is there, either." She waved her hand before Peabody could inform her. "Find me the head French cop, the one who handles the area where Rouche's ex lives. I want her watched. I need her communications monitored."

"You might have better luck with Global."

"They're greedy. They'll want her for their own. Let's try the locals first."

It took persuasion, cajolery, and in the end the mention of illegal funds and considerable merchandise purchased with those illegal funds—all housed in France—to ensure cooperation.

The possibility of confiscating a few million was worth the time and effort to sit on one Luanne Debois, and to monitor her communications.

"It'll take time," Eve complained as they rode down to the garage. "Proper authorization—meaning bureau-cratic crapola—before they can implement the watch. But he got a sparkle in his eyes when I outlined the money laundering, seeing as the result of it's sitting, pri-marily, on his turf."

"You get that, and Callendar comes through, we'll pin Ricker. Doesn't pin or even identify his next in command here."

"Working on it."

Peabody stopped and narrowed her eyes when Eve stepped up to her vehicle.

"I don't get it. I just don't get how come you have to pick something so ugly when you could have anything. Like the 2X-5000, or the big, burly all-terrain, or—"

"I didn't pick it; Roarke did."

"You're shattering all my hopes and dreams."

"Because he's smart enough to know it blends. Nobody'll look twice at it. Do you want a ride home or not?"

"I'm not going home." Peabody jumped in before Eve. "I'm going back to your place. All my stuff's there, and that's where McNab's coming when he gets back. Plus, brunch."

Eve felt the warning throb behind her eyes. "They're not still there. Are they? Why?"

"Because that was the plan, and yes, they are. I checked in."

"I was going to go by the morgue."

"Why?"

"Because. We could've missed something."

"I'll tag the morgue from here while you drive us to a magolicious breakfast buffet."

Life had to be, Morris had said, or what was the point? At the moment she might wish it would be elsewhere, but she accepted defeat. She could work from home, she told herself. Hide out in her office until the houseload of women finally went away. She could work on pinning down that last link while she waited for Callendar to come through.

She'd need to deal with Rouche, and needed to discuss that deal with the DA's office. Well, ADA Cher Reo was sleeping off a night of drunken revelry like the rest of them, so that would be handy.

Plus, she had Mira right on-site, too. Mira would be good with additional profiling.

They wanted brunch? she thought. Fine. But they were going to work for it.

She slid her gaze right and noted that Peabody was slumped against the door and out like a light.

Okay, they'd work for it as soon as they woke up.

Dawn pearled the air as she approached the house. Probably just as well they were sleeping, Eve decided. It would give her time to recharge, think, pace, work on some angles without a bunch of distractions.

Quiet, she thought. She could definitely use the quiet.

She shoved Peabody's shoulder and got a shocked snort out of her partner. "Wake up, go in, go up, go to bed."

"I'm awake. I'm good. Where . . . oh. Home again."

"Don't get used to it. Take a couple hours down. You can eat when you get up, then you're on the roll until I say otherwise."

"Okay. All right." She rubbed her eyes as she followed Eve to the door. "Are you going down?"

"I want to take advantage of the quiet until—"

She opened the door, and the high-pitched scream had her reaching for her weapon. Peabody grabbed Eve's arm. "Don't draw down. It's the baby."

Eve kept her hand on her weapon while her ears rang with wails and screams. "That's not possible. Nothing that small can make those sounds."

But she followed the sounds to the parlor, where a pajama-clad Mavis walked a shrieking, red-faced Bella.

"Hey!" Mavis walked, patted, swayed. "You're back. Sorry, she's a little fussy."

"It sounds like she's being hacked up with an axe." More, Eve thought, like she wanted to hack somebody else up with an axe.

"She's got good lungs."

Eve jolted as Mira—a Mira in a peacock blue robe—rose from the sofa. "Here, sweetie, let me take her awhile. Come to Aunt Charley, baby girl. Yes, there we are."

"Whew." Mavis grabbed a mug off the table, glugged. "I brought her down here to keep from breaking eardrums upstairs. She sure is pissed."

"Why? What did you do? That can't be normal. You're a doctor," Eve added, pointing at Mira. "You should do something."

"I am." Mira walked, stroked, crooned. "She's just teething and feeling mad, aren't you, poor thing? Poor Belle. I bet you could use some coffee."

"I bet she could," Eve muttered.

Mavis rose, handing Mira some pink-and-blue device that Mira plugged in Belle's mouth, then Mavis poured another mug of coffee. "Here you go. Peabody?"

"Yeah, thanks."

Since whatever Belle gnawed on took the shrieks down to sucking sounds and whimpers, Eve drank. "So . . . everybody else is asleep."

"As far as I know," Mavis told her. "Some conked downstairs watching vids. Others crawled off to their assigned rooms. Everyone had a mega-blast. Sorry you got called away."

Eve kept a wary eye on Belle, whose eyes were going glassy as she sucked. "Is that thing tranq'd? Is it legal?"

"No, it's not tranq'd; yes, it's legal. It's cold. The cold makes her inflamed gums feel better." Mira stroked Belle's cheek with her own. "She's worn herself out. Haven't you, sweetheart, just worn yourself out. The call was connected to the Coltraine case?"

"Yeah, one of our prime suspects is in the morgue." Eve stayed braced, in case the baby decided to erupt again. "Callendar hit hot on Omega. I'm waiting to hear back from her. I've got a couple of lines to look down. I could . . . I'll go up."

"Do you want my input?"

"It can wait."

"I can take her." Mavis moved over, reached for Belle. "She's about ready to go down again. Poor little Belly Button, Mommy's got you. Thanks," she said to Mira.

"I loved it."

Baffled, because the statement seemed sincere, Eve started upstairs. "Reo's still here, isn't she?"

"Yes. She went up to bed about two, I think. Are you looking for input from the ADA, too?"

"At some point, yeah."

"Why don't I go get her?"

"It could wait . . . But why should it? Yeah, why don't you go get her?" Eve continued up to her office, and glanced back at Peabody. "I said you could have a couple hours."

"I'm awake. And I'm hungry. I'm going to get some breakfast stuff out, if we're going to have a consult. You looking for protein or carbs?"

"Whatever." Eve turned into her office. She went straight to her board and updated it. As she started to run probabilities, Peabody set a plate and a fresh mug of coffee on her desk.

"Bacon and eggs seemed right. Dr Mira, how about some breakfast? I'm serving it up."

"Oh. That's an idea." Mira came in, walked to the board. "Whatever Eve's having is fine." She studied the dead photo of Sandy. "One wound?"

"Yes. One stick, dead in the heart."

"Personal again. Close work. Different weapon, different methodology than Coltraine, but the same sentiment, if you will. He likes to watch them die. Likes to be connected. Businesslike about it, but not removed."

"Killing's business for cops. You could say."

"Leaving him naked. Humiliation, as with using Coltraine's own weapon on her, taking it and her badge from the scene."

"I guess so." It threw her for a moment—and Eve realized it shouldn't have—to see the woman who'd been cuddling and soothing a screaming baby one minute coolly profiling a killer the next.

"It's a cover-up, a way to make it look like he got rolled and done," Eve continued. "Like taking Coltraine's jewelry, her wallet, were or could be interpreted as a cover-up, to make it initially appear as robbery. But the humiliation follows. It's a benefit. He was covered with ratty blankets, dirty clothes, filthy tarps."

"The killer disliked him, found him of little worth. Easily disposed of."

"Ricker likes to dispose of people who outlive their usefulness to him."

"Ricker may have ordered the murder, but the person who carried it out would—or certainly could—choose the method. The time, the place. Thank you, Peabody." Mira sat with the plate Peabody brought her. "You're focused on Coltraine's squad. Let's look at them."

"I smell food." Cher Reo, disheveled in pajamas covered with yellow daisies stopped on her way into the room to sniff the air. "And coffee. Food and coffee, please."

"I can be the waitress." Mavis followed Reo into the room. "Belle's sleeping, and I'm starved. I feel like French toast."

"Mmm," Reo said. "French toast."

"I'll make it two. Hey, Nadine, want to be a threesome with French toast?"

"I'd be a fool not to. Who got killed?" Nadine demanded as she strolled in. "Mira wouldn't spill."

"Jesus, go away," Eve ordered, but resisted yanking at her hair. Or Nadine's. "I'm working."

"I'll keep it off the record." Nadine grabbed a slice of bacon from Eve's plate. "I can help. We're the smart girls. Let's solve some crime!"

When she reached for Eve's mug, Eve grabbed her wrist. "There'll be another murder if you touch my coffee."

"I'll go get my own." But she walked to the board first, and found Sandy's photo. "One in the heart. No muss, no fuss."

Eve frowned as Nadine strolled to the kitchen. The hell of it was, they *were* the smart girls.

"Okay, all right. Reo, shut the damn door before somebody else wanders in here." Then she blew out a breath when Louise did just that.

"I couldn't sleep so . . . oh, French toast!"

"She's a smart girl," Nadine pointed out, and went over to shut the door herself. "Mavis, Louise wants French toast. We're helping Dallas on a case."

Eve resisted—barely—the urge to beat her head against the desk. "Everybody just sit down and shut up. Nadine, I don't want anything in here on-air, unless I clear it. And I don't want to see any of it in a damn book."

"I won't air anything without your go-ahead. As to the book? Hmmm, interesting."

"I mean it. Louise, you take your medi-van down to Pearl, don't you?"

"Sure."

"Have you ever treated a couple of scavengers called Kip and Bop?"

"As I matter of fact I have. They—"

"You can stay. I might have questions. Reo, let me tell you about this guard on Omega."

Since they were there, Eve started on the eggs while she summed up Cecil Rouche's connection to Ricker.

19

It was ridiculous, briefing a bunch of women—mostly civilians at that—on murder. Women in pajamas, Eve thought as she ran it through for Reo. Women in pajamas eating French toast and nibbling on bacon.

Smart girls, okay. But still. Other than Peabody, Reo, and Mira, what did they know about cop work? She could stretch it for Nadine, she supposed. Working the crime beat gave Nadine some insight. And she could be trusted not to put a story ahead of ethics. That was something.

Maybe Louise wasn't so far out of the box. As a doctor, she'd treated plenty of victims. As for Mavis, she knew the streets, which didn't really apply here. But she was basically serving coffee anyway.

What the hell.

"So, you want to make a deal with Rouche, give him incentive to flip on Max Ricker—and his New York contact who you believe killed both Coltraine and Sandy."

"Yeah. If Rouche has the name."

"If he has it," Reo agreed. "And to pressure him to flip on Max Ricker as the orchestrator of the murders. Ricker, who's already serving multiple life sentences in the toughest penal facility we have. We can't do any more to him, in any real sense, but Rouche, an accessory before and after, possibly conspiracy to murder—he'd pay for it. If Callendar gets you what you hope, you'd have enough for that, and enough to push him to giving you the name of the actual killer—if he has it."

"That's not the point. If Ricker pushed the button, and he damned well did, he has to be held accountable." Eve couldn't—wouldn't—budge on that single point. "Charged, tried, and convicted of these two murders. One of them a cop. Maybe a couple more life sentences added on doesn't mean anything, practically. But they matter. It matters for Coltraine."

"The law may not be able to make him pay, in any real sense, more than he already is." Louise looked to the murder board, and Coltraine's photo. "But if he isn't held accountable, it's not justice, is it? Two people are dead because he wanted them dead."

"Justice also includes the families and those who loved the victims," Mira added. "They're entitled to it."

Reo blew out a breath. "I don't disagree, and I'll have to pull all that out—and more—to convince my boss to take this metaphorical slap at Ricker, and let another fish off the line to do it. But he doesn't walk on this, Dallas. Rouche and the tech, they don't walk."

"I don't want them to. Accepting and exchanging bribes, tampering with security, falsifying documents, money laundering. We can pin his ex-wife, too, which adds more pressure. He'll do cage time, but I'm betting

Rouche will consider a stretch of ten a gift against life."

"Charge him with conspiracy to commit," Reo projected, "then deal it down. I'll take it to my boss if you get what we need. But that deal's going to depend on what Rouche brings to the table. Do you think he knows the name of the killer?"

"The actual identity, no. I figure he went through Sandy. But he may know enough to narrow the field. And he may know enough to help us plug up the funnel Ricker's using to fund his operation. If he's got one cop in his pocket still, he's probably got more."

"You're sure it's a cop?" Nadine asked.

"Not only a cop, but one of Coltraine's squad." She ordered data on her wall screen. "Delong, Vance, her lieutenant. Authority figure who likes to keep things low-key. Family man. Twenty years in, with more administrative interests and skills than investigative. He rarely works in the field, but does so on occasion."

"He prefers a steady flow," Mira said when Eve nodded to her. "While he does possess solid leadership qualities, he's better suited to running this small squad than he might be in helming a larger, more complex department."

"O'Brian, Patrick. Detective," Eve continued. "The senior man in the squad. Experience. Claims he prefers the slower pace of his squad to the work he used to do. His personal relationship with Coltraine is reputed to be a kind of father–daughter deal. With the way the squad's set up, he—and the others—would partner up when Delong paired them."

"He would be, in my opinion, the most trusted member of the squad. The others respected him," Mira added. "My read of the files and Dallas's notes indicated that the squad trusted his opinion more than their lieutenant's. He's the team leader."

"Coltraine wouldn't have questioned him," Peabody said. "If he contacted her, told her he needed her on a case, a follow-up, any kind of op, she'd have done exactly what we believe she did that night. Get her weapons, walk out to meet him. But . . . Well, he looked really sad at her memorial. And his wife came. It felt sincere."

"Sometimes, for some, killing's just business," Eve said.

"True." Mira nodded in agreement. "And that business can be held separate from sincerity. Cops separate their emotions very often. One with his longevity could potentially commit the act, as a job to be done, and regret the loss of a friend or coworker. He has the maturity needed for the control of the kills, and the experience. But the personal elements of the acts don't quite fit his profile, again in my opinion. The humiliation of both victims."

"It may have been part of the orders," Louise suggested. "Part of the assignment."

"True enough," Mira admitted.

"He wouldn't have used 'cunt'. In the message to me." Eve studied O'Brian's face. "It's too crude for his type. 'Bitch' but not 'cunt'. Plus I don't think he'd have screwed up the tail on me. He's too experienced. Delong would have, but not O'Brian. At this point, he's last on my list."

She brought up the next. "Clifton, Dak, Detective. Now, he'd use 'cunt'. And he'd screw up a tail. He's cocky, full of himself, and not nearly as good as he thinks he is. Youngest male in the squad, thinks he's a ladies' man, and hit on Coltraine. She deflected."

"Guys hate that." Nadine cut another piece of French toast. "Killing's a little extreme, but they hate that."

"There are elements of anger in the killings," Mira pointed out. "That need, or that enjoyment, in the close-up kill. The delay in killing Coltraine, so she'd know what was coming. The humiliation again. I would expect from his type to have signs of some sexual abuse. If not actual rape, some molestation. Proving his power over her."

"He may have done so without leaving a mark, a sign." Louise considered the data. "Touching her, or verbal abuse. You don't think it's him," she said to Eve. "Why?"

"I'd like it to be him. He's a prick. But he's a hothead, with a jacket that lists excessive force, insubordination. Ricker tends to go for smarter, cooler. Then again, he might've been all Ricker could get in this case. He's not out of it, he's just not top of my list."

She moved on. "Newman, Josh, Detective. Light touch, takes it easy. Keeps his head down and does the job."

"He's not top of your list either." Mavis stood at the board, a plate in her hand. "It's the woman." She ate another bite, turned to where Eve sat. "It's got to be the woman. She's the best fit."

"Why?" Nadine wanted to know.

"Well, jeez, Coltraine might've respected her lieu-tenant, and the old guy. She maybe liked the asshole okay, even if she brushed him back. Because, hey, Morris and she had good taste. Maybe she got on fine with this last guy, too. But she and this one? Only women in the club, right? They're going to have a dif-ferent kind of thing. Women say shit to each other and talk about stuff they don't with penises. Look at us. Sorry," she said abruptly to Mira. "Stepping on your spot."

"No, it's interesting. Your idea is that Cleo Grady killed Coltraine because they were women."

"I just figure she'd get closer than the others, know more about what the what was when Coltraine was off—you know, the R&R time. Like she's not going to tell the asshole she's got her period and wants a hot bath, or the old guy how she's got the hornies and can't wait to jump Morris. Like that. This one probably knew all that."

"And would've known, more than the others, that she'd be home alone that night." Nadine pursed her lips. "Good one, Mavis."

Mavis grinned, shrugged. "Okay," she said to Eve, "am I right or am I wrong?"

"You win the Smart Girl Award."

"Uptown!"

"Grady's your prime? You could've told me," Peabody complained.

"I didn't bump her up until this morning. She's cool-headed, but she's got something under there that runs hot. There's the ring. Okay, you take it because you're playing at making it look like robbery. But you don't send it back with the badge and weapon. You keep it. A man might do the same, for a trophy. But she likes jewelry—the subtle, classy kind. So it's an element. Coltraine might've told the entire squad she was taking an evening at home alone, but given her type, she was more likely to talk about it with Grady. Plus, she and Grady were working a case together. More opportunity. And the opportunity for Grady to tag her, tell her she had something go hot on the investigation. And Ricker likes using women. He likes using them, hurting them, disposing of them. It's icing for him to pit one against the other."

"Sandy." Peabody set her plate aside and rose to go to the board. "It would be easier for a woman to get close to him. Play on his ego, and he'd have less cause—in his mind—to worry about her, physically."

"Physically's a factor though, isn't it?" Nadine pointed toward Grady's photo. "Didn't the killer carry Coltraine to the basement? Or do you think Sandy was there and did the heavy work?"

"Maybe. But she could've done it."

"I carried Dallas down." Peabody smiled. "We reen-acted."

"Going on the assumption this is your killer, she wouldn't have wanted him there. Or anyone else there." Mira gestured with her coffee cup. "Factoring in the theories, this would have been a one-on-one, woman-to-woman. On orders perhaps, but personal."

"You need more than theories. Sorry." Reo spread her hands. "You've got no probable cause, no witness, nothing putting your suspect at either scene. Unless Rouche worked with her directly, and can give us some chapter and verse—or Ricker gets a wild hair and decides to flip on her for the fun of it—there's no physical evidence, and no real circumstantial."

"Crap City." Mavis plopped her butt on Eve's desk. "Because all my tinglies are saying the bitch is guilty."

"Usually it takes more than the tinglies to convict," Reo pointed out. "First Callendar's got to come through. Then, given that, Rouche has to spill. I might like the theory, in principle, but from where I'm sitting, you don't have any more on her than you have on any of them. Which is not anything."

"Tinglies should count," Mavis protested. "Besides. Oops!" She slid off the desk. "Bellamina's awake," she said tapping the big pink butterfly pinned over her ear. "Cha!"

"Mavis," Eve called out as Mavis dashed for the door. "Thanks for the input."

"Hey, us double-X chromos have to stick together."

"Some of the others are probably stirring by now." Louise got to her feet. "I'll gather them up and steer them into the dining room and keep them out of your way."

"I guess the party's about over." Nadine stretched out her legs. "I can do some research, see if I can find anywhere Ricker's path might've crossed with this Cleo Grady's. They had to connect somewhere. I take it you've checked her pockets. It's unlikely she killed two people for love or the fun factor."

"I've looked at her financials as far as I can without the probable cause to dig deeper. I figure she's been paid, but I don't discount the fun factor—or what people like her consider love. Ricker liked younger women.

"It'll go back, though," Eve mused. "It won't be recent, that connection. She didn't turn up in the sweep after we busted him, but she's no new recruit. That means she's got some layers over her, and some time in."

"If you find me a connection between her and Ricker—something solid—I can use that and her connection to Coltraine. I may be able to finesse a search warrant, and authorization for that deeper dip into financials." Reo considered it. "If you can get Rouche to say Ricker has someone in Coltraine's squad. I don't need a name, just the verification that Ricker has someone inside that unit, I can get the warrants. Maybe IAB—"

"They don't have anything on her," Eve told Reo. "I checked."

"Well, maybe they should look again."

"I'll take another look at her file," Mira said. "And her background data. I'll work up a more comprehensive profile."

"I'll write it up, run probabilities." Peabody got up to gather empty plates. "While Nadine's looking for that crossed path with Max Ricker, I can look for one between Grady and Sandy. Maybe he recruited her."

"Or she recruited him." Eve ordered more data on-screen—split screen. "Sandy, Grady, Alex Ricker.

They're all about the same age. Yeah, that might be something. Go back ten years, fifteen. College pals. If she was Ricker's that far back, he might've used her to get to Sandy. Let's—hold it."

She swiveled back to her 'link. "Dallas."

"What do you want first, Dallas?" Callendar asked. "'Cause I got a shitload for you."

"Did you break the encryption?"

"Damn fucking-A tooting. Gee, I'm really tired now. Booster's wearing down. Text, Omega to New York." She yawned, blinked. "Sorry. Text: 'Hit target within forty-eight. Complete disposal. Complete arrangements with hunter. Usual fees cleared when disposal verified.'

"Second text, Omega to New York," Callendar continued. "Oh, this is the one we matched with a toss-away down there. Text: 'Go. Coordinate with mole. Don't disappoint me, dear.'"

"Are there any more?"

"Isn't that enough?"

"Nothing within the last twenty-four from Omega?"

"Not on this. But to jump ahead, there's one from New York to Omega, same 'links as the second trans. Text: 'Disposal complete. I never disappoint.' That was sent an hour after Coltraine's TOD, to the unregistered 'link we dug up in Rouche's quarters. We also dug up a nice bit of accounting. He kept records, Dallas, of income. Payments listed by date—going back for ten months—and the accounts, by number, where he stashed the funds. It was a romp through the daisies. Then there's the e-mail. We pulled them off his in-room comp. All e's are required to go through security, but it looks like he got his buddy Art to bypass. The receiver's account is under Luanne DeBois."

"Yeah, I bet it is."

"Lots of lovey-dovey. And lots of instructions and communication about where and how to access funds, what to do with them. He is so screwed."

"Wrap him up and bring him in. But keep it under the radar. I don't want Ricker knowing his boy's pinned. Security breaches, fraternizing with prisoners, suspicion of collusion. That's enough to get them down here. Keep them separated on the trip back. Full security from here to there. If you need it, have the warden send a couple of people he can trust with you. I'll contact him directly, clear it. Get it going, Callendar."

"Sisto, we're getting the hell off this rock!"

"Good work," Eve added and signed off.

"That gives us goods on Rouche, but unless we can put that 'link into Ricker's hand—"

"Don't screw with my mood, Reo. I've got work, and I'm really happy."

She contacted the warden, then Whitney. Then, because under the circumstances being an informant for IAB didn't make her sick, she contacted Webster.

She stared at the blue screen of blocked video.

"Jesus, Dallas, it's Sunday morning. I'm off."

"I have information for IAB, but if you're too busy to—"

"What, what, what?"

"Are you alone?"

"What's it to you?" He cursed into the silence. "Yeah, yeah, I'm alone. I'm also in bed, mostly naked. I

x

356

can unblock the video to confirm, if you want to dream about me."

"I've already seen you mostly naked, and it never caused me to dream."

"Cold."

"Listen up. I'm informing IAB that I strongly suspect Detective Cleo Grady of colluding with Max Ricker, of being on his payroll, and of the murders of Detective Amaryllis Coltraine and Rod Sandy."

"Hold it. Hold it. You're making an arrest?"

"Did I say I was making an arrest? I'm informing you, as a member of IAB, that I suspect a fellow officer is involved in illegal activities, for gain, with a known and incarcerated criminal. I suspect that fellow officer killed Detective Coltraine on the orders of Max Ricker, and that she killed Rod Sandy."

"Who the hell is Rod Sandy?"

"Alex Ricker's personal assistant. He's in the morgue. I suspect, again on Max Ricker's orders, that Grady and Sandy worked together to murder Coltraine, and to splash some suspicion on Alex Ricker."

"What's your evidence?"

"I don't have to give you evidence," Eve said as Webster, dragging on a T-shirt, came on-screen. "I'm relaying my suspicions, and that's enough for IAB to start the ball rolling. If you consider that mostly naked, Webster, it's no wonder you're in bed alone on Sunday morning."

"I put clothes on. Stop yanking my chain. We don't release the hounds on a cop just on another cop's say-so."

"You know that's not what this is. Take a good look at her, Webster, and for Christ's sake, don't tip her off.

I'm building a case, and it's taking shape. If I'm off, I'm off, and no harm done. But I'm not. I've got some expert corroboration on that."

"What corroboration?"

"The tinglies," she said and cut him off.

Ball's rolling, ball's in the air, she thought. Nothing more to do just then but wait. She started to go out, remembered all the women who were probably swarming around the house. She detoured to the elevator. When it opened in her bedroom, she snuck over and closed the door. Then she walked to the bed, let out one sigh, and dropped face down onto it.

Coltraine sat at her desk in the squad room while Eve stood by Grady's.

"She was never a friend, never a partner." Sorrow weighed down Coltraine's voice. "Not to me, not to any of us. She'd have killed any one of us if Ricker ordered it."

"I doubt you were her first. It usually takes more than one to do it that cold. She doesn't have any kills on the job. Probably too bad as Testing after a termination's pretty intense. More intense than the screening, the evals, to get a badge."

"You seem so sure it was her."

"You looked in her face when she killed you."

Coltraine swiveled her chair from side to side. "Your dream, Dallas, your perspective. I can't tell you anything you don't already know."

"Fine, we'll play it that way. Yeah, it's her. That's my perspective."

"Because we're women."

"Plays into it, yeah. I think Mavis had some good points. But she was in my top two right along. Newman was up there with her because he keeps his head down, stays off the grid. Does the job, pleasant guy, doesn't make waves. A man who can do that makes a good tool. Which is why Clifton just didn't fit. Too volatile. The LT? Too much of a by-the-book guy, and O'Brian . . . He just plays straight for me. A good cop who takes pride in the job. You can't take pride in what you abuse, in what you betray. Plus the wife, the family. Why struggle to pay the bills, give the kids the education if you've got this well to dip in?"

"You like him."

"I guess. Delong needs the squad—they're family, and he needs that dynamic. Clifton's posturing, hanging out with the guys so he can brag whose chops he busted that day, and use that to get under a skirt when he can. Newman, he plods his way through, maybe has a drink after a long shift with his partner of the day, then goes home to his wife and dog.

"Grady, she's a loner. Nobody's there when she comes home. I know how that is. But she doesn't live the job, that's not it. If she did, she's smart enough, savvy enough to be second grade by now—closer to making first—to work out of a more powerful unit, a sexier squad." Eve tapped her fingers on Grady's desk. "But she's not and she doesn't. Because too much attention makes it so some people look too close. She's got something to hide."

"So did you. Hacking your father to death when you were eight's a big secret for a cop."

"I didn't remember it, not clearly. It wouldn't have mattered if I had. I did live the job. I needed it like I needed to breathe. And Feeney wanted me—" She broke off, angled her head. "Someone wanted me. That was a first. Someone saw me, wanted me, was willing to *invest* in me. That was a rush. Maybe Ricker saw her. What if—" She broke off again, cursed.

"Cat's on your ass," Coltraine said.

Eve woke feeling Galahad's paws kneading her ass. Then the considerable weight of him was gone. She rolled over and saw Roarke with his arms full of sulky cat.

"Sorry," he told her. "He's fat, but sneaky. He beat me to you."

"Were you going to knead my ass?"

"I think of little else, night and day." He sat beside her, stroking the cat. "I'm told you were called away from the party last night. Rod Sandy."

"Yeah." She sat up. "I don't think anyone missed me especially, so—"

"I did."

Now she smiled. "Yeah?"

"Yeah." He leaned forward to kiss her.

"I guess I should ask if you had fun."

"I was with a group of men, friends, in casinos, in strip joints of the highest, and the lowest, class."

"You took Trueheart to a strip dive?"

"He almost glows in the dark when he blushes. It's charming, actually. The boy also hit for over five grand on some ridiculous slot called Pirate Quest."

"Five? Yo-ho, Trueheart."

Roarke laughed. "And I've heard every variation of that ever since."

"Oh my God. My sweet blushing Jesus, wait. Rewind. You took Mr Mira to strip joints."

"He's a big boy, and enjoyed himself. He has a pair of pasties to prove it."

"No, no, no." She clamped her hands over her ears in defense. "I don't want to hear Mr Mira in the same sentence as pasties."

"And he won about twelve hundred at craps. McNab came out two thousand, three hundred dollars, and eighty-five cents ahead. Precisely—which he informed us of often. Charles ended up down just over that. Feeney won about twenty-five dollars, keeping the reputation of his lucky shirt intact. Baxter broke even."

"How about you, hotshot?"

"As it was my casino, if I win, I lose—in a matter of speaking. What about you? Did you have fun?" When she sat there, frowning, he flipped a finger down the dent in her chin. "That wasn't a trick question."

"I had to think about it. I have to say I did, in a weird way. I'm surprised. Then this morning, I end up running a breakfast meeting with the core group. Through no plan of mine. And Mavis puts her finger on the killer."

"Mavis?"

"Yeah. I've got all these brains—I don't mean Mavis is stupid, but I've got the police detective, the profiler, the ace reporter, and the doctor. And it's the former grifter turned music disc star and mother who nails it. I'll fill you in later if you want, but I guess I've got to go down and do whatever I'm supposed to do with everybody until they go the hell home."

"They've all gone the hell home."

"Don't toy with me."

"With many thanks for a wonderful party."

She started to grin, caught herself. "That's bad, right? That's being a crappy hostess. I was just going to go down for an hour while the rest of them were getting breakfast and all that. I was supposed to be down there waving bye-bye and thanking everyone for coming."

"I can tell you everyone who was still here when we arrived hoped you got some much needed rest. McNab had to come up and wake Peabody, so you weren't alone. I think you did very well."

"How long have I been down?"

"I don't know when you finally fell on your face, but it's nearly four now."

"Shit. Shit. I have to check, make sure Callendar's on her way."

"I can tell you she is, along with the other detective, two prisoners, and a representative of Omega. They had to clear the shuttle with me. So." He shifted, moved back to sit at the head of the bed, patted the space beside him. "Why don't you come over here and tell me what prisoners my shuttle is transporting to New York, and how they're connected to Ricker, Coltraine, and Sandy."

"It's going to take a while," she warned him.

"Believe me, after nearly twenty hours of gambling, naked women, strip music, and extraordinarily filthy jokes, I'm ready for home."

She rolled over until she was snuggled against him. "I missed you, too."

And while the cat sat at the foot of the bed washing himself, she filled Roarke in on the progress of the case.

20

Roarke listened, relaxing with his wife curled up against him. The cat padded up the bed to bookend him at the hip.

Yes, it was good to be home.

"They'll shut him down for a while," he said, thinking of Ricker. "But down the line he'll find another Rouche, another way. His power's diminished, his freedom gone—he needs some outlet. Some . . . entertainment."

"He has enough power, and freedom, to have caused two murders. Or one, anyway," Eve considered. "I don't think he ordered Sandy's. If Callendar didn't find a transmission on that, I have to believe it wasn't there. Grady did that one for free, for herself."

"Ricker wouldn't object. Not in the long run. Sandy was on shaky ground, enough to let it show. Ricker might have decided to snip that thread even as he arranged for Coltraine's murder."

"I don't know." She started to roll away, and Roarke tightened his grip on her. "I'll be back. He's used Sandy for years—more than likely," she continued as she got off the bed. "Sandy, shaky or not, was his best line to his son. His infallible way to keep tabs on Alex. That's gone now."

"Grady might think she can find a way to make that work for her." Roarke watched Eve go to the panel, open it to select a bottle of wine.

"I got ambition from her, and couldn't figure out why she's stuck at third grade, working out of that small, low-level squad. Now it makes sense, because her ambitions lie elsewhere." Eve chose a Tuscan red, opened it. "So yeah, I've got to figure she's got plans. And she's got to think she's in the clear on Coltraine. Sandy takes the rap there. Or I work on trying to tie Alex up along with his dead pal. That's how it's going to look."

"You've got plans."

"I'm working on some." She poured two glasses of wine, then carried them to the AutoChef. She programmed an assortment of cheeses, breads, crackers, fruit. She brought the wine over, handed a glass to Roarke, put hers on the night table before going back for the food. When she laid the tray on the bed, both the cat—who'd propped his head on Roarke's thigh— and her husband studied her.

"Well now, isn't this homey?"

"Some . . ." She reached over him for her wine, brushed her lips over his on the way back. "Might consider it groveling."

"It might be a start."

She spread cheese on a small round of crusty bread, offered it. "Alex and Sandy hooked up in college. Father and son weren't on the best of terms at that point. So it could be Ricker enlisted Sandy to get close, to develop a friendship." She spread another round for herself. "The

365

thing is, from what I've got at this point, Grady went to college. Not the same college, but she did six months in Europe. Some sort of exchange deal."

"You're wondering if she was Ricker's even then, and she recruited Sandy for him."

"It's a thought. She'd have been pretty young. But then so were you when you had business with Ricker. You don't remember her? She might've used a different name when she came around, maybe had a different look."

"There were women, certainly. Young women. He enjoyed them. Used them. Sexually or for whatever purpose best suited. I saw her ID shot, and got a look at her at the memorial. She didn't look familiar."

Eve brooded over it. "It doesn't fit that she's new to him. He couldn't know Coltraine would transfer to New York before she knew it herself. Grady's been in that squad for three years, and a cop for more than eight. And he'd never trust someone that new with an assignment like this. Plus, he's been in a cage longer than Coltraine's been in New York, so how would he select and convince Grady to kill her? *Hunter*. That was his term for her in the transmission. She's done this before."

"So she was in place, and it happened to be the right place and the right time for this purpose."

"Yeah. If not her, he'd have someone else. But it was her, so how, why, and when did she turn, did she sign up? She didn't join the force right out of college. She took another couple years. I've got no employment on record for that period."

"It's not unusual to take a few months or a year between graduation and the start of a career. In this case, it would've been time for more specific training and education."

"Detective third grade, small squad—not much notice there. She lives alone, nobody to wonder where she is, what she's doing. She takes every day—always has—of her vacation and sick leave."

"Unlike someone we know," Roarke said to Galahad as he offered the cat a small cracker and a smudge of cheese.

"Flexing time regularly," Eve added. "Not enough to raise eyebrows, but considerable. Enough time, when you add it up, for her to take other *assignments*. I need to know where she was during that period between college and going on the job. If she crossed with Sandy during that six months in Europe. Where she goes during her off time. I only need one connection, one time paths crossed. Reo can get me a search warrant on that."

"I take it we're working tonight."

Eve popped a grape into her mouth before she carried the tray over to her dresser. "It's not night yet." She crawled back onto the bed, and onto her man. "And I have to finish groveling."

"That's right, you do." In a quick move he reversed their positions. He lowered his head, caught her bottom lip in his teeth. Tugged. "There's quite a bit of groveling to be done here. So this might take a while."

"What choice do I have? My word is my bond."

*

Sleep, sex, a little food—it was, Eve thought, the trifecta of energy boosts. And since she was going to use that energy to work, she deserved her most comfortable clothes. In ancient jeans and an even more ancient Police Academy T-shirt, she brought coffee out of her office kitchen. And found Roarke studying her board.

"Because she's a woman?"

Eve passed him one of the mugs. "I know it sounds shaky. I guess you had to be here. It could be any one of them, but she's the best fit. And fitting her . . . it's all head and gut. That's the problem. Without more, without some bump along the way, I can't get the search. And the search may be the only way to find the bumps."

"If bumps are there, we'd find them with the unregistered."

"Can't do it. Before, that was for Morris." She shook her head, knowing as logic it was again shaky. "I'm going after another cop. I have to do it straight. Every step I take has to be by and on the book for the investigation. And for me. She made a mistake somewhere, overlooked something, sometime. She made one by sending Coltraine's weapon and badge back. By botching the ambush on me."

"Assuming it's Grady. This one." Roarke tapped Clifton's photo. "He's trouble. I know his type."

"Yeah, and I won't be surprised to hear at some point he's ordered to hand over his pieces and badge. And if Coltraine had been knocked around, he'd be top of my list. That was a mistake," Eve considered. "Grady did it too clean. It just wasn't physical enough, either of the hits. That's pride. She's proud of her work. She does well on the job, she gets kudos from her LT. She does well on her mission, she gets them from Ricker. She covers both."

"'Don't disappoint me, dear,'" Roarke remembered. "It does strike as a warning to a female. One that puts her in a subordinate position, and one that implies a relationship."

"Do you ever call your subordinates 'dear'?"

"Good Christ, I hope not. It's a kind of backhanded slap, isn't it? If I need to slap an employee, I do it face-to-face."

"Exactly. Ricker can't, being all busy in a cage off-planet. The whole phrase is an insult, and a warning. His history with women, it just fits again. So where did she catch his eye? I figure I'll start with that six months in Europe, the college stint. I might find some intersect with Sandy, then I can work back, and forward from there."

She went to her desk to do just that. Roarke continued to stand, studying the board.

Attractive woman, he thought. Compact, athletic, a strong face, but very female in the shape of the mouth, the line of the jaw. Certainly one of Ricker's type, he mused—as far as he could recall. And still, if that connection went back as far as Eve seemed to think, she'd have been eighteen, perhaps twenty. Ricker certainly hadn't been above using youth for sex, but had he ever taken an actual interest in a girl of that age?

Not in Roarke's memory of him.

No, that part didn't fit, not with the man he'd known in his own youth. Women had been commodities, something to be used. Easily discarded. Paid off, discarded, disposed of. Or, as with Alex's mother, eliminated.

"Look at her mother."

"What?"

"Her mother," Roarke repeated. "Run her mother, her parents. Indulge me," he said when she frowned at him.

Eve ordered the run, and Lissa Grady's data appeared on-screen.

"Attractive woman," Roarke commented. "Works part-time in an art gallery where she and her husband retired. Suburban Florida. Respectable salary."

"No criminal. I ran everyone's connections before. The father's clean, too," she pointed out. "Had his own accounting firm. Small company with two employees. Clean. Now he plays a lot of golf, and works freelance."

"Hmm. They must have sacrificed considerably to give the daughter the kind of education she had. Where were they when she started college?"

Eve ordered the history. "Bloomfield, New Jersey."

"No, the employment. She's a clerk, and he's working for an accounting firm. Go back on her. Where was she, let's say nine months before she gave birth?"

"Chicago," Eve announced. "Working her way through graduate school—art history major—as an assistant manager in a private art gallery. She moved to New Jersey, where her parents lived, during the pregnancy. She took maternity benefits, then the professional mother's stipend."

"And was single until, what would it be, she was about four months along."

"Like that never happens. It's . . . Wait."

"Run the gallery, Eve. Where she worked when she became pregnant."

She began, shook her head. "It doesn't exist anymore and hasn't for six years. It's an antique store now. Oh, big, giant pop. I'm an idiot. Not a protégée, not exactly. Not an employee—not only. Not a lover. His freaking daughter."

"Alex said he'd spent most of his life trying to please his father. Maybe she's doing the same. Ricker owned several art galleries, an excellent front for smuggling and art forgery. Lissa Grady—or Lissa Neil at the time—could've caught his eye."

"And if she turned up pregnant? He'd get rid of her?"

"Unless she was carrying a son, I imagine so. She's tested, it's a female. He might—if he was feeling generous—give the young woman some form of payment. If not, he'd issue a warning."

"And Lissa took either the payment or the warning, moved back home to New Jersey. Gave up her chance at her graduate degree, her job, had the kid. Married some guy."

"The some guy's stuck, more than thirty years. So I'd say Lissa found someone and made something."

"Would he have kept tabs on her?" Eve wondered. "Looked up the kid?"

"I wouldn't think so, no. The woman and the child wouldn't have existed for him."

"Okay. Okay." She pushed up to pace. "So, at some

point, they tell her. Or maybe they've been up front about it all along. Maybe she always knew the guy raising her wasn't her biological. She gets curious, she starts digging."

"And finds Max Ricker."

"Most people, they're going to be sick if they're looking for a biological and turn up a criminal kingpin, one suspected of being responsible for more deaths than a lot of small wars. If this is right, if this"—she pointed at Lissa's image on the wall screen—"is the connection, Grady went to him. She made the contact. I'm your kid, asshole, what are you going to do about it? What would he have done?"

"Depends on his mood again," Roarke said. "But he might have been entertained by a direct approach. And as he and Alex weren't on the best of terms at that point, it might've intrigued him. The idea of having a chance to mold an offspring."

"Educate her, train her. Use her." She knew all about that, Eve thought, all about the methods a father might use to *mold*. She blocked it out, focused on Grady. "And God, wouldn't it be sweet to use her to screw with the son who *disappointed* him?"

"And for her, wouldn't you think?" Roarke walked back to the board. "For her, also sweet to have a part in undermining the son—the prince, as he'd appear to be from the outside. The one who had all she didn't. The wealth, the advantages, the attention. The name. It all falls into place with this single element. But then you have to prove this single element is fact."

"I can do that." Eve grinned fiercely. "DNA doesn't

372

lie. I'm going to write this all up, toss it to Mira to add to the stew for the profile. I still need something that puts her and Sandy together, even just the same general place, same general time."

"That would be my assignment."

"It would, but you have to play it straight."

"You're always spoiling my fun."

"You already had fun. I groveled."

"True." He walked over, laid his hands on her shoulders, laid his lips on hers. "I know you." He rubbed her shoulders, lightly. "The part of you who isn't working the case in your head is wondering if all this is true, is she what she is, did she do what she did because of that DNA."

Yes, she thought, he knew her. "It's a question."

"And the mirror turns so you wonder next about your own blood. What passes from father to daughter."

"I know I'm not like her. But it's another question."

"Here's an answer. Three fathers—hers, mine, yours—and three products of that blood, so to speak. And all of us have done what we've done with it. Maybe because of it. You know you're not like her, you're sure of that much. I know you. I'm sure you never could have been."

He kissed her again before he left her.

She put it away, put away that part of her that wasn't working the case in her head. That was for later.

She stitched the theory together for Mira, and thought it was a shame Grady's DNA wasn't on record. She'd have her warrants in a fingersnap if she proved Grady was Max Ricker's daughter. Still, it wouldn't take much. A little spit, skin, hair, blood—whatever came handiest—was all she needed.

She sent messages to her commander, to Reo, to Peabody, and after a brief hesitation, to Morris.

Sitting back, Eve calculated the best, legal, and most satisfying method of collecting Cleo Grady's DNA.

"Here's an interesting bit of trivia," Roarke commented as he came back in. "The football team representing the university where Alex and Sandy became mates happens to play against the team representing the university where Grady was a visiting student."

"Is that a fucking fact?"

"It is. In fact, these teams hold a deep-seated rivalry and their matches are what you'd call events. Rallies, dances, mad celebrations. They held two of these events—one on each team's home pitch, during the time Grady was there."

"I like it."

"Alex got a bit of press as he scored goals in both those matches. I didn't find Sandy's name in any media, but he is listed as a member of the team."

"Second-string benchwarmer. Has to be a pisser. Reo's going to make noises—or make noises that her boss is going to make noises—that thousands of people must've been at those games. Hard to prove that Sandy and Grady actually met up. But it's going to be enough. It's going to weigh. Maybe Alex met her," she speculated. "Or saw Sandy with her. Would he know about her, about having a sister?"

"Max would only have told him if it was useful. More useful, to Max, to keep it to himself."

"Still, it has to be addressed. I have a lot of people to talk to in the morning." She angled her head. "What you said before about her education and her parents' finances. If Ricker paid for it, there's a record somewhere, however deep it's buried. I can't look at Grady's any deeper than I have, but Ricker's an open book. I can go anywhere I want there. As long as I play it straight."

"I knew you were going to say that, and just as I was getting excited."

Eve smiled. "Let's find her college fund. Add a little more weight to the scale for Reo."

She set up what she could, then refined the steps in a briefing the next morning at Central.

"It's not just my ass in the sling if I push for this warrant and you come up empty," Reo told her. "It'll be yours, and the department's in there with me."

"We'll find something. The warrant's not out of the box with what we have. Add in the blood tie with Ricker and Mira's profile, it's not only in the box, it's a lock."

"Alleged blood tie," Reo reminded her. "And the profile hinges on that. The need to impress her father, to punish her brother, and the rest of the psycho-shrink babble—no offense."

"None taken," Mira assured her.

"All that stands on her being Ricker's kid, and knowing it."

"We'll be substantiating that today. You're up for this, Morris?"

"Yes. Yes, I am."

"Peabody and I will pull Alex Ricker in, work him. If he knows about a sister, even suspects he may have one, we'll get it out of him. And letting the word get out that we've got Alex Ricker in the box, are interviewing him in the matter of Coltraine and Sandy? It's going to give Grady a feeling of accomplishment. I'll bet she'll want a pat on the back from Daddy."

"It would fit," Mira agreed. "She may try to contact him through her usual sources."

"Which we'll have, also in a box, within hours. Rouche will give us Ricker, and he'll give us Sandy. We may get lucky and get another log to add on the Grady fire." She looked at Feeney. "We need to know asap if she tries for the contact. You'll be set."

"We'll be set. She sends anything to the 'link Callendar found in Rouche's quarters, we'll nail it down. Once you work the return process out of Rouche, we'll send her whatever return you want."

"We're a go then. Get me the damn warrants, Reo. Peabody, wait outside, please. McNab, set it up. Morris, another minute."

Eve waited until the room cleared. "McNab's going to have ears on you the whole time you're with her."

"I'm not worried about it."

"She's a killer. It's her job. You should worry about it. If she senses anything off, she'll do you first, think about it later. You just have to—"

"We've been over what you want me to do, how you want me to do it, three times. I can do this. And I should be the one to do it, not only for Amaryllis, but because I'm the only logical choice. You have to trust me to do my part. I'm trusting you to do yours."

No choice, she thought, but to back off. "Call it in, either way."

"I will."

Eve watched him walk away, then stuck her hands in her pockets as Peabody stepped up. "He'll be okay, Dallas. McNab'll be right there. Practically."

"If he tips it the wrong way, and she pulls out her weapon or a knife, McNab will get it on record. Morris is still down. I couldn't work out a way to do it myself. She'll be on alert with me. I thought about pushing her into taking a swing at me, so I could swing back. Then, oops, I've got her blood on my shirt. But then I've provoked her into giving up DNA instead of her—essentially—volunteering it."

"He'll get it done. He needs to, so he will."

"Right. Contact Alex Ricker, and ask him real nice to come on down so we can chat."

"He'll bring a bunch of lawyers."

"I'm looking forward to it."

She went into her office to prep, to line up all the threads she intended to tie together. She could wrap that knot tight around Cleo Grady, but she needed all those threads to put the bow on it.

Now it was wait, she thought. Wait for Reo to get the warrants, wait for Callendar and Sisto to deliver Rouche, wait for Morris to play out his role.

Alex Ricker? At this point he was more a pawn than a thread. She'd use him—and prove his father, his friend, and his half sister had used him. And she'd prove all the threads ran out from him, simply because he was.

She wouldn't be sorry for it. He'd made his choices—to follow in his father's footsteps, or close enough alongside them to cross the lines. He'd chosen to stay on that path rather than change it for a woman who must have loved him. A woman who died because she'd loved him, and left him.

She stood at her window, drinking coffee, considering choices. When she heard the knock on her door, she called out, "Come on."

Mira stepped in, closed the door behind her. "Do you want me to observe when you interview Alex Ricker?"

"I've got it."

"All right. I will want to observe if and when you interview Cleo Grady."

"When. The DNA's going to lock it. I need that because the law says I do. But I know who she is. She's Ricker's spawn. What I don't know, what I'm curious about is what she wanted, or needed, from him. Was it the recognition, the money, the thrill? Maybe all of it. It fits that she sought him out rather than the other way. It fits their profiles."

"Yes. She'd be nothing to him, and he'd be important to her. She could make herself important to him."

"He educated her, so she must have. The college money, coming through a scholarship—with her the only recipient. That was stupid and greedy on Ricker's part. Why not spend some bucks to send off a few other kids? He'd buried the payment, putting it through one

378

of the arms of one of his fronts. He could've made it a legit deal, done the same a few times. Gotten the tax break or whatever."

"He wouldn't give a dollar to anyone without a purpose, a personal interest. It's not in his scope."

"Once she took it, he owned her. Was she too stupid to see that, or didn't she care? She didn't care," Eve said before Mira spoke. "I read your profile. I'm just talking out loud."

"It troubles you, all of this. The genetics of it."

"Maybe it does. But that only makes me more determined to put her away. She had a pretty good life from what I can see. Parents who stuck, a decent home. She tossed it. Some people are just born fucked up. I know that."

She studied Grady's photo on her board. "Maybe she was, maybe she was always going to go bad—even without knowing Ricker, without knowing she came from him. And maybe needing to know where she came from and finding out turned her, just enough. Just enough so she kept going, and couldn't go back. I'm curious."

"Will it make a difference in what you do?" Mira asked her. "Or how you handle what you've done, afterward?"

"No to the first. I'm not sure to the second. I'm not going to say taking her down isn't personal, because it is. Because she's a cop, because of Ricker. Because of Morris and because of Coltraine. It's personal, right down the line."

"And it's easier, clearer, to take the steps, do what has to be done when it's not. Or not this personal."

Eve met Mira's eyes and spoke calmly, coolly. "I want to hurt her, to use my hands on her, get her blood on them. I want that for all the reasons I just said. And I want it just for me."

"But you won't."

Eve shrugged. "I guess we'll see."

"You won't jeopardize the case for your own satisfaction, however much you'd enjoy it. That alone should answer one of your questions, Eve. Genetics stamp us, we can't deny it. But we build from there. At the end of the day you'll do what needs to be done, for all the reasons you named. But at the core of it, at the heart, you'll do what needs to be done for Amaryllis Coltraine."

"I didn't give her a chance, you know?"

"In what way?"

She let out a breath, shoved at her hair. "When she was alive, with Morris. I didn't give her a chance. It kind of irritated me for some reason that he was stuck on her. Stupid."

"Not stupid, really. You didn't know her, and you're very attached to him."

"Not that way."

Mira smiled. "Not that way. But you're not one who trusts quickly, or easily. God knows. You didn't trust her yet."

"I've been having dreams, kind of conversational dreams with her. It's weird. Weird because I know it's my head holding both ends of the conversation, but . . . I had this thought the other night at the shower deal. This thought that I guess comes out of those weird conversation dreams. I think I would've liked her okay if I'd given her more of a chance, when there was a chance. I think if that shower deal had been another six months or so down the road, she'd have been there."

"It's harder knowing that."

"It's fucking brutal actually."

"Dallas. Sorry, Dr Mira." Peabody poked her head in the door. "Alex Ricker's on his way in."

"Good. Set up for interview."

Wait's over, she thought.

21

Alex sat with his complement of lawyers while Eve and Peabody set up. Eve engaged the recorder and read off the salients. Though she'd Mirandized him before, she did so again.

"Questions?" she asked pleasantly. "Comments? Snide remarks?"

As she expected, the head suit went into a prepared riff on Mr Ricker's voluntary presence, on his willingness to cooperate, the previous examples of his cooperation. She let it run through, then nodded.

"Is that it? All finished now? Or would you like to give examples of Mr Ricker's kindness to the little orphaned children and small puppies?"

Harry Proctor looked down his important nose. "I'll make a note of your sarcasm and discourteous attitude."

"My partner here keeps them on disc."

"I can get you a copy," Peabody offered.

"And here's what I'm making a note of. The cooperative and civil-minded Mr Ricker comes into interview with not one, not two, but three—count them, three—lawyers. Makes me wonder just what you've got to worry about, Alex."

"I believe in being prepared, particularly when it comes to the police."

"I bet you do. But, golly, it's strange that someone who's prepared, a businessman of your . . . caliber would be, as he claims, oblivious to the machinations—don't you love that word, Peabody?"

"Top-ten favorite."

"Let's say it again, to the machinations of his personal assistant and longtime best pal, Rod Sandy. That you'd just be blissfully ignorant of Sandy and your father's plotting and planning. It makes you kind of an idiot, doesn't it?"

It got a rise of color along his cheekbones, but Alex's voice remained neutral. "I trusted Rod. My mistake."

"Oh boy, wasn't it just? We're talking *years* here, Alex. Your boyfriend's been socking away money your daddy paid him to spy on you, to pass info on. You can probably think back to a deal that didn't pan out the way you wanted, and wonder if it's because your old man had the inside track and felt like screwing with you."

"Am I in here to admit a trusted friend used me for his own gain, and my father enjoys complicating my life? Admitted. Freely. Is that all?"

"Not even close. It's got to piss you off."

"Again, freely admitted."

"In your shoes I'd want some payback." Eve gave Peabody a speculative glance. "If my partner here worked me that way and I found out? She couldn't run far or fast enough."

"And I can run pretty fast given the right incentive."

"I'd make her pay for it. How do you think I'd make you pay for it, Peabody?"

383

"In the most painful and humiliating way possible."

"See how well we know each other? The difference in the situations and personalities as I see it is I wouldn't end her. I'd want her to hurt and fear me for a long, long time. But we all have our different definition of fun. Did you have fun killing Sandy, Alex?"

"That accusation—"

Alex simply lifted a hand to cut the lawyer off. "Rod's dead? How?"

She'd kept a lid on it and saw now she'd been right to do so. He hadn't known, Eve thought. His network hadn't found Sandy, or hadn't been ordered to look quite deep enough. "I'm asking the questions. He betrayed you, made a fool of you, now he's dead. That's a one plus one equals two kind of deal around here. Of course, that's if we believe you were the goat."

She tipped back casually in her chair. "We could speculate that you and Sandy were duping your father. Take his money and Sandy feeds him what you want him to eat. You're smart enough to do that."

"It's exactly what I would have done, if I'd known."

"You're in a tough spot here, Alex. Say you knew and it could take you off the hook on Sandy's murder. But say you knew, and—since he's implicated in Coltraine's murder—that could tie you to a cop killing. Say you don't know, and you come off a fool who'd probably want some of his own back."

"Lieutenant Dallas," Proctor began, "my client can hardly be held responsible for the actions of . . ."

Eve didn't bother to listen, didn't bother to interrupt.

She just kept looking at Alex. It was Alex who finally shut the lawyer down, and leaned toward Eve. "I don't know when my father got his hooks into Rod. I intend to find out, but I don't know how long ago. I don't know why Rod betrayed me for money. Now I'll never know. You may not think the why would be important. It's essential to me. I didn't want Rod dead. I wanted to know why, I wanted to know if he had anything, anything at all to do with Ammy's death. I wanted to look in his face and know if he could've done that to her, to me. And why."

"He not only could have, he did. Why? Money's often enough. Add sex and the potential for power, and you've got it all. Hell, Alex, he's probably been banging your sister regularly since college."

"I don't have a sister, so the supposition is—"

"Christ, Peabody, maybe he is just an oblivious idiot." Eve pulled out Cleo Grady's photo, tossed it on the table. "Not much family resemblance, but that's understandable with half sibs."

Alex stared at the photo, and Eve watched his color fade shade by shade. "Get out," Alex said to the lawyers. "All of you, get out."

"Mr Ricker, it's not in your best interest to—"

"Get out now, or you're fired." He stared at Eve as the lawyers packed up their briefcases and left the room. "If you're lying about this, if you're playing me on this, I'll use every means at my disposal to have your badge."

"Now I'm scared."

"Don't *fuck* with me!"

It was the anger, the raw emotion through it, that

gave Eve some of the answers she'd wanted. "We'll remain on record. You have dismissed your attorneys?"

"Yes, I've damn well dismissed them. Tell me who this is, and what she has to do with me."

Morris opened the door of Ammy's apartment for Cleo Grady. She stepped forward, said only, "Morris," and gave him both her hands.

"I'm sorry I pulled you into this, Cleo. I wasn't thinking."

"Don't be. You shouldn't try to do this alone. She was my friend. I want to help."

She sounded so sincere, he thought. With just the slightest catch in her voice. How easy it would be to believe her, if he didn't know. He shifted to let her inside, closed the door. "I don't know if I could do it alone. But when her family asked, I . . . They don't want to come back here. I can't blame them. But going through her things, packing them up . . . There's so much of her. And none of her."

"I can take care of it. I've got the personal time coming. My LT knows I'm here today. Why don't you let me deal with this, Morris? You don't have to—"

"No, I said I would. I've started, but I keep, well, bogging down." Successful lies, Morris thought, were wrapped in truth. "The police still have her electronics, her files, but I started on her clothes. Her family told me to keep whatever I wanted, or to give what I thought appropriate to her friends here. How do I know, Cleo? How can I?"

"I'll help you." She stood, looked around the living

room. "She always kept her space nice. Here, at work. Made the rest of us look like slobs. She'd want us to put her things away, nice, if you know what I mean."

"With care."

"Yeah, with care." She turned to him. "We'll do that for her, Morris. Do you want to finish the clothes first?"

"Yes, that's probably best." He led the way into the bedroom where he had painfully begun the process of packing Ammy's things. Now he continued the task with the woman he believed had murdered his lover.

They spoke of her, and other things. He looked straight into Cleo's eyes as she folded one of Ammy's favorite sweaters. He could do that, Morris thought. He could let this woman touch Ammy's things, speak of her, move around the room where he and Ammy had been intimate, had loved each other. He could do whatever he needed to do, and for now—at least for now—feel nothing.

A twinge, just a twinge cut through when she began to box and wrap jewelry.

"She always knew just what to wear with what." Cleo's eyes met his in the mirror, smiled. "It's a talent I don't share. I used to admire . . . oh." She held up a pair of small, simple silver hoops. "She wore these a lot, for work anyway. They're so her, you know? Just exactly right, not too much, not too little. They're just . . . her."

It hurt, heart and gut. But he did what he had to do. "You should have them."

"Oh, I couldn't. Her family—"

Bitch, he thought as he watched her. You cold bitch. "Her family told me to give what was appropriate to friends. She'd want you to have those since they remind you of her."

"I'd really love to, if you're sure. I'd love to have something of hers." Tears sheened her eyes as she smiled. "I'll treasure them."

"I know you will."

There were so many ways to kill, he thought, as they closed and sealed boxes. Slow, painful ways, quick, merciful ways. Obscene ways. He knew them all. Did she? How many ways had she killed?

Had she felt anything when she'd taken Ammy's life? Or had it been simply a task to be done, like sealing a box for shipment? He wanted to ask her that, just that single thing. Instead, he asked if she'd like coffee.

"I wouldn't mind, actually. Why don't I get it? I know where everything is."

When she went out to the kitchen, he followed as far as the living room and crouched in front of the droid kitten. He activated it, then stepped away to carry boxes and protective wrap to a chair.

He began, meticulously, to wrap the pale green glass vase she'd used for the roses he'd sent her. And the kitten mewed, as programmed. It stretched its silky white body as Cleo came back with the coffee.

"Thanks." He kept his hands full—coffee, wrapping—while the kitten wound through Cleo's legs.

"She loved this thing." Cleo looked down as the kitten gave a plaintive meow and stared up at her with adoring eyes. "She just loved it. Will you keep it?"

"I suppose I will. I haven't thought that far yet."

Cleo laughed a little as the kitten continued to rub, meow, stare. "Do droids get lonely? You'd swear it's desperate for a little attention."

"It's programmed for companionship, so . . ."

"Yeah. Okay, okay." Cleo set down the coffee, bent down.

Morris continued to wrap even as he held his breath.

"It is kind of sweet if you go for this sort of thing. And she did. She bought it little toys, and the cat bed." Cleo picked up the kitten. Gave it a stroke. Cursed.

"Don't tell me it scratched you." Morris put aside the wrapping to go to her.

"No, but something did." Cleo held up her hand, and blood welled in a shallow cut on her index finger. "Something on the collar."

"Damn rhinestones." His own blood pumped hot, but his tone, his touch were both easy as he took Cleo's wounded hand. "It's not deep, but we'll clean it up."

"It's nothing. A scratch."

"You should wash and protect it." He took a handkerchief out of his pocket, dabbed at the blood. "She'll have what you need in the bathroom. Doctor's orders," he said.

"Can't argue with that. I'll be right back."

He folded the cloth, tucked it into an evidence bag. He removed the collar from the droid, studied—just for a moment—the faint smear of blood on the glittery stones he'd sharpened himself. And he bagged it as well.

Then he picked up the kitten, nuzzled it. "Yes, you'll come home with me. You won't be alone."

When Cleo came back in, he was sitting in one of Ammy's living-room chairs. "All right?" he asked.

"Good as new." She held up her finger with the clear strip on the tip. "Where's the cat?"

"I turned it to sleep mode." He gestured absently toward the ball of white on its pillow. "Cleo, I want to thank you again for all you've done today. It's been more help than you know. But I have to stop, for now. I think I've done all I can do in one day."

"It's a lot." She walked over, laid a hand on his shoulder.

He wanted to surge out of the chair, close his own hands around her throat and ask his single question. *What did you feel when you killed her?*

"Do you want me to come back tomorrow, help you with the rest?"

"Can I contact you? I'm just not sure."

"Absolutely. Anytime, Morris. I mean it. Anything you need."

He waited until she'd gone before he balled his hands into fists, kept them balled and tried to envision all his rage inside them. When his communicator beeped twice—McNab's all-clear—he rose. He walked over to pick up the sleeping kitten, its pillow, its toys.

He took them and nothing else from the home of the woman he loved. But the blood of her murderer.

In the interview room, Eve faced Alex across the table. "You want me to believe your father never told you that you have a half sib?"

"I want to know why you seem to believe I have one."

"Did you ever see Sandy with this woman?"

"No."

"You answered awfully quick, Alex. You've known Sandy since college, but you're absolutely sure you've never seen him with this woman."

"I don't recognize her. If you're trying to tell me she and Rod had a relationship, I didn't know about it. I haven't met every woman he's ever been with. Why do you think she's my sister?"

"Her mother was involved with your father."

"For Christ's sake—"

"Your father sent this woman to college. Paid the whole shot," she continued as she saw annoyance turn to bafflement. "She did six months at University of Stuttgart. Big rival of your alma mater's, right? Football rivals. Take another look."

"I tell you I've never seen this woman before in my life."

"Maybe you ought to think back to college. Sophomore year, and the big game. You made the varsity. Your pal was still a benchwarmer."

"We weren't . . ."

"Pals yet." Eve smiled.

"We knew each other. Of course. We were friendly enough."

Eve took out another photo, one of Cleo when she'd been eighteen. "Try this one, taken back in the day."

"I don't . . ." But he trailed off.

"Yeah, she looks different there. Younger, but that's

not all. Lots of long blond hair. The face is fuller. She looks girlier, fresher. Ring any bells?"

"You're talking about more than ten years ago. I can't remember every woman I've met or seen."

"Now you're lying to me. Fine, we'll just move on."

He slapped his hand on the photo before Eve could pick it up. "Who is she?"

"I ask the questions, you answer them. Now do you remember her?"

"I'm not sure I do. She looks like someone I saw around, during that time. With Rod. We were becoming friends, real friends. I saw him with her a few times, or someone who reminds me of her. I asked him about her, since we were starting to hang quite a bit— and, frankly, I liked the look of her. He was cagey, wouldn't say more than she went to Stuttgart. I only remember because I called her Miss Mystery. Just a lame joke between us that lasted for months. Long enough that I remember it, and her. She's not my sister."

"Because?"

"Because I don't *have* a sister. Do you think I wouldn't find out? That he—my father—wouldn't use it against me in some way? He'd—"

He broke off, and again Eve waited while he thought it through.

"You think my father sent her to Rod. To recruit him, to enlist him as a spy. To get close to me. That all this time, right from the beginning, Rod was my father's dog?"

He pushed up from the table, walked to the two-way

glass, and stared through his own image. "Yes, I see. I see how that could be, how he could and would orchestrate that. It doesn't make this woman my blood. My sister. It just makes her another of Max Ricker's tools."

Peabody's communicator signaled. She glanced at the text, nodded to Eve.

"We'll be able to verify that shortly. If you're being square with me on this, and if you were being square with me on wanting to know who killed Coltraine and why, you'll do what I tell you now."

"What are you telling me?"

"To stay here. It's going to take some time to wrap this, and I want you inside."

Alex continued to stare through the glass. "I've nowhere I have to be."

Eve stepped out to the corridor to confer with Peabody. "Morris pulled it off."

"McNab signals a go there. She left Coltraine's. We're on her, and she's heading back to work. That's a big plus as they're not done at her apartment. I'm getting like a zillion signals during the Ricker interview. Her comp's passcoded and it's got a fail-safe. They're bringing it in to Feeney. They haven't found, as yet, a toss-away 'link."

"She'd keep it with her. That's what I'd do."

"If she kept Coltraine's ring, it's not with her other jewelry. They haven't found it yet. Callendar's shuttle's on schedule. Morris is taking the sample to the lab, personally."

"Dickhead won't mess with him," Eve muttered,

thinking of the chief lab tech. "Not with Morris. I want to pick her up, but we don't have it. Not yet. Need the DNA, need the ring, the 'link. Any one of them would do it."

"We could get her down here. Use the Sandy homicide with the Alex Ricker connection. We believe he's responsible for both murders. We want to pick her brain, anything she might know, any take she might have. How we're trying to put him away, but we're hitting walls."

"Not bad, Peabody. Make it happen. Set up a conference room away from Interview. I don't want her running into Rouche when Callendar delivers him."

She turned away to contact Baxter herself. "Why haven't you found what I need?" she demanded.

"Working on it. We found a passcode. False bottom of her weapon's lockbox. It's a bank box. And before you tell me to contact Reo, I already did. We can't stretch the warrant to the bank box. We need a separate warrant, and we don't have enough for that."

"Damn it."

"Second that. There's nothing here so far that doesn't jibe with a cop's life, a cop's salary. No high-end electronics, jewelry, art. She's got some pretty serious weaponry though. Six pieces over and above her departmental issue. A freaking army of knives. Not all under the legal limit either, but she's got a collector's license. We checked for prints, for blood. They're showroom clean. She takes care of her tools."

"Is there a stiletto?"

"Several. We culled them out for forensics."

"Keep digging."

She clicked off as Peabody came back. "Grady's clearing it with her lieutenant. She's juiced, I could see it. The idea of coming in and bailing us out, of finding a way to put the screws to Alex. She's pumped."

"Good. Keep on Dickhead, will you? But not enough to put his back up. I'm going to move Alex to one of the visitor rooms, put a babysitter with him. We'll be working Grady, Rouche, and Zeban simultaneously, the way it's panning. You take Zeban. He's low rung, but that means he's going to flip. He just helped out his drinking buddy, and now he's in the soup. Work him quick and hard, Peabody. Scare the shit out of him."

"Oh, boy, oh, boy." Bouncing on her toes, Peabody rubbed her hands together. "Who's juiced now?"

Eve moved Alex, arranged for Cleo to be taken straight to the conference room upon arrival.

She paced awhile as she worked out the best strategy. And was ready when she got word Detective Grady was in the house. She grabbed a mug of coffee, a file bag, and timed it so she swung into the conference room a few minutes after Peabody.

"Appreciate you coming down." She kept her voice clipped, just a hair over into resentful.

"Not a problem for me," Cleo assured her. "Everybody in the squad wanted a piece of this. Now we've got one. I hear you have the son of a bitch in holding."

"For now. He's got three lawyers with him and more on tap. I want to record this. Okay with you?"

"Sure."

"Want some coffee, Detective?" Peabody asked.

"Sure. Thanks. I heard about the second murder. Rod Sandy? That's on Ricker, too?"

"Has to be. Okay, this is the way it's playing out." All business now, cop to cop, Eve sat across from Cleo. "Ricker and Sandy kill Coltraine. Ricker does Sandy to put the first murder on him. Could work, but where's Sandy's motive? There's no evidence of anything between Coltraine and Sandy. Sandy's Ricker's tool. Was. Like father like son," Eve said with a shrug. "You use the tool until you're done, then you break it so nobody else can. Ricker's blood? It's poison."

Cleo only smiled. "That may be your opinion, but that's not going to put Alex Ricker away for Ammy. If that's all you've got, you're not as good as everybody says you are."

"I put the old man away." Eve let anger—and some pride—punch through the words. "Nobody else ever did, or could. Don't forget that. I'll get his spawn, too. Count on it."

"Then why do you need me?"

"You worked with her. Morris, he's too close. I can't get what I need out of him. Everything's colored with emotion there. You worked with her, were friends with her. According to my partner, the fact you're female adds another layer to that."

"You said it yourself," Peabody told Cleo, "women talk about things to each other. Maybe they don't talk about those things even to guys they're sleeping with. Plus, you were both cops."

"She never mentioned Ricker to me, not by name.

But like I already told you, she talked about a guy she'd been involved with. How they'd broken it off, and she'd come here."

"She must've given you more than that," Eve pressed. "Are you saying you never asked what happened? Nothing?"

"It was her business. Maybe I poked a little." As if reluctant, Cleo hesitated, then sipped coffee. "I don't know how it helps, not with a solid case, but she said a few things off and on. Like he had money, and she'd traveled with him some. It just wasn't meant to be, and that kind of thing. She did say once he was too much like his father, but she didn't get into it. I didn't push because I didn't know we were talking about Ricker, for God's sake."

She frowned a moment. Eve could all but see the wheels turning in her head. How much to add, how much to fabricate. "You know, I remember she said something about how he had this friend. How they were practically joined at the hip, and that was annoying. She said she'd have thought they had a love affair except he was too busy doing her."

No, she didn't, Eve thought. Coltraine wouldn't have said that in a million.

"The friend didn't like her," Cleo added. "Tension there. Resented her. They had words at the end. He called her a cunt."

Eve picked up her cue, narrowed her eyes. "You're sure of that. That exact word?"

"Cunt cop, that's what she said he said. Said it to her as she was walking out with stuff she had at the boy-friend's place. She just kept walking. That was Ammy.

No point in mixing it up when it was done, you know? She was glad it was over, and that was that. She decided to transfer up here. That's what she said."

"But?" Eve prompted.

"I've gone over and over it, trying to read the nuances. Hindsight. I guess I'd have to say she was into Morris. She really cared about Morris. But she was still hung up on the guy back home. If I had to judge it, to judge her, I'd say if Ricker contacted her, made the play, she'd have gone for him. To him. He could've used her feelings to get at her."

Eve started to speak, broke off when her communicator signaled. "Crap. Sorry. I have to handle this."

"We can use some of this," Peabody said as Eve walked out. "The nuances, like you said, to try to pressure Ricker."

Keep it up, Peabody, Eve thought, and answered Morris's signal.

"Dallas."

"I'm at the lab. Cleo Grady is Max Ricker's daughter. We're doing a second test, but—"

"It's all I need."

"I'm coming in, Dallas. I need to be there when you take her."

"I've got her now, working her now. She thinks she's helping me nail Alex Ricker. I don't want her to see you, Morris."

"She won't."

He cut her off, so she contacted Baxter. "DNA's confirmed. Contact Reo. I want a warrant for that bank box."

She cut him off in turn, pulled out her 'link when it signaled. And her communicator beeped in her hand. She saw Roarke on the readout of the 'link, answered with a, "Hold it a damn minute," then switched to the comm.

"Hey, Lieutenant! We are back on Planet Earth."

"Get your ass in here, Callendar. Turn over your prisoners. Go home."

"Affirmative to one and two. Negativo on three. Come on, Dallas, I want to see it through."

"Your choice. Peabody will let you know which interview rooms. Nice work, Detective."

"Fucking A."

Eve ended the transmission, switched to 'link. "Yeah?"

"Busy girl."

"Yeah, and I've been trying to fit in a manicure all day."

"I had a meeting cancel, and have a bit of time on my hands. To echo Callendar, I'd like to see this through."

"There's going to be plenty to see here. If you really want to come down, maybe you could hang with Morris. Feeney's on the electronics. Unless he decides he needs super-geek, I'd like Morris to have a friend nearby."

"I can do that."

Yes, he could, she thought. "Then get your ass in here."

"Fucking A."

She shoved her 'link back in her pocket, dragged her communicator out again to tag Feeney. "Any hit?"

"No attempt to contact the Ricker 'link."

"I'll give her more time to try to talk to Daddy." Like a boxer before the big match, she rolled her shoulders. Then walked back into the conference room.

22

The trick, Eve thought, would be to pit all the players against each other and take them all down. Timing would be essential. Too much time and Grady would get suspicious.

"You're going to take Sisto and work Zeban. You're in charge."

"I love the 'in charge' part." Peabody grinned happily. "What about Grady?"

"I'm going to handle her in a minute. Meanwhile, we need to give her time and space, enough for her to use if she wants to call her daddy for kudos or instructions. But . . . little brainstorm." Eve contacted Feeney again.

"Don't give me grief, kid. I can't make the woman use the damn 'link. And as for the unit, McNab's on it."

"Here's the thing. The civilian consultant's coming in because he wants to play. But I want you to give him another assignment, in case she doesn't use the 'link. You'll need to clear it with Whitney, and Omega, but here's what I have in mind."

"I like it," Feeney said when she'd run it through. "I like it just fine."

"Can you make it work?"

"Kid, up here's where the magic sits. We'll work it."

"Within the hour?"

"That's pushing, but with the civilian we can shove it through."

"Then, I'm going to set up down here. Beep me when you've got it."

"It's devious," Peabody commented when Eve clicked off. "But how can you be sure they won't, well, band together instead of turning on one another?"

"Because it's who they are. Let's go give Grady some busywork, and get this rolling."

She walked back into the conference room, letting a little frustration show. "Sorry. I'm getting a lot of pressure to make an arrest on Coltraine. I'm going to work Ricker again, but he's a hard nut. Listen, if I clear it with your lieutenant, can you hang with this? I've got some files I'd like you to look through, to see if you can add anything, or if something in them pops for you. I've got plenty of dots, but I need to connect them to hang this bastard."

"I'll clear it. My boss wants this wrapped up as much as the rest of us."

"Great. Do you want to work with someone else from your squad? I can—"

"No, not yet anyway. I'll take a look at the files. We'll go from there."

"Your call." Eve pulled out discs. "If you want more eyes, just let me know. I appreciate this, Detective, appreciate you not holding back because I had to come at you and the rest of the squad in the first pass."

"It's the job." She held out her hand for the discs. "Anything that takes that fucker down works for me."

"Does this space suit you?"

"Coffee in the AC?"

"Sure."

"Then I'm solid."

"I'll check back in with you as soon as I can. Peabody, with me."

"What did you give her?" Peabody wanted to know when they headed down the corridor.

"Bullshit. Busywork. Enough to keep her occupied, enough to have her coming up with other little lies. Set up for Sisto and Zeban." She spotted Reo heading in her direction. "Flip him, Peabody. Fast and hard."

"This is the *best* day. Hey, Reo."

Eve waited while Reo caught up. "Ricker's daughter and my prime suspect is in the conference room. She thinks she's helping me hang Alex. I'm going to put a couple uniforms on the door, just in case, but the room's wired."

"You wired the room? You—"

"I asked her, straight off, if she minded being recorded. She said no—on record. It's slippery, but it'll hold. Alex is in one of the visitor areas. I could spring him, he's got nothing else to give me at this point. But I think he should stay for the finale. He's a criminal, but he cared about Coltraine. His father, his sister, and his best friend tried to frame him—however casually—for her murder. I figure he's entitled to the payoff."

With her shorter legs and snappy heels, Reo hustled to keep up with Eve's long, booted strides. "Which is?"

"Peabody's going to flip Zeban on Rouche. I'm flipping Rouche on Ricker, which should include Sandy and possibly Grady. Then I'm going to get a confession

403

out of Grady for Coltraine and Sandy, and flip her on her father."

"Is that all?"

"They're all connected. It's going to fall like a house of dominoes."

"I think that's house of cards, maybe rows of dominoes."

"Whichever, it's coming down." She paused by Vending, pulled out credits. "Get me a tube of Pepsi. I don't want to interact with the damn machine. I'm on a roll here, and I'm not jinxing it."

"You've got some strange habits, Dallas."

Eve studied Reo's high, elegant shoes while the APA ordered up the Pepsi. "I'm not the one wearing stilts. This show's going to require a lot of hiking from one room to another. Your feet are going to cry like babies before it's done."

Eve drank, explained the setup. "I want Morris to observe—anything he wants to observe. Mira wants to observe when I interview Grady."

"I can take care of that. If your men find anything in the bank box, and I'm betting they will, you won't need all the bells and whistles."

"It's not enough. Sure, that ring's going to be in there and probably more to take Grady down, and that's enough for the arrest. But it's not enough payback, not on my scale. I promised Morris justice for Coltraine." And, Eve supposed, she'd promised the same to a dead cop. "I'm going to get him every ounce of it."

"If you pull this off, you'll have made my job very easy."

"I'm counting on you to do it."

"Yo." A very hollow-eyed Callendar bounced up. "Swig of that?" she said and snatched the tube out of Eve's hand. Glugged some down. "Thanks."

"Keep it."

"Double thanks. Sisto hooked with the Peameister. I've got your asshole in interview A as ordered." She glugged down more Pepsi. "This shot ought to get me through observation while you fry his ass."

"You're not in observation. You're taking him with me."

"In interview?" Callendar's tired eyes popped wide. "Hot shit, this is uptown and over the bridge."

"You earned it."

"I'll get started on my end," Reo said. "Good luck."

"How'd you swing with this guy?"

"Kept it low and chill," Callendar began. "I'm just the girl." She fluttered her exhausted eyes. "He's interested in my tits, but they all are. Who could blame?"

"Yes, they're exceptional. Use them if it works."

"He hasn't said the L word yet, but he's thinking about it. I can tell."

"He can lawyer. It won't matter. If he does, he won't get the deal. I'm going to be mean. You can be shocked. Let's go."

She stepped in. "Record on," she said briskly, barely glancing at the big, bulky man huddled at the table. She read off the salients—pointing a finger at him to shut him up.

Wide face, she noted, short, bristly hair. Fear in his eyes.

405

She sat. "Officer Rouche, welcome to Earth." And smiled. "You have the right to remain silent," she began, keeping her eyes hard on his until she'd completed the recitation. "Do you understand your rights and obligations in this matter?"

"Yeah, I understand. I *don't* understand why the hell I need rights and obligations. I don't understand why the hell I got dragged off my job and down here like some criminal."

Eve leaned forward. "Oh yes, you do. And when you go back up, it won't be to the job. It'll be to a cage. Maybe real close to your good pal, Max Ricker."

"You gotta be crazy. I want a—"

"Say lawyer and we're done." She pointed her index finger at him, cocked her thumb. "I don't give you a shot, just wrap you up and dust off my hands while you're charged, tried, and convicted of conspiracy to murder a police officer."

"Con—" He literally choked while his face went raw-beet red. "I never—what the hell? I never killed anybody."

"Hence the word 'conspiracy'. You don't have to do the kill to go down just as hard, just as long. That's life, Rouche. But, hey, not so bad since you already live on Omega. I mean, it's not like you were planning to retire and relocate to, say, the south of France."

She grinned when he lost every ounce of angry color.

"Here you go, Rouche." Callendar moved to him, offered a cup of water. "You really look like you need this. Jeez, cop murder. You're so burnt. I mean, wow. And putting a former guard in up there, with the major badasses he used to dick around? Ouch. Majorly sucks to be you."

"Your pal Zeban's in another room just like this right now," Eve added. "And he's going to roll over so fast he'll look like a circus dog. I get a knock on that door before you do your trick of the day, and I don't need you."

Callendar let out a whistle. "Boy howdy, I'd jump, roll, and stand up and beg."

"I don't know what she's talking about." He spoke directly to Callendar now as little beads of sweat formed on his upper lip. "Hand to God, I never killed anybody. I don't know anything about killing a cop. Why would I do that?"

"I hear you." Callendar gave his arm a sympathetic pat. "But—and I'm sort of sorry to say it, under the circumstances—you were chummy with Max Ricker. I found the data myself. Feel kinda responsible for what's going down now. But, you know, I just did my job. The doctored logs, the toss-away 'link in your quarters. The text message. Plus . . . oh south of France!" Callendar looked at Eve as if she'd just understood. "The transmissions with the ex-wife!"

"Which puts her ass in the same sling. She's being picked up right now, and that's conspiracy to murder on her, in addition to the tax fraud, money laundering, bribery, and the host of others."

"Luanne didn't have anything to do with it. She just did like I said. What the hell *is* this?"

"Max Ricker ordered the assassination of a police

officer, one Detective Amaryllis Coltraine, through the 'link you provided him. You took payment from him. Multiple payments, which we've now documented. You arranged for the visitor's log to be altered, and for the transmissions sent and received by Ricker to be eliminated from record. You handed him the fucking weapon that took Coltraine's life.

"Look at me, at *me!*" she snapped when he turned desperately to Callendar. "I knew Coltraine. Believe me when I tell you I have a personal stake in this, that I won't give a goddamn if you and your greedy ex spend the rest of your useless lives in a cage. In fact, I'll have a small celebration over that fact daily. Do you believe me?"

"Yes."

Callendar made sure her gulp was audible. "Wow. Me, too."

"Here's the deal. Onetime offer, and I hope you're too stupid to take it. The conspiracy charges will be dropped on you, and on your wife, if you confess to the charges of bribery and collusion, to altering records. You'll do ten to fifteen, on-planet, provided you cooperate and tell us everything you know regarding Ricker's communications."

"Ten to fifteen on-planet's cake compared to life without parole on Omega." Callendar gave Rouche another little pat on the arm. "If I were you, I'd sing like a bird on a spring morning. What do you think?"

Rouche wiped his sweaty lip with the back of his hand. He cleared his throat. And he sang.

When it was done, Callendar stood outside interview

with Eve. "That rocked. Seriously. He just popped open and poured it out like . . . something that pops and has stuff in it. I'm really tired."

"Go home, get some sleep. You did solid work here."

"I am so all over that. Hey, Peabody. I helped Dallas cook the turkey. See ya."

"She looks beat, so did Sisto. But we cooked our own turkey."

"We'll compare notes." She nodded to Reo as Reo came out of observation. "Walk and talk. We need . . . Morris."

"He's an idiot. A greedy idiot. And that greed and stupidity helped kill her."

"I know ten to fifteen may not seem like enough, it may not seem like—"

"No." He interrupted, shook his head. "It's enough. For him."

"You can go with Reo. The two of you and Mira can watch the next phase. We've got a room set up for you." She pulled out her communicator when it signaled, noted it was Baxter. "You go on ahead. We're nearly ready to start."

She waited until Morris was out of hearing before she answered. "Tell me."

"A whole shitload of cash money, credit cards and IDs in fake names, more passcodes, which I'm reading as bank accounts. Unregistered 'link and PPC, not yet activated. And the money shot, Dallas: Coltraine's ring."

"Bag it, log it, bring it. You earned your doughnuts today, Baxter."

"Fry her ass, Dallas."

"You can depend on it."

She clicked off Baxter to tag Feeney. "Did she bite?"

"Not a nibble on the 'links."

"How about her unit?"

"Through the passcode and fail-safe—she has some skills, but I've got more. I'm just starting on the data."

"Plan B, then. Roarke?"

"Ask him yourself. Hey, hotshot, your wife wants you."

Eve winced at "your wife", then shrugged it off as Roarke came on. "Hello, darling."

"Don't *do* that. I'm clocking time. Did you hook it up?"

"Ready when you are. And let me just say this is a brilliant idea on so many levels. I'm pleased to have a hand in it."

"Thought you would be. I'll beep you twice when I'm ready."

"I like 'darling'," Peabody commented. "It's old-fashioned and romantic. Especially with the accent."

"Peabody."

"Just thinking out loud. So can we fry her now?"

"Right now."

When she reached the conference room, she stopped to give the uniforms new orders. "She won't get past me, but on the off chance she does, take her down."

She walked into the conference room. Grady sat at the conference table, drinking coffee, studying the screen. Looking, Eve thought, very pleased with herself.

"I was just about to hunt for you. I think I might have something."

"Funny, I have something, too. You helped me get to it."

"Yeah?" Genuine pleasure lit Cleo's face. "Can I be there when you arrest the fucker?"

"Front and center. Do you think it comes down in the blood?" Eve asked conversationally. "You know, bad blood begets bad blood? I think that's a cop-out myself. You're in the job long enough, you see it's not that simple. You see people who come from shit and crawl out of it to make a decent life. Others who come from decent and crawl into the shit. Because they like it. Then again, Ricker's blood's partially foul."

"Alex Ricker doesn't have his father's brains. He's just been coattailing. No offense, but somebody was going to nail him sooner or later."

"Maybe. His problem was getting stuck on the woman. Not enough to make him change his ways, but enough to mess him up. Guy's got a soft streak in there, sentimental, I guess. Men." She shook her head. "They think they're stronger, tougher than women. We know better. The coldest killers I've known have been female.

"But back to blood. I'm curious. Were you a cold, murderous bitch before you knew you had Ricker's blood, or did you turn into one after? Don't answer yet," Eve continued as Grady rose slowly. "Let's deal with the formalities. Cleo Grady, you're under arrest for the murder of Amaryllis Coltraine, the murder of Rod Sandy. Other charges include—"

Even as Cleo reached for her weapon, Eve reached for hers. They drew together.

"I'd love to do it," Eve said. "I'd feel joy in my heart

411

watching you drop. But maybe you'll drop me. Maybe. Then my partner, who's got her weapon at your back will drop you. You're not walking out of this room, Grady. Lower your weapon, or you'll get a taste of what you gave Coltraine."

"Mine's on full. You go down, you won't get up."

"Maybe. My partner's still going to drop you. Put down your weapon."

"The fuck I will. You move away from—"

Eve fired. Her weapon was on its lowest setting and did no more than jolt Cleo, sent her stumbling back as her own weapon clattered to the floor. "That felt good. Small of me, but damn, that felt good. Got her weapon secured, Peabody?"

"Yes, sir, I do. And it felt good over here, too."

"Hands behind your back, Cleo." Eve secured her own weapon, took out her restraints. "Oh, and please make a try for the door," she invited, "so I have an excuse to kick your ass."

"Easy to say when you and your partner have weapons on me."

"Yeah, it is." Eve grinned. "Want me to say it again?"

"You can't make this stick. None of it's going to stick."

"Bet?" She shoved Cleo into the chair, looped the restraints through the back rungs and chained her to it as she completed the Revised Miranda.

No blood on my hands, Eve thought. "I guess Mira was right," she muttered, then shook her head at Peabody's questioning look. "Nothing. I know you're Max Ricker's daughter," she said to Cleo. "I know you recruited Rod Sandy to pass data re Alex Ricker to Max Ricker. I know you've been in communication with your father since his incarceration on Omega, and that you communicated with him the night of Coltraine's murder."

"You can get me a slap on the wrist for that, you can cost me my job. But you can't pin murder on me."

"Oh, I will. You went looking for him, didn't you? Went looking for Daddy."

"What if I did? No crime."

"Hoping for his love and affection. Maybe a puppy. Pathetic."

Insult had Cleo yanking against the restraints. "I know about you, how you were raised by the State. You don't even know where you came from. That's pathetic."

"I know where I landed." Eve brought a chair around, straddled it. "Max Ricker sent you to college, paid your freight."

"So what? No crime."

"But it wasn't free. No free lunch from Max. Not for anyone. But then, it had to be a pleasure for you to find a way to stick it to your brother."

"Half."

"The half that got all the attention, all the bennies all those years. The son. Men are so freaking high on having sons."

"Depends on the son."

"Rod Sandy was easy to mold. He was so jealous of Alex. You just had to plant the seeds, show him the opportunity and the rewards."

"Can't prove it because, oh yeah, that's right. He's dead."

"Got your stiletto, Cleo."

"I'm a collector. I'm licensed." She yawned deliberately. "I'd lawyer but this is too entertaining."

"We've accessed your bank box. We have Coltraine's ring. That was stupid. A cop taking a trophy that can tie her to a murder."

Cleo merely jerked a shoulder and looked bored. "She lent it to me, a couple of days before she died. I put it in there out of respect."

"Yeah, that'll fly. You think it'll fly, Peabody?"

"Not even in a world where pink fairies sing and dance." Shaking her head, Peabody boosted up to sit on the conference table. "I bet Max told her to get rid of it, along with everything else. But it's a really pretty ring." She smiled at Cleo. "I guess you just wanted it."

"She lent it to me. You can't prove otherwise."

"You think Max is going to fix all this for you?" Eve allowed a quick chuckle to rise through the question. "That he has the power, the means, the connections to fix this? Maybe he does. But he'd have to care. He doesn't."

Cleo pulled against the restraints again, and in her eyes Eve recognized the desire for blood. "You don't know shit."

"I know he used you. You used each other to get what you wanted. To hurt Alex. And if Coltraine had to die to really screw with him, she meant nothing. Means to an end. How many other times have you killed for him?"

414

"You tell me. You've got circumstantial, you've got speculation. Bitch, you've got *nothing*."

"I've got plenty." Eve rose. "He loves nothing, Cleo, puts nothing over himself. You were interesting, and useful to him for a time. But your value to him just bottomed out. He'll cut you out like a tumor."

"You've got nothing," Cleo said between her teeth. "You know nothing."

"Okay. Why not get it right from the source." She signaled Roarke. "You can watch on-screen, Cleo. I'll say hi to your father for you."

It was strange to be in the conference room, to know she remained there, yet see her image form on the wall screen. To know she remained in place, and to look around and see the cold concrete cage. To see the man on the thin, narrow cot inside the unadorned gray box.

He hadn't weathered prison well, she noted. His hair was going, his body had begun to sag, his skin to sallow. But his eyes, she thought, they were as vital and vicious as ever.

"Hello, Max."

He sat up slowly. She saw the tremors—shock, excitement, fear? She couldn't be sure. "Lieutenant Dallas." His teeth showed in a ferocious smile as he sprang.

He passed through the holographic image, and scraped his hands on the wall when he threw them up to stop his forward motion.

"Yeah, nice to see you again, too. Why don't you sit down? We'll chat."

He came back, stood so their faces nearly touched.

Though she knew better, she almost felt his breath on her skin. "I'm under no obligation to speak to you. Your holo-presence is interfering with my rights."

"I think you're going to want to talk to me. Regarding rights, let's refresh your Miranda." Once she had, she smiled. "Gotcha again, Max. Conspiracy to murder a police officer. We know you ordered the hit on Coltraine. We've got a lock on it. Chapter and verse. I wanted to be the one to tell you about it, to let you know, personally, you'll be charged and convicted, and given another life sentence."

He did sit, laid his hands on his knees. "I don't know what you're talking about. But if I did, do you think it matters to me? Bitch is dead, isn't she?"

"We got Rouche, so he won't be at your beck. Added to it, now that the warden's aware of your activities, you'll be cut off. No more chatting with friends and family on-planet, Max."

His face tightened. "There's always someone willing to deal. Always someone. One day, they'll add another life sentence on for your murder. I'm giving that a lot of thought. A great deal of thought."

"Sandy won't be able to help you with that. He's dead."

She watched anger ripple over his face before it went tight and cold. "A pity. But there's always another Sandy."

"Your son's onto you. Lost your whipping boy there, Max."

"My son's useless. Couldn't even keep the woman in line, could he? Had a cop in his bed but wouldn't put her in his pocket." A smile, thin and sly, slid onto his lips. "He was happy to help kill when I suggested it, when I arranged it."

"Please. Alex is nothing but a disappointment to you because he wouldn't do things just your way. He didn't kill Coltraine. I've got your girl, Max."

"I don't know what you're talking about." He turned away now, shifting his body like a sulking child. "I've had enough of you."

"Cleo's in custody. Two murder counts. She didn't check in with you before she killed Sandy. Bad girl. She screwed it up, Max, and now you have to pay. It's her fault this didn't work out for you."

All sympathy and reason, she leaned back against the wall when he shifted toward her again. "You really batted zero in the progeny department. But maybe, seeing as you're already completely fucked, you want to help her out. Take the full rap, give her something for her defense. You forced her, you blackmailed her, you brainwashed her, threatened her. You might be able to convince me to go for a lesser charge. Hell, she's a cop. I'll deal. I could maybe get her twenty instead of life. She's your blood, after all."

"She's nothing. Never was, never will be. Less than nothing. Cleo's gotten all she'll get from me, and that's more than she deserved. Coltraine's on her. I'm an old man, in prison," he added with a sneer. "I have no control over what some bitch does on-planet. You won't prove otherwise."

"The bitch is your daughter, Max."

"She's nothing, and she'll get nothing from me. She

417

hated Alex—hated him because he was my son, my heir. Obviously she killed the cop whore to get back at him, and that's nothing to me."

"A minute ago you tried to tell me Alex did the murder."

"Alex doesn't have the *balls*. At least Cleo knows how to go after what she wants, whatever it takes. But she doesn't have Alex's brains. Between them, they barely make up one useful person."

"Do you have knowledge that Cleo Grady murdered Detective Coltraine."

He smiled again. "She wanted to do it two years ago when the cop lived with Alex in Atlanta. I advised against, so this is nothing to me. She's nothing to me. Lock her away. Stupid bitch. Stupid bitch." He pounded his fist on the bunk. "Stupid bitch," he repeated again and again.

"End holo," Eve ordered, and heard the bitter refrain echo in her ears as she stared at Cleo. "Daddy's in a very bad mood," Eve commented.

There were tears, Eve noted, just the faintest glimmer of them behind the fury in Cleo's eyes. "He's a liar."

"Oh yeah, but not about this. We've got him, Cleo. We've got you. And unless you're a complete fool you know he won't lift a finger to help you out."

"I want a deal."

"You won't get one." Eve sat again, made sure Cleo could read the solid truth of it on her face. "Murder in the First for Coltraine. We've got you wrapped on it. Your connection to Ricker will help put it over."

"I want a fucking deal."

"You're not going to fucking get one! Not for

418

Coltraine. Not as long as I'm breathing. You wanted to please your father and hurt your brother so you murdered an innocent woman. A fellow officer, a squad-mate. You're going to pay with the rest of your life for that. And for Sandy. He doesn't mean the same to me, that's a fact, but that's the job. You're going to pay for him, too."

"Then we've got nothing to say."

"Up to you. Let's book her, Peabody, two counts of Murder in the First."

"Give me something, goddamn it."

"You want something, *Detective?* You want some sort of consideration from me? The fact that you're conscious and not bleeding's all the consideration you're going to get."

"I know Max's contacts, the ones you missed. I know where he has accounts, accounts that hold enough to keep paying those contacts."

"I don't care. A good cop is dead, so believe me, I don't care about your pitiful trade. You've got nothing I want half as much as I want you living out your life in a cage."

Eve paused a moment as if considering. "But I'll give you the chance for retribution on Max Ricker. I'll give you the chance to drop the hammer on him."

She watched the interest, and the rage kindle. And played on it. "He says it doesn't matter, but you know better. Another life sentence, no more holes to slither through to push buttons down here. Strip him of whatever power he has left. I'll give you a shot at that, right here and now. I walk out, and you lose even that. Pay him back, Cleo. Pay him back for tossing you out like garbage."

"It was his idea. Coltraine. He wanted her dead, so he set it up. She's not the only one."

Eve came back to sit. "Let's start with her."

"He's still got some pull, and some connections in Atlanta. He used them when she started talking transfer, to clear the way to New York, to my squad. If she didn't bite, I'd have transferred to wherever she went. But she made it easy."

"He targeted her because of Alex?"

"He and Alex had words, before Max went down and right after. Yeah, he thought about payback there for a long time—hell, he promised Alex he'd pay. Coltraine was the payment."

"You contacted her that night."

"Max set it up. Had Sandy persuade Alex they needed to come to New York for a while, deal with some business here. Sandy knew Alex had some regrets about Coltraine, and he played on them—nudged him into contacting her, asking her over. After that, it was easy. Sandy talked Alex into going out, taking a walk. I tagged her, told her I had a solid on the Chinatown case, needed her to come. Max told me how he wanted it to go down, and I did exactly what he wanted."

"You waited for her in the stairway."

"Just a stun there. Max wanted it done a certain way, so it was done a certain way. I carried her down to the basement, brought her back so I could give her Max's message. 'Alex is killing you, bitch. Alex is taking your own goddamn weapon and pressing it to your throat.

Feel it? You don't walk away from a Ricker and live.' He wanted her to die thinking Alex ordered the hit. If Alex went down for it, so much the better. Either way, it was payback. And the kicker was it would happen on your turf. A little needle in your arm.

"He thinks about you a lot."

"So will you," Eve said.

Epilogue

When it was done, when Eve felt as much disgust as satisfaction, she ordered the uniforms to take Cleo to booking.

"Do you want to walk it through?" Peabody asked her.

"No, I really don't."

"I'll take care of it," Peabody offered. "It leaves you a little bit raw. She killed over a dozen people for him. Just because he said to."

"No, not just because. That's only part of it. The rest? It's just in her. God knows why."

"I'll write it up. I'd like to," she added before Eve could speak. "For Coltraine."

"Okay."

Alone, Eve simply sat down in the conference room. Too many things churning, she realized. Too many thoughts buzzing.

Morris came in quietly, sat across from her. "Thank you."

For reasons Eve couldn't name she braced her elbows on the table and pressed her fingers to eyes that stung.

"You feel some sympathy for her."

"I don't know what I feel," she managed.

"Some small seed of sympathy for a woman whose

father could have such contempt for her. I saw her face when he spoke to you about her. His words cut her to pieces. I was glad of it, and still I felt it, too. That small seed of sympathy."

Eve dropped her hands. "She deserved it. All of it. More of it."

"Yes. And still. That's what makes us different than she is, Eve. We can feel that, even though. I'm leaving tonight for Atlanta. I'd like to tell her family her killer— her killers—have been brought to justice. I'd like to do that myself."

"Yeah, okay. Sure. Are you . . ." She was nearly afraid to ask. "Are you coming back?"

"Yes. This is my place, this is my work. I'm coming back." He put a box on the table. "This was hers. I want you to have it."

"Morris, I can't—"

"It's a small thing." He opened the lid himself. Inside was a glass butterfly, jeweled wings lifted. "She told me it was the first thing she bought herself when she came here. That it always made her smile. It would mean a lot to me if you'd take it."

She nodded, then laid a hand over his. "It wasn't just the job this time."

"I know. But then, for you, it never is." He rose, crossed over. He took her face in his hands and kissed her softly on the mouth. "I'll be back. I promise," he said and left her with the jeweled butterfly.

She lost track of the time she sat there, waiting for herself to settle, to smooth out. Lost track of the time alone before Roarke came into the room.

Like Morris, he sat across from her. He studied her face in silence.

"I'm tired," she told him.

"I know you are."

"I want to feel good about this, but I can't quite get there. It was good work, I know that. Everybody did good work. But I can't feel good about it. I just feel tired."

She took a breath. "I wanted her cut to pieces, and I knew Ricker would do just that. I knew it. I wanted it. I had enough on her for the arrest without it. But—"

"Coltraine and Morris deserved more. And we both know an arrest isn't a conviction."

"Reo would've nailed her. But, yeah, Coltraine and Morris deserved more."

"They betrayed each other so easily. Used and attacked and betrayed each other without hesitation, without remorse. While I enjoyed watching you work Ricker, enjoyed seeing him in that stone box, it's just hard to feel good watching people who should feel some loyalty—bugger that—feel *something* for each other tear in like vultures on a corpse."

"She did feel something for him. Maybe that's the problem."

"You're right, yes. But it didn't stop her. You knew she felt something, however twisted, and used it. And that, Lieutenant, is good work." He tapped the open box. "What's this?"

"It was Coltraine's. Morris . . . he wanted me to have it."

Across those jeweled wings he smiled at her. "I think

you'll be able to look at that in days to come, and feel good. Can you go home?"

"Yeah. Peabody's handling the grunt work."

"Let's go home, and have an evening being grateful for who we are."

She closed the lid on the box, slipped it into her pocket. She came around the table, put her arms around him. "I am. Grateful. God. I want to watch a vid where lots of stuff blows up, and eat popcorn, drink a lot of wine, then have drunken sex on the floor."

"Strangely, just what I had in mind." He shifted her, took her hand in his. "We're perfect for each other."

Maybe she wasn't quite up to good, Eve thought as they left the conference room and started for the glides. But she was definitely feeling better.

GLORY IN DEATH

*The dead were her business. She lived with
them, worked with them, studied them. She dreamed
of them. And because that didn't seem to be enough,
in some deep, secret chamber of her heart,
she mourned for them …*

The first victim is found lying on a sidewalk in the rain.
The second murdered in her own apartment building.
Police lieutenant Eve Dallas has no problem finding connections between the two crimes. Both victims are
beautiful and highly successful women; their glamorous
lives and loves were the talk of the city. And their intimate
relations with men of great power and wealth provide Eve
with a long list of suspects – including her own lover,
Roarke. As a woman, Eve is compelled to trust the man
who shares her bed. But as a cop, it's her job to explore
every avenue … no matter where it might lead.

'Compelling characters, absorbing mysteries and a wonderful sense of both time and place, J.D. Robb's *In Death*
novels are can't-miss pleasures' Harlan Coben

978-0-7499-3407-1

SURVIVOR IN DEATH

*Murder was always an insult, and had been since
the first human hand had smashed a stone into the first human
skull. But the murder, bloody and brutal, of
an entire family in their own home, in their own
beds, was a different form of evil.*

When Eve Dallas is called to a multiple homicide at the Swisher family home, she discovers a blood-bath. The killers breached an elaborate security system, slashed the throat of each victim while they slept and were in and out of the house in less than ten minutes. Bu they did make one mistake. They left a survivor …

While her parents, brother and best friend lay in their beds, oblivious to the danger, nine-year-old Nixie Swisher was in the kitchen and saw far too much. Offering Nixie temporary refuge is easy, but dealing with the emotional needs of a girl who has lost everything isn't. Eve can at least promise Nixie justice, but she's chasing professionals who don't like leaving loose ends. And leaving Nixie Swisher alive is one loose end too many …

'Sexy and unpredictable, these books are first-rate suspense thrillers with wit, character and heart' Janet Evanovich

978-0-7499-3584-9

VENGEANCE IN DEATH

*In a time when technology links the law and
the lawless, predators and prey can be one
and the same ...*

He is an expert with the latest technology ... a madman
with the mind of a genius and the heart of a killer. He quietly stalks his prey. Then he haunts the police with cryptic
riddles about the crimes he is about to commit – always
solved moments too late to save his victims' lives. Police
lieutenant Eve Dallas finds the first victim butchered in his
own home. The second loses his life in a vacant luxury
apartment. The two men had little in common. Both suffered unspeakable torture before their deaths. And both
had ties to an ugly secret of ten years past – a secret shared
by none other than Eve's new husband, Roarke.

'Anchored by terrific characters, sudden twists that spin the
whole narrative on a dime, and a thrills-to-chills ratio that
will raise the neck hairs of even the most jaded reader, the
J.D. Robb books are the epitome of great popular fiction'
Dennis Lehane

978-0-7499-3413-2

CREATION IN DEATH

*For him, death was a vocation. Killing was not merely
an act, nor a means to an end. It certainly was not an impulse
of the moment or a path to gain and glory.
Death was, in and of itself, the all.*

When the body of a young brunette is found, artfully positioned and marked by signs of prolonged and painful torture, Lieutenant Eve Dallas is catapulted back nine years to a killer the media tagged 'The Groom' because he put silver rings on the fingers of his victims.

Now, 'The Groom' has returned – but this time he's made it personal: the victim was washed in products from a store Eve's billionaire husband Roarke owns, and laid out on a sheet his company manufactures. Familiar with his methods, Eve knows he has already grabbed his next victim and that time is running out. But, unbeknown to the police, 'The Groom' is already working up to his biggest challenge yet – abducting a woman who will test his skills on every level: Eve Dallas …

'Creation in Death is a witty, dark, page-turning tale of futuristic crime fighting. Raymond Chandler meets *Blade Runner* meets *Silence of the Lambs*. The techno-toys may change, but evil never does' Jonathan Kellerman

978-0-7499-3871-0

SALVATION IN DEATH

The ministers moved forward, stopping short of the altar as the priest lifted the chalice to his lips. He was dead the moment he drank the blood.

A priest is conducting the funeral service for a beloved member of his congregation. But when he lifts the chalice to his lips, he dies suddenly and horribly – poisoned by the blood of Christ.

Who would want to murder a parish priest in such a way? And who could get access to the closely guarded communion wine?

Lieutenant Eve Dallas is called to the scene to investigate. Although initially there seems to have been nothing out of the ordinary about the priest's life, there is something about the situation that just doesn't add up. And then she starts to uncover the evil lurking behind the ceremonial robes. The dead priest was not who he seemed to be – he harboured a dark, deadly secret that could bring Eve's own demons rushing back …

'Curious corpses, tangled twists, and one sizzling sleuth. *Salvation in Death* is a triple-whammy winner' Kathy Reichs

978-0-7499-2985-5

J.D. Robb & Nora Roberts

J.D. Robb is the pseudonym for Nora Roberts, the #1 *New York Times* bestselling author of nearly two hundred novels. Born in Maryland, USA, Nora Roberts has been writing for almost thirty years and with more than 300 million copies of her books in print and over 150 *New York Times* bestsellers to date, she is indisputably the most celebrated women's fiction writer today.

Nora Roberts is truly a publishing phenomenon. However, the remarkable Ms Roberts did not become a success overnight. By the time her first novel was published in 1981, she already had several rejected manuscripts languishing in drawers. Today, she is one of the world's leading novelists, translated into over twenty-five different languages. 'I always have stories running around in my head,' she explains. 'Once I start putting them down on paper, I just keep going; I just keep writing.'

Born into a family of readers, Nora had never known a time that she wasn't reading or making up stories. During a famous blizzard of '79, she pulled out a pencil and notebook and began to write down one of those stories. It was there that a career was born. Her first book, *Irish Thoroughbred*, was published in 1981.

In the spring of 1995, Nora released her first novel written under the pseudonym J.D. Robb. The pragmatic reason for creating J.D. Robb was the astounding pace at which she produces books. With nearly 100 published books to her credit by 1995, she had built up a surplus of titles to be released by her publishers, and still was creating more. Reluctant to publish romantic suspense books akin to what she was already writing under a pseudonym, Ms Roberts decided that readers would enjoy romantic suspense with a difference. Thus J.D. Robb was born. The initials were taken from Ms Roberts's sons, Jason and Dan, while Robb was a shortened form of Roberts.

Strong women. Powerful suspense. Fall into the grip of a Nora Roberts novel and it will never let you go.